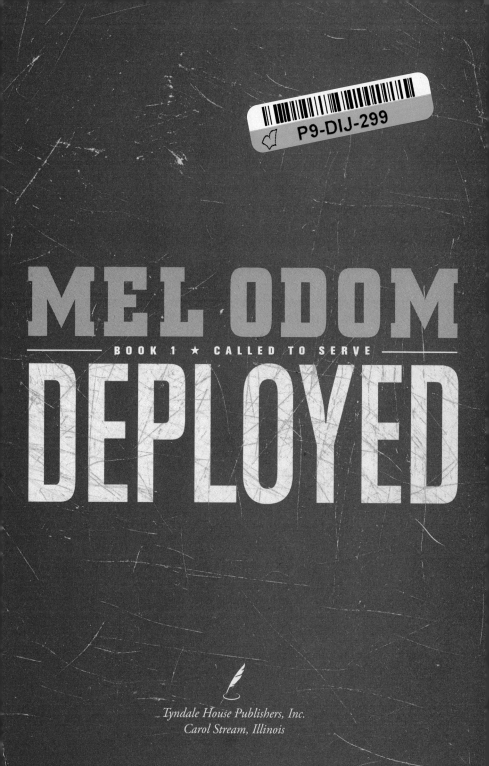

P9-DIJ-299

MEL ODOM

BOOK 1 ★ CALLED TO SERVE

DEPLOYED

Tyndale House Publishers, Inc.
Carol Stream, Illinois

Visit Tyndale online at www.tyndale.com.

Visit Mel Odom online at www.melodom.com.

Deployed

Designed by Ron Kaufmann

Edited by Caleb Sjogren

Published in association with the literary agency of Ethan Ellenberg Literary Agency, 548 Broadway, #5-E, New York, NY 10012.

Library of Congress Cataloging-in-Publication Data

Odom, Mel.
  Deployed / Mel Odom.
    p. cm.
    ISBN 978-1-4143-4930-5 (sc)
1. Afghan War, 2001—Fiction. 2. United States. Marine Corps—Fiction. I. Title.
  PS3565.D53D46 2012
  813'.54—dc23   2012019599

Printed in the United States of America

18   17   16   15   14   13   12
7   6   5   4   3   2   1

To my family, with all my love.

ACKNOWLEDGMENTS

I am always surprised at the things God puts before me, the tasks he gives me to do when sharing with others, and the vision I have for writing about the kinds of heroes I've gotten to write about in these books. I appreciate Tyndale's support and the efforts of Jan Stob, Caleb Sjogren, and Cheryl Kerwin to get these stories out there.

The brave men and women of the armed forces who have to leave families and other responsibilities have been the backbone of this nation since it was formed. I want to help keep them remembered and appreciated. These people lay everything on the line every day, and they have just as many reasons as anyone else to stay home.

God bless and keep you.

1

THE PAST SWAGGERED through the door of Darlton's Bar &
Grille in cowboy boots. United States Marine Corps Lance
Corporal Bekah Shaw blew out a disgusted breath as she took
in the man wearing those boots.

Tall, lean, with hair the color of straw and eyes the color
of sapphires, Billy Roy Briggs looked about the same as he
had when he'd caught Bekah's attention back in high school.
He definitely hadn't changed since Bekah had seen him walk
out on their marriage six years ago, right before their son,
Travis, was born.

Billy Roy wore faded jeans, a dark-blue cowboy shirt
rolled up to mid-forearm, and a beat-up Stetson his daddy
had given him when he'd still been throwing fastballs back
in high school. The ostrich cowboy boots stood out because
he'd tucked his pants legs into them—in true cowboy fashion, as he'd told her on more than one occasion. Red stubble

gleamed on his chin and cheeks. The dark tan had come from working at oil rigs around the state. He'd been on the road for the last few years and seldom returned home.

Bekah hoped he wouldn't notice her. The last thing she needed tonight was another round in that unwinnable fight. She'd learned to let go of Billy Roy, and she liked the direction her life had gone since she'd become a momma and a Marine. Her brunette hair normally dropped to her shoulders, but tonight she'd worn it up because she'd been working in the barn at her granny's house before being invited out.

Darlton's Bar & Grille was a small place where the scent of working men lingered in the air. Diesel fuel, oil field, fresh-cut hay, and barnyard smells all contributed to the mix. The dining area held a couple dozen tables and booths, had sawdust on the floor to absorb spilled beer, and had framed pictures of country-and-western singers on the wall. Connie had chosen a table under concert pictures and album covers of Taylor Swift.

Callum's Creek was a small town, but it held all of Bekah's life except for the last couple years when she'd been activated—first to Iraq, later to Afghanistan. Her daddy was buried in this town after his eighteen-wheeler went out of control when she was four. Her mother, grieving and unstable after losing her husband, had run off and stranded her there when she was six. So her grandpa and granny had finished raising her. Four years ago, she had helped her granny bury her grandpa, and Bekah had never felt more alone in her life.

Even though she'd had a baby six years ago at age nineteen, she'd kept her figure, but she knew that was more from her Marine reservist career than anything she'd done on her own. Working and being a mom didn't allow much time for an exercise regimen. But the Marines made up for that.

Unfortunately, with everything going on in the world lately, she had also been called into trouble spots around the globe. She hated being taken away from Travis, but she took pride in serving her country and knew that she was making a difference. She'd been activated twice, most recently to Afghanistan's Helmand province.

In fact, she'd only gotten back a month ago and was still struggling to reacclimatize to the civilian world. There was a big difference being back home in Callum's Creek, Oklahoma, and being in Afghanistan, where her life was in constant danger from the Taliban. She was dark from the unforgiving sun, and her lips felt like they were going to be chapped for life. Walking around in civilian clothes—jeans and a T-shirt and a baseball cap—instead of desert fatigues and BDUs felt strange. She kept looking for the assault rifle she normally carried as well.

"Well, well. Look what the cat dragged in." Connie Hiller sat up in her chair at the table she shared with Bekah. Connie glared daggers at Billy Roy and his companions. "He's got some nerve showing up here."

Connie was five feet four inches tall—a couple inches shorter than Bekah—and had more generous curves. The years since high school had added a few pounds that she hadn't needed, but she was attractive and knew how to make it all look good. Tonight she wore a silky red blouse and jeans that looked like they'd been painted on. Her hair was frosted blonde with two blue streaks through it and cut so that it ended at the nape of her neck.

For a moment, Bekah thought Connie was talking about Billy Roy. Then she realized that Connie's ex, Buck Miller, was with Bekah's ex-husband. Getting back from Afghanistan and discovering that Connie and Buck had stopped dating— because Buck had found someone else—wasn't surprising. Neither Connie nor Buck had a good record when it came to being committed. One of them had been bound to break it off. Connie was just miffed that Buck had pulled the trigger first.

Buck was one of Billy Roy's typical hangers-on. Rawboned and raucous, with a shock of brown hair and tattoos showing along his bare arms because he wore a work shirt with the sleeves ripped off, he looked small-town. A stained and frayed John Deere hat was pushed back crookedly from his sunburned face. He wore a lockback knife on his belt, which also sported a huge oval buckle. The wary way he looked around the bar and grill reminded Bekah of a coyote scenting the wind. Coyotes tended to be timid unless they were in a pack. But Billy Roy was all wolf.

Billy Roy usually attracted a crowd around Callum's Creek. He'd been the best pitcher the high school had ever turned out, and he'd been the one everyone thought would make it as a major league baseball player. Instead, after the first year on the road, the triple-A team he'd been playing for had cut him and sent him back home. Billy Roy had performed well in front of a small-town crowd, but he hadn't been able to convert that to success in triple-A ball. He'd claimed he had a shoulder injury that none of the team doctors could find.

The drinking and carousing hadn't helped his career. Bekah had discovered her then-husband's infidelity on Facebook when Connie and some of her other friends had brought their computers over to show her. That had nearly killed Bekah. Especially the fact that she was the last to know. Even her granny had known what would happen, because she'd seen right through Billy Roy from the start. Bekah had felt foolish and it had been a hard thing to accept, but she eventually got over it. She had more going on in her life these days than Billy Roy could have ever given her.

"Do you see them?" Connie was seething. That was one of the things she did best. "They come in here like they know no shame."

Jeanne Salver and Karol Tatum added their own disapproving noises to Connie's scathing comment, following her lead the way they usually did. These two were more Connie's friends than Bekah's. Bekah had known them back in high school, but she'd never gotten close. Jeanne and Karol looked and dressed enough alike that they could have been mistaken for sisters.

"Just stay put," Bekah whispered and reached out to take Connie's upper arm. "You don't want this to turn into something. We just came here for a drink. Not an argument."

Connie swiveled her heavily mascaraed gaze onto Bekah. "Buck cheated on me. Don't tell me you've already forgot how that feels."

"No. But I don't want this to be a scene. This was just a night out. A couple of beers, remember?"

"Well, Billy Roy and his crew shouldn't have shown up

here then, should they?" Connie pulled her arm from Bekah's grip. "I thought maybe you being in the Marines would teach you something about not being such a doormat."

That stung. Bekah took pride in her service as a Marine reservist. But just because someone put on a uniform didn't make them a superhero—or radically change that person's life. Becoming a Marine reservist three years ago did change Bekah's life, though. She made a little more money for those weekends and training camps, and she was able to use other programs to better her life and Travis's. It was a slow, small change, but it was welcome. She'd gotten a little more in control of things. She enjoyed that.

Billy Roy went to the bar and leaned over the counter. He slid over a little and half-sat on one of the stools. Then he proceeded to flirt with the girl working there.

The bartender blossomed under Billy Roy's attentions. She was blonde and pretty, probably all of twenty-one years old. The young woman leaned into the bar and devoted all of her attention to Billy Roy, who preened like a tomcat. Bekah could practically hear him purring as he grinned at the young woman and told stories.

During their high school years, Billy Roy had told Bekah stories about how he was going to become a big-time Major League Baseball pitcher and how they'd go off to see the world together. She had believed those stories because she'd wanted to, because she'd wanted more than the little town that she'd grown up in.

After being a Marine reservist for three years and being stationed overseas for two short support tours that had been filled with violence and death, Bekah had begun to think the world outside Callum's Creek wasn't as wonderful as she'd imagined. In fact, she knew several parts of that world weren't wonderful at all. Those experiences gave her a greater appreciation for the smallness of her hometown, but they also made Callum's Creek feel *very* small.

Connie stared at Bekah in disbelief. "Are you just going to let him stand up there like that? Hitting on that girl in front of you?"

Bekah gripped the icy-cold glass of Diet Coke in front of her. She'd only had one beer because she'd driven herself tonight. She'd insisted. Primarily so she could go home when she was ready. Connie had a tendency to stay too late, and Bekah had gotten trapped with her every now and again when they'd been younger.

"He isn't my problem anymore."

The bartender's laughter pealed over the jukebox playing Toby Keith in a corner of the room.

"Do you see the way Billy Roy's carrying on with that tramp?" Connie's eyes blazed.

"If she buys into whatever Billy Roy is selling, then he's her problem. Not mine. I've already had my cure." Bekah picked up her drink and drained the contents. She glanced at her watch. "It's after midnight. I think I'm going to call it a night and go on home."

"It's still early." Jeanne and Karol joined in on the chorus of that particular guilt song.

Bekah forced a grin at Connie and the other women. "One of us is raising a six-year-old. Mornings come a lot earlier."

Connie shook her head. "Don't let him run you off. It's taken me almost two weeks to get you to go out."

"He's not running me off. And I've been busy."

"A steady diet of slinging hash at a greasy spoon and working on your granny's place isn't any way to spend your life."

"It is for me." Although she didn't want to, Bekah felt more than a little angry at Connie. The constant onslaught of Coke and rum was taking its toll on Connie, stripping away her good judgment, and that always made for a bad time. Bekah had had reservations about coming out with her friends tonight for just that reason. But she'd been hungry for the companionship of friends and maybe a little more than ready for the illusion of a normal life. Whatever that was.

"You don't have to back down from Billy Roy." Connie frowned in displeasure.

"I'm not backing down."

"You are."

Bekah sighed. "Look, I'm not going to sit here and argue with you. I don't have anything to prove where Billy Roy is concerned. It's late and I'm leaving." She stood up.

"Sure." Connie looked away from her and stood up as well. Bekah knew something was going to happen, and she knew there wasn't a thing she could do to stop it. "Billy Roy Briggs, since you're so quick to flash that cash around and buy your buddies drinks, do you have any of that child support money you owe for your boy? 'Cause if you do, Bekah is right here and you can pay her."

Silently, Bekah cursed the circumstances. If Connie hadn't been drinking, if Billy Roy hadn't shown up, if Connie's ex-boyfriend hadn't been in the entourage, if Billy Roy hadn't skipped out on the court-arranged payments, tonight wouldn't have been so dicey.

And if Billy Roy hadn't been so prideful.

Stung by Connie's accusation, Billy Roy wiped beer foam from his upper lip with the back of his hand and turned to face her. He was instantly the center of attention in Darlton's, and he stepped into the limelight with the authority of one of those old Hollywood leading men Bekah's granny loved watching so much. He craved attention and knew how to play the hometown crowd. He leaned back against the bar and hooked his elbows on the smooth wood. Theatrically, in a move he'd practiced, he shoved his hat back with a thumb. And smiled.

2

"**CONNIE HILLER.**" Billy Roy drawled her name like it was something he'd stepped in. A couple of the patrons chuckled, obviously knowing what was coming. "As I recall, you always was a busybody. Always sticking your nose into things that you should have paid no attention to."

"Bekah's my friend, and your son is my godbaby. That makes you not paying what you owe them my business." Connie reached out and roped an arm around Bekah, instantly bringing her onto the battlefield.

Bekah knew that Connie's logic wasn't true. She'd just wanted to horn in on the argument, get her licks in.

Billy Roy grinned. "Seems to me I remember Megan Dinwiddie flattened your big nose our senior year right before picture day. That portrait that hangs in the school was shot another day, but the yearbook's still got some pictures of your nose all swole up. You might want to be careful before that happens again."

Crimson stained Connie's cheeks. She'd hated those year-book pictures and had even thought about cutting them out of her yearbook and asking Bekah to do the same. "You owe Bekah and your son money. The court told you that too. I've got half a mind to call the sheriff and have a deputy come pick you up as a deadbeat dad."

Bekah stood there when all she wanted to do was leave. She'd already had her arguments with Billy Roy over Travis and money and everything else that had come up, and none of them had ended well. Billy Roy hadn't wanted to stay or be responsible, and he didn't want to be a father to Travis. All of those things had hurt at one time, but there was nothing she could do about it. She preferred to just let those problems go and focus on what she could do. Even the Department of Human Services hadn't been able to get a steady payment out of Billy Roy. He didn't always work, and when he did he often got paid under the table. Or he worked just long enough for the DHS child support paperwork to catch up to him, then moved on to the next job or the next town.

Not smiling anymore, Billy Roy shook his head. "I don't owe that woman a dime. That boy she has ain't mine. Anybody with eyes in his head can see that."

Listening to Billy Roy deny Travis made Bekah angry, but she curbed her anger with discipline she'd learned in the Marines. Arguing with Billy Roy was just a waste of time, and she wouldn't give it another minute.

Connie's voice rose. "That's a lie and you know it. Anybody with eyes in his head can see Travis *is* yours. Boy looks just like you."

"He's got dark hair."

"He gets his hair from his momma's side. The Shaws got Cherokee blood in them. Black hair is going to show up. That's no more surprising than you having a redheaded son because your family runs to Irish."

"Well then, maybe that boy should have had red hair."

"You can't just walk away from your responsibilities."

Billy Roy reached over his shoulder and snagged his beer with ease. He always seemed to know just where things were. And he knew where Bekah was right now too.

"That boy's not my responsibility. She had him while I was on the road playing baseball." Billy Roy sipped his beer. "I wasn't home to father a child."

Bekah regretted giving in to Connie's invitation. Her private life was becoming a spectacle, a sideshow in Callum's Creek, where such things happened a lot unless a person lived really small. Billy Roy didn't live small. He loved the attention, and he counted bad attention just as worthy as good attention. In a town that ran on rumors and half-lies, a lively personal life made someone a rock star.

"She had your son while you were on the road because you were out there cheating on her with every pretty little thing that looked your way." Connie had her hands on her hips now, and Bekah knew her friend had lost it. "There's a lot of girls out there that don't have a brain in their pretty little heads." She looked meaningfully at the bartender, who had backed off a little.

Bekah silently turned and made herself walk toward the exit. There was nothing graceful about leaving, but staying was pointless. She told herself this was a parade drill at the Corps, that she was going to execute it and be gone.

"You going to just sneak on out of here, Rebecca Ann? That how you going to do this while your friend runs her mouth and talks trash about me?" Billy Roy's tone carried that old, familiar taunt. "Let your friend slander my good name while you walk out with your holier-than-thou attitude?"

Don't turn around. Don't talk to him. He's not worth it. You've already had this fight hundreds of times, and you can't win. There's nothing you can do tonight to change that. Bekah kept her focus on the door. It was less than ten feet away. She'd be gone by the time she drew another breath.

Connie didn't lighten up on her tirade. "You're a loser, Billy Roy. You're a wannabe baseball player, and you're a no-account daddy."

Bekah had her hand on the doorknob when she heard the rapid footsteps behind her, the squealed curse from Connie, and the sudden scrape of chairs as the bar patrons cleared a path. Turning around, she fully expected to see Billy Roy making a beeline toward Connie even though she'd never seen him strike a woman in her life.

Instead, Buck Miller stopped just in front of Connie, grabbed her by the wrist with one hand, and backhanded her across the face with the other. Buck's face was florid, and Bekah knew the man had been drinking even before he'd come to Darlton's.

Blood sprayed from Connie's nose and mouth at the impact, and she sagged to her knees on the floor. Buck kept hold of her arm and didn't let her go. He leaned over her and shouted into her shocked, frightened face.

The crowd drew back. A couple of men acted like they were going to intervene, but they easily let their friends haul them back. Buck Miller had a reputation as a fighter, and most of the crowd in Darlton's that night probably hadn't ever been in a real fight. One of the men protested and threatened to call the cops, but Buck glared the man to silence, then turned his attention back to Connie.

"You never did know when to shut your mouth! That was your biggest problem! Always had to have the last word! Well, you ain't getting the last word tonight!"

Methodically, Buck slapped Connie in the face again and rocked her head back.

By the time she realized that no one in the place was going to do anything to stop Buck, Bekah was already in motion. She stepped around the tables and chairs and made straight for the man.

Buck saw her coming and grinned. He stood up a little straighter, putting himself a full head taller than Bekah. He was broader and heavier too, and that gave Bekah some pause, but she regularly trained with male Marines in hand-to-hand combat who were bigger and heavier than her. Granted, that was under the supervision of a sergeant who made sure things only went so far.

If Buck didn't listen to reason, this was going to get ugly. But she was not going to stand by and let him manhandle Connie. She couldn't respect herself if she did.

"Let her go." Bekah stopped just out of Buck's reach.

"You've already hurt her, and you don't want to hurt her any more."

Buck laughed at her, then looked over his shoulder at Billy Roy to make sure he was laughing too. Billy Roy wasn't laughing, but he had on that stupid, cocky grin that Bekah had come to hate. It had been cute when they'd first gotten together. Now the expression just made her sick.

Laughing harder, Buck turned back to her. "The Army lets you give orders? Is that what's going on here?"

"The Marines." Bekah kept her voice flat, neutral.

Buck shrugged. "Whatever. Just because you get to tote around a rifle and sing songs while you're marching don't mean you got britches big enough to come up against me. Do yourself a favor. Tuck your tail between your legs and sashay right on out of here."

"Fine. Let Connie go with me." All Bekah wanted was to get her friend safe. Nothing else mattered. She didn't have to prove herself. She only needed to get her friend out of harm's way. That was her job as a Marine.

Connie sniffled at Buck's feet and mopped at the blood streaming from her nose.

"Me and her got a few more words to share, now that I got her attention for once. I'm gonna teach her a little respect and to hold a civil tongue." Buck drew his hand back again.

Without thinking about what she was doing, acting on instinct and fired by concern for her friend, Bekah stepped forward and turned sideways. With a quickness trained into her through hours of practice, she caught Buck's hand and wrist as it came down. She added her strength to her opponent's and torqued the captured arm around, down, and behind Buck's back, missing Connie by inches.

Propelled by the sudden motion and the leverage Bekah had, Buck squalled in pain and left his feet in a rush as momentum spun him into a flip. He released Connie and landed flat on his back on the floor.

Bekah caught Connie under the arm and helped her friend to her feet. "Let's go."

Connie nodded weakly. Her eyes were glazed and she looked half out of it. Bekah had guided her three steps toward the door before Buck shook his head, pushed up to his feet, and screamed in defiance. He came at Bekah at a dead run with his arms outspread.

Moving quickly, Bekah shoved Connie out of the way and stepped in front of Buck. Again, she took a profile stance, and the movements came automatically from all the training she'd had. She knew she couldn't meet Buck head-on. His size and strength would break through every aggressive defense she had to stand her ground. Speed and technique were the only skill sets that would help her. At the last minute she stepped to one side, to Buck's right so that her left shoulder was toward him. Buck instinctively grabbed for her, as she'd expected, because most attackers coming at speed didn't want their prey to get away.

Bekah slapped down Buck's arm with her right hand, then chopped him across the throat with the edge of her left hand. Buck lost his balance and started gagging, trying desperately to breathe. Under combat conditions, Bekah could have killed someone with the move, but she'd never used it with lethal force and she'd held back the strength of the blow now.

Buck caught himself over a table and stopped his forward momentum. Hacking and coughing, he turned around and screamed hoarse curses at Bekah.

Unwilling to let go of the upper hand while she had it—and knowing from watching him in past fights that Buck wouldn't quit—Bekah stepped toward him, spun, and kicked him in the chest. A shock ran up her leg as her boot made contact. Buck was solid, strong. The impact almost knocked her from her left foot, but she recovered and remained standing, fists raised in front of her. Ready.

The kick knocked Buck back into the wall. A framed picture of Loretta Lynn and Conway Twitty dropped to the floor, and the glass shattered. Buck grunted in pain, touched his chest with his right hand as if making sure nothing was broken, then pushed off the wall and came at her again.

This time he was more wary. He put up his fists and pulled his chin down to his chest. He'd boxed some, but only with friends. Bekah saw immediately that his stance was too wide, something she would not have known without the martial arts training in the Marines.

By now the crowd had gotten a taste of the bloodlust. A few of the less raucous patrons headed for the door, but the majority of them remained. A fight was just local entertainment. Callum's Creek had a lot of UFC and WWE fans.

Fear thrummed through Bekah as it always did before an encounter, but she controlled it. She'd been in firefights out on the battlefield, had exchanged shots with enemy soldiers, had shot enemy soldiers, but she'd never been face-to-face with any of them during a struggle. Buck was up close and personal, and she grew even more aware of his size.

He swung at her, and she easily dodged back out of the way. He punched at her again, grinning when she dodged away.

"What's the matter? Scared?" Buck licked his lips. "You ain't begun to get scared yet. Just wait."

This time when Buck swung, telegraphing the effort, Bekah blocked the blow, catching his forearm against hers and stepping inside. She didn't punch for his jaw or his chin or his forehead. Those would be too hard and could break her hand. Instead, she planted her feet, pushed with her knee, swiveled her hip to transfer her weight and strength to the punch, and hit him squarely in the nose. Blood gushed immediately and his head snapped back. Before he could react, she retreated.

"This doesn't have to go any farther." Bekah was breathing easily now, and that surprised her. "I just want to take Connie to the emergency room and get her looked at. Just let us pass."

Surprised and hurt, Buck halted his advance and stepped back. He touched his bleeding nose, and his fingers came away stained with crimson. He snarled an oath. "Oh, you're gonna pay for that, Bekah!" He came at her again, fists flying like a threshing machine.

Bekah stayed ahead of him, dodging through the chairs and tables, and managed to get to the door. She kept going out into the parking lot, hoping she'd have the chance to get to her pickup truck and get away. She had her keys in her pocket. All she needed was an opening. As long as she could get Connie out of there too. She wasn't leaving without her.

Even as she was digging for her keys, though, the other guy with Billy Roy ran over to her pickup and took a position beside the door. The message was clear: she wasn't leaving till they were ready for her to go.

Loose gravel covered the parking lot, and potholes still held a small amount of rainwater and gray sludge from the rain yesterday. Fifty yards away, the two-lane highway sat dark and empty. Callum's Creek lay at the west end of the highway, and the east end led back toward Oklahoma City, an hour away. Thready gray clouds covered the quarter moon.

"Come back here and take what's coming to you." Buck roared like a bull and lumbered after her. Blood had leaked from his nose, down his face and neck, and was soaking into his shirt. "You're gonna be sorry you ever started this."

I didn't start this. Bekah thought briefly of trying to run to the highway. The first rule of every fight was to survive. But she knew that Buck would only pursue. She'd also be leaving Connie there. And one of Buck's buddies might even fire up a pickup and follow her. That way even more people risked the chance of getting hurt.

She stood her ground in the middle of the impromptu battleground. Gravel popped and crunched under her boots. She took in a breath and let it out, relaxing a little, feeling her muscles loosen. And she waited on Buck to make his move, determined to end the fight.

3

BILLY ROY LOUNGED on a nearby car hood. He'd pushed himself up and sat with his legs hanging over the side, like he was sitting at the drive-in waiting for the movie to start. A beer bottle dangled in his fingers. "You should have stayed home tonight, Rebecca Ann. What kind of momma are you to go off and leave your granny to watch your baby while you're out on the town?"

Bekah hated the sanctimonious tone in Billy Roy's voice. But she hated it even more because it touched on the guilt that had been bubbling around inside her all evening anyway. Her granny had insisted she go out with her friends, but Bekah hadn't felt good about doing it. Still, she'd wanted to know how much of a normal life could exist for her outside of being a momma and serving with the Marines. She'd joined up to hang on to her life and get in a better financial situation, but lately she felt like she was just losing more and more of her days. The two tours had chipped away six months each, and she'd come home to see Travis more grown-up every time.

That bothered her. She should have been there. A hard knot formed in her stomach, and she knew it was more fear. But it wasn't fear of Buck. It was fear of her boy growing up without her because wars seemed to be breaking out all around the world, and the United States government appeared determined to get involved in all of them.

She hadn't counted on being away from her son so much. It was just a part-time job. But the things she'd helped do were amazing. The lives she'd saved were precious. She hated being torn the way she was between the two.

Connie stood out in front of the bar and grill. "She's a better momma than you'll ever be a daddy, Billy Roy."

Billy Roy scowled but didn't even look in Connie's direction. He sipped on his beer and stared at Bekah.

"I gotta warn you, Billy Roy." Buck wiped at his face but only succeeded in smearing more blood. "I'm gonna mess up your old lady now."

"She's not my old lady."

Bekah stared at Buck and waited for the big man to make a move. She had to wait. She couldn't be the aggressor with all the weight and size she was giving away. She was surprised at the calm way she could stand there. But she'd always stood her ground. That was one of the most important things her grandpa and granny had taught her: to stand up for herself and to do what was right. She'd stood quietly at her daddy's grave when they buried him, and she'd stood holding her granny's hand when her momma drove off in the rain two years later, fueled by alcohol and worn out by anger and betrayal and the need to be free of a child.

"C'mon." Buck waved for Bekah to come closer. "Let's see what you have."

Bekah ignored him and kept her fists up. When Buck started circling her, she followed him with small steps of her own.

"Go on, Buck. Step in there and paste her one. Knock some sense into her." That came from the other man who had followed Billy Roy into Darlton's. He still stood guard by Bekah's pickup.

At least two dozen onlookers stood out in front of the bar and grill, all of them up on the wooden boardwalk in front of the place. Shadows fell over them except for the soft light coming from their cell phones. Bekah would have bet none of them were calling the sheriff's office and that all of them were texting neighbors and friends.

For a moment, Bekah detested them all. She'd always known Callum's Creek was small, but she hadn't truly realized how cold the town could be till she got ostracized by Billy Roy's claims that Travis was someone else's son. Until that time Bekah had been the lucky girl who had landed the town's baseball hero.

Before that, she'd been a nobody, a kid who'd been orphaned by her parents and taken in by her grandparents. Now she was the girl who had gone off with the Marines and come back a stranger. Most of the people she'd known didn't treat her the same anymore. They were too afraid that she'd changed, that she now looked down on their small-town ways.

"What?" Buck kept moving. He feinted a couple punches, but Bekah didn't react because his footwork gave away the fake efforts. "You ain't got nothing to say now?"

Bekah kept moving as well, placing one foot at a time, never crossing a foot over the other, just like she'd been trained. Then, when Buck lunged at her, she gave ground, stepping back quickly, gliding her boots over the uneven surface and feeling the rocks shift. She set herself, ducked beneath his outstretched arms, spun, and stomped her right foot on the back of his right knee as he went past her.

Off balance, flailing wildly, Buck smashed into the side of a large Ford F-150. The pickup's security system screamed to life, and the lights flashed in stunning syncopation. Buck recovered faster than Bekah would have thought, though. He pushed off the truck's side and came at her again. His boots dug into the gravel.

Bekah tried to get away, but her left foot slid into one of the sludge-filled potholes. Buck was on her before she could slide out of his grasp. Triumphantly, he lifted her in a bear hug, threatening to crush her ribs. He rammed her back into a parked car and nearly bent her over it. Her head smacked into the hood. The breath went out of her in a rush as he roared victoriously.

"Now you're gonna—"

Buck never got to finish. Bekah slammed the palms of both hands over his ears and sent shock waves through his eardrums. Head filled with exploding pain, Buck released her and staggered backward. Bekah slid to her feet and drew in a painful breath. Her senses spun from the impact with the car. Double vision threw her depth perception off.

The crowd was yelling in a fever, but Bekah didn't know whose name they were calling. She tried to focus and square herself up, but her legs felt rubbery. She rolled her hands into fists and watched in mixed disbelief and dismay as Buck reached for the knife at his belt. He brought the weapon out and flicked it open with a thumb. The blade gleamed sharp and strong in the red and blue lights streaming from the neon Darlton's sign.

He'd lost all control. And nobody was stepping in to talk sense into him.

"I'm gonna kill you." Buck advanced on her with more confidence. Blood leaked from one of his ears as well as his nose now.

Desperate, Bekah turned and clambered on top of the car because Buck was close enough to intercept her before she could get around it. Once atop the car, she took a step and vaulted into the back of a pickup parked nearby. When she landed, the L-shaped jack handle in the pickup bed bounced and clanged. Seizing the jack handle, she vaulted over the other side, toward her vehicle.

Her legs nearly collapsed beneath her as her knees threatened to give way. She remained standing through sheer determination and stubbornness. But Buck came around the vehicle from the rear and slashed at her with the knife.

Automatically, Bekah grasped the jack handle in both hands the way she would a baton. She blocked the knife blow, and the clang of metal on metal rasped over the other sounds of the crowd. Moving forward, she snap-kicked Buck in the crotch like she was going for a fifty-yard field goal. He yelped in pain and sagged backward.

Mercilessly, Bekah let her Marine baton training take over, still dazed and only thinking that she wanted to make it home to her son that night. Stepping back again, she swept the jack handle down onto Buck's knife wrist. The blade glinted as it spun free and dropped, and the crack of wrist bones sounded like gunshots.

She moved to the side and swung the jack handle again, hitting Buck in the side of the knee. Something crunched, and Buck fell sideways. He curled into a fetal position and held his injured knee, screaming in pain like an animal. Still on autopilot, Bekah stooped to deliver a final blow, then caught herself and kept the jack handle raised. With a fearful yelp, Buck covered his head with his hands. As she drew a shaky breath, the *whoop-whoop* of a police unit roared over the parking lot.

Still breathing rapidly, her legs feeling like spaghetti beneath her, Bekah stood and let the jack handle dangle at her side. She didn't let it go. Buck might get up one more time, or someone else in the crowd might decide to take sides.

The sheriff's department cruiser slid to a stop in the parking lot and emptied several potholes along the way. The whirling light splashed over the crowd, and they stepped back, unwilling to get caught up in the legal repercussions.

The deputy climbed out of the cruiser with his hand on his pistol. He was tall and lanky, with a dark crew cut and a square jaw. His uniform was neat and pressed. Bekah recognized him as he came forward. He was one of the Trimble boys. She couldn't remember which one other than it was the one who had played baseball with Billy Roy and Buck. Her hopes sank because she knew the deputy wouldn't be inclined favorably toward her.

The deputy waved at her. "You put down that jack handle."

Without a word, Bekah dropped the jack handle. All of a sudden, she felt incredibly tired. Adrenaline crash. She recognized the symptoms from her previous tours.

Buck still rocked in pain, but he no longer screamed hoarsely.

"How bad is it, Buck?" The deputy stood over the fallen man almost protectively.

"Feels like my knee's broke. So's my wrist."

"Lemme call for an ambulance." The deputy did that, speaking into the handi-talker pinned to his shoulder. When he was finished, he glanced back at Buck. "Want to tell me what happened?"

"She went crazy, Alvin. Plumb loco. Attacked me with that tire iron. Musta been one of them flashbacks from the war or something."

"That's not what happened." Bekah took a step forward.

The deputy, Alvin Trimble, threw up a hand. "You stay right there." His other hand eased his pistol from its holster. "Not another step."

Bekah froze, but she couldn't stop talking. She was going to be heard, and the record was going to be set straight.

"Buck attacked Connie Hiller in Darlton's. I was just defending her."

"With a tire iron?"

"Yes. Buck had a knife."

"A knife?" Alvin took a mini Maglite from his utility belt, flicked it on, and shined it around the parking lot. "I don't see no knife."

Bekah didn't either. The blade had been there only a moment ago. "It was here. Somebody picked it up." That was the only answer she could come up with.

"Yeah. Well, we'll see about that. In the meantime, you're under arrest."

"For what?"

"Drunk and disorderly. Assault and battery. Disturbing the peace. I'll think of some more along the way." The deputy put the flashlight away and took a pair of handcuffs from his belt.

"I was defending myself. I was defending Connie Hiller. Take a look at her. Buck beat her before I stepped into it."

"We'll let the judge figure that out. Now you just turn around and don't start nothing."

Bekah almost ran. She'd never been in trouble with the law before outside of a speeding ticket when she was seventeen. She'd always lived her life quiet and small and never got in anybody's way. Billy Roy, on the other hand, had been arrested a number of times—for speeding and fighting and drinking. He hadn't been quite that way when she'd married him, but he'd turned on the trouble afterward. She'd had to bail him out of jail three times, and it had taken her grandpa's money to do it.

Silently, she steeled herself, turned around, and stuck out her left hand when she was instructed to. The narrow, cold steel clamped around her wrist just short of biting into the flesh. Several of Darlton's clientele had their phones out now and were taking her picture. In minutes the news would be up all over Facebook and Twitter. Callum's Creek had embraced the technology that enabled faster gossip with pictures.

Alvin wheeled her around so that her back was to him while he clamped the open cuff around her other wrist. Her hands were now secured behind her, and she had to squelch the immediate claustrophobic feeling that snaked up from her belly. All she could think about was what this was going to do to her granny and to her son. Granny would understand, but there was no telling what kind of stories Travis would hear.

Alvin grabbed her by one arm and pulled her away from the vehicle. "Let's go."

Bekah nearly tripped because her legs weren't quite keeping up with her thoughts. She made a quickstep to keep up, and the deputy shook her irritably.

"Don't you try nothing, missy, or I'll clock you."

Holding in her anger and a scathing retort, Bekah marched resolutely toward the waiting cruiser. The Marines had taught her to march, and she did it now with all the skill she had. Just kept putting one foot in front of the other. And she held her head high.

Phone flashes went off around her, bright sparks against the neon-threaded night.

Alvin opened the back door of the cruiser, put a hand on

top of her head, and shoved her in. Sitting with her hands cuffed behind her was hard and uncomfortable. She leaned back and tried to keep herself calm. The mesh that separated her from the front seats was a constant reminder of where she was and how much trouble she was in. *Just breathe. Keep breathing. That's all you can do right now.*

Leaning her head to the side, she peered out the window and watched as the crowd closed in around Buck. They acted like they were concerned and worried, but Bekah knew from experience that most of them just wanted to see what had been done to him. The deputy tried to keep them back, but everybody had a story to tell. Hands gestured and called for attention. Alvin shook his head and talked, but nobody was listening.

Finally, after fifteen minutes according to the dashboard clock, an ambulance pulled into the parking lot. Two EMTs, both guys she recognized from high school, got out of the vehicle and brought out a stretcher. They worked quickly, putting Buck on a backboard and strapping him to the gurney. When everything was in place, they pushed Buck into the ambulance.

A shadow fell across the window an instant before Billy Roy stepped into view. He flashed a mocking smile at her. "Appears you got some bad trouble on your hands, Rebecca Ann. I would say I'm sorry . . . but I'm not. This may be better than watching Buck take your head off. I figure you're gonna get some county time out of this. You and your son have caused me plenty of grief these past few years."

Bekah had nothing to say. She knew the sheriff's cruiser

had audio and video pickup equipment in the back. That was standard these days even in Callum's Creek.

Deputy Alvin Trimble approached the car and touched his hat to Billy Roy. "Hey, Billy Roy."

"Hey, Alvin." Billy Roy grinned like a possum. "Got you a bad 'un tonight, huh?"

"Man, you sure knew how to pick 'em, didn't you?"

"We all make mistakes." Billy Roy nodded toward Bekah. "You'll want to watch yourself. Them Marines have sure riled her up."

"I get her back to the jail, she'll gentle down pretty fast."

Billy Roy nodded and touched his beer bottle to his hat brim. "I'll leave you with it." He turned and walked away.

Bekah took another breath and worked on the next one.

4

WHEN THE FOUR-WHEEL-DRIVE JEEP rumbled down the narrow street, Rageh Daud ducked into the nearest alley and attempted to hide. The early-morning light filtering through Mogadishu betrayed him, though. Or perhaps the men in the jeep were wide awake and looking for opportunities, and the sudden movement merely landed him on their radar.

Whatever the reason, the jeep pulled into the alley after Daud, and he hardened his heart for what he knew he must do, for what he must accept. *Only for the moment.* That was a promise he silently made to himself. Hardening the heart these days didn't take much. Sometimes he was surprised at the violence that he could unleash. Perhaps he was not so different from his father.

"Hold on there. We want to speak to you." The voice was blunt and heavy, full of authority.

Daud kept facing the other end of the alley and walking.

He wore khaki pants that were a little too big for him and a lightweight cotton shirt that had once been white. He was slim and of medium height, his skin dark except where months-old scars crossed his arms, neck, and right cheek. His hair was short and curled tightly in toward his scalp. He no longer looked like the man he had been. His losses had marked him and changed him forever. He was a hollow man now, filled only with hate and a desire to make others hurt.

One of the men released the slide on an AK-47. The sound was immediately distinctive, and Daud knew it well. He stopped and held up his hands.

"Now you understand." The men laughed in the bullying tone that made Daud so angry. Lately, there were many bullies in Somalia, many killers and defilers who did atrocious things in the name of God.

Daud hated those men and knew they were worthy of his attentions. Slowly, he turned to face the three killers. His gaze swept over their faces, and he knew them in a glance more deeply than they would expect. After all, he had grown up around such men. His father had commanded them, keeping them in line with his hard fists and a bullet when necessary.

The one holding the AK-47 lowered it. He was young and brash, a youth who had taken to the hard side of life because he feared being a victim. His scraggly beard barely shadowed his cheeks. He couldn't be more than fifteen or sixteen. Still, even small children were dangerous when armed with assault weapons as they often were these days.

For a moment, though, Daud thought of his own son, how he had held him after he'd been born, and how he'd held him the last time only a few months ago when he'd laid him in the same grave as his mother. Daud quelled the flicker of pity he felt for the boy holding the rifle and instead focused on the ice-cold intensity of the ever-present rage that wore him like a suit of clothes.

The driver was a slightly older version of the boy. Not a relative. He was just what the boy would become if he lived so long and learned no other direction in his life. Older, heavier, with eyes that were totally dead and uncaring. He picked at his yellowed teeth with a fingernail.

In the passenger seat, their leader sat and glared arrogantly, filled with self-importance. He was in his early thirties—the oldest of the men—and wore better clothes. A gold tooth gleamed at the front of his mouth. That tooth told Daud that the man wasn't a native of Mogadishu, and probably not of Somalia either. The Somali people knew better than to choose something like that gold tooth because it would mark them for thieves who would take that very tooth out of their mouths to put food on the table.

Daud guessed the man was from the Middle East, come down to be a leader among the al-Shabaab faction. Many were arriving from the Middle East since they had more training than the local people.

"What do you wish?" Daud lowered his hands to his sides.

The leader nodded curtly, his lips curled cruelly. "We are al-Shabaab, and we are raising funds for our efforts to retake our city. We wish for you to donate."

The al-Shabaab were Islamist militants warring with the Transitional Federal Government. When the TFG had taken over the city, the al-Shabaab had retreated to the jungle, but they hadn't entirely gone away. Mogadishu was too big and scattered for the TFG and the African Union Mission to Somalia (AMISOM) to effectively police. Plus, the TFG and AMISOM units got distracted watching over each other as well.

There was little trust left in Somalia. The al-Shabaab were believed to be funding the pirates that captured international ships and held them for ransom. Even if that were not true, the Islamist faction still raided the city and left decapitated citizens in their wake as a message.

Daud quietly regarded the men for a moment. They claimed to be al-Shabaab, and he had no reason to doubt them, but he knew they were truly there merely to rob him. He was a man alone in the city. "I have only a little money."

"I do not believe you." The leader cocked his head. "Your shoes say you have money."

Daud resisted the impulse to look down. He had deliberately chosen worn clothing, but he'd been loath to jettison the hiking boots. Somalia was rough country. A person had to have a four-wheel-drive vehicle to get around. Traveling the land on foot was no easier.

Now it looked as though his boots might be the death of him.

Reluctantly, Daud reached into his pockets and pulled out a thick wad of paper Somali shillings. The paper currency was almost worthless in the present economy. Buying a loaf of bread took a fistful of banknotes.

The man in the passenger seat climbed out and stepped forward. Daud resisted the impulse to smash the man's face in when he came to a stop in front of him. Such an action would only get him killed. Perhaps the young man with the rifle might not respond quickly enough or accurately enough, but the driver would. Daud was certain the man already had a hand on a pistol beneath the jeep's dashboard. At this distance, he would not miss.

The leader took the currency from Daud and quickly riffled through it. The bundle held a mixture of old notes and new, and even some of the Canadian notes that had been brought into the country when the Transitional National Government had been formed in 2000. The influx of additional monies had almost bankrupted Somalia. The people of Mogadishu had revolted and forced the TNG to buy back the foreign currency.

Smiling coldly, the leader shoved the bills into his shirt pocket. "This isn't the money I was referring to. I want the real money."

Daud didn't try to hide his subterfuge. He had prepared for this as well. He reached into his other pocket and brought out the thin sheaf of American money he had hoarded for his trip to Mogadishu.

The leader stared at him suspiciously. He flipped his thumb idly over the money. "American bills. Where did you get these?"

"I sold personal belongings. A computer. Some jewelry." His wife no longer had need of her wedding rings or the other things he'd bought her during their marriage. He'd still felt guilty about not putting those things into her grave with her, but he'd needed money if he and his son were to survive.

Then, after his son had died, Daud had needed the money to get supplies, information, and a pistol. He was going to survive, and he would recognize few friends and few allies.

"Liar." The word cut the air like a bullet.

Daud stood quietly in front of the man. "I am telling you the truth."

"The American CIA pays our people to spy on their brothers."

"I am no spy."

"I do not believe you."

"I am sorry, but that is the best answer I can give you. Months ago, I was a businessman. The attacks within the city killed my wife and son." Daud felt the wetness gathering in his eyes, and it surprised him. He'd felt certain he had no more tears left. But he told the truth so the man could sense no falsehood. "My business was destroyed. I sold what I had left."

"And you did not leave the country?"

Daud shrugged. "Where would I go? This place has always been my home."

The man waggled the American currency. "I do not believe this is all the money you have."

Daud stood still and silent.

"Give me the rest of it."

"There is—"

The man moved more quickly than Daud would have believed possible. With a practiced economy of motion, the man smashed his pistol butt into Daud's forehead.

Stunned, head suddenly throbbing with pain, Daud

dropped to his knees. He almost reached for the man's legs to yank them out from under him, but he stopped himself just in time. If he did that, the man or the boy with the assault rifle might shoot him. Still, he was tempted, and he could be fast when he wanted to be.

The man hit him with the pistol again, then whipped Daud down to the rough ground. At one time the alley had been covered by concrete, put there by the Communists who had been in control of the country in the 1970s, when Somalia had been the Somali Democratic Republic. But time and use had worn the concrete back down to bedrock. The rough surface dug into Daud's face, but he could barely feel the heat or the abrasive texture against his nerve-deadened cheek. He tasted his blood, though.

Although he was not completely stunned, he pretended that he was. The leader was very thorough in his search of Daud's clothing. The man found the thicker sheaf of American currency hidden in Daud's belt. As a last insult, he took Daud's boots and socks, leaving him barefoot in the alley. Then he kicked Daud in the head.

As the new explosion of blood filled his mouth and his senses faded, Daud mocked himself. *Welcome back home, Rageh.* His vision blanked, but he heard the leader walking back to the jeep. *Enjoy your newfound wealth, Gold Tooth. I will come for you.*

★　★　★

When Daud regained consciousness, his face had swollen considerably and a small child was laboring to rob him. The boy had his hand deep inside Daud's pants pocket and was rummaging for change. Feeling the shift of Daud's body, the boy looked at his victim and squeaked in alarm. He knotted his fingers into a fist, seized all the coins he could, and withdrew his hand; then he took off running.

Head spinning, thinking he was going to be sick, Daud glanced up and stared into the bright sky that temporarily blinded him. Sharp lances of agony fired through his brain. The slap of the boy's bare feet against the alley ground echoed inside his skull. At the other end of the alley, glimpsed through spots that swam through his vision, the boy joined a few other children in a pack and they all ran as if for their lives.

Daud touched his nose and felt the caked blood on his upper lip. He'd been unconscious for a while. He took another breath, then forced himself to his feet. When he glanced at his wrist, he discovered the al-Shabaab men had taken his cheap watch as well. He'd bought it for an American dollar from a sailor at the harbor.

He started walking, and the sharp rocks along the alley bit into his feet. Thankfully, the thick pads that had formed on his feet as a young boy hadn't completely gone away. The feet were not nearly so much of a problem as his head.

★　★　★

A half hour later, Daud arrived at Afrah's house. The home was a small building covered in corrugated metal in the middle of a small sea of such structures. Half of those had been destroyed not so long ago, and their charred remains stood out like meteor craters among the other makeshift houses.

His son had never had to live so hard, and Daud took pride in that. But Ibrahim had died hard, suffering from infections that had taken three days to steal his life from him. Daud had been forced to open his wife's grave to lay their son with her.

After that, Daud had given up. His heart had turned to stone, and he had walked away from everything he'd believed in. Now he was back in the old neighborhood where his father had raised him, a place that was just across the city but a world away. His wife had never seen this part of him. She had known only the college graduate and the businessman he had become, not the son of a brigand who had grown up hard and hungry until his loving father had set him on another path.

Daud stood to one side of the door and knocked, out of the way in case Afrah was drunk and paranoid. Afrah had taken to alcohol when he'd renounced the thin veneer of Muslim faith he'd learned from his mother. The metal covering the door felt hot beneath Daud's hand.

"Who is it?" The voice was deep and husky, not quite alert.

"Rageh Daud."

A moment passed. Then the door edged open. A huge, bearded face peered out through the opening. Afrah's face looked like a threatening storm cloud as he peered at Daud over the muzzle of a Tokarev 9mm pistol. After he had renounced Islam, Afrah became a Communist for a time and learned to drink from the Russians while they were in-country.

"I do not have business with you." Afrah's eyes narrowed and his finger rested on the pistol's trigger. "Go someplace else or you will regret it."

"Afrah, friend to my father, do you not know me?" Daud knew that he was more gaunt than he had ever been. His face had suffered from the injuries received from the bomb as well as the sudden weight loss, and the sadness that had turned him numb inside had stamped his features.

"Your father?" Afrah looked at him a moment longer. The man was in his fifties, though he still looked to be in his physical prime, but Daud feared that his mind was no longer as true as it had once been. "Rageh? Can that be you?"

"Yes."

Whooping with unrestrained joy, Afrah shoved open the door and stepped outside. He was a bull of a man, wide through the shoulders and shaggy now because his hair had grown long. Wisps of gray showed at his temples and in his beard. An old scar—but new to Daud—ran down the man's left cheek and caught his upper lip, puckering it up into a madman's leer.

He wrapped his arms around Daud and lifted him from his feet. The huge embrace and the sudden movement drew a groan of pain from Daud.

Gently, like he was handling a babe, Afrah placed Daud once more on his feet. "You have been ill-treated, Rageh."

"I have."

Afrah trailed fingers over the fresh scarring on Daud's face. "And you have been mightily wounded."

"Yes."

"Your father would have killed the man who has done such a thing to you."

"I know. May I come in?"

"Of course." Afrah opened the door and gestured inside.

"We have many things to speak of, and I would learn what you know of an al-Shabaab man who has a gold tooth." Daud touched his front tooth, though pulling his lip back to show Afrah hurt. "Here."

"I know of such a man."

"Good. Because I am going to kill him."

5

AT THE JAIL, Sheriff's Deputy Alvin Trimble guided Bekah in through the back way. She went without speaking, wishing everything she was experiencing was just a bad dream, wishing again that she had stayed home with her granny and Travis. That was where she should have been. She had no business going into town. She hadn't even enjoyed hanging out with Connie and the others.

"Did you try to kill Buck?" Alvin's tone was flatly accusing. He halted beside a security door and buzzed for admittance.

"No." Bekah refused to look at him, but she knew that not answering would make things worse. Alvin Trimble wasn't much different from Buck Miller as she recalled, but he was on the side of the law.

"Buck says you did."

"Buck pulled a knife on me. That's why I got the jack handle."

"That's not how he says it."

"You need to look for that knife." Bekah said that, but in her heart she was sure that someone had scooped the weapon up. Maybe it was to protect Buck, or maybe it was just theft, pure and simple. It could have been someone looking for a souvenir.

"I need to get you booked and in a cell, that's what I need to do. And you need to be praying Buck survives."

"He has a broken wrist and a fractured knee. He's not going to die."

"And what makes you the expert of that?"

Bekah looked at Alvin then and spoke calmly. "I've seen men die. I've held a couple of them in my arms while they talked to their mommas, then crossed over to someplace else. I know what a dying man looks like. Do you?"

Alvin shrank back from her for just an instant, then came back filled with anger and embarrassment. She'd forgotten how prideful small-town men were. Or maybe she hadn't cared. She wasn't sure which. "I've seen my share of dead people. We get traffic accidents out here, and I worked the Hickerson killing."

Bekah vaguely remembered the Hickerson killing. The murder had been a domestic dispute that had turned deadly a couple years ago. Bekah resisted the impulse to tell him that a shooting was nothing like having to go out and help gather pieces of a fellow Marine who had gotten blown up by an IED only a few feet away. She turned her attention back to the security door as it buzzed.

"You said I was drunk and disorderly."

"You are."

"Then hook me up to a Breathalyzer. Give me a blood test."

"Why don't you just be quiet." Alvin grabbed the door and opened it, then shoved Bekah ahead of him. She kept pace, following the narrow hallway past the jail cells. Low-wattage bulbs filled the area with pale light that barely penetrated the darkness.

Bekah barely kept herself calm. She wanted the cuffs off, and she wanted to know how badly getting arrested— even under these bogus pretenses—would harm her career as a Marine reservist. She needed that job. She needed the income and the insurance. She needed a way to take care of her son and herself.

And she liked what she did as a Marine. Billy Roy couldn't be allowed to take that away from her.

For just a moment she considered prayer. That was an automatic response left over from her childhood days. Her grandparents had always taken her to church. Her daddy had been on the road a lot, and her momma had worked all the time. Or been gone. Bekah wasn't quite sure which was the truth there. Rumors still persisted about her momma even though that was nearly twenty years ago. Callum's Creek was a town that relished hanging on to dirty laundry. Kids inherited all those troubles the day they were born and carried them around forever.

As long as they remained in Callum's Creek.

Sometimes Bekah had thought about getting out of town, but her granny lived here, and she knew the woman would never leave. Not with Grandpa buried in the small family cemetery on the property her granny kept.

Bekah didn't pray, though. God had stopped answering her prayers a long time ago. She didn't think God even knew she was alive these days.

★   ★   ★

The female jailer expertly rolled Bekah's fingers on an ink pad, then rolled them again across the ten-card, the document that held her fingerprints. The woman was gray-haired and in her late forties. Bekah could almost recall her name, but it eluded her. She was heavyset and looked more like a momma than a peace officer.

"You need to get some ice on that hand." The jailer held up Bekah's right hand. Bruising was already swelling the knuckles and turning the flesh purplish. "I'll see that you get some."

"Thank you."

"Surprised that all you got is a little damage to one hand." The jailer kept rolling Bekah's fingers, taking it easy with the wounded hand. "You take on a bruiser like Buck Miller, I'd expect them to have to cart you out of there. The way I heard it from dispatch, you pretty much cleaned his clock." The woman smiled at her admiringly.

Despite the circumstances, Bekah grinned a little. "I suppose I did."

"Some of the gals around here should send you a thank-you note. Buck's rode roughshod over a few of them."

"I know."

"If the world was fair, I'd be booking him into a cell tonight. Not you." The jailer finished the last finger and handed Bekah a towelette to clean up with. "But we both know the world ain't fair, don't we?"

Bekah wiped the ink from her fingers and didn't say anything.

"Still, coulda been worse."

"How do you figure?"

"They coulda been carting you off to the hospital tonight. You got to be thankful for that."

"Yes ma'am."

The jailer looked at Bekah. "They said you're a Marine."

"Reservist."

The woman nodded. "Marines are a tough bunch. My daddy was a Marine. Fought back in World War II, then again in Korea. He was a good man. One thing he always remembered and took pride in throughout his life—and there were precious few things to take pride in where I grew up—was that he was a Marine."

"Yes ma'am."

"You just keep your head up, Marine. You'll get through this."

"Thank you."

"Now let's get you back to one of those cells. You look like you could use some sleep."

Bekah didn't think she could sleep, but the adrenaline drain had left her empty.

★   ★   ★

The eight-by-eight jail cell felt as closed-in as a broom closet and smelled of disinfectant and old urine. The county was poor and struggling; it didn't put a lot of money into its criminal-holding facilities.

Bekah sat on one of the two cots bolted to the cinder blocks and looked at the blank wall. There was nothing else she could do. Besides the two cots, there was only a toilet and a sink—bare essentials. In another cell, a drunken man sang church hymns and another man growled curses at him and told him to shut up.

She had no idea of how much time had passed before Alvin came back to the holding area. He held a fresh cup of coffee, and the smell cut through the stink of disinfectant and urine. "Just wanted to see how you were holding up."

"I'm fine."

"Did the Marines teach you how to handle jail time?"

Bekah ignored that. "Don't I get a phone call?"

"Who would you call? Judge has gotta set bail before you can bond out. That won't come till the hearing in the morning. If you can get before him in the morning."

Bekah didn't even know a bail bondsman, nor how that process worked. The only person she could call would be her granny, and she didn't like the idea of waking the old woman in the middle of the night.

"How is Connie?"

Alvin shrugged. "Just had a nosebleed. Nothing much." He sipped the coffee. "Buck is gonna live."

Bekah ignored that. "Did Connie swear out a complaint against him?"

"No."

Confused, Bekah looked at Alvin again. "Why not?"

"You'd have to ask her."

"Buck *hit* her. More than once."

"That ain't how she's telling it. She says she slipped and fell, and you went off half-cocked, screaming and yelling at Buck. Attacked him."

The floor seemed to drop away under Bekah.

"Yeah, you're in a world of hurt." Alvin shook his head. "I'm betting Judge Harrelson throws the book at you in the morning. You get a good night's sleep. We start early tomorrow." He turned and walked away.

Bekah sat in the darkness, alone and uncertain about what her immediate future held. She didn't know what she was supposed to do. *Suck it up, Marine. Take things one step at a time.*

Because she'd stood post in enemy-occupied areas, she knew how to turn off her mind when she needed to sleep. She lay back on the cot and tried not to think about what might live there. None of it could be any worse than the bugs and lizards and snakes she'd had to put up with in Helmand province. At least there was no sand.

After a while, she slept.

★　　★　　★

At eight o'clock the next morning, Bekah filed into the judge's courtroom behind four other prisoners and ahead of two. Two of them had on orange jumpsuits. All of them were in handcuffs. The guys in the orange jumpsuits had leg irons as well. The bailiff directed them to sit in the front rows, which were marked for detainees. A scattered double handful of people occupied the rows farther back.

Bekah was mortified to see that her granny sat in one of those rows beside Travis.

"Momma!" Travis tried to get up and run to her, but Granny caught him and held him back, talking quietly into his ear. Travis wasn't happy but finally went back to his seat.

Bekah smiled at her son and mouthed *I'm sorry* to her granny.

The old woman smiled back and shook her head. Granny was in her late sixties—past retirement age—and was thin. Grandpa had always said Granny was made out of rawhide and bone and filled with sheer cussedness, because she never backed down from anyone or anything. He'd also told Bekah that she had a lot of her granny in her and that she should take pride in the fact.

Bekah did. When her granny had been younger, she had broken horses, roped cattle, and done every nasty job required around the ranch. She'd mucked out stalls, then cleaned up and had supper on the table when everyone came in tired and hungry.

Age had turned Granny's hair white, and she'd cut it short years ago so it wouldn't be a bother. She was in one of her Sunday dresses today, not the everyday jeans and blouse and boots she normally wore. Time had slowed the woman down, but she still put in full days. Helping raise Travis had guaranteed that. That chore made Bekah feel guilty, because her granny shouldn't have had to raise her granddaughter, much less her great-grandson. She should have been able to enjoy her twilight years.

Whenever Bekah brought that up, though, her granny

just waved it away. *"Both of us are here just doing the Lord's work, girl. He don't ever give you more than you can handle. We'll get through this just fine. And with your grandpa gone, the Lord knows I needed something to do so that I didn't just wither away. The boy makes life new again, and I give thanks for that."*

Even when Bekah couldn't manage her own belief, she clung to her granny's faith. That was what she had always done. She took her seat on the bench and waited a few minutes till the bailiff told them all to rise. Then she stood as the judge entered the courtroom.

Warren Harrelson had a reputation as a hard-nosed judge. Repeat offenders were not welcome in his courtroom. Habitual drunk drivers and meth dealers found permanent homes in prison on his watch.

Now in his sixties, Harrelson had been doling out justice in the county for over twenty years. Standing over six feet tall, brown hair finally giving way to gray, freckled, broad across the chest, and only ten pounds over his best weight, the judge was an imposing figure. He didn't wear robes this morning, since these were hearings and not actual court trials. He wore slacks and a golf shirt. He took his place at the bench and told everyone to be seated.

Most of the cases appeared to be everyday business. The two men in orange jumpsuits pled guilty and got prison time, which ratcheted up Bekah's feelings of unease. She'd never been to court before and had only seen trials on television. This didn't seem much like television.

One of the women pled out to a charge of prostitution, and that shocked Bekah because the woman had been picked up in Callum's Creek. Bekah hadn't known that particular vice existed in her hometown. She received an additional thirty days to the probation sentence she'd already been under.

The other woman pled guilty to a charge of dealing meth, but the public defender interjected, "Her circumstances were still pending, Your Honor."

"Means she's gonna rat somebody out." That came from the young man seated beside Bekah. His breath was harsh and his body odor was severe. The sniffles he kept having and the jittery way he sat there told her that he was probably a meth addict.

The judge was quiet a moment as he read over the next sheet of paper. Then he called out her name. "Rebecca Ann Shaw."

6

"HERE, YOUR HONOR." Bekah stood and tried to ignore the man chuckling beside her.

"This ain't homeroom, girl."

Harrelson adjusted his reading glasses and looked over the paper again. "Says here you attacked a man last night."

"I defended myself." Bekah wanted that distinction made very clear.

"With a tire iron."

"He had a knife."

Harrelson gazed at the paper again, then cut his gaze over to Alvin Trimble, who stood in one corner of the courtroom. "You're the arresting officer, Deputy Trimble?"

"Yes sir."

"Did you find a knife?"

"No sir, I did not."

"Did you look?"

Trimble hesitated just a second before answering. "Yes sir, I did. Long and hard."

"No knife?"

"None, Your Honor."

Harrelson glanced back at Bekah. "Buck Miller has been in my courtroom a time or two. In my opinion, the man outweighs you by a hundred pounds, Ms. Shaw. That about right?"

"I wouldn't know, sir."

"Well, we'll just take my estimate into account for now."

Bekah nodded.

"That's a considerable size difference. Knife or no knife, you might feel you needed a tire iron to fight him."

"There was a knife." Bekah spoke coldly and precisely. "I saw it. The knife was there. Someone picked it up."

"Do you have any idea of who might have done that?"

Billy Roy's name was at the tip of Bekah's tongue, but she shook her head. "No sir. There were a lot of people at Darlton's."

"Says here you're a Marine reservist."

"Yes sir."

"Seen action?"

Bekah nodded. "One tour in Iraq. One in Helmand province. Afghanistan."

"I know where Helmand province is." Harrelson stroked his jaw with the backs of his fingers. "That's rough country. Marines are having a hard time there."

"Yes sir."

"I was a soldier too. Served in regular Army back when

Vietnam was the hot spot. I remember coming back home and how hard it was to adjust after being in-country. Felt like I was going to jump out of my skin every time somebody moved too fast. Those were hard times."

Bekah didn't know what to do with that, so she let it pass.

"What I'm trying to say, young lady, is that sometimes those experiences lead us to make mistakes when we're trying to integrate with the civilian populace again."

"That isn't what happened. Buck Miller attacked a friend of mine. I tried to get her out of there. Buck Miller turned that into a physical confrontation."

Harrelson looked back at Alvin. "Has anyone talked to the friend?"

Alvin nodded. "Yes sir. Says she slipped and fell, and then Bekah Shaw went wacko." He shrugged. "I think it must have been the sight of blood."

"You do, do you?" Harrelson's tone turned chilly. "You're an expert in combat fatigue, Deputy?"

Alvin's face turned red. He straightened up self-consciously. "No sir."

"Then maybe you'll keep your opinions regarding such matters out of my courtroom."

"Yes sir."

Harrelson glanced at the sheet again. "Drunk and disorderly? Was Ms. Shaw given a Breathalyzer test?"

"No, Your Honor."

"Why wasn't she?"

"I didn't see the need for one. I smelled the liquor on her."

"I see."

"My expert testimony, Your Honor. Lots of experience in field sobriety testing."

Clearly irritated, Harrelson placed the paper down in front of him. He looked back at Bekah. "Were you drunk?"

"No sir."

"Had you been drinking?"

"One beer an hour before this happened."

Harrelson nodded. "It would help if your *friend* would come forward—or anyone else who was at Darlton's for that matter—and tell this story your way. Any chance of that happening?"

Bekah swallowed and thought about it. There was a chance that most of the people in the bar and grill didn't know what had happened that night and weren't sure who started the fight. But Bekah was willing to put money on the fact that Buck Miller and his cronies had already put pressure on anyone who might be willing to testify on her behalf. They'd handled things that way in the past, and everyone in Callum's Creek knew that.

"If it hasn't happened before now, Your Honor, I don't think so."

Harrelson sighed. "Me neither. And that being so, I have no choice but to carry your case over to trial. Is there someone here to post bail for you?"

Before Bekah could reply, her granny stood up. "I am, Your Honor."

Harrelson looked out into the audience. "Who are you?"

"Mrs. Alice Shaw. Her grandma."

"That's fine, Mrs. Shaw." Harrelson nodded toward the

bailiff. "Have someone help Mrs. Shaw." He turned back to Bekah. "We should have you out of here in just a little while."

Gratefully, Bekah nodded and resumed her seat. She couldn't wait to get out.

★   ★   ★

A half hour later, Bekah stood at the booking desk with her granny and Travis. Her son rested in her arms, holding on fiercely while he looked around at the strange surroundings.

"This is a police house." Travis's voice was a whisper.

"It is." Bekah didn't bother trying to make the distinction between police and sheriff's deputies.

"They're the good guys."

"They are." Bekah wasn't feeling too friendly toward the law enforcement department at the moment, though.

"Did you do something wrong, Momma?"

That was a hard question to answer, and Bekah hesitated.

Granny came to her rescue, smiling up at the boy and patting him on the shoulder. "No, sweetie, your momma didn't do anything wrong. The police just don't have their facts straight. Everything's going to be just fine."

"Good."

Bekah shot her granny a look, but the old woman shook her head. There were things they didn't talk about around Travis. When the deputy handed her the manila envelope containing her personal effects, Bekah checked them over, then signed the sheet.

Granny reached over and took her arm. "Let's go get

you something to eat. I didn't have much of a breakfast this morning."

Travis rubbed his stomach. "Me neither. Can we have McDonald's?"

Bekah grinned at her son and bumped heads with him playfully. "Of course you can have McDonald's."

★   ★   ★

Murchison, Oklahoma, was the county seat, so it was a lot larger than Callum's Creek, but it was still small-time next to Oklahoma City, Tulsa, or Houston. Bekah hadn't traveled much in the United States, so she hadn't seen the cosmopolitan cities like New York or Los Angeles.

However, the town did boast a McDonald's, and Travis loved to go there every chance he got. He sat through half of his Egg McMuffin, then begged to be set free. Now he was crawling through the brightly colored PlayPlace.

Bekah picked at her breakfast, but she was hungry enough and sensible enough that she knew she was going to work her way through it. Once Travis had gone to find "new friends," Bekah told her granny what had happened the previous night.

"This is all my fault."

"Nonsense." Granny lightly slapped her hand. "You were defending Connie Hiller. I'd have thought less of you if you hadn't. I'm just thankful you weren't hurt. Things could have gone the other way."

"I know. I got lucky."

"I think maybe there was more than luck involved, Bekah

Ann. You're a good Marine. You knew what to do and you did it."

At first, Granny hadn't embraced the idea of Bekah serving in the military. And that was before Bekah's activation and first tour as part of the support teams from the First Battalion, Twenty-Third Marines based in Houston.

For a time they'd been at odds over the kind of momma Bekah would be for Travis. Bekah had argued the point, saying she needed training for something, and she couldn't manage college on her own. The money she earned as a Marine would help with that.

Then she'd felt guilty about leaving Travis with her granny, knowing taking care of the boy would be a hardship. Granny had made that easier for her, pointing out that Travis would have to live with his closest relative while Bekah was gone, and that there was no one else around since Billy Roy Briggs and his family weren't going to have anything to do with her son.

Granny shook her head angrily. "What chaps my hide is the fact that none of those people in Darlton's will come forward and tell the truth."

"Buck Miller and his friends have a reputation for hurting folks who cross them." That said, Bekah felt an uneasy feeling slide through her. "We might need to watch ourselves for a while."

"Pshaw!" Granny waved that away. "I keep a loaded shotgun at home and I'm carrying my pistol in my purse. Buck Miller and his trash had better not come around and try to start trouble."

Bekah glanced at Granny's purse. "You carried the pistol into the courthouse this morning?"

"Of course not. I left it out in the truck, in the glove box. I just put it back in my purse while you were taking Travis to the bathroom."

Smiling, Bekah took a deep breath. Her granny had carried the .38 revolver for years. Her grandpa, a retired volunteer peace officer himself, had insisted on it. He'd given Bekah her first pistol, a .38 just like her granny's, when she'd turned sixteen and started working at Hollister's Fine Dining, the local greasy spoon where Bekah picked up shifts when she wasn't with the Marines. She hadn't carried it, though, and had left it at home in the box it came in. She'd grown up with shotguns and .22 rifles, and she'd been qualified as a marksman on the Marine range. She took pride in that skill because shooting was something her grandpa had taught her.

Travis climbed through the PlayPlace, squealing with joy as he chased after his new friends. Bekah watched him. "I'm in a lot of trouble, Granny."

Her granny reached out and took her hand, squeezing it briefly. "Trouble's something this family is familiar with, baby girl. You just remember that, and remember that we've always seen it through. We'll see this through too. Just you wait and see."

"The courts are calling this a felony. I can't have a felony on my record and stay a Marine. Not something like this."

"You don't know that yet. One step at a time. Just like me and your grandpa taught you to do. No matter how hard you try, you can only live life like that."

★   ★   ★

After excusing herself and leaving Travis in her granny's care, Bekah walked into the McDonald's parking lot and punched in Connie Hiller's number. The phone rang and rang at the other end of the connection. When the voice mail picked up, Bekah hung up and called right back. She was mad and couldn't let it go.

Finally, Connie picked up and her voice was thick and sounded congested. "What do you want?"

"I want to know why you're telling everyone that you *slipped* in Darlton's."

"Are you recording this phone call?"

Bekah couldn't believe it. "No. Of course not."

"Because if you are, I slipped and fell. You can't make me say anything else."

"Buck Miller was slapping you around like a rag doll." Bekah's voice got higher than she'd intended. An older couple with three grandkids stepped away from her on their way into the restaurant.

"I don't know what you're talking about. Are you trying to make yourself out to be some kind of hero, Bekah Ann?"

"No, but I'm in trouble with the law, and I'm in that trouble because of you."

"I didn't ask you for no help."

"You weren't exactly able to, as I recall." Bekah wanted to scream, but she knew it wouldn't do any good.

"I got my nose broke and stitches in my cheek trying to help you get your child support."

"Fine. Then tell it that way. But tell it."

"This wouldn't have happened if you stood up to Billy Roy. I was only doing what you're too afraid to do."

"That's insane." Bekah couldn't believe it. "I stood up to Buck Miller, and he had a knife."

"I got hurt because you wouldn't take care of your own business. Now you want to blame this all on me? You want me to stick my neck out where Buck Miller and his thugs will snap it off? And you know he's running with some of those methheads now. You're not a very good friend, Bekah. I can't believe it's taken me this long to figure that out."

The phone clicked dead in Bekah's ear.

Angry and frustrated, Bekah looked at the phone and thought about calling back. But she knew it wouldn't do any good. Connie had already chosen her path through the current mess. There was nothing she could do to change her mind. Feeling down and whipped, Bekah retreated back into McDonald's.

7

THE NEXT DAY, Bekah parked her twenty-year-old Chevy pickup out behind Hollister's Fine Dining. The day's heat had already started to kick in, but the Chevy's air-conditioning had played out a couple years ago and she hadn't wanted to replace it because it was so expensive. She drove the pickup with the windows down, but that didn't help much except to give her a driver's tan, left arm darker than the right.

She listened to the last bit of one of her favorite Kellie Pickler songs, then shut off the radio and picked up the brown waitress apron with *Hollister's Fine Dining* in gold thread across the bottom. At least Hollister's allowed casual wear while waiting tables. She wore jeans, tennis shoes, and a kelly-green blouse. As she walked around the restaurant, smelling the burgers and fried onions, she tied the apron around her waist.

Hollister's wasn't "fine dining," but the small brick

restaurant was the place in Callum's Creek where all the locals came to eat when they were tired of eating at home. Or Sundays after church. The church crowd was always good, but the servers had to dress up a little better then. It was not a hardship to Bekah. She liked the energy that filled the restaurant on those days. Things just seemed more positive.

She'd worked there since high school. Her grandpa, though she hadn't known it at the time, had arranged her job through Mr. Evan Hollister, the original owner. Grandpa had always looked out for her, and it was embarrassing when Bekah found out a couple years later. But Grandpa had meant well, and Mr. Hollister had been a good boss, training her on everything.

The present Mr. Hollister—the original had died a few years before Grandpa—wasn't so good. Dwight Hollister was in his forties and tight with a penny, and he made sure every employee he had worked hard for their wages. He could call the shots on that because there weren't too many places in town where high school kids—and single moms—could work flexible schedules.

The jobs at the Beep 'N' Buy got handed down by the Morton family, and they were picky about whom they hired. The rest of the work around Callum's Creek was all ranch and farm related. Nobody wanted to work at Fancher's pig farm. The smell lingered even miles away. The only other choice for work was Murchison, which was a seventeen-mile drive, one way. The cost of gasoline would eat into whatever check she brought home.

The bond money, which she had insisted on paying back to her granny, had cut deeply into Bekah's savings, and finding a lawyer to represent her at trial was going to be even more costly. She'd gone to bed with that in her mind last night, and it had been the first thing she'd thought of this morning.

Things were bad enough that she was beginning to hope her unit might get activated again. The increase in pay would be awesome, but she would have to be away from Travis again for God only knew how long.

Who are you kidding? God doesn't see you. You're invisible on that particular radar screen.

Drawing a final breath, looking forward to the air-conditioning inside, Bekah pushed the door open and walked in. The restaurant was casual—tables and chairs that mostly went together, checked curtains that were faded but regularly cleaned. The concrete floor had wear patterns between the tables and booths, but the restaurant still smelled like home cooking: chili and cornbread and fried chicken.

She inhaled, remembering those cold nights in Afghanistan when all she'd had to eat was an MRE that certainly didn't fit the description printed on the package. Outside of her granny's kitchen, Hollister's was the place that smelled most like home.

It was a quarter to seven and a dozen or so regulars, most of them seniors who spent most of the morning gossiping, sat in the dining area. Conversation stopped for a moment as they all looked at her.

Glad to see the local grapevine is still in effect. Bekah nodded and focused her attention on the door to the kitchen. She needed to punch in and get started. She was pulling a double today.

Once she was through the back door, Dwight Hollister called her name. He sat in the small office off the kitchen, a squat little man with too-perfect hair, a short-sleeved shirt, and bland brown eyes behind thick-lensed glasses.

"Can you come in here for a minute?" Dwight rested his hands over his paunch and leaned back in his chair.

Bekah had a bad feeling. Dwight was being polite. The man was *never* polite. Uneasily, she took the chair he waved her toward. She sat and waited.

"Bekah, there's no good way to put this to you, but I'm going to have to let you go." Dwight looked sour.

"Let me go?" At first the words didn't make any sense to Bekah.

"Yeah. I'm sorry, but that's just how it has to be."

"Why?"

Dwight waved a hand. "Cutbacks. It's this recession we're in. Gotta make some adjustments. Nothing personal."

"I work on tips, Mr. Hollister. And you don't provide benefits. It's not like the restaurant is out a lot of money having me at this job."

"I'm sorry. It's just the way it has to be." Dwight looked down and wouldn't meet her eyes. He reached into a drawer and came out with an envelope. "I've got your final check here. I added an extra week's pay."

Numbly, Bekah took the envelope because she didn't know what else she was supposed to do.

"It's not like you really needed this job, Bekah. Your grandma looks out for you and your son."

That brought some anger back to Bekah and she tried to rein it in. "I make my own way, Mr. Hollister. I work hard to make my own way."

"Don't make this any more difficult than it has to be."

"Why does it have to be difficult? What has changed?"

"Bekah." Dwight looked at her calmly, and she saw that there was maybe a little shame in his gaze, but it wasn't going to affect his decision. "You've worked at this restaurant for nine years, off and on. Since you were a girl. The Hollister family has taken care of you."

"And I've worked hard, Mr. Hollister. I've worked every shift that was asked, and I've picked up slack when there was some. The only time I've ever missed is when I was having Travis."

"You missed while you were off with the Marines too. I took care of you then, and I made sure you had a job when you came back."

Bekah wanted to point out again how hard she worked, but she knew it wouldn't do any good.

"I just can't do that anymore. I'm sorry."

"This is about Buck Miller, isn't it?"

Dwight hesitated, then gave her a short nod. "Yes. It is. I can't afford to have him or his friends come in here and bust the place up. Darlton's was lucky to get by with just a little damage the other night. Those people Buck is running with these days?" He shook his head. "Some of those folks are dangerous. I can't risk anybody getting hurt. Buck's gonna get back on his feet again, and he might just come looking for you. I can't take that chance." He paused. "I'll be happy to give you a recommendation for somewhere else. Anywhere else you want to go."

"Where am I supposed to go?"

"They got restaurants in Murchison, secretarial jobs, other things. You can find something. I know you can."

Bekah had already thought about those options a long time ago. The truth of the matter was that she was a blue-collar girl with little training. The Marines hadn't expanded her knowledge base like she'd hoped. She'd learned to shoot and to guard and to march wherever she'd been ordered, just to do more of the same.

"Let me know if I can help you."

Knowing that was her cue to leave, Bekah stood. "Thank you."

Dwight nodded.

Head high, ignoring the emotions sloshing around inside her, Bekah walked out of the restaurant and back into the heat of the day. She paused at the front of the building and dug in her pants pocket for change, then bought copies of the *Oklahoman* and the *Murchison Gazette*.

When she returned to her truck, she went down to the Beep 'N' Buy to fill up the gas tank. As the pump cycled, draining her bank account of more money, she leafed through the classified ads and circled jobs that looked like something she could do.

She wasn't going to give up. She had too much of her grandparents in her for that. But it felt like every direction she faced was uphill, like she was climbing out of a well.

Then she remembered something her grandpa had always

told her. *"No matter how tough the way looks, little girl, all it takes is that first step to get you going. Just take that step."*

She took out her phone and started calling the numbers she'd circled in the *Gazette*. She'd start there, see how far she got.

★   ★   ★

The truck hesitated a few times on the old country road that led back to the Shaw farm. The engine coughed and sputtered and wheezed like an asthmatic.

Tired and frustrated, spent from a day relentlessly pounding pavement and talking to strangers about jobs that didn't exist or required more experience than she had, Bekah stomped the accelerator. "C'mon. Don't quit on me now."

She gazed at the fuel gauge and saw that she had used just under half a tank. The heat gauge was well within range as well.

With a final spastic cough, the engine died completely and the power steering went out. Thankfully the brakes were manual. She stomped hard on the brake pedal and muscled the truck to the side of the road.

Resisting the urge to cry or curse, Bekah popped the hood and got out the small toolbox she carried behind the seat. Walking around to the front of the truck, she smelled gasoline and guessed at the problem she was going to find.

She loved the truck for two reasons: because her grandpa had given it to her and because she could work on it. They had rebuilt the engine together, and it had run like a top.

Until today.

The spark plugs and coil wires had been changed right

before she'd headed to Afghanistan for her last tour, so they should still be in fine shape. That left the carburetor or the fuel pump. Both of which were expensive. All the local auto shops and salvage yards would be closed up tonight, and tomorrow was Saturday. Most of them closed at noon, even in Murchison.

Disheartened, Bekah closed the hood and put her tools back behind the seat. She guessed she was still four miles from home. She did the only thing she knew to do: she called home.

★   ★   ★

"She give out on you, did she?" Clyde Walters, as big and affable as ever, climbed out from behind the steering wheel of his tow truck. He was tall and broad, and he looked like a wild-maned Santa Claus in overalls. A Texas Rangers ball cap held his white hair in place. The truck's bright lights carved holes in the darkness that had settled over the deserted road.

"Yes." Bekah tried to put on a smile, but she really wasn't feeling it. She'd placed road flares around the truck, and the glow left spots dancing in her vision.

"Well, don't you worry, little missy. We'll get you and your truck home tonight. We ain't gonna leave either one of you stranded out here." Clyde started hauling chains from the back end of the tow truck. "Do you know what's wrong with her? Got plenty of gas?"

"Half a tank. I think it's the fuel pump or the carburetor."

"You know how to fix those, right?" Clyde crawled under the back of her truck and started attaching the chains. "Big Travis, he was right proud of the way you took to mechanicking and hunting and fishing."

After Travis was born, everyone started calling her grandpa Big Travis.

"I know how."

"You're lucky you got a model you can work on. Most cars these days, you gotta be a computer technician to climb up under the hood."

"I know. That's why Grandpa insisted on this truck and why he helped me rebuild it."

"Your granddaddy was a smart man."

"He was."

Clyde grabbed hold of the truck's bumper and levered himself up. He wiped his hands clean on a red rag. "I miss talking to him."

"Me too." Bekah swallowed an unexpected lump in her throat. "I appreciate you coming out here to get me, Mr. Walters."

Clyde waved that away. "I can't refuse your grandma anything. I promised your granddaddy I'd help look after her, so that means I'm helping look after you and your young'un too. Let's get in my truck. I got a couple sodas in the cooler. I bet you could use one about now."

★ ★ ★

Driving carefully over the cattle guard at the entrance to the small ranch, Clyde honked the horn a couple times and headed on past the house to the barn in the back.

"I suppose you want the truck in the barn?"

Bekah nodded. "I'll probably pull the carburetor tonight."

"Mighty ambitious, aren't you?"

"It's not going to fix itself."

"True enough, and the Good Book always noted that God helps those who helps themselves. Or maybe that was Andy Rooney."

Bekah smiled a bit, but she couldn't help thinking that, given everything going on in her life lately, God had been a little shy on the helping-out part. She finished the Coca-Cola Clyde had given her from the cooler between the seats. "Stop for just a second and I'll open the barn."

"Yep. It's a lot easier that way. Won't have to replace the doors." Clyde grinned at her, and his good nature was infectious. He brought the truck to a halt and she got out. By that time her granny was standing on the front porch with Travis.

"Hi, Momma!" Travis waved excitedly.

"Hi, Travis." Bekah set herself and shoved the barn door open, then walked inside and switched on the lights. The stalls were empty at the moment, but tack for horses hung on the walls along with milking stools. A hoist for working on the tractor and the vehicles hung from the ceiling rafters.

Deftly, Clyde slipped the truck into the barn, and they each took a side to unhook the vehicle.

Bekah coiled the chain and put it on the back deck of the tow truck. Then she headed back to her own truck to get her tools and get started.

Clyde wiped his hands on the red rag again. "Your grandma's got supper waiting."

"The sooner I get started on this truck, the sooner I'll have it running again. I need it running."

"Let me make you a deal. Your grandma invited me to supper tonight too. What say we go eat, and then I'll come back and help you tear down that carburetor? Four hands work faster than two."

"Mr. Walters, I already owe you for the tow."

Clyde waved that away. "No, you don't. Least I can do for one of our soldiers. And for your grandma. From time to time, she makes a meal and asks me to stop by. I'm getting a home-cooked meal out of this tonight. The way I figure it, I'm coming out ahead. My good fortune. And I like working on cars. Don't get to do it as much as I used to because everything's so new and can be cantankerous."

Grinning in spite of her situation, Bekah held out her hand. "You've got a deal."

"Good. I'll try not to feel bad what with me getting the better end of things. Let's get on to the house."

Bekah led the way across the yard that she had mowed countless times while growing up. She loved the smell of the dark all around her, the way the world was cooling down and the breeze was finally sighing through the trees. Fireflies glimmered in the deep shadows around the yard, and moths bumped the light hanging from the second floor of the old house she'd grown up in.

She was home, and that felt better than it had in a long time.

Travis came running toward her, and she scooped him up in her arms. He hugged her tight. "I thought you were never coming home."

"Me too."

Then he looked at her seriously. "Did you break your truck?"

"A little bit."

"Can you fix it?"

"I can."

"I'll help."

"All right." Bekah bumped heads with him. In that minute, she didn't feel all the disappointment and setbacks of the day. She was home and she had her son, and there wasn't much else she needed. Then she saw the official-looking letter in her granny's hand.

"This came for you today." Her granny looked at the letter with displeasure. "I was going to hold it till after supper, but I didn't figure it would be any more welcome then." She held the letter out. "And I figured you'd want to know now."

Bekah took the letter with a mixture of emotions. She didn't think the Marine Corps could be writing her about the felony charges. That had only been two days ago. They couldn't find out that fast, could they? And they'd wait until the trial was over before taking any kind of disciplinary action, wouldn't they?

Of all the military branches, the Marines were strictest about legal infractions and personal backgrounds. Almost anyone could get into the Army, but tattoos—even non-gang-related ones—could keep an applicant out of the Corps. Bekah didn't know how they would react to the felony charges she had pending.

She shifted Travis to her hip to free up both hands so she could open the letter. When she had it open, she had to turn slightly to catch the light from the lamp on the house. The letter was simple and direct.

"I've been reactivated. My orders are to report to Twentynine Palms in California by the end of next week."

Travis looked up at her with mournful eyes. "You're going away, Momma?"

It broke Bekah's heart to have to tell him, but part of her was thinking about the battle pay and how that money would help straighten out everything at home. "Yeah, baby, I have to go away."

Travis held her tightly, and she carried him into the house.

8

RAGEH DAUD CREPT through the jungle, surprised by how much at home he felt. All the years that he'd been away melted, and he became the creature that he had been back then almost as easily as drawing breath. He slid effortlessly through the trees and brush even in the darkness, despite the bruises and pains that still plagued him from the beating he'd received. The AK-47 he carried in his arms felt natural, and it was like he'd found a piece of himself that he had been missing these past ten years.

When he was a child, Daud had lived in ruins outside Mogadishu with his father and the bad men his father had led. His father had never tried to hide his nature or the nature of the men from Daud. They were thieves and killers, men who took what they needed from those who had it.

His father, before he had died from sickness, had been on the cutting edge of the pirates who now worked the Gulf of

Aden and the Indian Ocean. Before his death, his father had even started capturing some of the ships out in the harbor. The work—and all of the men with his father considered the piracy to be work—had kept them alive. And the pay was important to the survival of their families.

In fact, for a time Daud's father had served with the local coast guard. That was where many of the pirates learned the skills they now used to take the cargo ships. When the jobs they needed went away, they turned to the business that had supported the country hundreds of years ago when their ancestors had plied the seas. Piracy was a very old trade in Somalia.

So was raiding, and that was what Daud and his group were here to do tonight. Returning to the old ways, giving in to the violence that he knew so well, felt right and good. He felt stronger, able to reach out and seize his own fate from the jaws of uncertainty.

But he knew his wife would have been ashamed of him.

She had known nothing of the things he'd done before she met him, and he'd always told her different stories about the scars she discovered on his body. Mogadishu was filled with violence. People were easily in the wrong place at the wrong time. She had believed him without question.

A momentary twinge of guilt over her innocence assailed him as he went forward, but he quickly walled it off with the anger and pain that threatened to consume him over the deaths of his wife and son. Images of Ibrahim's wide, unseeing eyes haunted Daud's sleep. He had spent days and nights praying at his son's bedside, and all of those prayers had gone unanswered.

Now he had no prayers left in him. Only the violence that he was about to unleash.

Voices sounded from up ahead. Men laughed and joked, and the golden glow of a campfire cut through the darkness. Those men had no idea they were being stalked.

The day after the beating he had received in the alley, Daud had lain abed to recover. He'd come a long way on foot to reach Afrah, and that had been draining enough—he'd had to dodge the TFG and AMISOM units struggling to lock down the city so peacekeeping efforts could be made. When the al-Shabaab had pulled out of the city, a power vacuum had been created that the transitional government and the United Nations were struggling to fill. Hundreds of thousands of people had been displaced by the constant warring, and many of them remained scattered in the surrounding countryside. The al-Shabaab held some of them as hostages in order to extort more money and to ensure their own protection from retaliation.

All of those displaced people needed food and water and medicine. Children died every day. The peacekeeping efforts were too little too late, and they did not appear to be growing in number.

God had truly turned his back on Mogadishu.

But Daud had not. When he had buried his beloved wife and child, he understood what he was meant to do. He took a better grip on the assault rifle and peered through the darkness toward the fire as he waved his group to ground.

Afrah, only a few feet away, hunkered down behind a boulder sticking up from the ground that was just large enough to shield him. Daud thought maybe time had robbed the older man of a step or two, but he moved silently in the shadows, like *Qori ismaris*, the hyena-man who switched between animal and human form.

Daud could remember being fascinated as a child by the old stories that his father and the other men told him. They'd done it to scare him, of course, but he had loved the old tales; he had loved being scared of things that didn't exist. There were too many real fears in his life, but borrowing nonexistent ones that could be banished at daybreak was another matter. Those make-believe terrors had contributed to his tattered childhood. Those stories had been one of the constants in his life with his father. The other had been learning weapons and small-unit tactics.

Taking cover behind a banana tree, Daud concentrated on the clearing ahead. All of the trees in the area were short and stunted from the drought that had claimed Somalia, but they were big enough and thick enough to hide Daud and his men. The ground was almost as dry as dust, and when the wind picked up, the earth lifted with it and was blown away.

Gone were the pasturelands that had fed the cattle so many Somali people depended on for their livelihood. Only farmlands along the Jubba, the Shebelle, and the other rivers still prospered. However, many rivers were under al-Shabaab control, and the water was auctioned off to those farmers who could pay. People downriver from where the dams were built had to struggle even harder to survive and keep their cattle alive.

Men like Gold Tooth were behind those selfish enterprises.

Daud knew his father might have considered it worthwhile to attack his enemy directly, but it would mean having a much larger force than he presently had. It was one thing to take an area; it was another to hold it. His father had always survived by striking, taking what he wanted, and fading back into the countryside. Daud intended to follow the same plan until his group grew, which would foster new problems. Feeding all of them while on the move would be difficult.

Reaching into his military chest pack, Daud took out a set of binoculars he'd gotten on the black market and focused the lenses on the campsite. With the way various armies—the Russians, the French, the Ethiopians, the British, and the Americans—had come to Somalia to shore up one government after another, getting military surplus was easy. Just costly.

A dozen men sat around the campfire in folding lawn chairs. They kept assault rifles next to them and wore pistols and knives. Many of them chewed *khat*, a native plant that created a state of euphoria. The drug was easier to get than alcohol and wasn't forbidden by Islam. *Khat* was also being exported to Scandinavia, and the profits funneled back into the pockets of Muslim terrorist groups.

Beyond the men, two jeeps and two four-wheel-drive pickups sat parked in the shadows surrounding the hollow that protected the group from the wind. The scent of braised lamb rode the wind, mixed with herbs. Evidently the men had dined well and were settling in for the night.

That suited Daud. Silently, he put away the binoculars

and rose into a crouch, holding the rifle in both hands as he advanced. Afrah and the four other men with them—three of them men who had accompanied Daud's father years ago—rose like dark ghosts and followed.

Daud kept putting one foot in front of the other. The al-Shabaab had posted no guards, no lookouts, obviously complacent in their hiding place. A local herdsman who had ventured into Mogadishu looking for food for his family had brought news of Gold Tooth, whose real name was Liban. The herdsman had contacted one of the men Afrah had sent out to find information about the al-Shabaab contingent. In return, the herdsman had received food for his family.

Life was sold cheaply in Mogadishu even after the al-Shabaab had been driven from most of the city.

Fifteen feet out, one of the men got up and wandered outside the firelight, probably to heed nature. Daud froze, but the man saw someone in the brush anyway.

"Look out, my brothers! Look out!" The man scrambled to yank the rifle from over his shoulder and find cover.

Daud stood and fired at once. His bullets caught the man and drove him backward into the flames where his hair caught on fire. The foul odor of burned hair and cooked flesh filled the campsite. The man didn't move and didn't make a sound as he burned.

The al-Shabaab terrorists grabbed their weapons, but they were blinded from looking into the campfire and addled by the *khat*. They fired long bursts that cut through the trees over Daud's head. Daud stayed low and fired at the targets that presented themselves. The rifle recoiled against his shoulder again and again. He kept moving forward, watching as the bodies of the al-Shabaab hit the ground.

One of the terrorists turned and fled into the trees. Light glinted at the man's mouth when he shot a frightened glance over his shoulder.

Gold Tooth. Liban.

Daud's head ached from where Afrah had put in eight stitches to close a cut on his temple. The wound still threatened infection. Other cuts inside his mouth made eating an unpleasant chore, and two of his teeth were loose.

"Afrah."

The big man glanced at Daud.

"Secure the camp. Kill them all."

Afrah nodded and surged forward.

Dropping his rifle, Daud took up pursuit of Liban and drew the Tokarev pistol from the holster at his hip. The Russian-made pistol wasn't as accurate as its American and British counterparts, but it would serve. He ran, and the effort amplified the painful pounding in his head. He guessed that he was at least a decade older than his quarry, but he knew the wilderness better than the other man did.

Liban slipped and fell, narrowly avoiding collisions with trees. Daud gave chase in a distance-eating lope, easily making his way through the stubby trees and scrub brush as if it had been only yesterday and not ten years.

During those ten years, Daud had taken college courses and learned what he needed in order to become a warehouse administrator. He had used some of the money his father had bequeathed him to buy a modest house and try to live the life he'd thought he wanted instead of the violence he had always known. He'd met a beautiful woman and had a beautiful son. Life had been good.

Until it had all been taken from him. Memories of the bombed-out house skated through his mind as he ran. His rapid inhalations and exhalations sounded like the screams of his son and his wife after the mortar had blown their house to pieces. He had been outside when the explosion had occurred, and that was when he had been wounded with the scars he now carried on his cheek. But those remembered pains were nothing compared to the ones that still writhed through his heart. Soon, though, he knew those sharp aches would dim and die, and he would have nothing except his hate and anger to sustain him.

He came up fast behind Liban, pointed the pistol at him, and thought then of shooting the man point-blank. But that wasn't how Daud wanted to deliver his message. Liban and his cronies had made everything personal. The al-Shabaab and the TFG had made things personal. The Ethiopians and the Americans and all the other foreigners had made it personal.

Now Daud was going to make his war against them personal. He would live and he would become strong. And they would all pay.

Screaming in fury, giving in to the anger and desire for vengeance that filled him as Liban crested a hill and headed down, Daud topped the hill as well, then hurled himself headlong after the man. Sailing through the air, Daud crashed into Liban and knocked them both sprawling to the ground.

The impact knocked the wind from Daud's lungs, but he held on to the pistol and rolled. Disoriented by the dark and the brush he landed in, he scrambled for a moment and pulled himself to his feet with the pistol pointed at Liban.

The al-Shabaab man pushed himself to his feet, spotted Daud ahead of him, and immediately reached for the pistol at his belt. Then, seeing that he was already too late, he slowly lifted his hands.

"Don't shoot me. I beg you."

Daud's voice was cold and hard. "You can beg all you wish to, dog. But it will do you no good."

"I am protected by Haroun."

"I am hunting this man. Throwing his name at me affords you no protection."

"He will kill you. He will kill all of you for what you do."

"Do you know me?"

Liban studied Daud, cocking his head first one way, then the other. But his attention was divided between Daud and the pistol he held. "You're the man in the alley."

"I am. And tonight I am your executioner." Daud squeezed the trigger and the pistol roared. Now that the rifles of his men and the other al-Shabaab had fallen silent, the explosion sounded incredibly loud.

For a moment, Liban stood. Then his legs gave way and his body toppled to the ground. Daud stood above the man, hoping to feel something fill in the awful emptiness that consumed him. But there was nothing. Even the vindication of striking back at a man who had caused him so grievous an injury did not help. Eventually it would, though. He was certain of that.

He knelt and went through the dead man's pockets, taking money, jewelry, and weapons. Daud reclaimed his hiking boots as well. Afrah found him there in the darkness as he was lacing them up.

"You are well, Rageh?"

"I am. Did we lose anyone?"

"No." Afrah shook his shaggy head.

"Are the al-Shabaab all dead?"

"Yes. To the last man."

Daud stood and stomped his feet. He reloaded the pistol, once more filling the magazine. "Did they have much?"

Afrah shrugged. "Food, water, medicine. Some weapons beyond what they carried." He grinned. "But now we have four more vehicles than we had. From these things, we can grow and become more powerful."

"All right." Daud headed up the hill, back toward the terrorist camp.

Walking beside him, Afrah clapped a hand on Daud's shoulder. "You are as your father was. Aggressive and merciless. He would be proud of the son he sired. And I will follow you as I followed your father."

Daud kept walking, but his mind was already restlessly turning over his next steps. They needed more men. They needed more weapons. And to get those things, he would have to steal more. He looked forward to it; the task gave him purpose.

9

BEKAH'S HEAD BUZZED with questions and possibilities as she walked into the AutoZone store in Murchison with the old carburetor she'd pulled out of her pickup. The letter from the Marine Corps had been short and succinct as always, letting her know where to be and when, and that a ticket would be waiting for her at Will Rogers World Airport in Oklahoma City.

She dreaded the thought of going back to Afghanistan. Being a woman there, especially a female Marine, was hard. There were a lot of rules for engagement that women military personnel had to obey even when working among friendlies.

Wearing his Texas Rangers ball cap, Travis walked beside her. It was a little big on him, but he was proud of it because his great-grandpa had given it to him. Bekah didn't think Travis could remember that since he'd been so young, but she and her granny had told him a lot about his great-grandpa.

She placed the carburetor on the counter, then gave Travis

a quarter to buy gum from one of the small vending machines at the front of the shop. While she waited, she stared at the television behind the counter. The Fox News broadcast showed footage of Mogadishu and some of the fighting that had broken out in the northern sections of the city.

"Pretty intense, huh?" The young man on the other side of the counter looked all of eighteen or nineteen. Small and compact, with his hair high and tight, he looked like he'd stepped off a high school football field somewhere. His grin was open and friendly, and his blue eyes flashed.

"Yeah."

"I just found out I'm going over there."

"Mogadishu?"

The counter man nodded. "I'm a Marine reservist. We got activated this week. Supposed to be in California by the end of next week."

Bekah smiled back. "Always good to meet a fellow Marine." She extended her hand.

"You?" The guy looked surprised but took her hand.

"Lance Corporal Bekah Shaw currently tasked to Charlie Company. I'm headed to California too."

"Lance corporal. I'm a private. Am I supposed to salute?"

"The officers, yes, but I'm noncom."

"First time I've been activated." He hesitated. "I've got to admit, I'm a little nervous."

"When you get over there, stick with the guys who have the experience. Do what they do. Don't take chances. Watch over your buddies and trust them to watch over you. Just like you've been training."

The guy nodded. "My name's Ralph. Ralph Caxton."

"Pleasure to meet you, Ralph Caxton."

"Likewise."

"How do you know you're shipping out to Mogadishu?"

"Got an older brother in the Marines who works in intel. He went to officer's school. Says I should be doing the same thing, but I want to get my boots muddy first before I commit to something like that."

"It's a good way to go."

"You didn't."

Bekah smiled and shrugged. "I don't have the necessary college. Can't get it right now. But it's definitely something you should think about if you decide you like the Corps."

"I will. Maybe we'll see each other."

Bekah nodded, amazed how at home she felt in the presence of another Marine she'd never even met before. She felt more connected to Ralph Caxton than she did to any of her friends back in Callum's Creek. "Could be. You get overseas, the world gets pretty small. You tend to notice each other."

Ralph turned his attention to the carburetor. "I suppose you'll be needing one of these."

Bekah nodded and glanced at Travis. He was standing in the plate-glass windows watching with rapt attention as traffic whizzed by. She marveled again at how small his world was—and how small hers had at one time been.

Ralph left the counter and came back a few minutes later with the necessary part. He arranged for a military discount after checking her ID, then rang her up. As he did, Bekah kept watching the television station. The words *hostage*, *piracy, looting, famine, drought,* and *deaths* kept scrolling across the bottom of the screen.

Almost immediately, other footage rolled that described the struggling supply lines trying to get food, medicine, and water to the people displaced by the constant warring. That was followed by images of sick children wasted away to nothing, looking like stick puppets with bulbous heads and lifeless eyes. It was almost more than Bekah could bear. Even though she knew Travis would never face such circumstances, she couldn't help knowing how she would feel if she were the momma of one of those children.

"Looks pretty bad, doesn't it?" Ralph's voice was quiet.

"It does." Bekah wrote out a check for the carburetor.

"But it's okay. We'll be over there soon. We can do something about that." Ralph gave her a winning smile and handed her the box. "When you want something done right, you send in the Marines. Semper Fi."

"Semper Fi, Marine." Bekah tucked the box under her arm and called Travis over to her. They headed out of the building and back to her granny's truck and were on the road before eight thirty.

★   ★   ★

"Thought maybe you could use a glass of lemonade."

Sitting on her truck's fender, Bekah glanced up and saw her granny standing nearby with a tall glass in one hand. She also held a small saucer of fresh-baked peanut butter cookies.

"I can. Thanks." Bekah wiped her hands on the cloth she held, then spun around and stepped to the ground. Her back and shoulders hurt from working in the slumped position she'd had to endure. She took the glass and drank half the contents.

Her granny set the saucer on the fender. "Not too fast. You've been working hard, and it's hot out here. You don't want to make yourself sick."

"I won't." Bekah took a cookie and bit into it. The smell instantly brought back all those memories of baking with her granny when she was a small girl. These days there was precious little time for that. They both worked harder than they'd ever worked just to get by. "Your timing is about perfect, by the way."

"How do you mean?"

"I've got everything back together. I'm ready to see if the truck will fire up."

Granny's eyebrows lifted in surprise. "That was fast."

"Grandpa and me built this truck. I know my way around it."

Granny smiled. "I suppose you do."

Bekah finished the cookie, took another sip of the lemonade, and climbed behind the truck's steering wheel. She pumped the accelerator, took a breath, and cranked the ignition as she watched the engine through the space between the open hood and the truck body.

The engine turned over a few times, and just when Bekah was beginning to think maybe she'd gotten something wrong, the V6 caught and the *chug-chug* became a throaty roar. Bekah smiled and felt the expression pulling across her face.

Granny looked at her, nodding and smiling.

In the yard between the ranch house and the barn, Travis

whooped in delight and came running over. "You fixed it! You fixed it, Momma!"

Proud of herself, feeling a little more in control of her life, Bekah stepped out of the truck and caught her son in mid-rush. She lifted him up high and beamed at him. "I did, baby boy. So what do you think about your momma now?"

Travis hugged her. "You're a good mechanic, Momma."

It wasn't what most mommas heard from their kids, but Bekah was willing to take it. As she hugged her son back, she hated the thought that she was going to be taken away from him again so soon.

★　★　★

Standing at the kitchen sink, Bekah washed the vegetables she was going to put into the stew for supper. She did the chore mechanically after years of practice. Her attention was on Travis. Bekah could see him out the window as he threw a stick for Shep, his border collie puppy. Travis was convinced Shep could learn to fetch. The only thing Shep truly wanted to do was follow Travis around.

Travis threw the stick, and Shep sat and watched. Exasperated, Travis turned and talked to the pup, explaining how the trick was supposed to work. Finally, Travis got down on hands and knees and crawled over to the stick, which he hadn't thrown very far. Shep laid his head down on his paws and closed his eyes.

Bekah laughed out loud.

"What's going on?" Granny stood up from the oven where

she was baking a fresh pan of cornbread. The smell filled the kitchen and made Bekah's stomach growl.

"Travis is trying to teach Shep to fetch."

Granny smiled, wiped her hands on a dish towel, and joined Bekah at the sink. "That should be entertaining."

Out in the yard, Travis knelt and talked to Shep. Then he pointed at the stick. He talked some more and pointed to the stick again. Shep just stared at him and occasionally wagged his thin little tail.

"Not making much headway with that pup, is he?"

Bekah shook her head. "Gonna be interesting to see which one of them gives up first."

"Have you told Travis when you're going back to the Marines?"

Bekah drained the water from the pan she'd used for scrubbing the carrots, potatoes, onions, and celery. Lifting the vegetables from the pan, she placed them on the chopping block and raised the Japanese-style knife she'd picked up at Walmart after she got back from her last tour. She wasn't Rachael Ray or Guy Fieri, but the Marines had taught her to have the proper tool for the job. She loved the knife and the way it sounded so authoritative when it hit the block. "Not yet."

"Gonna have to be done. He don't need to be surprised."

"I know. I just want to let him have another day or two without thinking about it."

Granny rested her thin hand on Bekah's shoulder. "I know, darling girl, but he has to deal with it. We all do."

Lowering her head, Bekah tried to focus on her task. But

it was hard. "I keep telling myself that this is for the best. After losing the job at Hollister's, I need the money."

"You don't need the money. I've told you more than once that you and Travis are welcome to stay here as long as you need."

"Granny, please. I can't talk about this right now." The argument was an old one, and Bekah couldn't bear to rehash it again.

10

THE WIND STIRRED the August heat that surrounded Oklahoma State Penitentiary but only succeeded in making the air feel like it poured from a convection oven. Heath Bridger sweltered in his suit as he trudged up the white stone steps leading to the main building. His sunglasses blunted the sunlight, but he felt it beating down on him with physical force. He remained steadfast, though, and carried himself with dignity, attracting the ire of a few of the prison guards as he drew closer to the main building. The antagonism that radiated from them was thicker than the early-afternoon heat.

The prison guards knew who Heath was there to see, and their disapproval showed in scowls and muttered curses. Heath ignored the behavior the same way he had for the last five months. Some days he wanted to tell the guards and administration that what they dished out to him on these weekly visits paled in comparison to what his father handed out almost daily.

But he didn't. He kept his family trials and tribulations close, the way he had all his life.

Once inside the building, he handed over his briefcase and submitted to the electronic and physical search that had become routine. He'd gotten so inured to the process that he went through the motions automatically—not taking anything personal, just accepting the events.

On the other side of the first security door, Heath pulled his clothing back into order, ran a hand through his short-cropped dark-blond hair, and took his briefcase back from one security officer while another affixed a visitor's badge to his pocket.

"Stay in the designated areas, Counselor." The guard who had clipped on the badge stepped back. He was in his late twenties, maybe early thirties, probably about Heath's age.

"Sure." Heath tightened his grip on the briefcase's handle. He didn't bother pointing out that he'd heard the warning dozens of times.

"I'll walk you to the room."

Heath nodded and fell into step with the man. The guard was six feet tall—four inches shorter than Heath—but was wider across the shoulders and chest. Looked like he worked at it, maybe with the help of some steroids and muscle-mass hormones. His sleeves were rolled up to midbicep, and the material strained as he moved with an easy grace.

Lean and athletic, Heath paced the guard easily. Exercise, sports, and competition had helped him work out his frustrations and his father's disapproval. Endorphins were his drug of choice, and he kept in shape for the Marines.

"I heard you used to play football." The guard stopped in front of the next security door.

"I did." Heath stood quietly beside the man. He didn't want to talk to the guard, but he knew any reticence on his part would only add to the tension.

"Somebody told me you were a quarterback."

"I was."

The guard at the security door punched in the code, and the massive door slid back with a clang.

"Said you played at OSU."

Heath nodded and thought about the years he'd spent at Oklahoma State University. When he was on the team, he'd felt like he was part of something that mattered. His father hadn't respected football, though, and he'd never come to a single game. So Heath played even harder, getting enough ink in the papers that he knew his father had to avoid the topic when he was with his friends.

Lionel Bridger represented a few professional football players who got themselves into trouble, but he didn't care for the sport. For Lionel, it was all about the money. Professional athletes could pay a lot, and they generally got into the kind of trouble that warranted a crafty lawyer. Lionel Bridger was that in spades.

"I've always been an OU fan." The guard got under way again.

"The University of Oklahoma is a good school." Heath hated walking down the prison's gray corridors. Every time he did, it felt like the world was growing steadily smaller around him and would one day crush him beneath its weight. There wasn't a single time he left the building that he didn't feel like he'd just made an escape.

"If you were such a hotshot quarterback, why didn't you play at OU?"

"Couldn't make the cut." Heath decided to give the guard that, even though it wasn't true. He'd followed a girl to OSU, thought he'd been in love. Actually, he *had* loved her, but she hadn't loved him. Not enough. When he caught her cheating on him, all that was left for him was the team.

And when the collegiate football career was over, Heath went to law school because he hadn't known what else to do with himself. Lionel had insisted, and the confusion of his girlfriend's betrayal had left him anchorless. Stuck with a father who only saw him as a continuation of the bloodline.

Strangely enough, Heath had an aptitude for law and a good, quick mind. More than that, he loved winning. The competition in the courtroom didn't replace the action on the gridiron, but it awakened new areas in Heath's life. He'd found a new battlefield that gave him new rewards.

"OU's a tough program."

"Yeah."

"Somebody said they thought you were good enough to go pro."

Heath shook his head. "Not me." There had been offers, though. Never first-round choice, but he'd received some interest. After college, Heath just couldn't wrap his head around football anymore. He moved on, and he didn't have it in him to try to build that kind of relationship with anyone else. He'd wanted—*needed*—to be alone. Except for his service in the Marines. He enjoyed that camaraderie, but it had been limited—until lately.

After law school, he'd gone back to what he knew and began work at his father's firm. They had offices in Dallas and Houston, in Tulsa and Oklahoma City. His father kept a lot of work on the dockets. Lionel Bridger was a rainmaker in two states, and he handled civil as well as criminal cases as long as the client had the long green.

The guard stopped at the doorway to the interview room and gestured to the table and chairs inside. "You got privacy in there, Counselor."

"Thanks."

The guard crossed his arms and looked at Heath with a measuring glance. "I also heard you were a soldier."

Heath almost said, *"I'm a Marine,"* but he held himself in check. That would be Marine pride speaking, and the guard wouldn't understand it as anything other than self-aggrandizement. "Yeah."

"Weekend warrior." The guard's tone almost masked the sarcasm.

"That's right."

"But you've been in Afghanistan, other places like that."

Heath stood in the doorway. Darnell Lester hadn't been brought in yet, so he had time to kill. He didn't want to kill the time with the guard, but the man wasn't going to go away until he'd asked the question he was dying to ask. "I have."

"So you've seen some bad things."

The anger in Heath stirred like a snake, lifting and preparing to strike suddenly. "There's a war on over there. Maybe you've heard about it."

The guard smiled a little at that, and Heath knew the man was happy to have struck a nerve. "I have. Just seems to me you've seen brother soldiers go down."

Heath remained silent with effort. He made himself breathe out and relax.

The guard only waited a short time for a reply that just didn't happen. Then he forged on, obviously determined to say whatever he'd come to say. "After being there through something like that, it makes me wonder why you would defend a cop killer like Darnell Lester. I'd think maybe you'd sympathize with what we're trying to do here instead of taking it on yourself to interrupt the wheels of justice."

Heath flicked his gaze to the guard's ID tag. He hadn't taken note of the man's name earlier, on purpose. Giving the opposition names allowed them more power to get under his skin. "Do you have a personal interest in this, Mr. Cookson? If so, I'll need to see about having you relieved of duty here. Conflict of interest." He didn't know if he could do that, but the guard wilted under the threat.

"No. No personal interest." Duane Cookson tried to play off his intimidation, but he was young and probably hadn't been in the streets as a police officer.

Guys who had actually been out patrolling the streets gave off a different vibe than the one the guard had. Heath had learned to feel that vibe through experience in the courtroom. Those men hit his personal radar in the same fashion Marines did. They had a sense of purpose, a calling. At least the ones who had seen violence up close and believed in what they were doing.

"Because if you do, I need to know." Heath leaned in, towering over the shorter man.

Cookson bristled and gritted his teeth. "Darnell Lester is a cop killer. He confessed to the shooting. He's scheduled to die, and he probably wants to after fourteen years of being in this place." His nostrils flared. "I'm thinking maybe you should just let him."

Keeping his voice cold, his words like chipped ice, Heath met the man's gaze full measure. "Are we done here? Or do I need to speak with your supervisor?"

Cookson held his position for a moment, and Heath knew the man had a lot of pride on the line. Maybe the other guards had put Cookson up to the confrontation, or maybe the man had taken it upon himself, but he wasn't going to let it go easily.

Then he subsided. "Sure. We're done. Just lemme know when you're ready to leave." He turned and walked away.

Breathing hard, Heath went to the table in the center of the room and sat down to wait. He focused on what he needed to say, and he tried to find the best way to say it.

★　★　★

The other door leading to the interview room abruptly clanged open a few minutes later while Heath was still considering his options. Darnell Lester shuffled into the room wearing the orange prison uniform and shackles on his ankles and wrists. He glanced at Heath and nodded slightly. Another guard, this one older and heavier, followed the prisoner into the room.

Heath stood and looked at the guard. "Take the cuffs off my client, please."

The guard scowled but did as Heath ordered. During the process, Darnell never acknowledged the guard. He kept his eyes on Heath. When the guard had the shackles off, he glanced at Heath. "You need me, I'll just be outside."

Heath nodded. "I'll let you know when I'm done."

The guard walked away and closed the door behind him.

"Hello, Darnell." Heath waved to one of the chairs at the table. "How are you holding up?"

"Fine. I'm holding up fine. Thank you." Darnell eased himself into the chair across the table. He was fifty-four years old—not an old man, but fourteen years of prison had weighted him down. He was thin and knobby, a man who looked put together with ball bearings and piano wire. His head looked too big for his body, but his face had at one time been handsome.

That had been years ago, before the violent arrest that put him in intensive care and cost him the use of his right eye. Now age and physical abuse had weathered his features. The cottony fringe of hair that encircled his bald pate stood out against his ebony skin. Scars showed on the knuckles of his big hands, and burn scarring from the First Iraq War left his skin spotted and pink from the tips of his fingers to his mid-forearms. Faded gang tattoos, rendered in blue ink, barely stood out against his arms, but they remained indelible.

"I see you still ain't winnin' no friends here." Darnell grinned and showed his tobacco-stained teeth. A few on the sides were missing, and his pink gums showed.

"I didn't know we were in a popularity contest." Heath took off his jacket and hung it from the back of his chair.

Darnell laughed, and the sound was soft and delicate. His voice sounded melodic when he spoke, and there was a cadence to it that Heath always took note of. "I suppose not." He paused a moment. "So what are you doing here, Counselor?"

"I came to catch you up on where we stand." Heath took a yellow legal pad from his briefcase and placed it on the table. He added a tape recorder, then took a pen from the briefcase as well. "I filed a motion to get a new judge to look over your files."

Darnell clasped his hands in front of him and shook his head. "Why would you go an' do a thing like that?"

"Because I don't think Judge Winters is willing to look at an appeal."

"Ain't no reason he should. Nothin's changed. That man's still dead, an' I'm the one that done it."

"I know." Heath had seen the video footage himself. Darnell Lester's case had reached a swift end. The convenience-store footage showed Darnell robbing the store clerk, then shooting Keith Jointer, an off-duty Oklahoma City police officer who had stopped by for gas at the time of the robbery.

Jointer had pulled his weapon and started ordering Darnell to put his gun down. He hadn't identified himself, and Heath didn't fault the young officer for that. Adrenaline sharpened the senses and reflexes during conflict, but it also sometimes dulled the thinking. Experience with similar situations would change things, but that day had been the first time Officer Jointer had drawn his weapon during the commission of a crime. Jointer had fired first, missing Darnell by three feet.

Darnell, heavily under the influence of the drugs that had consumed his life back in those days, had turned and fired automatically. His bullet had caught the young officer dead center in the chest. When he saw what he'd done, Darnell had immediately tried to give first aid. He was still administering CPR when the patrol cars arrived.

Once the arriving officers learned that Darnell had shot Jointer, they had pulled Darnell from the body and beaten him with their batons. Darnell was unconscious before a shift sergeant arrived and finally got control of his men.

For six days, Darnell had lingered in a coma, and the doctors caring for him couldn't say if he would live or die. When he finally came to, Darnell was in a world of hurt. His left arm had been broken in two places, both knees shattered, several ribs broken, and he'd been blinded in his right eye. On top of that, his drug dependency made it hard to administer the proper pain meds to keep him from agony and from overdosing.

As soon as he'd recovered enough to leave the hospital, Darnell had been taken to lockup. He'd gone from jail to prison and hadn't been out in the world again except for his brief trial. Darnell's original attorney had tried to plea-bargain, willing to take life imprisonment without any chance of parole over a death sentence. Darnell had been fine with that too. He'd never tried to deny his responsibility for Jointer's death.

The district attorney had rejected the offer, insisting on making an example of Darnell Lester. After all, the man had shot a cop, the case was ironclad—with video footage and witness testimony as well as Darnell's own continuing admission—and it had been an election year. The trial was everything a politically minded district attorney could hope for, and he wanted to personally pound the nails into Darnell's coffin. It had been like shooting fish in a barrel.

Now, all these years later, Darnell was facing death by lethal injection within seventeen months. And the wheels of justice turned slowly.

If they turned at all.

Heath looked at Darnell, into the man's good brown eye and not the dead blue one. "You don't deserve the death penalty, Darnell. You're not the same man you were when you pulled that trigger."

Darnell took in a breath of air and let it out. His rounded shoulders rose and fell. "None of us stays the same, Counselor. That officer I shot had boys that ain't the same as they was. Prob'ly gonna be glad when I'm dead. Won't have to think about me no more."

The man spoke without emotion, just a flat expression of a truth he believed in. Darnell Lester wasn't a cynic. He was just a realist. All those years of being in prison had worn away whatever hopes and dreams he might have had.

"You have a daughter yourself." Heath watched Darnell

and saw the words hit him hard. His good eye blinked in pain, but he quickly compartmentalized it and put it away.

"I know I do. I take pride in that girl. She didn't turn out to be like me."

"I think she turned out more like you than you know." Heath chose his words carefully. Most of the time Darnell would listen, but sometimes—when the pain he kept shut away so long and so hard slipped its bonds—he wouldn't hear a thing Heath had to tell him.

Darnell started to object.

Heath kept speaking. "She's a survivor. She's tough and she learns quickly. She doesn't give up."

For a moment, Darnell sat silent as stone. Heath feared that he'd lost the man and the interview would be over. Then Darnell leaned back in his chair and laced his hands behind his head. "Shoulda been easier for her. I made her life hard."

"Deshondra has a good life. She's a schoolteacher. She has two healthy children. A good husband." Heath reached into his briefcase and took out a small envelope. "She sent new pictures of the kids." He took the pictures from the envelope and placed them on the table, turning them so they were right-side up for Darnell. "Things aren't easy for her, but they're manageable. She and her husband are about to close on a house."

As he gazed at the two pictures, Darnell's lips quivered for just a moment and he blinked away a tear. Then, once more, he was stone. "Trashae is looking more an' more like her momma ever' day." Tenderly, he touched the photograph of the seven-year-old girl with wild hair and a gap-toothed smile. "An' Keywon gets bigger every time I see him." The little boy was five and had tried to look serious in the photo, but his dark eyes glimmered with suppressed merriment.

Darnell cleared his throat. "You see them lately?"

"This morning."

"They lookin' good?"

"They are. I had breakfast with them at McDonald's."

A chuckle rumbled from deep inside Darnell's chest. "In the play area, I suppose."

Heath hesitated, thinking that maybe he shouldn't have been so specific. Something as simple as taking his grandkids to McDonald's was never going to happen for Darnell Lester.

"Yeah."

Darnell smiled a little and put his fingers on the two photographs. He dragged them to his side of the table, and the paper sliding across the metal surface whispered loud enough to be heard in the silence. "Onliest place to take kids that size. I 'member takin' Deshondra. Her favorite place to go." He smiled again and darted a look at Heath. "Till she met Mr. Ronald McDonald himself. Had a guy there in the clown suit. Deshondra didn't care for that at all. Put her off goin' to McDonald's for a week."

"Some people have problems with clowns."

"You?"

Heath shook his head. Clowns had never scared him. He had worse fears than any guy dressed in a shaggy wig, a red rubber nose, and pancake makeup could give him. Lionel Bridger was the only thing Heath had ever feared.

"Me neither." Darnell picked up the photographs and slid them into his pocket.

"Deshondra also asked me to tell you that she was praying for you."

"That's good. But she should save her prayers for her ownself. Two kids like that can be a lotta hard work."

"She's up to it. But she's worried about you."

Darnell shook his head. "Nothin' to worry about when it comes to me. Ever'thin' that's gonna be done to me, that's already in the book. I'm just markin' time till we get it over with. I've made my peace with God."

"That's what I want to talk about." Heath leaned forward then. "That peace you've made."

That was one of the things that had first stood out when Heath had met Darnell Lester five months ago. The man was staring death in the face, constantly watched and surrounded by other death row inmates. During that time, over a dozen condemned men had been executed by lethal injection. Darnell had known a few of them. The condemned were a special breed in the prison, and they had an unstated respect for each other. In the cell blocks, each man stood tall on his own two legs or he died inside.

But Darnell had found God years ago. Warden Billy Wilkins had told Heath that himself when he'd first come to the prison five months ago. Wilkins had a soft spot in his heart for Darnell and had wished Heath well in his endeavors.

"If there's any man that deserves a change from death sentence to life imprisonment, it's that man."

When Heath had first met Darnell, the man had brought his Bible into the interview room, been polite, and read the whole time Heath tried to talk to him. Heath had explained that his father's law firm had taken on Darnell's representation pro bono, part of the volunteer work they had to do every year. At the end of that, Darnell had gotten up, thanked him for his time, and left the room.

Heath hadn't known what to do. He discussed the matter with his father, who had thought this should be a simple pro bono, probably the easiest Heath would ever get the chance to represent. Most of them tended to try to drain a firm's resources and often wore on the attorney. Lionel had told Heath to let it go.

Although he'd tried to walk away, Heath hadn't been able to. There was something about Darnell that drew his interest, something that kept pulling him back. Darnell's calming words about his faith always gripped Heath in a manner he couldn't explain. After a couple more visits, Heath had gone to find Darnell's ex-wife, discovered that she'd passed on six years earlier, and found Deshondra and the grandkids.

The next time he'd come to see Darnell, Heath brought Deshondra, who had been visiting her father on a regular basis throughout his incarceration. Deshondra implored her father, and Darnell had agreed to listen.

"It ain't my peace, Counselor." Darnell grinned good-naturedly. "It's the Lord's peace, an' he was kind enough to give it to me."

Since taking on Darnell Lester's case, Heath had studied instances where the death penalty had been enforced. He'd read a lot of testimony about how the convicts' last words were of forgiveness and sorrow and God. Heath didn't believe that those men truly meant what they were saying. It was just their last time to be heard, and many of them were still in denial about what was going to happen to them. They'd watched too many movies and had wanted to go out as stars.

Or maybe they were just scared, afraid of what might be waiting on them for their sins. Some of them were probably afraid that nothing at all awaited them on the other side.

Heath wasn't a true believer. He had his doubts and fears. Darnell had talked to him about those, always pointing to Jesus and the sacrifice he made to wipe away all of Heath's sins. Heath had listened out of politeness, but he hadn't bought in.

Lionel Bridger had attended church with his family. A lot of his clients did, and it had been good for him to be seen there. Church was good PR.

When he had been small, Heath had marveled at all the events in Jesus' life and how Jesus had gone through his service to his Father. Especially that story with the money-lenders. Heath had particularly liked that one.

If he was pressed, Heath would admit that the closest he had ever seen God work was in Darnell Lester. Lester clung to his faith wholeheartedly but with a sense of peace and forgiveness, not some kind of fervor of the holy righteous.

"The fact is, Darnell, you're a force for good in your daughter's life and in the lives of your grandchildren." Heath spoke earnestly. "That shouldn't be taken away because of the man you were all those years ago."

"That man was me. Ain't no gettin' around that. I pulled that trigger, an' I killed that young man stone dead. All for a twelve-pack an' a carton of smokes, an' maybe enough cash money to buy my next chunk of rock cocaine."

The image of that wild-eyed man in the convenience store filled Heath's mind. Darnell Lester had looked a lot different. His hair had been unkempt. He'd been wearing his old Army jacket and stained slacks he'd kept from working at some fast food restaurant. His addictions had leaned him out to flesh over bone, and his eyes had been red-rimmed and jaundiced yellow. The doctor said if Darnell hadn't been brought in, he'd probably have died from his organs crashing within a matter of weeks.

Heath shook his head. "No. You're not the same man you were then. And you're not as bad as you think you were then."

"I killed that man."

"You shot him, then you tried to save him." Heath paused. "Jointer came in shooting. You were out of the Army maybe a year. Someone shot at you, and you shot back. That was misjudgment and you were under the influence, but that was also how you'd been trained to fight in Iraq. That was reflex."

"Murder's murder, Counselor."

"It is. But there are degrees of murder. Different penalties for crimes committed." Heath leaned forward. "You shouldn't die, Darnell. Not by lethal injection. I can't get you out of here. That's nowhere even close to the table. But I think, under the right circumstances, I can get the sentence flipped to life imprisonment."

Darnell leaned back in his chair. "You don't understand what it's like to be in here. It's hard. Powerful hard. Lotsa long hours an' rememberin' what life was like on the other side of these bars an' walls." His voice quavered for just an instant. "Hard to keep it together some days."

"I understand that, but there are other days when you see Deshondra and those grandchildren."

Darnell closed his eyes for a moment. "Those are good days."

"Deshondra doesn't want to lose you. You're the only parent she has left. Even with you in here, she'd rather have that than nothing at all. I'm hoping that you would too."

"Okay, Counselor. I hear you."

"I have to have your permission to continue pursuing this. There are people who will ask you."

"Let me pray on it. I'll get back to you."

"All right, but there's something else I have to tell you. My unit got activated. I'm leaving for California on Friday. I don't know for sure where I'm going from there or how long I'll be gone."

"That's fine." Darnell put one of his knobby hands over Heath's. "Then I'll be askin' God to look over you too."

11

"MR. PIKE?"

Lying on the creeper under the eight-year-old Ford pickup that had shelled its transmission, Pike Morgan dropped a leisurely hand down to the heavy crescent wrench lying on the ground beside him. He kept a high-capacity .45 and a shotgun in his apartment not far from the garage where he worked, and he kept a .38 revolver in his boot. Getting to the boot would be too obvious in his present position, but a mechanic having a wrench close to hand was no immediate red flag.

Unless a professional killer had finally caught up with him.

Then again, if one of those guys had found him, if his luck had finally run out, he would already be a dead man. They didn't hand out warnings to someone like Pike. They wouldn't want to give him a chance.

Pike reached overhead, caught the pickup's frame, and propelled himself on the creeper. He slid out from under the vehicle but held on to the crescent wrench and the frame in case he needed to strike or scoot back to safety under the truck.

The second bay of the small garage held an older SUV that needed transmission repairs as well. Monty hadn't come back from lunch yet. The small office on the other side of the room was empty. Classic rock blared from the boom box sitting on the office window ledge, an old one by the Rolling Stones. *"Hey, you, get off of my cloud."*

A small boy, maybe eight or nine, stood a few feet away. He was Hispanic, his hair sticking out and uncombed, wearing a frayed Dallas Cowboys jersey that was too big for him. The short sleeves had been rolled up to his elbows. That little detail told Pike the kid had a mom. A lot of them in the neighborhood didn't. He looked scared, but that was the reaction Pike usually got from people.

Pike was big and broad; he didn't work at it, but putting in long hours in a garage helped fine-tune his naturally powerful physique. He preferred working on motorcycles. That was what he'd done since age fifteen. Most of the time. The last four years, though, he'd had to stay away from bikes.

Mulvaney had offered to get Pike some other kind of training, something that would take him away from mechanic work entirely, but Pike didn't want that. He'd given up too much of his past already. He wanted to hang on to part of it. Mulvaney and the US Marshals hadn't been happy about that, but it was his life. He allowed the deal he'd been forced into to compromise his way of living only so far.

Pike released his grip on the crescent wrench and sat up on the creeper. The kid backed away a step. Dressed in work boots, grease-stained jeans, and a T-shirt with the sleeves torn off, his long hair wild and three weeks of beard on his face, Pike knew he looked like a Neanderthal. He was tan, and some of the color came from Indian heritage. He blamed his dark eyes on his blood too, but he couldn't have named which tribe it had come from. He was state-raised and had never known his parents. Muscles rolled in his arms as he folded them on top of his knees and looked at the kid.

"I know you?" Pike's voice was a deep bass rumble.

The kid shook his head. "No, Mr. Pike."

"Just Pike. I don't answer to *mister*."

The boy nodded. "I'm sorry."

Pike waved that away. "You got a name?"

"Hector."

"Like the Trojan warrior?"

A shy smile twisted Hector's lips, but he was still nervous. "Yeah, like that."

"Cool name." Pike wiped his hands on the red rag beside the creeper. Through the open garage doors, out on the gravel parking lot, he didn't see a vehicle waiting. Sometimes, in this neighborhood, the kids were bilingual but the parents weren't. The parents would send the kids in to tell him or Monty they needed someone to look at their cars.

Only the trio of cars awaiting pickup and the two junkers Monty had bought for parts sat in the lot. Beyond them and the security fence, the narrow street ran through a neighborhood that had been challenged by poverty and dismissal by the rest of the city. Tulsa was like that, split into subdivisions between haves and have-nots, between whites, Hispanics, African-Americans, and other ethnicities and financial brackets.

The city was a lot like Dallas, actually. Pike still didn't exactly feel at home here, but it was familiar terrain. Mulvaney had wanted to send Pike somewhere north or back east, or maybe out to Phoenix. Lots of witness relocation took place out there. Pike hadn't wanted to go that far. People were still looking for him for what he'd done, for those he had betrayed, and he didn't want to be anywhere he would stick out. Oklahoma was as far as he'd been willing to go.

"I don't see a car, Hector. Maybe you got a bicycle?" Pike had gotten a reputation in the neighborhood for repairing kids' bicycles for free. Monty usually didn't have the time between running the business, working on the trannies, and raising a family. At closing time, Monty went home to his wife and three kids, and he coached little league baseball and basketball teams. That schedule didn't leave a lot of time for free work.

Pike usually worked late because he didn't have anywhere to go or anything to do. He got paid for piecework, a percentage of each job, instead of hourly—almost like a partner—so Monty didn't kick about it. After Monty went home at six, Pike cracked open a beer, blasted the jams, and turned wrenches. As a result, Monty was bringing in more work than ever.

Working on the bicycles paid off too. The kids told their parents about the big guy down at the garage who was so nice, and the parents who needed repairs and could afford them came calling.

Hector shook his head. "No bicycle. I'm not big enough."

Pike grinned at the kid. "Sure you are. They got bicycles your size."

A flush of embarrassment darkened Hector's face. "I'm not big enough 'cause the other kids would take it away from me."

"Oh." Pike muted the anger that instantly vibrated inside him. He remembered being Hector's age. The only thing that had saved him in the state-run facility and the foster homes that had followed for a while was his size. Still, he hadn't had eyes in the back of his head.

Not until Petey had come along.

That old pain rocketed through Pike and caught him by surprise. Memories returned in a deluge: the young teen Petey had been, all rawboned knees and elbows and attitude. Then the piece of bullet-ruptured meat the Diablos had left behind. Pike clamped down on those feelings quick.

Hector fidgeted.

"So what are you doing here, Hector?" Pike felt the strain in his voice, but he thought maybe the kid wouldn't notice.

"It's my sister. Erendria." Hector stopped speaking.

Pike waited, knowing the boy wouldn't go on until he was ready. Pike understood—he'd been the same way at that age. There wasn't much that Pike had control over as a kid, so he'd worked at controlling himself. He still did. When you didn't have anything, you concentrated on keeping your world small: nothing you cared about, no friends, nothing to carry when you had to move on.

The kid didn't have it that bad. He had a sister, and that meant he had family. Of course, a family brought a lot of trouble, too. You could maybe protect yourself, but you couldn't protect a family all the time. Petey had taught Pike that. Living outside yourself, looking out for something more than was inside your skin, was risky.

The kid wet his lips and squeezed his hands into small fists. "I've heard people say you sometimes do things. Sometimes you help people that can't help themselves."

Pike shook his head. "You heard wrong, Hector. I work on cars. I work on bicycles. That's what I do."

"I know. I heard that. You work on people's cars and you let them pay you out."

Monty hadn't been a big fan of that, either. He hadn't wanted to get known as a garage that gave out credit. If he started doing that, he'd lose his shirt, and the profit margin was thin as a frayed shoestring anyway.

Pike had invested in people on his own, after hours so Monty wouldn't get caught up in all the work or the financial risk. Monty knew about it, but it was something they just didn't talk about. A few times, Pike had gotten burned on deals. People had stiffed him, or they'd gotten themselves in jams and couldn't pay him back. It was no big deal. Money came and money went. That's how it was with money. Petey never had understood that, and he'd gotten killed trying to hang on to too much of it.

"You said you didn't have a car."

Hector shook his head. "No car."

"Your sister have a car?"

"She wishes. Erendria is seventeen, but she's loco." Hector twirled a finger around one of his ears.

"Girls can get like that." In fact, they could get completely psychotic. Pike had seen those.

"She's not a bad girl. She's my sister. But she's in trouble."

Pike pushed himself up and walked across the garage to the ice chest where he and Monty kept their drinks. He opened the chest, sorted through the bottled water and the beer, and found two Cokes. The kid had followed at his heels. Pike handed one, dripping wet from the melted ice, to Hector and kept the other for himself.

"What kind of trouble is your sister in?" Pike didn't want to ask, but he couldn't help himself. He figured maybe the sister was hanging with the wrong guy, something the kid should tell his parents, not a stranger who worked at the garage.

"There's this guy—"

Pike held up a hand. "Hector, your sister is going to meet bad guys. She'll figure it out. And if you're really worried about her, you should tell your momma and your daddy."

"I don't have a father. He ran away after I was born."

Pike cracked his Coke open and took a sip. The tune was as old and familiar as the Led Zeppelin song playing on the boom box. He let the kid tell it, though, knowing that telling it would at least help a little. There were things in this life that couldn't be controlled. That was just how the world worked.

"It's just my mom taking care of us. She has two jobs and is barely home. If I told her what Erendria was doing, it would break my mom's heart, and there still wouldn't be anything she could do about Erendria."

"Look, Hector, I can see you're worried about your sister. I get that. I respect that. But I ain't no family counselor. Whatever this guy is to your sister, you should work that out with her and your momma."

"What he is, is a drug dealer. He's turning my sister into his mule. And she's too stupid to see that."

Pike looked into the kid's dark eyes and knew he wasn't going to go away. "You could go to the police."

Hector expelled a disgusted breath. His voice became high-pitched and strained. "I go to the police, you know what they're gonna do? They're gonna bust Juan Mendoza and Erendria too if she's there. She wants to be a nurse, like our mom. You think she's gonna get to be a nurse with a drug arrest on her record? After she gets out of jail for who knows how long?"

Pike took a long, slow drink of the Coke. Then he pulled over an empty plastic five-gallon bucket that he and Monty used to soak car parts in to clean them. He turned the bucket upside down. "Why don't you have a seat and tell me about this Mendoza guy?"

★   ★   ★

Standing in the dark shadows that lined the street, up against the closed doughnut shop across from the house and dressed in a black hoodie, Pike knew he was invisible in the night. He wore a pair of urban combat pants from his kit, a pair of military boots he'd gotten from the Salvation Army, and black leather gloves that molded to his big hands. He carried no ID. If he got busted, he'd make one phone call and be out in an hour.

Mulvaney wouldn't be happy about that. Neither would the US Marshals assigned to Pike. He didn't care. What he was doing here tonight was a risk. He felt good taking a risk. For the first time in a long time, he felt alive. Working at the garage was good and clean, but it wasn't the kind of thing Pike felt like he'd been born to do.

He kept watch over the house, but he was constantly aware that Petey wasn't with him and hadn't been in four years. That was a long time to go without eyes in the back of your head. Sometimes, though, Pike thought he felt Petey there, just over his shoulder, a half step gone so he'd just missed seeing him.

Juan Mendoza was biracial: half-Hispanic and half–African American. He ran a crew of hardcases—four in all—who were from both communities. Mendoza had staked out a section of the neighborhood and settled in. Crack cocaine, meth, and prostitutes flowed through the house.

Most of the residences around Mendoza's house belonged to honest people struggling to make a go of it despite the economy and the cultural pressure. But none of them were brave enough to stand up to Mendoza.

Hector had explained it all two days ago. And the kid had provided pretty good recon, which Pike had confirmed.

Twenty-five years old, Juan Mendoza had been in and out of lockup since he was twelve. His history read a lot like Pike's, except for the drug-related arrests. Pike had never had anything to do with drugs, but he'd run with people who had. All he'd ever done while running with the Diablos was provide protection, keep other biker gangs from preying on them, recover lost money or goods, and take care of Petey. Pike didn't like drugs, but most biker outlaws did because the profits were good.

Mendoza hadn't taken a fall in six years. The last time had been a three-year shot for dealing. Once he'd gotten out, he'd gone straight back to the business he knew, but he was smarter about it this time. Mendoza's operation consisted of having kids haul his merchandise. If they got busted, they got juvie— a short haul through the justice system—and released.

And kids could be scared into not talking.

Even when they were trying to save their big sister.

According to Hector, Erendria was in love, and she was trying to help Mendoza make his fortune so they could move away. That was the dream Mendoza had been selling her. Of course, the guy was also selling that dream to two other girls Pike had spotted during his surveillance of the house. Mendoza kept the girls staggered pretty well too. He was cunning—and totally ruthless.

The four guys with him were ruthless; not so much in the cunning department. But they were all strapped.

Pike was surprised the police hadn't already flagged the operation and taken it down. But Mendoza lived small, like a tick feeding on a dog's ear, taking just enough to survive without getting too large. He was low-profile all the way, living in the neighborhood and controlling everything he needed to.

The delivery system was good too. The house was a front. Buyers came up to the curb and delivered the money to one of Mendoza's men. Then the car drove halfway down the block, and one of the kids working for Mendoza delivered the goods. If an undercover cop popped one of the kids, they were experienced enough in the system to close their mouths and ride it out.

Mendoza never kept the drugs in the house, and it wasn't against the law to have money. He even had a storefront loan office that explained why people were there dropping off the money. Simply paying off their loans, Officer. Just business.

Across the street, a sports car loaded with college students pulled up to the curb and honked the horn. One of Mendoza's men came out, talked briefly with them, and took the money they passed over. Then he waved them down the street.

A few doors down, a young boy ran out from between the houses and gave the guys in the sports car a small package. The driver stepped on the accelerator hard enough to burn the tires and sped off down the street.

They weren't regular customers. Just wannabes who decided to go slumming. What they'd been given probably wasn't even drugs.

Pike returned his attention to the house. He headed to the corner, rounded the block, and approached Mendoza's house from the rear.

★　★　★

The plan was simple. The best plans always were. Pike knew that from experience. He darted down an alley between houses, then hopped over a bridge railing and dropped into the drainage ditch. Houses fronted streets on either side. Dogs barked and yapped, but most of them just picked up the excitement from the others and carried on the hue and cry. A few men and kids came out of the houses to check on the dogs, but Pike knew how to move through the shadows and remain unseen. A couple of security lights flared to life, but none of them came close to him.

He paused long enough to pull a black ski mask over his face. His mouth and nose were covered, but the eyehole was big enough that his vision wasn't restricted. He kept moving.

Fifty yards farther on, he came up out of the ditch and crouched beside a tall tree just beyond the fence around Mendoza's backyard. Peering through the back windows, he couldn't see much. All the windows were covered by blinds. One of them shifted, and Pike knew someone inside had gotten concerned over the barking dogs.

Paranoia and the drug culture went hand in hand.

After letting five minutes pass, breathing slowly and evenly, Pike vaulted the fence and crossed the backyard, which had become a repository for an ancient and rusting Chevy, two refrigerators, and a stove. Maybe once the backyard filled up, Mendoza would have someone haul the junk off. Or maybe he'd just move.

The front door was reinforced steel. Pike had taken notice of that on his first tour of recon. But the back door that opened into the garage was a no-frills, hollow-core wooden door. Mendoza must have figured any attack would come from the front, or that cops would only come from that way.

The rap music streaming from inside was almost deafening even on the other side of the back door. Pike timed the percussive beats and pulled the ASP baton from his hoodie pocket. The weapon was short and easily concealed when unexpanded. He flicked the release and had sixteen inches of matte-black steel in his fist. Because of the tight confines presented by the house, he'd gone for the shortest length. Other batons expanded to over two feet.

With the next wave of bass percussion, Pike let out a breath and rammed his shoulder into the door. Wood shattered and screws shrieked, and the door flew open. He stepped into the garage, the ASP held in close and ready.

On the other side of the garage, two men leaned on a lowrider and stared at Pike. They'd evidently been sharing a joint, maybe talking about the car. The thick, musky haze of marijuana filled Pike's nostrils.

The men reached for the pistols shoved into the fronts of their belts, but Pike was still in motion, never halting once he'd broken through the door. He swung the baton and shattered the hand of the man on the left before he could get his pistol clear. Pike planted his empty hand in the center of the man's chest and shoved.

By that time the second man was lifting the pistol, his finger already sliding inside the trigger guard. His thumb flicked for the safety, missed, and immediately tried again. Too close now to go for the hand, Pike swung a backhand blow that caught the man on the shoulder. Bone crunched under the assault. Pike felt the shoulder go, but he didn't hear anything over the music.

The man opened his mouth to scream as his pistol tumbled from his nerveless fingers. Moving quickly, Pike hit the man in the throat with the Y of his open hand, catching his opponent between his thumb and forefinger and hitting him hard enough to shut his wind off but not to kill him. Pike didn't want to leave any bodies. Cops looked harder and longer when someone got killed, even when the dead were people like Mendoza and his crew. The neighborhood would be scared.

Gagging and choking, the man went down. Pike swung the ASP again, catching him on the temple and knocking him unconscious. The guy sprawled like a dead man.

The other guy flailed at his gun with his shattered hand, but his fingers weren't working and couldn't close properly. He took a breath to try and yell. Pike kicked the man in the face, no mercy in him as he thought of Hector and his sister. Pike didn't think of himself as a good man by any stretch of the imagination, but he wasn't a Juan Mendoza, either. Pike figured his own road to hell was already paved, but there had to be a special place for guys like Mendoza and his buddies.

The man's head thumped into the wall behind him, and he went slack-jawed as his eyes rolled back up into his head. Heart beating slightly faster, Pike checked the door that led to the house.

It was still closed, and men's voices punctuated the rap music that streamed endlessly.

Kneeling, Pike flipped both men onto their stomachs and secured their hands behind their backs with zip ties. He took out a roll of gray duct tape and ran strips over their mouths and around their heads.

He took one of the pistols, checked the load, and slipped it into the back of his waistband. He wasn't going to kill if he could help it, but he wasn't there to die, either. If he had to shoot someone, it would be better if he shot them with one of their own guns. Whatever story they told the police—if they talked at all—would be confused.

A quick search of the garage revealed the breaker box on one wall. Pike found the master switch, then closed his eyes and counted off thirty seconds, allowing his eyes to adjust to darkness.

Then he threw the switch.

The music died instantly, and even though his eyes were closed, Pike noticed the absence of light. He blinked his eyes open and could see the dim outlines of the garage because the door to the outside allowed moonlight in. With the ASP in one hand, he headed toward the door to the house.

At least three men were still waiting inside.

Pike opened the door, slid inside, and found himself in a utility room. After a brief glance to orient himself as to where the washer and dryer were, he pulled the door closed behind him and walked through the room and into the kitchen.

Violent cursing filled the silence that had fallen over the house.

"Man, what happened to the lights? Jervay! Hey! *Jervay!*"

Hearing the footsteps closing on him, Pike paused beside the refrigerator. Using his peripheral vision so he could see better in the darkness, Pike waited, trusting the light coming through the window on the other side of the kitchen to help him.

"Yo! This is stupid, homes! I'm gonna break my neck wanderin' around in the dark."

"Use your lighter, *ese*. Don't be stupid," the man said in Spanish.

The shadow paused in front of Pike and reached into its pants pocket. Pike reached out, caught a fistful of the man's shirt by feel and yanked him forward, then lifted a knee into the man's crotch. Air whooshed out of the man's lungs along with a thin, gurgling cry of pain. Then Pike clubbed him behind the ear with the ASP and let the unconscious body drop to the floor.

"Hey. You listenin' to me? Light up."

Taking long strides, trusting his night vision and the light leaking through the window blinds in the other room, Pike closed on the remaining two men.

One of them had a penlight attached to his key ring. Drunk or high, he struggled to thumb the penlight on. His hair was done in cornrows that stuck out like tiny pigtails in the darkness. Pike rapped him on the temple with the ASP and he crumpled.

On the other side of the room, Juan Mendoza suddenly struck life to a lighter with one hand while he raised a big-bore pistol in the other. He cursed and fired immediately as the dancing flame atop the cigarette lighter spun shadows around the room.

The muzzle flash ricocheted off the light-colored walls and ignited a small, dark sun inside the room. Pike dodged to one side, and the bullet zipped past him and emptied the guts from a large-screen plasma television. Glass tinkled to the floor.

Mendoza rushed his next shot before he'd recovered from the recoil of the first. His second round bored through the ceiling and drew a tumbling fog of plaster dust that lit up against the lighter flame. He yelped curses and tried to correct his aim.

By that time, Pike was on him. He closed a big fist over Mendoza's hand and held the pistol to one side as the drug dealer fired another round into the wall. Pike whipped the ASP around in a backhanded blow that caught the man in the ribs. The meaty *thunk* was punctuated by breaking bones. Pike had heard the sound plenty of times before and recognized it easily.

Mendoza screamed but had little air left in his lungs. He squirmed and tried to pull the pistol back on track, firing yet another round into the ceiling. Pike stabbed a thumb into the nerve cluster on the back of the man's hand, and the pistol dropped to the carpet with a muffled thud.

Before Mendoza could yell again, Pike whipped the ASP across the man's face and broke his jaw. The yell turned into a bloody mewling. Mendoza dropped to his knees and fell back against the easy chair behind him.

A frightened scream came from a few feet away.

Glaring through the gloom, Pike barely made out the young woman standing in the hallway door. She was of average height but seriously underweight. Her dark hair was pulled back, and all she had on was a T-shirt.

"Get out of here." Pike snarled the command and spoke in Spanish. When the girl didn't move, he stood, picked up the fallen pistol, crossed over to the girl, grabbed her elbow, and hustled her toward the front door. Lights flashed over her from a car just pulling to the curb. An instant later someone honked. A customer was waiting.

The girl got the message and took off running.

Pike closed and locked the door, then went back to Mendoza. The drug dealer was reaching for where the pistol had been and using his other hand to hold his broken jaw. The pain alone from the fracture should have knocked him out. Pike suspected that the pharmaceuticals in his system had kept him functioning.

"It ain't there, Mendoza." Pike dropped into a squatting position beside the man. "Now you need to listen to me."

"Gonna get you, man. Gonna kill you." Mendoza's words were slurred and almost incomprehensible.

Pike pushed the pistol into Mendoza's forehead, getting his attention at once.

Mendoza quieted and went still.

"Got your attention now, *ese*?"

Mendoza mumbled again, and this time Pike recognized the words of the prayer. He'd had religion thrown down his throat in juvie and in some of the foster homes.

"Call on God all you want to, but it's just me and you in this room, Mendoza. If he does exist—and I ain't convinced of that—God don't care about nobody."

Mendoza kept praying, shaking from the pain or the fear—Pike wasn't sure which.

"This is the only warning you get." Pike pressed the pistol muzzle harder against Mendoza's head to get his point across. "You don't know me, but I know you. When you get free of the cops—if you get free of them—you get yourself gone. You don't come around here again. You do and I'll put you in the ground. Do you understand?"

"Yeah." Mendoza nodded and his eyelids fluttered.

"Give me your phone." Pike collapsed the ASP and shoved it back into his hoodie.

Mendoza fumbled in his pants pocket and brought out a cell. Pike took it and headed back through the house. He didn't know if the neighbors had called for the police.

Outside the house, with no one following him, Pike flipped the phone open and dialed 911. When the dispatch officer answered, he gave her the address and told her to send an ambulance with the cops. He spoke in Spanish. Then he hung up, vaulted the back fence, dropped the phone into the spillway, and disappeared into the darkness.

12

PEOPLE HUNKERED in the shadows of the boswellia and commiphora trees and watched fearfully as the trucks rolled to a stop in the tall weeds that somehow managed to sprout from the parched earth. Seated in the passenger seat in the lead truck with an AK-47 in his lap, Rageh Daud watched the people and wondered how many men among them had weapons. It wouldn't be much of an arsenal, a few old single-shot rifles that had been carefully cared for and perhaps a few pistols.

His men, fifteen strong now, rode on the trucks in prominent positions while brandishing the automatic rifles they carried. They would look fearsome and lethal to the displaced people.

Afrah drove the truck and sipped from a whiskey bottle. The al-Shabaab hadn't just had food and medicine in their stolen cargo. There had been a case of whiskey. Some of the men in Daud's group were like Afrah, men who had turned from their Muslim ways to embrace only death.

A man was born and then he died. The time in between was measured in blood and weighed in suffering. Daud's father had told him that, and he had refused to believe it as a young man. His father had even seemed to turn from it when he had set Daud up to go to school.

But Daud had learned that lesson now. This world was the hell the Christian Bible had spoken of, and there were many demons that lived within it. Daud intended to become stronger than any of them, and to do that he needed to raise an army. He couldn't have too many, though, because a large group would slow him down and become more detectable. They had to stay lean and hungry.

They could make safe places for themselves, though, and that was what he intended to do here.

The gathering of shelters wasn't a town. It was a pocket of survivors who had thrown in together in hopes of living. They'd made *aqals*, traditional homes constructed from long branches bent to create ceiling arches and covered in blankets. In earlier times, such structures had been covered in animal skins. This group might have had blankets, but they weren't far removed from those long-ago days. Starvation shadowed them even in the brightest sunlight.

Naked, emaciated children hid behind trees with the women. The men formed a loose line in front of them, armed with the few firearms they had as well as spears and clubs.

"Foolish primitives." Afrah shook his head and took another sip from his bottle. He didn't drink enough to be drunk. Daud made certain of that. "One man with a full magazine could take them all out."

"Perhaps. But they're not just foolish. They're brave enough."

"Do not confuse a lack of somewhere to run with brav- ery." Afrah hawked up phlegm and spat out the truck win- dow. "If they'd been brave, they would have attacked us along this pitiful excuse for a road before we got here."

"They might have hoped we'd drive on by."

Afrah waved at the arid plains that stretched out before them. "And go where? There is only thirst and starvation in any direction."

"Yet they live here."

"Only because they lack the sense to lie down and die."

"They haven't given up, Afrah. Even after all the hardship and turmoil they've been through. You should respect that."

"I do." Afrah glared through the dusty, bug-encrusted windshield at the people. "But they make my heart hurt because I know there is still much pain coming their way."

Daud slapped the bigger man on the shoulder. "We came to alleviate some of that, so let's get to it." He opened the door and stepped out onto the truck's running board. Even just moving from the truck cab to the outside meant an immediate rise in temperature. By the time he touched ground, most of his men had also stepped down with their weapons at the ready.

Afrah came around the truck and stood near the bumper. His fierce visage drew the attention of most of the people.

Daud waved his men to stay back, then walked forward

as he slung his rifle over his shoulder. He wore a white shirt, a blue bandanna over his head, sunglasses, and khaki pants. His boots thudded against the ground and raised small puffs of dust.

From within the sparse trees, goats and sheep bleated and a few of the children cried out fearfully. Chickens occupied small crates that served as coops. The people hadn't been totally without resources.

Daud stopped ten feet from the line of men. He faced them from behind his sunglasses, his small army at his back. "I would talk with your elders."

A middle-aged man held a single-shot rifle to his shoulder. His aim was on Daud. "Who are you?"

"I wish to speak with your elders."

"You are in no position to make demands."

Daud swiveled his attention to the man. "Put your rifle away. Otherwise I will kill you, then bury your woman and your children with you."

The man stubbornly held on to his rifle, but his hands started shaking.

One of the old men in the group stepped forward and placed his hand atop the rifle, gently pushing the barrel toward the ground. "Put your rifle away, Ghauth. If they meant us any harm, they would have killed us from the trucks."

"Then why did they come out here, Nishaaj? There is nothing for men such as these out here."

The old man had a gray beard that trailed nearly to his stomach. He looked thin and frail, and his belly was distended. Daud knew the old man wasn't fat. Probably he was more starved than anything. He wore a traditional long white cloth wound around his body, a *benadiry kufia* on his head, and a pair of tennis shoes. He carried a gnarled shepherd's crook, but that looked like it was more for support these days than for tending a flock.

"The only way we can know the answer to that is to ask them." Nishaaj looked at Daud. "I am Nishaaj. I am the elder of the people."

"I am Rageh Daud, and I would welcome the opportunity to speak with you, father."

"Of course." The old man shuffled forward, and his fear was evident in his small steps and the way he kept scanning the rest of Daud's men. Still, despite his fear, he walked to Daud and stopped. "Is there anything I may get you?"

"No, but there is much I can give you."

Nishaaj looked at him curiously. "Who are you with?"

Daud looked past the man to the people in the sparse trees. "I am not with the al-Shabaab, if that is what you fear. My warriors and I kill those animals wherever we find them." He pointed back at the trucks. "That's where these vehicles come from. From the al-Shabaab. Only a few days ago, my warriors and I killed a band of them and took the trucks. They are loaded with goods the al-Shabaab took from the Westerners who say they are here to help us but seek only to shore up the Transitional Federal Government to serve as their puppet. I came here today to share with you our good fortune."

The words hung in the hot air. Slowly, Ghauth and the

rest of the men relaxed and lowered their weapons, but the hate did not die from their eyes. Daud did not fault them for that. His presence there struck their pride, and that could be as deadly as fear, just slower to react.

"I have food and medicine on those trucks." Daud spoke loudly, letting his voice ring out. "I have clothing and other supplies that will make your lives easier."

"And what do you want in return for these treasures?" Ghauth spoke bravely and in disgust. His pride was obviously stung at being upstaged. "We have nothing you could want. You can look around this place and see that."

Afrah's voice was a low rumble that only reached Daud's ears. "That one, he will be trouble."

"I do not want to hurt any of these people, Afrah."

Afrah growled in displeasure and spat again.

Daud addressed Ghauth. "I want nothing from you. I only want to share our good fortune."

"Your misery, you mean." Ghauth turned to the men around him. "Do not let his smooth tongue fool you. Whoever he took those trucks from, they will come looking for them. They will punish anyone who has anything of theirs."

"The men I took these trucks from will not come looking." Daud lifted his voice and made it strong. "Those men I left stretched out for buzzards to pick clean their bones." He shifted his gaze from Ghauth back to the elder. "Is that what you wish for your children, father? Do you wish them an unkind death and only carrion birds as their pallbearers?"

Nishaaj hesitated only a moment; then he firmed his jaw

and stood more erect as he spoke in a low voice. "I know what you want here, Rageh Daud."

Daud nodded and spoke gently enough that only the old man could hear him. "I knew that you would, father, but there is nothing to be done for it. I have already won and will have what I want. The question is, do you want what I have to offer before I take my leave?"

"God will punish you for what you do."

Daud grinned coldly. "If there is a God, he has already punished me more than I can bear, and I did nothing wrong. So if he is there, and if this is his doing, then he will have to strike me down himself before I will stop."

"Do not taunt God. That is an evil thing to do."

"That will be the least evil thing I will do, old man. Now do you want these medicines and supplies?"

"Yes." Nishaaj turned and waved to his men. "Come. Help me welcome our new friends."

Daud walked back to the first truck and hauled himself up into the cargo area. He threw wide the tarp and revealed the cargo that he'd carried to the outskirts of Mogadishu. Within minutes he stared down at a pack of half-starved men and women who began celebrating and thanking God for all the things they saw before them.

★　★　★

That night the people threw a big party. There was a lot of food to eat. They opened cans and poured the contents into large cook pots. In only a short time the smell of broth, meat, and herbs filled the air.

Daud sat on a crate with his back to the large tree behind him. He kept his AK-47 close by but did not in any way act fearful. From across one of the cook fires, Ghauth kept watch over him, but the man was also aware that he was under Afrah's scrutiny. There was no doubt that he would be dead before he could more than think about acting against Daud.

One of the young women approached Daud with a bowl of meat and vegetables. If she hadn't been so malnourished, she might have been pretty. There was something in her eyes that reminded Daud of his dead wife, some simple innocence, and that recognition sent a sharp pain through his chest.

"For you." The woman bowed as she handed him the bowl.

"Thank you." Daud took the bowl and returned the bow from his seated position. "You should eat, sister."

"I will." She looked at him. "Thank you for all you have brought."

"It was my pleasure."

"It was God's will. I will ask that you be blessed for your kindness."

Daud nodded and smiled, but he didn't think the God this woman believed in would have wanted men left torn and twisted the way Daud had left them in his wake.

The woman hurried back to her mother and younger siblings.

Daud spooned up the broth, blew on it, and ate. The women had enhanced the canned goods with herbs, and the food tasted fresh and good—better than it had any right to. The fact that he was eating it here, away from the city and among simple people, might have had something to do with that.

Mogadishu had held danger not only from the al-Shabaab but from the outsiders. His job also had been filled with unaccustomed pressures. Even the TFG, with their attempts to bring a different and freer government to Somalia, had been dangerous. The TFG soldiers didn't always wait to verify someone's identity before opening fire. The pirates who had gone into business over the last few years had added another element of danger. All three factions fought for Somalia, and the Western military forces only added to the deadly mix.

The people gathered around the cook fires and talked excitedly. Some of the women worked with three of Daud's men who had some medical training. Together, his men and the women cleaned and cared for the children. Many of the children were covered with sores caused by near-starvation and infections. His men worked tirelessly, medicating the children and educating the women on dressings, medicines, and giving injections.

The children played in the shadows, running among the trees and darting in and out of the firelight. Watching them play hurt most of all. Daud had too many memories of his son.

And here you sit, Rageh, unashamed of your intention to take some of these people's children with you.

The truth, though, was that he did feel shame. However, there was no other way. In order to survive, he had to build an army, and that army demanded a fresh influx of bodies.

One of the young men came to Daud first. The man was nineteen or twenty—almost too close to a boy to stand as a man, but wilderness and hardship had aged the young man drastically. By the time Daud had been the young man's age, he had already killed several times. He wasn't proud of that, but it was a fact he knew he had to remember.

"Sir." The young man bowed slightly. He proudly held the spear that served as his weapon.

"Call me Daud."

"Daud."

"What is it you wish?"

The young man looked around nervously. "You have many men."

Daud waited, blowing on a new spoonful, then eating it. "I am aware."

"I did not know if you wanted another."

For a moment, Daud was silent and thoughtful. The young man was clean-limbed and could be strong if he ate regularly and was allowed to take care of himself. "There is always room for a man who is willing to fight for his life and the lives of others."

"I am one of those men. I swear to you this is true. You fight the al-Shabaab. I hate them. I will be glad to fight them as well if you will teach me how and give me proper weapons to do this. If you have none to spare, then I will fight them with my bare hands if I have to and take one from them."

"What is your name?"

"Usayd."

Daud smiled at that, understanding the meaning of the name. "Little lion."

Usayd looked uncomfortable. "I was given the name when I was very small. I am not so small now."

"No, you are not. Do you know how to use a rifle?"

"I have shot my father's."

"At a man?"

The young man hesitated, and Daud knew he was thinking of lying. Then Usayd shook his head. "No. Only at game."

"Guinea?" The birds were black with white speckles, raised domestically and hunted in the wild.

Usayd nodded.

"A guinea is much smaller than a man." Daud smiled. "If you can shoot a guinea, you can shoot an al-Shabaab man."

The young man smiled back. "I have shot many guineas."

"They are very tough to eat." The meat from the fowl was notoriously stringy and did not taste good no matter what was done to it.

"I have never enjoyed eating them." Usayd looked hopefully at Daud. "May I accompany you when you leave?"

"Why do you wish to go?"

"There is nothing here for me."

"These people are your family."

Usayd's face pinched tight. "My family is starving. You gave them food and supplies to get through a few more days, but what will they do then? Go back to dying slowly?"

Daud said nothing. His father had taught him that a man had to talk himself into something. Rarely could anyone be persuaded into something potentially dangerous, generally only through greed or lust. Survival, though, was a common goal for many. Finding out how much risk a person would tolerate to survive was best left to the individual.

"I do not want that for myself, and I do not want that for

these people. If I go with you, I will try to provide for them."
Usayd hesitated. "If that is permitted."

"Have you spoken with your father?"

"My father died before we came out here. Last year. He got sick."

"I am sorry."

"It was God's will. His time among us was done. Now we have to survive."

"You have your mother?"

"Yes. And three younger sisters." Usayd looked earnestly at Daud. "If I go with you, if I swear myself to your cause, I want you to promise me something."

"What?"

"That my family here will not be forgotten. That when we can, we will bring them more food and more medicine."

"I give you my word." If possible, Daud would keep that promise, but not at the risk of what he was doing.

"Thank you. When are we leaving?"

"In the morning."

"I will be ready." Usayd took his leave and retreated back to the cook fires and his people.

He wasn't the only one who came to see Daud. The others drifted in slowly, and he talked with them throughout the night.

★   ★   ★

Hours later, the people finally calmed down, sated by food and worn from fatigue. The cook fires burned down to smoking coals and barely showed in the dense darkness. Thin, black shadows spun like gossamer across the face of the quarter moon. A slight breeze cooled the night, and Daud lay beneath a blanket under one of the trucks. He kept a guard rotation going just in case some of the men turned greedy.

"The old man is coming." Afrah lay nearby on another pallet with his bottle close by. His alcoholic breath occasionally tainted the night breezes.

"I knew he would." Daud rose, resenting the old man for disturbing his slumber but knowing the man had no choice. "He could not let this go unchallenged."

Nishaaj stopped a few feet in front of Daud. The moonlight fell across the hard obsidian of his face and carved out deep shadows. "May we speak?"

"Of course."

"How many of our young men are you taking?"

Daud answered at once, knowing the old man had the right to know because he was looking out for these people. And he respected the blunt way the man addressed the situation. "Five."

"Five." The number seemed to strike the old man a blow. "So many."

"It could have been more. In fact, some may try to follow me when I leave in the morning even though I have rejected them. I give you my word that I will send them back." Eleven young men between the ages of fifteen and thirty-two had approached Daud. He had chosen from among them, taking ones who were older and didn't have as many ties to family members so they wouldn't get homesick and try to return.

He also rejected anyone over the age of twenty-five

because those would be too headstrong and, perhaps, ultimately untrainable. Most of them joined because they wanted something more than they had, or they were afraid of starving to death. They were young and selfish, and Daud knew he could work with that.

Usayd had been different. He saw joining Daud as a way to provide for his family. Others had seemed like rats deserting a sinking ship. Men who gave up that easily would give up when Daud needed them. He had rejected those as well.

"I suppose it could have been." Nishaaj shook his head. "You take our young men from us, and with them you take our future."

Daud looked at the old man coldly. "Out here, fleeing like animals, you have no future. I have given you much in exchange for five men. You should count yourself fortunate with the bargain."

Nishaaj's face tightened with displeasure. "You mock me."

"No. I speak the truth. You know that."

"These are young men."

"They can still be trained to fight. Those other men, like Ghauth, they don't know when to leave, when to acknowledge there is nothing here they can do. They will stay and die rather than leave their families and live to fight on a better day."

"A man is nothing without his family."

"Wrong. Without his family, a man is a powerful weapon. He can be strong and fearless. There is nothing left to lose, nothing that can be taken from him."

"There is nothing to live for."

"Wrong, old man." Daud's voice came hot and harsh. "A man such as that may live on the hate that is in his heart."

"A heart may not carry such a load."

"A heart may not *choose* such a burden, but it will carry it just fine."

"It will be a coal that burns too hotly, bright and then quickly ash."

"I will burn all those who come my way. Never doubt that. I embrace my fiery heart."

Wearily, Nishaaj shook his shaggy head and ran his fingers through his beard. "I will pray for your soul."

"Pray all you want, old man. Pray until your knees are bruised and bloody, but it will do no good. I have no soul. If there is a God, he took that from me and buried it in a hole with my wife and child."

Nishaaj looked Daud in the eye. "Go early in the morning, before the mothers know they are about to lose their sons." Without another word, he turned and walked away.

Daud lay back down and slept.

★   ★   ★

Shortly after the dawn broke over the eastern horizon and filled the sky with bloody-egg-yolk color, Daud roused his men and got them onto the trucks. The people were only then getting up from their beds, still too full from last night's feast. They watched in confusion as their visitors readied to go.

Daud's warriors weren't happy about leaving at such an hour either, but Daud yelled orders at them till they swiftly recognized that he was in no mood to be disobeyed. In minutes they were ready to go.

"Without breakfast?" Afrah was still half-intoxicated and his foot slipped from the running board as he sought to pull himself up behind the wheel.

"We will eat on the road." Daud briefly considered taking Afrah's place driving, but he knew the older man would control the truck just fine once they got under way.

Afrah snarled curses but climbed in and turned the motor over. The throaty rumble shattered the peaceful stillness over the area.

Standing on the truck's running board, Daud gazed back toward the people in their miserable huts. As he watched, seven young men ran toward the trucks with their meager belongings slung over their shoulders in packs.

Daud pointed to two of the men. "Not you two."

The two young men he'd singled out stopped, then glared at him belligerently and started forward again.

Daud drew his pistol and fired into the air. The two men came to a stop as he took aim at them. Terrified now, they slunk back. The other five men scrambled onto the waiting trucks.

Only then did the mothers of three of the young men realize what was happening. They cried their sons' names and ran toward them. Smaller children trailed after them, squalling and crying as well. The young men begged forgiveness from their mothers, but they maintained their positions aboard the trucks.

Daud glanced at Afrah and nodded. "Go."

Afrah put the truck into gear and released the clutch. The big wheels bit into the ground and rolled forward, bouncing over the rough terrain. The mothers quickly fell behind, and their plaintive cries drowned in the acceleration of the motors. Daud swung into his seat and closed the door. He pulled his sunglasses down and rested his rifle beside him while he replaced the spent cartridge in his pistol.

"Where to?" Afrah squinted against the bright sun and drove relentlessly.

Daud pulled a map from his shirt pocket and opened it. He had marked sites where pockets of desperate humanity were rumored to be, places he intended to exploit to grow his army. "There is another camp forty or fifty miles away. We will go there."

"This is a slow process, Rageh."

"Perhaps. But it is also a true one." Daud folded the map and replaced it in his pocket. Then he took up his rifle and began watching for any signs of the TFG or the al-Shabaab contingent that might be looking for them.

13

HEATH PLACED HIS CARRY-ON beside the table in the small restaurant inside Will Rogers Airport. His flight wasn't scheduled till 11:18 a.m. It was 9:37 now. Taking his iPad from his carry-on, he opened the cover and pulled up his e-mail.

Fourteen new pieces of mail popped into his in-box. Heath sorted through them at a glance. A couple were ads (couldn't ever seem to get completely away from those), four were Facebook updates from people he knew, five more were from personal acquaintances wishing him the best on his reactivation, and three were from the other attorneys with his father's firm whom he'd turned cases over to in his absence.

There was nothing from Lionel Bridger.

Heath hadn't expected there to be. Darnell Lester was a flyspeck on Lionel Bridger's radar.

Sighing with frustration, Heath took the lid off his coffee, poured in two creamers, and stirred. Then he took a sip and decided to let it sit for just a while longer. A few passersby took notice of him, and he knew it was because he was dressed in camo fatigues. Even though a lot of military people were on flights these days, they still attracted attention. He took out his cell and used speed dial to call his father's office.

The phone rang once—just once—and Margaret Atwater lifted it and answered precisely. "You've reached the office of Lionel Bridger. This is Margaret Atwater. May I help you?"

"Good morning, Ms. Atwater." No one called the woman by her first name. Not even Heath's father. She was extremely efficient, dedicated, and protective. No one encroached on her space or any space she defended, and she defended Lionel Bridger's schedule religiously.

"Good morning, Mr. Bridger. I know that you are on your way to a new posting, and I would like to take this moment to wish you the best of luck."

"Thank you, Ms. Atwater. I'd—"

The woman interrupted him with surgical precision. "However, you do know the rules. Unless you have an appointment with Mr. Bridger, you may not inconvenience him. I just checked his schedule, and you are not listed."

"This is about a case."

"I appreciate that, but it is not about Mr. Bridger's cases. Otherwise I would have a notation about this call."

"I've got a motion in front of a judge regarding Darnell Lester."

"I wish you the best of luck with that as well."

"Thank you, but I want my father to be aware of the motion and to be prepared to lend a hand getting it before

Judge Seaver. As I recall, my father and Judge Seaver play golf together occasionally."

"They do."

"I was thinking my father could give the judge a call, maybe nudge the motion onto his review docket."

"That would be a matter for you to discuss with Mr. Bridger, Mr. Bridger. I would suggest you set up an appointment."

"I don't know when I will be back from this tour of duty."

"Understood, but chances are you will be on the other side of the world and back again before I can find time for a meeting on Mr. Bridger's calendar. I'm looking at it now. It's quite full. And Mr. Bridger has made it plain to me that Mr. Lester's case is in your hands, not his."

Heath bit back a scathing retort. He made himself breathe out. "This case is important to me, Ms. Atwater. Darnell Lester is important to me."

"I believe you."

Although the woman's response was cold and impersonal, Heath knew she meant it. "The man shouldn't have to die."

"Mr. Lester is a convicted murderer. The jury has ruled. You were handed this case as part of a pro bono package, Mr. Bridger. No one will believe you haven't done your job, however the matter turns out."

"This isn't about the win."

"Don't let Mr. Bridger hear you say that. A legal case is always about the win."

"Darnell Lester has a daughter. He has grandkids. For the last twelve years, he's been a positive force in their lives. That should be allowed to continue."

"Don't attempt to try your case with me, Counselor. It will be wasted effort. Mr. Bridger's schedule is carved in stone."

"Can I at least leave him a note?"

"Of course. I suggest sending him an e-mail."

And that would be an exercise in futility. Margaret Atwater went through Lionel Bridger's e-mail, mail, and texts with a fine-tooth comb. If a person or case was declared persona non grata, nothing less than a nuclear weapon would get through.

"Thank you for your time, Ms. Atwater." Heath glanced at his watch and knew he was just wasting his time, as he'd feared.

"Of course, Mr. Bridger. And do let me know if there is anything I can do for you while you are wherever it is you're going."

Heath thanked her and hung up, immediately calling up his contact list and searching for Mark Kluger. He punched the button and listened to the phone ring as he sipped his coffee. He glared at the breakfast biscuit he'd bought, knowing he couldn't eat it until he'd resolved the issue regarding Darnell Lester.

Mark Kluger was a couple years older than Heath, and he'd been one of those attorneys whom Lionel Bridger had developed connections with early on, while Mark was still in law school. Mark was going to be an excellent trial lawyer, equipped with supreme poise, elegant diction, and a square jaw that could shatter granite.

"Mark Kluger, rising legal star of Bridger, Constant, and McClinton. I have a list of satisfied clients and a wake of broken hearts."

Despite the situation and the tension within him, Heath smiled. Mark's good nature was irrepressible, and he was generally a good person. If he had any downfall, it was that he was too much like Lionel Bridger when it came to business. But that was also his greatest strength, and it was what Heath needed now.

"I suppose you have caller ID on." Heath stared out the window as a Southwest jet sped into the morning sky.

The public address system came on and blurted one of the safety messages that routinely repeated.

"I do, and I suppose from the canned announcement you're at the airport."

"I am."

"Safe voyage, my friend. Where are you headed? Brief vacation?"

"Military assignment."

"Ouch." Mark groaned. "I wish you'd come to me when you first thought of signing up to be a soldier."

"A Marine."

"Whatever. The whole idea of taking orders gives me hives."

"Actually, I'm a lieutenant. I give a lot of orders."

"You're not a general. You take a lot of orders as well."

Heath didn't have a comeback for that because it was true.

"You know, you could have played softball for the firm if you'd wanted a physical activity."

"I like being a Marine." That was out before Heath even knew it was coming.

"Touch a nerve?"

"No."

"Sounded like I did."

"Must be the phone connection."

"I beg to differ. I'm very perceptive. One of my best skills."

"Inflated ego much?"

"Not at all. Your father, the Mr. Bridger who signs my checks, told me that himself."

That smarted a little too. Mark Kluger was one of Lionel Bridger's favorites. Heath had never made that particular list, and he was pretty sure he never would. He just wished it didn't matter to him.

"Terrific. Maybe I could convince you to use some of that perception to help me with a case."

"You? Need help? Say it ain't so."

"I filed a motion that I'd like to see moved to Judge Seaver's docket. Do you have any pull with him?"

"I let him win at golf and don't force him to cheat to do it. I'm not quite in your father's league. You do know why your old man puts up with the cheating, don't you?"

"Yes."

Mark went on as though Heath hadn't spoken. "Because Seaver hates knowing he isn't getting away with anything. And he's not good enough to cheat *and* beat your father." He chuckled. "Man, I love that."

"Great. A fan club."

"You old man is great at what he does."

"I've grown up hearing about it. Let's talk about how great you can be."

"Sure. One of my favorite subjects."

"Can you move a motion onto Seaver's calendar?"

"Probably. What kind of motion is it?" Mark's chair squeaked, and Heath knew the man was reaching for a pen.

"I'm working on getting a death penalty commuted."

Mark didn't speak for a moment. "This is that Lester thing, isn't it? The pro bono case?"

"Darnell Lester, that's right."

The sound of a pen tapping against a blotter echoed over the connection for a moment. "Man's convicted of killing a police officer, isn't he?"

"Yeah. I'm not trying to get him out of prison, Mark. That's not what this is about. I'm just trying to beat the death penalty. The guy made a mistake."

"The courts don't put you on death row for making a mistake, buddy. They put you on death row for killing other people who shouldn't have been killed."

"Review my motion and I think you'll get a better understanding of what's going on here."

"I already understand. At best, this is a slim chance."

"If I don't get the case out of Winters's hands, there's no chance at all."

"I get that. Winters's father was a highway patrolman who was killed by an escaping felon."

"Which is one of the reasons he should have recused himself from the case."

"Couldn't do that and you know it. A judge who admits to any kind of predisposition on cases isn't going to sit the bench long, or he'll get his rulings questioned ad infinitum."

"The motion, Mark. I need it to hit Seaver's calendar."

"Your father might not be happy about this. I've already heard him mention a couple times that he's not thrilled about the time you're putting into this case."

"Maybe it would be better if the firm got called under fire because there's some question about me going the distance on this one."

"Whoa, buckaroo. Don't leave the rails just yet. No one would dare say that."

"I want that motion on Seaver's calendar, Mark. That's the deal."

"What deal?"

"I'm getting pulled out of here in the middle of that case. That could be leverage by another attorney to not only file for Darnell Lester, but also to sue Bridger, Constant, and McClinton."

"No one would do that."

"If I was the attorney following up after me, I would." Heath knew it was possible, but he didn't know anyone that good who would be willing to work a pro bono case.

"Did you talk to your father about this?"

"Couldn't get past Ms. Atwater."

"Yeah, I've been there." Mark was silent for a moment. "Let me work on this. I'll get back to you."

"I'll owe you one."

"I pull this off, you'll owe me more than that."

"Let me know. And thanks." Heath punched off the phone and sat back in his chair. He hated leaving things hanging with his cases when he got called away. He knew he might have been able to postpone his reactivation under legal precedent, but the truth was that he didn't want to. When he left the offices of Bridger, Constant, and McClinton and put on that Marine uniform, he became more of his own man than he'd ever been.

He liked that feeling, and he liked knowing that everything he did as a Marine mattered. When it came to life-or-death decisions on the battlefield, things were generally black and white. He liked that. He knew what to do there. Dealing with the court and the law, that was something different. Things tended to come in layers of gray.

Trying to work out things with his father was closer to impossible.

14

PIKE MORGAN PASSED THROUGH security at Tulsa International Airport without a hitch. The TSA guys gave him a little extra room, and the two young security women gave him more attention. One of them even smiled at him. He gave her a wink as he strode from the checkpoint.

"You gonna be in the airport long?" She was tall and brunette, late twenties or early thirties—about Pike's age. She wore her hair pulled back, and there was enough of it that he wanted to see it let down.

"Couple hours." Pike pulled his carry-on over one shoulder and shoved his hands into the pockets of his leather jacket.

"I get a break in about thirty minutes." The woman nodded down the hallway. "Got a bar down that way on the right. Maybe we could talk a minute."

"I'll be there." He turned and walked away without

looking back, but he knew she was watching him. He could feel her eyes. Hooking up had never been a problem, but he'd never met a woman—had never met anyone—that he really wanted to keep in his life. He hadn't wanted Petey there either, but Petey hadn't had anyone else to look after him.

Pike found the bar with no problem and sat at a table in the rear. He ordered a whiskey and a beer back. He'd never cared for flying, and the drinks would take the edge off.

His cell rang after he got his drinks. A quick check of the caller ID identified the caller as "5-0." He smiled at that. The joke didn't get old. Caleb Mulvaney was a detective sergeant serving with Dallas homicide. The two of them had ended up on opposite sides of the law, but they'd reached an understanding that had surprised Pike. Mulvaney had a rapport with Pike that none of the marshals in the witness protection program had ever managed. And because the United States Marshals Service thought Pike was intractable, special dispensation had been made, and Mulvaney and Pike were still in touch.

Mulvaney was an old-school cop, tough and unflinching, a guy who didn't take any bollocks and didn't find a foxhole to avoid bad times. He stood up and got counted. Pike respected that, and he figured maybe Mulvaney saw some of it in him as well.

Why Pike got such pleasure from these calls was a mystery to him. Maybe it was because Mulvaney was safe, always at arm's length. He opened the phone and said hello.

"I heard you were shipping out today." Mulvaney's voice was a rough rasp. He was nearly sixty and had been a lifetime smoker, but he was a feisty guy and still had the chops to be dangerous in a fight. Pike had firsthand knowledge of that.

"I am."

"Know where?"

"Not yet. I get my orders when I hit the West Coast."

Mulvaney puffed—probably a cigar, his usual. "Could be Afghanistan. You ready to go back into that soup?"

"I go where I go, chief."

"Roll like a stone, that it?"

"Yep. I like the wind in my hair."

"Not as much hair as there used to be."

Pike smiled. "I cut mine, though. You, you're just getting thin."

"Hardy har, punk."

"You just call to tell me how much you missed me?" Pike sipped the whiskey.

"Not even. Called to tell you not to get yourself killed."

"Case is closed. We put the bad guys away months ago. I'm in the rocking chair right now. You don't have to worry about me."

Mulvaney grunted. "Except for that whole going overseas to get shot by al Qaeda."

"They ain't shot me enough yet." Pike had been wounded twice.

"You keep giving them chances, they're gonna get it right one of these days."

"I'm trying not to let that happen."

"Good for you. But you could let it go, you know."

Pike swirled the amber liquor in his glass. "Nah, I can't."

"Why?"

Thinking back to three years ago when he'd first enlisted with the Marines, Pike recalled how upset the United States Marshals Office had been when they found out. He'd gotten all kinds of flak over that, and he'd weathered it all. He was good at that.

"Truth?"

"Can I bear it?"

"Sure. You're always telling me you're a tough guy."

"Hit me."

"I miss the action." Pike listened to himself and was amazed at how truthful he was being. "I grew up on the streets."

"That's not entirely true. There were foster homes in there."

A *lot* of foster homes, and Mulvaney knew it. That was part of the problem. "Yeah, it's true enough. The parts of me that matter, the stuff that I respect, that's where it came from. This deal with Petey and the Diablos, that took me off the streets. Took me away from the action."

"Streets would have got you dead." Mulvaney sounded more serious now.

"Sooner or later they get everybody."

"You're better off away from that life."

"Maybe. I didn't plan for a future. All I wanted was a good run." Pike stared out at the passersby walking in front of the bar with unseeing eyes. He registered them, but he didn't care about them enough to even be curious about where they were going or why.

"You *had* a good run, kid. You got lucky. Otherwise you'd have been buried years ago."

Pike laughed. "Man, ain't you the optimist?"

"Call 'em as I see 'em." Mulvaney laughed too. "You'd think after three years in the Marines you'd be more than a private first class."

"I have been. A few times."

"I know. Even made sergeant once. Now you're back to private."

"Keeping tabs on me?"

"Some. I got resources. Easy enough to check. So what's the problem with advancing your military career?"

"They think I'm intractable."

"Can't imagine where they'd get that idea."

"Me neither."

"But I wasn't talking about what's the matter with them. I'm talking about what's the matter with you."

"Advancing that career don't cut no ice with me. I never signed on to be a lapdog."

"Then why not get out of it before you get your ticket punched?"

Pike sipped his beer and thought about the question. He never questioned himself, and he generally ignored other people's questions. But Mulvaney was different. Mulvaney had invested in him, and when the time had come, the old cop had laid his life on the line. That carried weight in Pike's world.

"I'm happy doing what I do. I make sergeant, or even lance corporal, they want me to take on responsibilities. I'm not there for that."

"You're there for the action."

"That's right." Pike enjoyed the camaraderie he had with Mulvaney, and that relationship continued to surprise him. Mulvaney's opinion of him mattered more to Pike than anybody's ever had . . . except Petey's.

"Speaking of action." Mulvaney took another hit on his cigar, and the sucking sound carried over the phone connection.

"If this is a segue to your love life, I ain't interested."

Mulvaney cursed Pike good-naturedly. "No, but it is about a crack house that got busted up a couple days ago. People are wondering if you had anything to do with that."

Pike sipped his whiskey and didn't say anything.

"The marshals got hold of me, told me about this crack house that suddenly went out of business not far from that place where you're turning wrenches."

"I blame the economy. It's tough all over."

"Some of those guys ended up in the hospital."

"Probably brought their own painkillers."

Mulvaney chuckled. "Could be. I didn't ask. The marshals thought maybe I should talk to you about it."

"Sure. I'm in favor of crack houses going out of business."

"Between you and me, I figure you had your own reasons."

Pike kept his silence for a moment, then decided that Mulvaney knew what Mulvaney knew, and him confirming it wouldn't make any real difference about how this bounced. "Kids were getting caught up in the machine. The machine needed to go away. It did. End of discussion."

"Yeah. I guess so. I'll tell the marshals that you don't know anything about it and they shouldn't bother you."

"I appreciate that."

"Just make sure you watch your six, amigo." Mulvaney had been a Marine too.

"Always do."

"While you're over there, you take care of yourself."

"My number one job."

"And if you need something, drop a dime. Lemme know."

"Thanks. And you do the same. Stay frosty."

"You too, kid. I'll keep you in my prayers." Mulvaney broke the connection.

For a minute, Pike looked at the phone. It was weird how he felt closer to Mulvaney, a cop who would have busted him all those years ago if he could have caught him, than anybody since Petey. He still didn't feel the same. He'd been like Petey's big brother, watching over him and trying to keep him alive.

Only Petey hadn't been looking out for himself. Got himself killed and almost got Pike killed too.

At that moment, the brunette security officer entered the bar and smiled at him. She glanced at the phone in Pike's big hand. "Bad news?"

"Nah." Pike put the phone in his coat. "Catching up with an old friend. You want something to drink?"

"I do, but I gotta go back to work. Maybe a Diet Coke?"

"Coming up." Pike went back to the bar to order another round.

15

BEKAH HATED GOOD-BYES at the airport. There were always too many people at Will Rogers, and all of them were strangers. It might have been better if Granny and Travis could have gone through the security checkpoints with her. There were more restaurants there, and Travis could have watched the jets take off and land.

The trip to the airport took a lot out of Granny as well. She looked exhausted, but Bekah knew a lot of the fatigue was from worrying about her and from driving through all the metropolitan traffic. Granny insisted on driving so Bekah could talk to Travis during the trip.

Bekah held her son and didn't want to let him go. He kept getting so big. Every time she came back from overseas, Travis always seemed so much more grown up. One of these days he'd be too big to hold, and she knew that day was coming quicker than she wanted it to. She wrapped her arms around him and inhaled his scent—the shampoo in his hair and the soap that clung to his skin, the freshness of his clothes because she'd just taken them off the clothesline that morning.

This is what you're supposed to be doing. You're supposed to be with this boy.

She remembered again how she'd felt the day she found out she was pregnant. Billy Roy had been on the road then. She'd wanted to tell someone how excited she was—and how afraid. Nothing ever came easy or just one way. Her life had always been complicated. And it seemed like things only got worse.

She struggled to keep the news to herself, but Billy Roy had been three weeks out from a return home. Two days after confirming the pregnancy, she told him over the phone.

Billy Roy hadn't taken the news well. The timing couldn't have been worse. He'd just taken the mound earlier in the evening and had learned that his pitching skills weren't as impressive against triple-A ballplayers. He'd gotten shelled, the batters hit everything he threw at them, and if it hadn't been for the outfield, he would have been trapped on that mound. The manager had pulled him in the second inning.

When he found out about the baby, he'd yelled at her, told her the pregnancy was all her fault. That taking care of something like that was her responsibility, and how could she be so stupid as to get knocked up?

His words. *Knocked up.*

That had hurt. From the beginning, Billy Roy had treated Travis like some kind of disease. Only a few months later, Billy Roy had started calling her drunk and accusing her of infidelity, telling her there was no way the baby could be his.

Those words and the raw anger behind them had broken Bekah's heart. The only thing she had to hang on to was the baby growing inside her. As soon as he got home, Billy Roy moved out. Bekah had been on her own ever since.

Travis leaned back in her arms and looked at her from under his baseball cap. "Are you okay, Momma?"

"I am."

"You're crying."

She thought about lying to him, but she didn't want to do that. Nobody deserved to be lied to. "Maybe a little."

"Because you're going away?"

"Yes."

"It'll be okay, Momma."

That hurt so bad Bekah could scarcely contain it. "I know. I know it will."

"I'm gonna draw you pictures every day."

"And I'll look forward to them."

"You're gonna come back soon, and me and Granny will be here waiting for you." Travis looked at his granny. "Ain't that right?"

"That's right, sugar." Granny gripped Travis's elbow and beamed at him. Then she shifted her attention to Bekah. "You gotta be strong, girl. This is the path God put you on, so you gotta be strong. You gotta serve his plans. When Jesus walked this earth, he didn't demand any kind of special favors from his Father. He emptied himself and came as a servant. Jesus sacrificed his own life for us, and now your sacrifice is for your son. You just gotta trust in the Lord."

Bekah had had this discussion before. When she was little, she believed everything her granny had told her about God and how he had plans for everyone. But Bekah didn't believe that it was in God's plans to take her away from her son when he needed her most. She couldn't believe that.

"I know, Granny." Bekah nodded. She knew the older woman was talking about being strong for Travis. He was already aware of the arrest and the night at the police station, and he was confused about that. He didn't need to see her upset before she left. "I will be. I am."

"That's good. You just hold on to that and get back to us as soon as you can." Granny folded her arms over her thin chest. She glanced at her watch. "About time for you to get going, ain't it?"

Glancing at the clock on the wall, Bekah saw that it was time. She made herself hug Travis tightly. Then she kissed him and handed him to Granny.

"I'll take good care of this'n." Granny threw an arm around Bekah's shoulders and held her tight for a moment. "Don't you worry none about that."

"I never do, Granny." Bekah kissed her granny's cheek, returned the hug, and shouldered her olive-colored carry-on. Her other bags had already been checked.

"And if you need something, you let us know. Me and Travis will get it to you."

"I will." Bekah took two steps back while waving good-bye, then turned and made herself march to the security checkpoint.

"Good morning, Soldier." A gray-haired woman in a security uniform took Bekah's papers when she offered them. She looked to be in her late fifties and had a working woman's hands, short nails and calluses.

"Marine." Bekah's reply was automatic.

The woman smiled. "Marine. That your boy?"

Bekah blinked back tears and nodded because she didn't trust her voice.

"Good-looking boy." The woman initialed the boarding pass.

"Thank you."

"Got to be hard to leave."

"It is. Every time."

The woman shook her head. "Don't see how you do it. I raised three of my own, and I can't imagine not being around them when they were that age."

It wasn't supposed to be like this. Bekah kept that to herself. She'd joined the Marine Reserve as a means of getting some extra income and insurance for herself. Travis, for the moment, was still covered by SoonerCare, the insurance provided by the state, but he would keep growing. She'd needed a way to provide for him and a means of getting more education for herself.

Being a Marine was supposed to be a part-time thing. She hadn't thought she'd ever be activated. That had just been bad luck, and she knew she shouldn't be surprised. She'd had a long line of it since Billy Roy.

"God bless you, Marine." The woman handed the boarding pass back and gave her a smile. "There's a lot of people here who appreciate everything you do."

"Thank you." Bekah took the boarding pass and headed for the line to the X-ray machines. As she dumped her belongings into the tubs, she glanced back to where Granny and Travis had been, even though she hadn't wanted to.

They were gone, like they'd never been.

Once she was past the checkpoint, Bekah headed for the bathroom. She found an open stall, dropped her carry-on, and got sick. It happened every time. She couldn't stop it. No matter what she did, no matter what antacid she took, she couldn't keep from being sick.

When she was finished, she wiped her face, picked up her bag, and headed to the sink. Thankfully, no one else seemed to have noticed. She surveyed her reflection in the mirror. Even after the years she'd been in the Marines, she still had a hard time seeing herself in the camouflage fatigues she had on. That wasn't her. It didn't fit the image she kept of herself.

She'd pulled her hair back in a French braid, applied foundation to her face to even out her complexion, and wore earring studs. Those would come out later, but for now she wore them.

Dark circles lay under her eyes. She couldn't help noticing them as she stared into that tanned face. Her eyes were red and puffy, and she hated the way they made her look weak and soft.

You're not weak and soft. You're a Marine. You're going to do whatever has to be done. Then you're coming back to be with your son. With your family. So get it together, Marine. Put that face on. Get into that mind-set. Get the job done. Get back home. That's the mission. That will never change.

Bekah squared her shoulders and dried her eyes. When she looked back at the mirror, she was once more the Marine she'd set out to become . . . because that was who she had to be to survive.

Lance Corporal Bekah Shaw. Today she was a Marine. When she got back, she'd be a momma again. She picked up her carry-on and left.

★　★　★

As she walked toward her boarding gate, Bekah noticed the man in camo fatigues seated at a table by himself in one of the restaurants. There were a lot of military guys in the airport, but this one drew her eye, and she wondered why. She thought he looked familiar and wondered if she'd served with him somewhere before. Then, after she got another look, she realized that she didn't know him, but she noticed the glint of the lieutenant's bars on his lapels.

He was an officer. Definitely off-limits for casual conversation.

Bekah went to the counter and ordered a coffee to help get rid of the sour taste in her mouth. She added cream and sugar, recapped her cup, and briefly made eye contact with the lieutenant. A shiver passed through her when he smiled.

She didn't smile back. She just ducked her head and headed for the gate, hoping the guy wasn't going to come after her. Being a woman in the military—where the ratio was dramatically different than in the civilian world— meant having to put up with a lot of stumbling passes. The fact that she was older than a lot of the eighteen- and nineteen-year-olds in the service made the situation even more awkward.

Few people were in the gate area, and Bekah took a seat near one of the large windows. She put her carry-on on the floor between her boots, reached inside, and took out the *Entertainment Weekly* and a couple paperback thrillers that her granny had packed. Granny had an addiction to crime and suspense novels and had read Nancy Drew mysteries to Bekah when she was a girl.

Thinking about that, Bekah wondered if Granny would read Hardy Boys mysteries to Travis. And that made Bekah feel guilty about not being there herself to read them to him when the time came. Good things had to be passed on to the next generations.

"Hey. Seat taken?"

Hearing the male voice, Bekah looked up, expecting to see the young lieutenant from the restaurant. She really didn't need that kind of attention right now, and she definitely didn't want it.

Instead, though, the guy standing in front of her was a familiar face. Ralph Caxton, from the auto parts store, grinned nervously at her. His camo fatigues looked like they'd just come off the shelf. The material was stiff and unblemished, and she knew he was going to take heat from the other Marines for that. He looked new and shiny, and really innocent with his hat on.

"Sorry." He looked flustered. "I didn't mean to interrupt— and if I am, just let me know."

"No interruption." Bekah smiled at him.

"Maybe you don't remember me." Ralph stuck his hand out. "I'm—"

"Ralph Caxton. From the auto store. I remember you, Marine."

"Okay. Good." Ralph plucked at his collar. "Get your truck fixed?"

"I did."

"Cool. That's good." Ralph looked around. "When I first got here, I wasn't sure if I would know anybody or not. Yours is the first familiar face I've seen."

"There'll be others once we get where we're going."

"I'm glad, because I gotta admit that I'm a little freaked out."

"Don't freak out." Bekah nodded to the seat beside her.

"Thanks." Ralph sat and dropped his carry-on to the ground.

Bekah looked at his hat meaningfully.

"What? Is it crooked?" Ralph reached up to his head.

"You did a lot of outside drills, didn't you?"

"Yeah."

"When you're inside, you should take your cover off."

"Cover?"

"Your hat." Bekah pointed. "Officially, as part of the uniform, it's called a cover."

"Oh." Ralph took off the hat, folded it, and put it on his thigh. "Thanks."

"Shove it into your pocket. You don't want to get caught outside without it. A first shirt will give you grief." Bekah knew lots of sergeants who liked to terrorize the newbies to get them on the straight and narrow really quick. Sometimes it was the only way to keep them alive.

"Right." Ralph shoved the hat into a thigh pocket of his camo pants. He leaned back in the seat and tried to act nonchalant, though his nerves showed through. He looked at her magazine. "Did I interrupt your reading?"

"Not really." Bekah closed the magazine and slid it back into her carry-on. "Just killing time till the flight."

"Yeah." Ralph thumped his blouse pocket. "Brought my iPhone loaded with jams."

Bekah nodded and sipped her coffee. "Being nervous is natural."

Ralph spoke quickly. "I'm not nervous. I'm just—" He stopped himself and looked embarrassed. "I guess maybe I am a little nervous."

"No big deal, Marine. Guys I've talked to that have been in twenty years still get nervous too. It's all the adrenaline spiking in your body while you're sitting around. Once you get out in the field, you're doing things. It works itself out."

Ralph nodded. "Good to know." He took a breath and let it out. When he spoke again, his voice was tighter. "I just don't want to screw this up, you know."

"I know." Bekah looked into the young man's eyes. "Just remember the training. Stick with your buddies. You'll be fine." That was what she told herself each time, and she hoped it was true. Of course the advice would be true.

Until it wasn't.

16

LYING ATOP THE HILLOCK overlooking the bare-bones trail that snaked across the plains west of Mogadishu, Daud watched through a pair of binoculars as the medical caravan ground across the rough terrain. Six vehicles—four trucks and two military jeeps—jolted and jerked as they rumbled along. A low-hanging dust cloud trailed after them like a determined old dog.

Afrah lay beside Daud with his own pair of binoculars. "I count twelve soldiers." The fine dust and grit covered his skin and made him look like something that had crawled up from the earth.

Daud flicked his binoculars over the caravan, taking count once more. Four soldiers in the front jeep and four in the back. Four more rode shotgun in the trucks. The soldiers in the lead jeep wore the dark-green helmets of the Somali military forces. The other soldiers wore the distinctive bright-blue helmets of the United Nations.

"I count twelve as well." Daud set his binoculars on the ground and scraped his grizzled chin with his knuckles.

"They are not so many." Afrah grinned in anticipation. "We have twenty-seven men. More than them."

"Yes, my friend, we do. And I want to make sure we keep all of those men. They have come very dearly to us, and I do not wish to waste them foolishly." During the past two weeks, Daud had worked hard to grow his little army, selecting young men from camps scattered across the backcountry.

The problem with young men, though, was they sometimes got themselves killed. Experience was a hard-won thing, and desperately needed, but it took time to acquire it.

Afrah grunted, and his breath stirred the dust in front of him. "We are in place, Rageh, but you are running out of time to do this thing if it is to be done. If we are to take this convoy, then we must do it."

Daud knew that was true, and the only way he was going to succeed was to be aggressive. If he hid out in the parched lands like so many of the displaced people who feared the city, he would die a slow death, gradually starved out or finally hunted by the al-Shabaab.

He could not allow such a fate; he had a lot more killing to do.

With a nod, Daud spoke quietly. "Give the order."

Afrah waved to one of the men acting as lookout for the rest of the bandit group. Quickly, the message spread along the land without alerting the convoy. Daud had men in front of the trucks along the road as well as behind them.

Taking up the binoculars again, Daud raked the convoy

with his gaze. The soldiers in the first jeep sat at attention and talked among themselves. They were watchful, but complacent. They understood danger could be lurking, but they didn't know they were already in the sights of a predator.

Then, across the road from where Daud and Afrah lay, a small section of the terrain shifted. Daud never saw the RPG-7 rocket launcher, but he spotted the contrail the warhead left as it sped across the fifty-meter distance to the jeep.

The man wielding the rocket launcher was one of the men Daud's father had trained, men who had served in the Somali army for a time, then abandoned it when things became too confusing and there was no loyalty. He kept his shot low so the explosion would impact the vehicle, not the men.

The warhead slammed into the jeep somewhere around the right front wheel. The resulting detonation rang in Daud's ears as the vehicle's front section became a twisted mass of metal. Knocked upward by the blast, the jeep acted like a wild pony rearing up on its hind legs. Then it slewed violently to the side and overturned.

Caught off guard, the four soldiers flew from the stricken vehicle and sprawled across the ground. One of them got caught under the rolling jeep and was either grievously injured or dead. Daud didn't truly care which. There were going to be casualties in war, and he preferred his enemies pay the necessary blood price.

The United Nations peacekeeping forces, as well as the American military reinforcements coming into Somalia, were there to follow their own plans. They would save whom they wished to save, but they wouldn't save everyone. The job was simply too big.

Daud wasn't looking for salvation. He was only looking for revenge against the al-Shabaab who had destroyed his family. He intended to kill until he could kill no more.

Pushing himself up, Daud shoved his binoculars into his chest pack and fisted his AK-47. At that moment, the second rocket team launched their attack on the rear vehicle. The second explosion caught the rear jeep almost center and toppled it forward, punching it into the truck only a few feet ahead.

"Let's go." Daud swung back to his own pickup. Two men with assault rifles already waited in the back.

Afrah slid behind the wheel and turned the engine over. With a throaty roar, the rear wheels engaged and threw out a rooster tail of dirt and rock as the truck plunged over the low hill and raced toward the convoy.

The first cargo vehicle behind the lead jeep tried to pull out around the wreckage. It rocked unsteadily, and the slow roll told Daud that it was packed full.

"Bring the truck around, Afrah. Quickly." Daud turned in the seat and shoved the AK-47's barrel through the open window. Heat from the noonday sun beat into him, and the wind plucked at his clothing and cooled the sweat that slicked his body.

Afrah pulled into a hard turn, grinding the tires into the dry and broken earth. The pickup shuddered and slipped across the terrain, then found a new hold as it veered to match the fleeing truck's path thirty feet away.

Taking aim at the front tires, Daud took up trigger slack, then loosed a burst of rounds. The bullets tore into the rubber tires and shredded them. Immediately, the vehicle lurched out of control and came to a stop.

"Stop the truck!" Daud slapped the dash to underscore his command. But Afrah was already braking, shoving his foot hard against the pedal and bringing the truck up short.

With athletic grace, Daud threw himself from the vehicle and hit the ground running. He held the AK-47 in both hands as he scouted the soldiers scattered across the ground as well as the ones in the four cargo trucks. He brought himself up twenty feet from the first truck and pulled the assault rifle to his shoulder.

"Everybody get out of the vehicles! Get out of the vehicles and you will not be harmed!"

Evidently the soldier in the lead truck didn't believe that, or perhaps he was disoriented from the sudden stop. He swung out of the door and tried to raise his rifle to his shoulder.

Daud raised his rifle to cover the soldier, taking aim at the man's helmet. Not much of the man was exposed above the truck's hood, only half of his head. Daud stared down the muzzle of the enemy rifle. He knew he was only a heartbeat from death, but he didn't care. If he died trying to avenge the lives of his wife and son, he would be content with that.

But he would not die easily.

He stood his ground and squeezed the trigger, listening to the harsh cracks of the rounds exploding. Wind from a passing bullet burned his unscarred cheek. His first round skimmed across the hood. The next two caught the UN soldier in the face and punched him backward.

Daud ran forward, covering the truck driver with his weapon. "Get down! Get down!"

Dazed and bleeding from a cut over his left eye, the driver slumped down to his knees and put his hands behind his head. He was at least forty, stocky and resolute, and had obviously been hijacked before.

Three of the soldiers in the first jeep—including the one the vehicle had rolled over—were dead or unconscious. Daud couldn't see more than that as he trotted past them. The fourth man fought to get to his feet and tried to pull his sidearm.

Daud whipped his rifle's buttstock into the man's forehead. The skull held together, but the man's eyes rolled back and showed white. His legs turned to jelly and he went down in a heap.

On the other side of the truck, Daud looked at the man he'd shot. The bullets had ripped the man's face to pieces. There was no question about whether he was still a threat. He no longer lived.

Remorse almost touched Daud then, as he considered that the man was only there trying to protect things that were supposed to do good for others. But that was what war was about: the casualties. Only casualties could end a war or convince an enemy that it was time to leave the battlefield.

A white man stumbled from the truck's cargo area. Bruises showed on his face, and his shirt and pants were ripped, exposing long, bloody scratches. He was ten years younger than Daud, perhaps thirty or so, and lean and tanned, with dark hair and light-colored eyes. Although he was dazed and shaken from his ordeal, he retained the presence of mind to stop where he was and raise his hands.

"Please!" The man spoke English with a Western accent— American, Daud thought. "Please let me help. I'm a doctor."

Daud shifted the rifle muzzle away from the man and looked down the line of trucks. His men were taking the others without any opposition. He glanced down at the dead man at his feet, then back at the American doctor. "There is no help for this man."

"Are you sure?"

"I know a dead man when I see one. I have seen plenty of them. Many I have killed myself."

The doctor paused and swallowed hard. "What about the rest of the people? There are other doctors and nurses and non-combatants in these trucks. If someone is injured, I can help."

Daud looked over to Usayd. Since joining, the young man had taken it upon himself to act as Daud's personal bodyguard every chance he had. The attention was starting to irritate Afrah, who had taken on the role of second-in-command within the group. "Usayd."

"Yes." The young man handled the AK-47 efficiently. His gaze was intense and serious. The innocence he'd had when he left the people he'd been with had melted away over the last few weeks. He now killed without flinching when there was a need.

"Accompany the doctor."

Slowly, the doctor lowered his hands. "Thank you. I need to get a medical kit."

Daud nodded to Usayd. "Let him get the bag. Check it first and make sure there are no weapons inside."

"It will be done." Usayd walked forward and pushed on the doctor's shoulder. "Move."

Stumbling, the doctor got under way.

Daud watched them go to the rear of the truck and doubled back to the first jeep. The surviving man, now conscious and on his knees, peered up at Daud in helpless frustration.

Afrah stood nearby, watching over Daud's shoulder. "One of the others still lives."

Daud examined the other three men. One of them did survive, but only just. Evidently he'd taken a devastating blow, because his right side was staved in. Ribs showed through the bloody mess of his shirt and torn flesh. His breath gurgled, and he tried to move but couldn't do anything more than twitch his fingers. His open eyes stared skyward, but the man wasn't really seeing anything.

The doctor hurried back with his bag, stopping only briefly to examine one of the dead men. Then he moved to the wounded one. He breathed some kind of prayer—Daud only heard bits and pieces of it—and reached into the black medical kit he'd brought with him.

Without a word, Afrah drew the large-bladed combat knife strapped to his thigh and walked toward the doctor. The American saw the big man coming toward him and leaned back, obviously thinking that Afrah meant to do him some kind of harm.

Silently, Afrah leaned down and drew the knife across the wounded man's throat. Bright-red blood pumped out.

Stunned, then jerked into motion, the doctor leaned forward and pressed his hands to the gaping wound. "Why did you do that?"

"To ease his passage into the next world." Afrah cleaned his knife blade on the uniform blouse of one of the dead men.

"I could have saved him."

Afrah chuckled as he returned his knife to its scabbard. "Out here? Without a proper hospital?" He shook his head. "No. You would have only been wasting your time and the medicines you're carrying. We are not staying here any longer than we need to."

The doctor turned and glared at Daud. "Why did you do this?"

"To get what you were transporting." Daud felt the accusation the man unloaded on him, but he accepted none of it. The people that the Western militaries and the TFG helped were like lottery winners. Those people chose whom they helped, but they couldn't rescue everyone.

Daud was doing no less. He would not feel guilty about the losses even when he instigated them.

"That's insane." The doctor looked like he couldn't believe it. "You attacked us. Do you even know what we're carrying?"

"Yes."

The man hurried on like Daud hadn't even spoken. "We're carrying medicines and supplies to groups of people who have been forced out of Mogadishu. We're on a peaceful mission. There was no reason to kill anyone."

"This is a war zone." Even to his own ears, Daud's voice sounded cold and merciless. "If I could take your caravan so easily, do you not think the al-Shabaab could do the same?"

The doctor gazed down at the dead man. "You shouldn't have done that. You shouldn't have done any of this."

Afrah took a step forward, put a big hand on the doctor's arm, and shoved him into motion. "Go. This one is beyond your care. Perhaps there are others who can use your help. You only have minutes to get them ready to travel."

Wordlessly, the doctor turned and walked away. He clutched his medical bag to him like it would protect him.

Daud glanced at Usayd meaningfully. The younger man nodded and tapped his rifle.

Standing only a couple feet away, Afrah reached into his hip pocket and took out the flask he carried. He took a sip and gazed at the dead men scattered over the ground. The surviving soldier glared at the big man.

"You are not al-Shabaab." The soldier's voice cracked and he spoke in Somali.

Daud turned to face the soldier. "No, we are not. We kill al-Shabaab where we find them."

"We are not al-Shabaab."

"No, you are not."

"Then why did you do this thing?"

Daud shook his head.

"We are not enemies. If you fight the al-Shabaab, we should be compatriots." The soldier relaxed a little, evidently trusting that he would not be killed.

"We are not compatriots. If you do not do as I tell you to, I will kill you. Believe that."

The man's mouth tightened and he looked at the ground. Afrah called one of their soldiers over, and together they tied the man up. Then he was led away to a small bit of shade at the side of the road where the other survivors were being kept under guard. The doctor was among them, working on a man who lay prone and bloody.

Daud walked along the uneven line of trucks, stepping up into the rear compartments to survey the cargo. As he'd expected, most of it was food, medicine, and clothing—all things that had been gathered from Mogadishu.

"Doubtless they were taking this to one of the displacement camps." Afrah walked at Daud's side.

Daud nodded as he crawled into the third truck. "It would be good to know where these places are. Get me one of the drivers."

Afrah nodded and walked over to the group of prisoners.

Making his way through the cargo, Daud glimpsed a tire near the front of the space. He shifted boxes and crates to get to the tire and found that there were four in all. He grabbed the top one and hefted it with difficulty, then rolled it toward the rear of the vehicle.

Afrah stood there with a small, older man beside him. Putting out a big hand, Afrah caught the tire and stopped it with ease. He lifted the tire from the truck with one hand and placed it on the ground. Daud returned for another tire and brought it out as well, then jumped down.

"This is Dido. He is the lead caravan driver."

The old man nodded and looked nervous. He was thin, and his skin had withered from age and from exposure to the elements. He had a mouthful of broken yellow stumps.

Daud looked at the man. "Do you know where these trucks were going?"

"Of course." Dido reached into the pocket of his shirt. "I have a map." He took out the map and unfolded it with trembling fingers.

The map was a good one, a printout from a satellite view that had been marked with computer legends rendered in neat white boxes. The destination camps had no names, only coordinates and some kind of key listing.

"Rageh." Afrah spoke softly.

Daud looked over to his father's friend.

"We have to get moving. Those jeeps have radios. It is possible that these soldiers were in contact with other military units. There may already be some kind of rescue being mounted."

Folding the map, Daud put it into his pocket. "You are correct. Find some strong backs to replace the tires on the truck with the flats. Have this man help you."

Afrah dropped a heavy hand onto the old man's shoulder, and they walked away.

Daud followed them and watched the doctor as he continued working on the prostrate man. The soldier was already somewhat alert and had an IV drip running into one arm. Bandages covered wounds that tracked along his left side. Daud didn't know if they were from bullets or shrapnel. The doctor ignored Daud and devoted all of his attention to his patient.

When the doctor leaned back briefly, evidently done for the moment, Daud spoke to him. "What is your name?"

The doctor hesitated. "Sykes. Brandon Sykes."

"You are very conscientious about what you do."

Sykes hesitated, obviously uncertain how to take that. "Thanks. I'm just trying to get these people out of here alive. Trying to help as many as I can."

"That's why you're coming with us."

17

AFTER AWAKENING in the temporary quarters the Marines had arranged in Mogadishu, Bekah Shaw mustered out earlier than the others to get a look at the city. She'd heard a lot in the news about the struggles going on in the nation, and she was aware of the movie *Black Hawk Down*, though she'd never seen it.

The city was a war zone, more or less, and the Marines were working against the pirates holding ships hostage out in the Gulf of Aden.

That wasn't what the Charlie Company reinforcements were there to do, though. According to their orders, they were supposed to shore up the peacekeeping efforts established by the United Nations and provide support to the Somali military in holding Mogadishu from the al-Shabaab and other insurgents.

Bekah had read all the handouts that the Marines had

given her, in addition to several local English newspapers she'd found lying around in the mess hall. She wore fatigues and carried her helmet by its chinstrap. The M4A1 rifle slung over her shoulder felt comfortable and familiar, as did the Kevlar battle armor.

The temperature along the coastal areas was moderate and even felt cool when the breeze lifted, but she knew that the heat climbed quickly toward the interior. The salt stink of the ocean filled her nostrils, but there was more that she could detect riding the wind. Diesel fuel, charred wood, and cooking meat added their scents.

Standing in front of the warehouse the Marines had been assigned as temporary lodging, Bekah stared out at the city. The buildings and streets bore scars from the decades-long power struggles that had been fought there. The Marines had cleaned most of the street to afford a clear field of fire for the guards stationed in posts atop the warehouse as well as other nearby buildings.

A hundred yards away, a group of scavengers worked the pile of old wrecked cars that had been bulldozed away from the warehouse. Several black and brown men and boys, and even a few white ones, worked the junkers.

Bekah knew what they were looking for: parts that could be harvested to keep other vehicles running, tires, and—when all else failed—copper wiring and other metals that could be salvaged for scrap prices. In places like Mogadishu, recycling was part of the lifeblood that kept the city working.

People back home in Callum's Creek operated by the same principles. They kept their old refrigerators and stoves so they could part them out too, either using the pieces themselves or trading them to other people.

Reaching into her BDU pocket, Bekah took out the small digital camera Granny had given her a couple Christmases ago. The gift was an extravagance by Bekah's standards, something she definitely didn't need, but Granny had insisted. Until then, Bekah had made do with an old 35mm Rebel camera she'd saved up for and gotten secondhand before Travis was born.

She snapped off a few shots of the men working the cars. Travis might enjoy the pictures when she got back to Callum's Creek.

"Shutterbug?"

Startled, surprised to find herself suddenly not alone, Bekah turned and found Gunnery Sergeant Francis Towers behind her. The man stood six feet six inches tall and was broad and thick. She didn't know how he could move so silently, but he did. His skin was black as coal, and he was ill-defined in the morning shadows that still draped the front of the warehouse. He smelled like Doublemint gum and Old Spice, but he'd leave those things behind in the field the same way Bekah would forgo deodorant and scented soap, which could give away her position to the enemy.

Towers was in his early forties and had been a Marine since age nineteen, when he'd discovered he wasn't going to cut it as a forward in the NBA. Bekah had already tapped into the scuttlebutt about the man. Activated reserves got dropped into new situations nearly each tour and had to learn the ropes and the pecking order quickly. Or get squashed.

Despite the fact that they were reinforcements and there to help the entrenched full-time Marines, those full-time Marines didn't always appreciate the activated units. There was usually a discrepancy in age, for one thing—a lot of the reserves tended to be older than the younger enlisted troops. And for another, reserves often wanted to know why orders were given and didn't obey them as blindly as the younger Marines. Those attitudes created friction.

"Good morning, Gunney."

Towers nodded. "Good morning, Marine. Lance Corporal Shaw, right?"

"Yes."

"So, are you?"

"Am I what, Gunney?"

"A shutterbug." Towers nodded toward the camera in her hand.

Bekah smiled a little and shook her head. "Not even close. Just got a hobby of taking pictures."

"Brass give you the lowdown on hanging pictures on Facebook and sending them off to friends back home? No bodies, that kind of thing?"

"Yeah." Bekah shivered. Since the world had entered the digital age, the hard face of war and death could show up on every computer in every home. "It's not my first time at the rodeo, Gunney."

"I knew it wasn't. I've seen your field service report. You're an outstanding Marine."

"Thank you, but it takes all of us to look good."

Towers smiled at that. "It does. It takes *all* of us. So

I wanted you to know that I've noticed you doing your part."

Bekah put her camera back in her pocket and closed the tab. "I know there's a reason the brass doesn't want photos on the Internet, but I sometimes wonder if maybe having everyone back home see everything we see would make a difference."

"What? Seeing bodies? Seeing folks blown all to bits and lying in the street days later? That what you mean?"

The coarseness surprised Bekah, but she nodded.

"You forget that there's always been pictures." Towers took a deep breath and let it out. "Ain't like a camera's anything new in the field. Soldiers have had them a good long time. The Internet makes it easier to show everybody, but magazines and newspapers done all right showing folks all them things before computers and smartphones come along. My father caught a couple tours in Vietnam. He had him some pictures too. Shot them on an old Instamatic. He never showed them pictures to my momma, but he showed them to me."

Vietnam was history to Bekah, fodder for films and conversation among some of the old-timers who swapped stories in Hollister's Fine Dining. She respected the men who had served, but she didn't have a true touchstone for that war.

"The problem with pictures is that there'll always be pictures." Towers nodded out toward the sprawl of the city, toward the broken buildings and cratered streets. "It was pictures that brought us out to this country back in the 1990s. Pictures of kids—starving, wounded, diseased. Kids nobody wanted. Somebody started showing those pictures around and telling the United States they could make a difference."

"Don't you think we do?"

Towers grinned, his teeth white and the gleam in his dark eyes showing the effort was genuine. "We do make a difference. Marines always do. Don't forget that." He shrugged his shoulders and rolled his neck. "The big drawback is when we gotta pull out of an area and people ain't ready to stand on their own two feet. They can't help but go back to what they were." He paused. "That's what happened to this place. It's even true of them pirates out in the Puntland. They just gone back to being what they've been before."

As she listened to the gunney's words, Bekah couldn't help but think about Billy Roy and how he'd been in high school. She'd thought marriage would grow him up, or at the very least being a daddy would. Instead, Billy Roy had gone back to being what he'd always been too. She thought about Travis, how she wanted more for her son's life than what Billy Roy and she had had.

"Lance Corporal."

Jerked back to the present, Bekah focused on Towers.

"You doing okay?"

"I am." Bekah nodded. "Just thinking about what you said."

"Well, let's go get chow. You and I have a debrief with the lieutenant at oh eight hundred."

Glancing at her watch, Bekah logged the time. She had fifty minutes for breakfast. "Sounds good, Gunney."

"Found a local place that I thought I could treat you to."

Bekah knew then that the meeting this morning hadn't been by chance, and her curiosity flared. "I can treat myself."

Towers cocked a skeptical eyebrow at her. "You really gonna turn down a free meal and a chance to pump the sergeant about the new lieutenant?"

Bekah grinned and relaxed, knowing that Towers had sought her out to bring her up to speed away from the rest of the unit. There weren't as many on the team who had served together as there had been in the past. Learning a new command infrastructure—and about the officers—was important. "When you put it that way, a free breakfast sounds great."

"I thought it might." Towers led the way across the street. "Get your pot on."

Bekah strapped on her helmet and followed. As soon as she left the warehouse she changed her mind-set, telling herself she was now in enemy territory.

★　★　★

Towers took his helmet off as he entered the small restaurant. The place was a small affair in the corner of a warehouse, what would be a mom-and-pop business back home. The resulting space seated maybe forty people.

Burning frankincense thickened the air. The décor was a loose collection of photographs that spanned dozens of years. In several of them, the harbor area looked industrious and relaxed, but that time was long past, as marked by the faded condition of the photographs and the cars and trucks visible in the images. Other photographs were of American soldiers seated at the small tables and mugging for the camera. The eatery wanted to establish a connection with the American soldiers; that was evident. But Bekah knew it was because American soldiers tended to have more money than other servicemen.

"I know," Towers said. "You didn't expect there to be a restaurant anywhere near the city, what with all the food shortages, but people gotta work and people gotta eat. You'll find little out-of-the-way places around the harbor area, but always under the loose protection of the military. The military pulls out, these places close up shop and disappear."

"Food is tight in this city." Bekah took her helmet off as well. "Where do they get the supplies?"

"From the ships passing in and out of the port. They make deals with captains and ships' crews. You find markets everywhere like this. People want things, a way is made to provide them. Basic economics." Towers looked around the room, and his hand didn't stray far from the sidearm at his hip. "I been in a lot of places. Always try to find someplace where I can clear my head, away from the rest of the team."

Bekah understood that. Sergeants got squeezed between enlisted and officers.

"Keep in mind, just because I bring you here today don't mean this place is safe." Towers looked at her.

"I get that."

"Bad people gotta eat too, and you're a woman. You walking around in that uniform, no *hijab*, and carrying that rifle—that marks you as a target in the eyes of some men."

"I know." Part of the briefing had included warnings about the strict Muslim code and the resistance to women military personnel. But the Marine Corps believed in its female Marines and knew they made a difference with the local women. "Not much different than it was in Afghanistan."

"There's a difference. In Afghanistan, you generally knew who was trying to kill you." Towers guided her to a small table near a wall. "Here, the scorecard seems to change every day. Make no mistake: we've got a dirty job to do. I'll go get us something to eat."

Gunney Towers went to the counter and placed their order, not bothering to ask Bekah what she wanted. She assumed that was because the menu was limited, or because Towers had learned what was more palatable to American taste buds.

Bekah sat in the uneven chair, placed her helmet on the table, and kept her rifle close to hand. Some of the men in the little shop eyed her, but they looked away when she glanced in their direction.

These customers were all old men already at their tea and coffee. The young men were laboring at whatever jobs they could find. Or they were sleeping in, hungover from a long night of chewing *khat* or drinking to excess. The diners spoke in their native languages or a mixture of Somali and Arabic.

Somali was totally unknown to Bekah, but she had picked up some Arabic in Iraq during her first tour. She eavesdropped casually. Most of the talk she could understand was about the sudden departure of the al-Shabaab and what it meant. The concern seemed to be whether the Muslim insurgents would stay gone and how long the Western military would remain this time. One of the men lamented that he was too old to become a pirate.

Turning her attention to the wall beside her, Bekah studied the young American faces she found there. They sat at tables with British and Nigerian military as well as Somali soldiers. All of them looked like they were having a good time.

Bekah couldn't help wondering how many of those men and women had actually made it back home alive.

After a few minutes, Towers returned to the table carrying two small trays containing unfamiliar food and two cups of hot liquid that looked like tea. But the scents made Bekah's mouth water and her stomach growl.

Towers placed one of the trays in front of her and sat on the opposite side of the table. He pointed at the food with his fork. "Over here they call breakfast *quraac*. That pancake-looking thing is *canjeero*. Break it up and drop it into that bowl."

Bekah started doing that and discovered the bread was more grainy and tough than she'd expected.

Towers passed her a small porcelain container. "This is *ghee*. Cow's butter, but it's different than anything you ever had back home."

"I've made butter before."

Towers looked surprised. "Grew up in the country?"

"Little town in Oklahoma."

"I come from Alabama. Born and raised in a sleepy little armpit of a town on a farm."

"Sounds a lot like where I'm from."

"My wife still lives there and we raised two kids, so I'm not gonna speak too badly of it. Small towns are the back-bone of America."

"Not everybody feels that way."

"Not everybody is as worldly as we are."

Bekah laughed. Despite the tension that pinged inside her, she liked Gunney Towers.

Towers passed over another small container. "Sugar. Add it to taste." He continued his presentation and pointed at a small serving of browned meat and soup in another bowl. "*Hilib ari.* Goat meat. Ever had goat before?"

"I have."

Towers chuckled. "Not many first-timers we get over here have."

"I grew up on a farm, Gunney. If my granddaddy raised it, we ate it."

"I hear that. You'll find the goat a little tough, but it's good enough. Beats an MRE or powdered eggs all to pieces." Towers pointed at another bowl that contained a pasty yellow substance. "That's *boorash.* Looks like porridge, right? That's 'cause it is porridge. Made outta cornmeal. Add butter and sugar. Pretty much pabulum. The real treat is the chunk of bread. They call it *malawax,* and it's a lot sweeter than *canjeero.*"

"I suppose salads and fresh fruit are out of the question."

"Yeah. But you can get those at the mess hall. Biggest thing is to stay hydrated. They got this stuff." He tapped the cup beside his plate. "*Shaah.* It's a weak tea, but it'll get you going."

Following Towers's example, Bekah added sugar to the tea without even sampling it.

"I know this looks like a mean breakfast, but you'd be

surprised at how many people in this city don't start their day out with anything like this." Towers dug into his breakfast with gusto, or like a man knowing he had an appointment in thirty minutes and wanting to be early. "You got a lotta displaced people living hard around here. If it ain't guarded or nailed down tight, it's gone. A lot of them are living outside of the city too, and they're like locusts, eating everything they can find and starving slow."

"How long have you been here?" Bekah tried the porridge and found it to her liking.

"Second tour."

"Why aren't you with enlisted instead of spare parts?"

"Spare parts?" Towers grinned. "Is that how you think of yourself?"

"No. But a lot of the enlisted do."

"I suppose they do." Towers broke up more *canjeero* and seasoned it. "I work with you guys because this is a dangerous place. You don't watch where you step every minute of every day, Lance Corporal, you end up going home in a box. Your boy needs his momma."

Bekah looked at Towers but didn't say anything.

"Yeah, I looked at your service record. I look at every Marine I work with. I try to get to know every one of you so I can keep you boneheads from getting yourselves killed out here when you don't need to."

"I appreciate the straight-ahead approach."

"You'll appreciate me getting you back home in one piece more." Towers sipped his tea. "I've seen enough of you people sent back home shot up, tore up, and dead." His voice grew deeper and softer. "When I was given this opportunity—and I do see it as an opportunity—to shepherd you folks, I took it."

Towers sipped his tea. "Regular Marines don't get a lot more training than you do, but they're out here in the soup every day. They don't get as much time back in the real world as you reservists do, and they ain't lived long enough to learn really bad habits or learn to think too much for themselves. Being a Marine is what they know. But you guys?" Towers shook his head. "You're green. I don't care how many times you got activated."

"I don't know why you bothered to sugarcoat it. Tell me how you really feel."

Towers laughed. "I teach you a thing or two, Lance Corporal Shaw, you might be able to keep yourself and your people alive."

18

"YOU'RE PART OF Rifle Platoon Indigo." As Towers talked, he kept food moving toward his mouth. "Gonna put you in charge of Fire Team Indigo Eight. What I read says you got some experience doing that."

"I have." Bekah had made lance corporal in Afghanistan on her second tour and had been in charge of a fire team. The unit was a four-man operation that worked with the two other fire teams to make up a squad. There were three squads in a rifle platoon, nine fire teams in all. The responsibility to coordinate efforts was demanding.

"Good. Then you should be comfortable there. You've done MOUT?"

MOUT was Military Operations on Urban Terrain—basically urban warfare, fought building to building instead of in the open. More and more of the training concentrated on urban warfare because that was where the wars were being fought.

"We've worked a lot with MOUT scenarios, and I spent some time door-to-door in Afghanistan."

"That's outstanding. Here in Mogadishu, though, you're gonna get a mix. When the Islamic Courts Union split up—that's the Islamist group that took over a bunch of the southern parts of this country, including Mogadishu—the al-Shabaab started stirring up trouble in the city. And they haven't all gone away—we've still got a lot of al-Shabaab waiting in the wings. You still have that nut job or this nut job trying to make a name for himself by taking down American or UN forces or Somali military. Or taking a profit here and there."

Bekah nodded. All of that had been covered in the reports.

Towers's dark eyes flashed. "Mostly I think those people just got to where they like killing folks. Gives them something to do when they get up in the morning. Gives me no end of pleasure to track them down and drop a hammer on 'em."

"The briefing I got said Charlie Company's Indigo Platoon was under Lieutenant Heath Bridger." Bekah sipped her tea.

"Yeah."

"He full-time like you too?"

"Nope. Part-timer. Like you."

That made Bekah nervous. Officers of the Marine Reserve usually came in two flavors: people who knew what they were doing and took care of their unit, or people who were trying to make a name for themselves and got a lot of Marines hurt.

"Has Lieutenant Bridger been in Somalia long?"

Towers shook his head. "Hit the ground the same day you

did. You guys probably came in on the same flight. He's from Oklahoma too." He grinned. "Only he speaks English a lot better than you and me."

"What's his background?"

Towers didn't hesitate. "College. When he's not toting an M4 and bleeding Marine green, he's a lawyer. His father is some kind of big deal in legal circles back in the States."

Bekah suppressed a grimace. He sounded like one of those glory grabbers who got people killed. "Is this your first tour with him?"

"No. I put some time in with him in Afghanistan. He's solid. Just, like the rest of you, not a full-time Marine. You don't have to worry about him being stupid with personnel."

Bekah finished her tea and pushed her plate away because it was time to go. "I'm one of nine fire team leaders, Gunney. You plan on taking us all to breakfast?"

Towers grinned. "You were the last one on the list, Lance Corporal, and that was only because you got here late." He stood and picked up his helmet and rifle. "Like I said, I get to know who I'm working with."

"Well then, Gunney Towers, it's been a pleasure to meet you."

"Likewise." Towers offered her his hand, and it engulfed hers for just a moment. She felt the strength in his grip, but he didn't have anything to prove. The calluses spoke volumes.

★　★　★

Back at Indigo Platoon's command post, Bekah was surprised to find that she'd already met Lieutenant Bridger. At least, she'd *almost* met him. He'd been the man with bars on his collar back at Will Rogers Airport.

As she sat in one of the folding chairs set up in the briefing room, she locked eyes with him for just a moment, and then he moved on. She doubted if he recognized her from the airport. She didn't stick out in the room full of Marines, other than being one of only three women. Quietly, she placed her helmet on the ground between her feet and secured her rifle at her side.

A quick glimpse around the room let her know that she was one of two women heading up fire teams. One of the squads was led by another woman, who looked like she was in her early thirties, a quiet, steadfast woman with a stern disposition but an easy smile. She evidently knew some of the other people in the group.

Lieutenant Heath Bridger stood near a small desk at the front of the room. A screen hung on the wall behind him and displayed a street map of Mogadishu. He held an iPad in one hand, and Bekah knew for a fact that the device wasn't military-issue.

So he brought some toys from home. Trying to impress the guys. Bekah decided she could resent the lieutenant on that alone, and the swagger that he made look so natural was another reason. He was handsome and clean-shaven, looking more like a poster board for a Marine than a real Marine.

"Good morning." The lieutenant stood in front of his assembled platoon leaders and smiled. Evidently he wasn't going for the no-nonsense approach that a lot of officers liked to try on for size at the beginning of new assignments. "I'm going to try to keep this short."

One of the guys next to Bekah cursed softly and spoke in a whisper. "Yeah, that'll be the day."

Officers either tended to be reluctant to speak and turned the meetings over to a more experienced sergeant, or they liked the sound of their own voices. Bekah figured a lawyer would like the sound of his own voice.

"We're being tasked to help bring some stability to Mogadishu." The lieutenant tapped the iPad, and the scene on the screen changed to another view of the street map with several sections shaded in red. "That's not an easy job. Despite the departure of the al-Shabaab and other Muslim terrorist entities from the city, Mogadishu is not yet free. Terrorist attacks continue to occur, and there are several underground efforts being made to strike out against us.

"From this moment on, none of you goes anywhere without your teammates. You work together, you bunk together, you eat together. As a unit. That means, fire team leaders, the three people under your command are going to stick to you like a bad shirt. And you're going to stick with them. When you get leave—*if* you get leave—you have leave together. This is a dangerous place. If one of your team goes down and you're not there ready, willing, and able to do something about it, you're going to wish you had been. And, squad leaders, you'd better make sure you stay up to speed on your fire teams. We live and die on communication, people, and I plan on us living."

The smile on the lieutenant's handsome face didn't mask the steel in his voice and in his gray-blue eyes. That caught Bekah's attention. She hadn't expected him to come off so strong—or to give such reasonable advice.

However, living that close and that tight with people you hardly knew was hard. Having to do that in a war zone made it even more difficult.

"That's my operating criteria." The lieutenant continued without missing a beat. Gunney Towers stood just behind the lieutenant on the right in a parade rest position that totally supported the younger officer. "That's what I expect of you. As part of our assignment from Command, we're going to be street sweeping." He tapped the iPad again.

This time the image was of a ragged line of apartment buildings and shops separated by narrow, curving alleys.

"This city is a rat's nest of blind alleys and underground warrens. Whatever you've heard whispered on flights over here or in the mess hall, put that on steroids. You don't know your way around, and you're taking your life in your hands. But you've each got three of my people with you. Take care of them by getting to know the terrain." The lieutenant flipped through the photos quickly now. Several showed different views of the alleys, and Bekah was impressed at how thorough he'd been for the presentation. "Gunney Towers and I took these pictures yesterday."

Bekah had been helping set up the temporary quarters, packing stuff off trucks and setting up cots. The fact that the lieutenant had been out on recon with Towers instead of hanging with the other officers impressed her too.

"The street maps you can get around here aren't up to date. The satellite pictures we get of these areas aren't up to date. An alley you went down one day might be blocked the next because of a terrorist attack that happened the night before. Do not enter an area unless you know of two ways to escape it. At least." The lieutenant paused. "Otherwise you've just killed yourself and taken your teammates with you."

That was a sobering thought, and one that Bekah had never been given by a commanding officer before.

"At nine hundred today, we're taking to the streets in an effort to find and secure a bomb-making facility Intel learned of through an informant." The lieutenant tapped the iPad again and brought up another image.

The man on the screen had dark and cruelly handsome eyes. He looked to be in his early thirties and wore a distinctive red-and-white-checked *keffiyeh* that covered most of his face. He held an SAR 80, a distinctive Singapore Assault Rifle that Bekah had gotten familiar with. Knowing an enemy's weapons—knowing how to *use* an enemy's weapons if the need arose—was important if she wanted to get back home to Granny and Travis.

"Intel says that the man responsible for the bomb-making operation, if we find it, is a guy named Korfa Haroun, a member of the al-Shabaab who's got a special interest in taking down American soldiers." The lieutenant paused. "This means you. Chances are if you meet Haroun in the streets, he's going to be wearing the *keffiyeh*, but you might also spot him without it." The lieutenant tapped the iPad again.

The next picture of Haroun showed the man more clearly, and unmasked. His face was chiseled, hard and sloped like a red-tailed hawk's face back home. His dark eyes were cold and distant too. Haroun stood in a small room lit only by an oil lantern. Bekah figured it was a bunker. He wore a beard and his hair was curly.

"This is the only picture we have of Haroun's face." The lieutenant spoke flatly. "It was taken by an informant the CIA cultivated within Haroun's circle before the al-Shabaab pulled out of Mogadishu." The screen blanked. "The informant was found dead a couple days after the picture was given to the CIA. Haroun or his followers nailed the man's body to a wall and laid the corpses of his family at his feet. His wife, his sister, his mother, and his three children."

Bekah closed her eyes and tried not to think of the children, but that was impossible.

A young lance corporal spoke out. "I guess maybe the CIA can't keep secrets."

The lieutenant remained unflappable. "Haroun's picture was also given to Marine recon teams. Nobody knows who let the cat out of the bag, Lance Corporal. At this point, the CIA isn't happy with the Corps. For all you know, a Marine showed Haroun's picture to the wrong person and word got back to the al-Shabaab. My point is that the terrorists are well connected in this city. Getting close to Haroun is going to be hard, and it's going to be dangerous." He looked around the room. "Are there any questions?"

No one said anything.

"All right." The lieutenant glanced at his watch. "I told you I'd keep this short. Make sure you and your people stick to the chain of command. I want this unit nice and tight. Your teams are waiting in the barracks. You've got forty minutes to get with them and get ready to move out."

Towers's loud voice blasted through the room as he stepped forward. "Dismissed."

Bekah picked up her helmet and got ready to go. As she stood, the lieutenant walked over to her. "Lance Corporal, I need five minutes with you."

The other fire team leaders and squad commanders looked at her like she'd done something wrong. "Yes sir." Bekah stiffened at the lieutenant's terse tone, and she didn't like being singled out.

19

BEKAH STOOD UNEASILY at attention until the rest of the Marines
filed out of the room. After they'd gone, she stood with the
lieutenant and Towers. She was grateful that Towers was
there. Whatever the lieutenant wanted, it couldn't be bad,
otherwise she wouldn't have been put in command of a fire
team. And Towers wouldn't have taken her out to breakfast.
She kept telling herself that, but she had her doubts. Things
had certainly soured back in Callum's Creek.

"At ease, Lance Corporal." The lieutenant stood only a
few feet away.

Automatically, Bekah fell into parade rest, eyes forward
and staring past the lieutenant. "Thank you, sir."

"I want to touch on a couple things." The lieutenant studied her, making no attempt to be polite about it. "There's a
piece of paper on my desk requiring my attention regarding
a legal matter you're involved in back wherever you're from."

"Yes sir. That would be from Callum's Creek. I need to show cause to change the court appearance I was scheduled for. My attorney said a letter from you would be fine."

"Maybe you've discovered that I know a little about the law."

"Yes sir."

"I'm sure Gunney Towers filled you in on me over breakfast this morning." The lieutenant shot Towers a quick glance, then returned his attention to Bekah. "He has a habit of doing that."

Since she wasn't required to make a response, Bekah let that one go.

"Since I've been in command, I've gone with sergeants to get men out of local jails back stateside. They'd gotten into all kinds of mishaps. Driving while intoxicated. Fighting with other Marines and with civilians. Some of them were arrested for dealing drugs. And once I had to get a man who had killed a fellow Marine over the attentions of an exotic dancer."

Bekah remained quiet and listened.

"I believe people can make mistakes. I've made a few myself. I believe in forgiving and forgetting. But if I have a Marine under my command who becomes a problem, I generally find a way to correct that problem or get that Marine out of the Corps."

Bekah swallowed and felt her face heat up. Her problem wasn't *her* problem. She'd been trying to walk away from the fight that night. She just hadn't been allowed to. And she hadn't scheduled her reactivation either. This wasn't her fault. She kept her gaze focused on the far wall and squeezed her emotions into a small box at the back of her mind. She thought about Granny and Travis and how the money she was making on this tour would help make their lives easier.

After a moment, the lieutenant continued. "I don't like to deal with Marines whose personal issues override their ability to be Marines. Is that understood?"

"Crystal, sir."

"Judging from the report I read, you were arrested for fighting in a bar."

Bekah's immediate impulse was to defend herself, but she knew she didn't have the time before they were supposed to get into the field, and she doubted the lieutenant would care. The man had his own agenda.

"I didn't get that paper till this morning. If I'd known this yesterday, I would have probably made other arrangements for the leadership positions among the fire teams. But I made the best decisions I could based on the information I had on you people."

You people. Like they were parts, not human beings. Bekah could feel resentment rising up in her again. Coming from such different backgrounds, she knew there was nothing she would have in common with Lieutenant Heath Bridger.

Still, Bekah couldn't completely hold her tongue. Not after everything that had happened back home before she'd left. "You made a good decision, sir. I'm a good Marine."

The lieutenant leaned toward her, invading her personal

space just a little, enough to ping her radar. "Good Marines don't get caught up in bar fights, Lance Corporal."

Bekah sipped her breath and kept her voice level with effort. She stared at the far wall hard enough to bore holes through it. "Yes sir. You're right, sir."

"I am." The lieutenant held his position for a split second longer, then leaned back. "Up until this point, you've had a spotless record. Don't go off the rails now."

"No sir. I won't, sir."

The lieutenant glanced at Gunney Towers as if to confirm what the big man thought. Then he shifted his attention back to Bekah. "I'll take care of the paperwork."

"Thank you, sir."

"There's one other thing I want to discuss." The lieutenant pulled up a file on his iPad. "One of the men assigned to your team could be a problem." He turned the device around to show her a man who looked a couple years older than her. "His name is Pike Morgan."

Bekah studied the face. Pike Morgan looked intimidating. His face was broad, and his dark eyes were watchful and predatory. The picture was file stock, a straight-on view that Bekah felt probably didn't give the man's true nature. His dark hair was longer than regulation, but that was allowed in some instances in the emerging war zones because the United States military didn't want its soldiers targeted just by their haircuts.

"Maybe you're wondering why he could be a problem?" The lieutenant sounded a little put out.

After the warning she'd received, Bekah had determined not to ask questions. Either the lieutenant would tell her what he wanted her to know, or she would find out for herself. Either way would work for her. She just wanted to get away from the lieutenant and get to her team.

Bekah cleared her throat. "Why is this man a problem? Sir." She put the emphasis on the *sir*.

"Pike's been activated more than you have. He's a true warrior, a guy who can get you there and back again in one piece." The lieutenant paused. "The downside is that Pike doesn't much care for authority."

Then why did you assign him to me? Bekah kept that question to herself with effort.

"Pike was all the way up to sergeant at one point; then he got busted back down to private for fighting with his commanding officer."

Bekah was pretty sure the commanding officer hadn't been Lieutenant Heath Bridger. Pike looked like a bruiser. He would have left the lieutenant marked, messed up those metrosexual good looks.

"I served with Pike back in Afghanistan. When I found out he was here, I asked that he be assigned to this unit. The brass was happy to have someone take him off their hands." The lieutenant put his iPad away. "The man's good in the streets. Pay attention to him."

"Yes sir."

"I put him with you because—until I received notice about this court case—you've always gotten good marks from your commanding officers. You have people skills, Lance Corporal, you can get creative within given orders, and you have obviously learned to keep yourself and your people alive in difficult situations. I thought maybe you could make a difference with Pike Morgan."

"Sir, permission to speak freely?"

The lieutenant didn't hesitate. "Granted."

"Pike has had higher rank than I now currently possess. Will that be a problem?"

"I don't know, Lance Corporal. Will it?"

Bekah kept her face unreadable, but she knew he'd deliberately avoided the question.

"My advice to you is, don't let that history make a difference. The reason Pike fails at command is because he doesn't function in a group. He's too much of a loner. You've got to find a way to bring him into the fold. Based on your past successes, I thought you might be the person to do that." The lieutenant paused. "Now I guess we'll just have to wait and see."

Anger and frustration stirred in Bekah, coiling in her stomach and pounding at her temples.

The lieutenant seemed surprised that she didn't have anything to say. "Any questions, Lance Corporal?"

"No sir."

"Then you're dismissed."

Bekah came to full attention with a snap and brought her hand up to her forehead in a perfectly executed salute. Her speed caught the lieutenant off guard.

The lieutenant brought himself up and returned the salute.

Lifting her foot and pointing her toe, Bekah spun in a tightly controlled 180 and marched out of the room. She shouldered her weapon and pulled on her helmet before she cleared the door.

★　★　★

Heath didn't speak until Lance Corporal Bekah Shaw exited the room. Then he had only a one-word rejoinder. "Wow." He turned to Gunney Towers and found the big man grinning. "Think I hit a nerve?"

"That one's got a lot of sand in her. I saw so this morning. She takes pride in what she does."

Heath retreated to the desk at the front of the room and picked up the cup of coffee he had waiting there. "Do you know what her story is?"

"Read the same file as you."

"Yeah, yeah, Gunney." Heath waved a dismissive hand. "I got the whole small-town, single-mom thing. But I'm talking about the between-the-lines stuff. What makes her tick?"

"I think that's what does it." Gunney Towers took a seat across from Heath. The chair teetered precariously under his weight. "My mom raised me and my younger brother by herself since I was seven years old. Takes a special kind of woman to do that."

"I suppose." Heath leaned back in his chair and sipped his coffee, which was bad, but it provided a hot wake-up and caffeine. He thought about Bekah Shaw and his preconceived notions of her. As he'd said, her file held several commendations. There was every reason to assign her as a fire team leader.

Until he'd gotten the notice about the legal problem, Heath had felt confident about her posting.

"You're overthinking it." Towers's voice was a deep rumble.

"Overthinking it?"

"The situation with Bekah Shaw."

"I don't need a loose cannon heading up one of my fire teams."

Towers's lips quirked a little. "She look like a loose cannon to you this morning?"

Heath sighed and worked his shoulders. He was tired from the long flight and from worrying about Darnell Lester and his family. Heath didn't want the ball to get dropped while he was gone, and he had yet to hear from Mark Kluger regarding the motion to commute the death sentence.

Finally, Heath had to admit his thoughts. "No, she doesn't."

"Doesn't to me, either."

Heath liked working with Towers. They'd met in Afghanistan and had gotten on well together. Heath knew he was fortunate in having a second-in-command with all the experience the gunney had, and he appreciated the fact that Towers was willing to place his life in the hands of such a green unit.

"You took her to breakfast this morning?"

Towers nodded. "I did."

Heath waited, then realized the gunney wasn't going to volunteer any further information. Towers had an irritating habit of parceling out what he knew, never giving too much without first being asked. The trait was a good training technique because it forced a new lieutenant to think independently.

"Did the court matter come up?"

"No."

"So you have no idea what it's about?"

"Not a clue."

Heath sipped his coffee again. "Doesn't it make you curious?"

"Not me." Towers looked utterly relaxed, not like a man about to go out into a war-torn city.

Heath sighed. "You're no help."

"Now my feelings are hurt."

"I'm sure they are."

Towers grinned at him.

"Keep an eye on her."

"I plan to do that for all of them."

"I know." Heath tapped the side of his coffee cup with a well-groomed fingernail. "Something happened back home. Something changed. We need to know if it followed her out here and if it's going to affect our operations."

Towers nodded. "Putting Pike Morgan with her is gonna be a stressor."

"I know. We'll want to keep an eye on that, too. In the meantime, you still have favors you can call in with the satellite communications people?"

"I do. I always keep on the right side of favors."

"See if one of those computer jockeys can ferret out information about Lance Corporal Bekah Shaw's legal problems."

"I can do that."

20

BEKAH MET HER TEAM in the barracks. They were the only three people left there. The other team leaders had met with their people, checked equipment, and pulled out. Being late made Bekah feel awkward and embarrassed, and it made her more dissatisfied with Lieutenant Heath Bridger. There would have been plenty of other times for him to have talked to her about the court appearance.

Still, she also understood the lieutenant's reticence about sending her out into the field without getting a feel for her mental state. If she'd been in charge, she would have probably done the same thing. Marines counted on each other for survival. If a Marine couldn't be counted on, the other Marines deserved to know.

And that line of thinking brought her to Private First Class Pike Morgan. She wanted to know how much trouble the man was going to be, and she had no doubt he was going to be trouble.

The makeshift barracks inside the warehouse reminded Bekah a lot of the war movies she'd sometimes watched with her granddaddy. Everything felt spartan.

"Bekah." One of the two Marines standing in a huddle in full combat gear looked up at Bekah's approach.

A smile lit up Bekah's face when she recognized the woman. Private Trudy Schultz was a year or so younger than Bekah. At five foot four and athletic, Trudy was petite and filled with boundless energy. She wore her blonde hair razored to chin length and always appeared bright and earnest, always peppy. Back in the real world, she lived in Georgia, a schoolteacher. She'd joined the Marine Reserve to help pay her student loans.

"Trudy." Bekah nodded. "Good to see you."

Trudy stepped forward and embraced Bekah. Normally Bekah didn't care to be hugged much. She preferred to keep her distance from everyone but Granny and Travis. But there was something special about Trudy that felt warm and inviting. She returned the embrace, then stepped back. Relationships between fellow Marines tended to be more casual than a lot of civilians thought.

Turning a hand to the other Marine standing nearby, Trudy cleared her throat. "Let me introduce Private First Class Tyler Bowdrie. He's from Austin, Texas. He's a carpenter and plays in a band when he's back home."

Tyler was a good-looking guy in his early thirties. The haircut looked new because his tan line only crept halfway up his neck. The tan was deep enough to let Bekah know he worked outside. A shade over six feet tall, he was broad-shouldered and ruggedly lean. He wore round-lensed John

Lennon glasses and had a shy smile, but his grip was firm from swinging hammers.

"Lance Corporal." His words sounded musical.

"Call me Bekah." It was important that the team be relaxed with each other, and having to remember call signs and rank during the heat of battle was hard.

Tyler nodded. "Yes ma'am."

"Sorry I'm late. I got held up by Lieutenant Bridger. I suppose Private Morgan went on ahead with the others?"

"Actually, he didn't." Trudy pointed to a bunk at the end of the long line. "When he saw that you weren't here, he went back to his bunk."

Irritation gnawed at Bekah. Lieutenant Bridger should have recognized that holding her up after the meeting would undermine her command right from the start. Pike lay on his back, one hand behind his head and an arm across his eyes. His thick chest rose and fell rhythmically.

"Private Morgan." Bekah's voice echoed off the empty interior of the barracks.

"Yeah?"

"Maybe you'd like to join us."

"We ready to go?"

"We are." Bekah refrained from saying anything sharper.

Pike rolled from the rack like a big jungle cat. One minute he was lying down, the next he was walking toward her holding his rifle in one hand and clapping his helmet on with the other. "Glad to see you could make it."

Bekah made herself ignore the sarcasm. "The lieutenant held me up."

Pike gave her more attention then and stopped in front of her. "Did he?"

"Yeah."

"Why?"

"Especially to annoy you."

Pike grinned at that, and the expression seemed more genuine. "I didn't know he still cared."

"Next time I see him, I'll tell him how much you were touched."

The grin grew bigger. "Where are you from, Lance Corporal Bekah Shaw?"

"A little town you've probably never heard of."

"Try me."

"Callum's Creek, Oklahoma."

Pike nodded. "You're right. Never heard of it."

"Where are you from?"

"Lots of places." Pike looked at the other two Marines, then back at Bekah. "We gonna go out there on this op? Or are we gonna campfire?"

"We're going." Bekah turned and headed for the door. Her Marines fell in after her, and her stomach spasmed a little when she thought about what might be waiting for them. The adrenaline pounded through her system and the stink of gunpowder and burned flesh from past engagements filled her nose.

★   ★   ★

"Do you see the Americans?"

On the third floor of the building, out of the sunlight

that gathered at the window, Pabest shifted slightly behind the RPG-7 rocket launcher he held and took better aim at the small group of United States Marines moving stealthily through the street below. "I see them, Ezaan. Do I not have eyes in my head?"

Ezaan slid to the side, changing his angle of view. "If you do not take the shot soon, you will have no shot at all." Like Pabest, Ezaan was short and angular, carrying no spare flesh on his frame. Both of them wore red-and-white-checked *keffiyehs* and long jackets. Pabest's bandolier carried extra magazines for the AK-47 assault rifle that sat canted against the wall. Ezaan held his own weapon, but his hands played nervously over it.

This was Ezaan's first fight against the American forces. Until now he'd only raided displaced citizens outside the city to strike fear into their hearts. That was an important job, almost as important as killing the foreign soldiers. The people who sought to turn from God's will needed to be reminded that they lived in the shadow of God's wrath and should not consort with the enemy Satans.

"Be quiet, Ezaan." Pabest took a fresh grip on the rocket launcher to relax his hand. "We must await Sadim's signal. Or would you rather face Haroun and tell him you ruined his trap for the Americans?"

Ezaan sighed. "No. We will wait."

Silently, Pabest tracked the Marines as they filed through the alleys and broken buildings below. Haroun had set the trap for the Marines, sending them information about the bomb factory the al-Shabaab no longer used. The place lay in a basement below one of the crumbling buildings. Last year, Pabest had worked there to build bombs. He had gotten quite good at the craft, and he missed the calm focus.

Skulking through the city and in the nearby wilderness was no life. He missed living in Mogadishu, missed the respect and dread the striking *keffiyeh* caused in the people who lived in the city. God made sure his warriors were recognized and feared.

"How many do you count, Ezaan?"

"Ten. Maybe twelve. It is hard to know for sure when they move so much and take cover."

"Cover will do them no good. They will all die today." Pabest prayed that it would be so. Briefly, he tracked one of the female Marines. They were the biggest offense to Pabest, abominations to God's will who needed to be subjugated or eradicated. He longed to administer such retribution himself. The American women were causing good Muslim women to question God's plans for them. That could not be tolerated. But there they were, flaunting their bodies, driving trucks that only a man should drive, and carrying weapons like they were warriors.

Pabest followed the woman Marine with his weapon, praying that the order would be given to fire. Instead, two steps farther on, the woman disappeared behind the remnant of a wall. He cursed his ill luck and shifted his aim back to an open area between two other Marines. The warhead would hit the ground and kill or wound anything in any direction for fifteen meters. He smiled in anticipation and stroked the trigger.

Suddenly a shot rang out, and one of the Marines staggered. Pabest knew that Sadim had fired the shot to start the battle, and he hoped that his commander had scored a kill. The message would be received by the American Satans.

Mastering the excitement that filled him, Pabest squeezed the trigger and watched as the RPG took flight and sailed out the window. All around him, the crackle of gunfire split the stillness that had hung over the area. A moment after that, the explosives that had been planted in the ruins erupted in sudden fury, throwing dirt, stone, and mortar into the air in long plumes. Craters opened up in the ground as Pabest fitted another rocket to his launcher and readied his weapon again.

There would be no escape for the American Marines.

★ ★ ★

"Get down! Get down!" As the explosions vomited up from the alley and ruins around her, Bekah swung around to survey her team, fearing she had already incurred a loss.

Trudy had gone to ground as a matter of course. She'd been under fire several times in Afghanistan. She lay on the ground only a few feet away, her right hand on her rifle and her left hand clamped reflexively on her helmet.

Tyler was stretched out as well, but he had his head moving, looking around.

Ten feet away, Pike Morgan squatted calmly against what remained of a stone wall. The building's foundation had become a maze of sorts, filled with half-destroyed walls where the structure had once been. Piles of rubble had been picked over for salvageable items, but they provided further hardships for anyone traveling through them.

A sandy-yellow haze created by the dust from the

explosives planted in the ground drifted slowly over the battle zone. That was what the area was now. Before, it had been a trap, and Rifle Platoon Indigo had stepped right into the middle of it. Harsh cracks of small-arms fire punctuated the ringing that filled Bekah's ears, and she tried in vain to track the sounds coming from all around her.

Bullets chopped into the ground near Trudy, tracking closer to her as the shooter adjusted his shots.

"Trudy! Get up! Move to your left to Pike!" As she yelled the order, Bekah tasted the alkaline dust on her tongue.

Immediately, Trudy got up and ran toward Pike, who still hadn't moved from his crouched position. A small smile quirked his lips, and Bekah would have sworn the man was enjoying himself.

"Tyler! Move!"

The Marine surged up and raced to join Pike and Trudy.

Bekah fell back as well and kept her M4A1 up and ready. She keyed her MBITR comm device when she heard the lieutenant calling for casualties. "This is Indigo Eight Leader. We're good."

Four of the other fire teams hadn't fared so well. Indigo Three and Five had wounded, and Indigo One—the point guys—had taken two casualties and one wounded. One of the casualties was the team leader, and the young private who had survived was totally losing his mind.

"I got two dead, Indigo Leader! Team leader is dead! The other guy looks like he's bleeding out! I need a corpsman!"

With the wall at her back, Bekah tried to figure out where Indigo One was. They had to be up ahead of her.

"Indigo Eight." Lieutenant Bridger sounded calm, but there was tension in his voice.

So much for keeping everyone intact, Bekah thought, then immediately felt guilty. Marines were dead. More might be dying. She replied in a hoarse voice. "I read you, Leader."

"You and your team are solid?"

"Affirmative. I think we're also the closest to Indigo One at this point."

"You are. They need you to assist. Can you provide support?"

"We're on our way."

"We're going to give you some cover."

Bekah rose into a crouch and motioned to her team as the firing from the Marine positions escalated. Pike stepped into the right-wing position beside Bekah like he'd been there all his life. His rifle was up and ready.

Bullets continued peppering the area from gunners in the surrounding buildings. Every now and again, a rocket warhead hit the ground and split the earth, throwing up another cloud of dirt and dust.

"Right side." Pike's warning came at the same time Bekah noticed him in motion, twisting to the right and bringing his rifle around.

21

THROUGH THE SMOKY, DUSTY HAZE that filled the immediate area, Bekah barely spotted the five men running toward them. All wore the red-and-white-checked *keffiyehs* and long jackets that marked them as al-Shabaab. They carried AK-47s and SAR 80s, already firing, and the harsh *crack-crack-crack* of the weapons sounded muted and far away because her ears still rang from the explosives that had detonated.

The bullets, however, weren't far away. They tore into the earth in front of her and pinged off the nearby rubble. Chunks of stone leaped into the air.

Something slammed into Bekah's helmet as she returned fire. Her head bounced back slightly, but she quickly recovered. She knew she'd been hit by a round but that the helmet had stopped it. She also knew the round had to have been one of the 5.56mm rounds from the SAR 80s instead of the heavier rounds fired by the AK-47s, otherwise the impact would have been much more serious.

But she'd come only inches from leaving Travis without a mother.

Pike fired from the crouched position, squeezing off exact three-round bursts into their attackers. Two of the al-Shabaab terrorists went down almost immediately. The three remaining gunmen recognized that they weren't going to easily overpower their prey as they'd believed and split up.

Slightly leading the gunman who had run off to her left, Bekah aimed for the center mass of the man's body and squeezed off two bursts. The gunman's gait suddenly lost rhythm, and he fell in a headlong rush as the AK-47 tumbled free of his hand. He rolled and landed on his back, reaching for the assault rifle. Bekah took aim again and fired another burst of rounds into the man's head and chest. The terrorist shivered and lay still, and the amount of bright blood spilling out across the ground under the late-morning sun told her that he wasn't getting up again.

When she'd first gone into combat, Bekah had never thought about the emotional consequences of killing others. That was something a person didn't talk about back in the real world. Sometimes a civilian asked a question like that, and she ignored it. Most military personnel who had been in combat acted the same way. When a Marine went back to the civilized world, they tried to keep the war in a different place.

She didn't think about the number of opponents she'd killed. Or possibly killed. With everything that happened in a battle, it was hard to know for certain.

But she knew she'd killed this man, and she accepted it just as she had all the others that had been confirmed.

The two remaining al-Shabaab fighters tried to reach cover, but a hail of bullets knocked them to the ground.

"Let's go." Bekah glanced at her team and made certain they were in one piece. Then she rose in a crouch and ran forward to confirm that the men were down.

All of them were dead.

Tyler looked at the men and quickly turned away. His eyes had rounded behind the John Lennon glasses. Whatever exposure he'd had to combat, it hadn't been this up close and personal. Bekah made a mental note to talk to him later, see where his head was at. Having him freeze up at some point would be dangerous for all of them.

On the move again, Bekah led the team into an alley on the other side of the broken remnant of the building and resumed her heading toward Indigo One's position. The firefight continued, only this time a new sound entered the fray: a roaring engine.

Glancing ahead toward the end of the alley, Bekah paused next to a doorway as a pickup truck with a 7.62mm machine gun mounted on the rear deck screeched around the corner and sped toward them. She lifted her rifle and opened fire, a half second behind Pike.

Their rounds bounced off the thick metal plate welded to the front of the pickup. More metal covered the windshield, giving the driver a narrow field of view. The vehicle looked like a bulldozer coming at them.

"The door! Move!"

Pike heaved himself at the flimsy wooden door and crashed through into the room beyond. Trudy and Tyler went through on his heels as Bekah brought up the rear. She crouched on one knee in the doorway, barely having time to drop into position before the pickup raced by. Thankfully the room was empty and no noncombatants were endangered by the exchange.

Pike was already down and swinging around with his rifle in his hands. "Get down!" Trudy dropped and went flat. When Tyler didn't react quickly enough, Pike kicked the Marine's legs out from under him just as the pickup truck drew even with the room.

The machine gun ripped a ragged line of bullet holes through the wall just over Bekah's head. She had seen that the machine gun's field of fire was limited by the sides of the vehicle and hoped her low profile would keep her safe. As the pickup roared past, Bekah stepped out into the alley and fired her rifle dry, but she got chased back to cover by the support riflemen using small arms on either side of the machine gunner.

"Indigo Eight, have you reached Indigo One yet?" Gunshots echoed over the connection to the lieutenant, and Bekah knew he and his group were taking heavy fire as well.

"Not yet. On our way." Bekah reloaded her weapon from the ammo rack across her Kevlar vest. Pike had already taken a support position near the door.

"Pickup's gone. Ran out onto the next street." Pike scowled and spat.

Bekah nodded. "Let's go."

Pike headed out the door and took point. Bekah followed close behind the big man, surprised at how athletically he moved despite his size. He was like the wind, every movement fluid and natural.

Less than a minute later, while the ambush continued around them, Bekah and her team reached what remained of Indigo One. They had to stay low because the al-Shabaab had a sniper's nest in a nearby building. The gunmen inside popped out occasionally to pepper the area with rifle fire or launch a rocket-propelled grenade.

The only protection Indigo One had was an L-shaped wall remnant no more than five feet tall. Pike and Bekah kept sporadic fire on the building window to pin the snipers down, but she'd already detected other terrorists running into the building. She didn't know if the men were trying to retreat or intended to provide additional support.

"Bekah," Trudy called out from a kneeling position beside a wounded Marine who was bleeding profusely. "I need another pair of hands." Tyler had joined her there, but he was providing cover fire with the surviving Indigo One Marine.

Bekah swapped looks with Pike. She had worked field medical triage with Trudy before.

The big man nodded as he reloaded his weapon. "I've got this. I'll cover you."

When Pike started firing, spraying rounds across the window where the snipers were, Bekah darted toward Trudy and the wounded Marine. The other two Marines in the fire team lay a few feet away in the open, torn apart by one of the ground-emplaced explosives. They'd never had a chance.

Bekah took up a position opposite Trudy over the wounded Marine. "What do you have?" She laid her rifle nearby and focused on the mass of blood-soaked material stretched across the Marine's midsection.

"Abdominal bleeder. Bullet must have taken a weird bounce and got up under his armor. Or he took shrapnel. I can't tell. I need to get under there and clamp it off if I can, or he's going to bleed out. Help me get the vest off him." Trudy pulled at the vest on her side, freeing the Velcro closures. Her hands were covered in blood.

Ignoring the sounds of the battle and the flying stone chips that rained down on her from the sustained sniper fire, Bekah grabbed the vest and tugged at the closures on the wounded man's side. They opened with a rip. Then she reached for the closures at his shoulders and saw his face for the first time.

"Hey, Marine." The young man smiled at her, and it took Bekah a second to realize the first time she'd seen his face had been at the auto parts store. His voice was hoarse and shaky, and his eyes looked dull and glassy from shock.

"Hey, Private Caxton." Bekah put a smile on her face even though she wasn't feeling it. He was in trouble, maybe dying, and they weren't far from that fate themselves. The young man was badly hurt and needed to know he was in good hands. "You're not supposed to get wounded on the first day of the job. I guess you missed that at the briefing."

Ralph Caxton tried another smile, but he broke into a coughing fit that left bloody spittle around his lips. He tried again. "It's just a flesh wound."

"Bekah."

Looking back at Trudy, Bekah noted the concern on the

other woman's face. She shifted her gaze to Caxton's stomach. There wasn't one wound there. The young man had suffered what looked like three, all close together, all jagged and irregular. Bekah realized then that he must have been standing close to the two Marines who had lost their lives. He hadn't caught a bullet. He'd been hit by shrapnel, and those shards were probably still inside him keeping the wounds open.

Blood poured out of the Marine like water from a boot.

Trudy gazed at Bekah helplessly.

There was nothing they could do for Ralph Caxton, and Bekah knew it. The pain of the loss coupled with the shock of recognition hit her like a fist. She pushed those thoughts away and took a breath.

Deal with this. He needs you to be strong. Deal with it. Maybe a corpsman will get here in time. Maybe he'll pull through. Don't give up on him.

"How bad is it?" Ralph's voice was barely more than a whisper, but he sounded calm.

Bekah made herself smile reassuringly while Trudy called for a medic over the MBITR. "I've seen worse, Private." Bekah reached out and took the young man's bloody hand. "We're not going to let you get out of this that easily."

"Okay." Ralph took her hand, but he had hardly any strength in his grip. The most noticeable thing was the shaking.

Suddenly he convulsed and gasped.

"Ralph." Bekah leaned more closely over him and looked into his eyes. "Stay with me, Marine. Do you hear me?"

Ralph's hand went slack in hers. His eyes turned glassy, and the pupils dilated into black pools that nearly filled the irises.

"Ralph!" Bekah squeezed his hand, willing him to be okay and knowing that he wouldn't be. He'd lost too much blood. A heart couldn't pump when it was dry, and his body was shutting down. Death was stealing him away.

Mechanically, Bekah released Ralph's hand, then straddled his body and started doing a series of chest compressions.

"Bekah." Trudy pulled at her. "Bekah. He needs blood. Lots of it, and we don't have any. He's gone. There's nothing you can do."

"No."

"Bekah." Trudy pulled at Bekah's arm again.

Stubbornly, working to wall the grief away inside her, Bekah shook off the woman's hold and got up off the dead Marine. There would be time to deal with the loss later. She told herself as much, just as she had before, but she knew from experience that a person couldn't really deal with losses like that. A Marine survived them, accepted another scar that no one else could see, and moved on.

She picked up her M4A1 as another rocket went wide of the wall and blew up inside the building that Pike used for cover. Trudy was canceling the call for the corpsman. Bekah crept to the surviving Marine's side. She looked him in the eye. He was just a scared kid, bony and angular, looking like he'd just graduated high school.

"What's your name, Marine?" Bekah made her voice neutral.

"Mike. Mike Carruthers."

"Mike, I'm Bekah. You're going to be all right."

He looked at her wildly and held tightly to his rifle. "They're going to kill us. We walked into a trap."

"That's right, we did. And we're going to walk back out of this. Are you listening to me?"

"Yes."

"You keep listening to me and you're going to be fine." Bekah spoke with more confidence than she felt. She kept reminding herself that other Marines were in the area and they were doing all they could to reach them.

"All right."

Another warhead detonated against the wall. More rubble showered over them as the wall quivered but miraculously remained standing. Bekah pressed herself against the stones and kept her head ducked, listening to the debris ping off her helmet. The dust gathered intensity and thickened so much she had trouble breathing. When the moment passed, she pulled away from the wall again.

Looking at the young Marine, Bekah knew he was frozen. Getting him out of here was going to be difficult with the snipers in place. She looked back at Pike, who was judiciously returning fire. His presence was probably the only thing keeping the terrorists from pouring out of the building and overrunning their position.

"Pike."

He looked at her as he reloaded his weapon.

"We need the high ground." Bekah shoved a fresh magazine into her own weapon and checked her webbing for grenades. She had a small assortment of flashbangs and antipersonnel explosives for urban encounters.

Pike nodded. "Me and you?"

"Yes."

He smiled grimly. "You think we're that good?"

"We'd better be."

"We get through this, I'll buy you a beer."

"I'll let you." Bekah turned to Trudy and Tyler. "Hold your position here. Give Pike and me cover."

The two Marines nodded and took up positions along the wall.

Bekah shifted behind the wall, crept toward the corner, and glanced back at Pike. "You take the door. I'll take the window next to it."

"Good enough." Pike rose and cradled the M4A1 in both hands. "Whenever you're ready."

Bekah took a deep breath and thought of Travis and her granny. *You're going back home. No matter how bad this looks, you're getting through it.* She let the air out of her lungs and raced around the corner of the wall. Pike ate up the distance with long strides and was on her heels as they crossed the alley to the building where the snipers nested.

22

BULLETS RAKED THE ALLEY around Bekah as she sprinted. At least two struck her body armor and another glanced off her helmet, but she never broke stride. Stopping or turning back was a certain path to death. On the other side of the alley, she slammed into the wall between the door and the window on the first floor.

Pike fell into position on the other side of the door.

In a former life, the building had housed a business. A faded sign with fresh bullet holes hung overhead. Bekah couldn't read the Somali words written there or on what was left of the shattered plate-glass window beside her. More scars from bullets cratered the building's front, and not all of those were new. War was an old thing here.

Tyler and Trudy kept a constant barrage of fire going, drawing the attention of several of the gunners inside the building, but Bekah knew the al-Shabaab were aware of Pike and her at the door.

"You ready?" Pike looked at her. Dust covered his broad face and blood wept from two long scratches on his left cheek.

Bekah nodded. "Do it."

Whirling around, Pike drove his shoulder into the wooden door. Hinges shrilled as screws tore from the jamb, and the door flew inward and broke at the same time.

Bekah spun around and raised the M4A1 to her shoulder as she peered through the broken window. The room held a counter and broken shelves that had been Swiss-cheesed by scavengers looking for wood and metal they could use or sell. A few pictures of breads remained on the wall, along with a chalkboard with more Somali writing and advertisements from other vendors.

Shadows moved on the other side of the room, and the dust filling the area gave Bekah pause for a moment. Then she spotted the red-and-white-checked *keffiyehs* and the assault rifles in the hands of the men. She opened fire as Pike rolled against the counter on the left side of the room.

Ejected brass spun and glinted as Bekah fired, and the rifle chugged repeatedly against her shoulder. Bullets cut the air around her and knocked jagged pieces of glass from the window. The two terrorists went down, sprawling at the foot of a narrow stairwell.

"Good shooting." Pike got to his feet with ease and took the lead.

Swapping out her empty magazine for a full one from her ammo rack, Bekah stepped up onto the window ledge and plunged into the room with her rifle at the ready. She followed Pike's lead as he checked the bodies of the men on the floor, then stepped over them to cover the stairwell. He paused as Bekah caught up with him.

She nodded and let him go first, covering him as he went as much as she could and making sure their exit route remained clear. Having a group of terrorists take away their retreat would leave them trapped on the stairwell like fish in a barrel.

Pike was almost at the landing when another terrorist peeked down from the next set of stairs. Bekah trotted up behind Pike and fired upward, driving the man back to cover as splinters ripped from the stairwell railing.

At the same time, a door in the hallway near Pike burst open and another terrorist aimed at Pike's head from only inches away. Bekah scrambled to get a clear shot but couldn't because the angles were all wrong. She knew she was about to see Pike die, either by the man beside him or from the guns hidden above.

Instead, Pike's left hand flicked out, caught the offending rifle muzzle, and yanked. The terrorist flew toward Pike and managed to squeeze off a burst of bullets that chipped plaster from the wall beside the Marine's head. A white cloud wreathed Pike as he stepped forward slightly while still holding his opponent's rifle. He swung his elbow into the man's face and knocked him into the wall behind him.

Tossing the AK-47 to the floor, Pike stepped forward again and wrapped one big hand around the back of the terrorist's neck. Spinning, Pike brought the man around and turned him into a human shield as he raised his M4A1 under the dazed terrorist's arm and fired the weapon one-handed.

Bullets chewed along the stairwell and ripped splinters and plaster from the walls and the railing. Return fire caught the terrorist as he screamed and tried to break free. But Pike's inexorable grip on the back of his captive's neck held him in place. In the space of a heartbeat, the fight left the terrorist and he hung limply against Pike.

Another terrorist spilled down the stairwell in a loose-limbed sprawl. Bekah followed the gunman's progress automatically, then pulled her aim off him when she realized the guy was dead.

Pike dropped the dead man he held and shoved another magazine into his assault rifle while he headed up the stairs again.

After a brief glance at the front of the shop to make certain there was no one behind her, Bekah followed Pike. The steps shivered and felt uneven, showing years of wear and tear as well as the newer damage from the bullets.

Another dead man sat on the next landing. His sightless eyes stared out of the gloom, and his weapon lay abandoned across his knees. For an instant Bekah thought the man might still be alive, but then she noticed that half of his head was missing, swathed in a torn and bloody *keffiyeh*.

She followed Pike up the stairs and had trouble breathing the thick air swirling with dust and smoke. She and Pike moved in unison, and she always made sure her weapon pointed away from her partner's back.

"Indigo Eight, what is your twenty?" Lieutenant Bridger sounded out of breath.

"Taking out a sniper nest that has my people pinned

down." Bekah swung around the next landing and stepped out into the hallway after Pike.

"Affirmative. All Indigo teams are en route, and we have air support coming."

Bekah pictured the building in her mind as she stepped after Pike. She tried to remember all the twists and turns she'd taken, struggling to figure out where the snipers would be.

The hallway was narrow, but the rooms on either side of it looked like they'd been small shops, not residences. Large windows held pieces of glass. There was a small drugstore with empty shelves, a clothing store with broken mannequins, and other shops, barren and unidentifiable.

Evidently Pike had a better grasp of the layout, though. He glanced back at her and waved to one of the doors ahead of them as he fell into position against the wall. He freed a grenade from his combat webbing.

On the other side of the door, sharp rifle bursts cracked. At first Bekah hadn't been able to get a handle on the direction the gunfire was coming from because the sounds of battle echoed all through the hallway.

Pike looked at her, and she nodded. He leaned around the doorway and tossed the grenade inside. Bekah closed her eyes to preserve her vision. Three seconds later, the deafening explosion filled the room, and bright light tore away the shadows in the room as well as in the hallway.

Immediately, Pike spun into the doorway and entered. Bekah followed and took a flanking position to Pike's right. There was a wall at the back of the room, obviously once intended to set off another room, but now the wall was filled with holes that had been knocked through the plasterboard.

Three al-Shabaab gunners struggled to overcome the effects of the flashbang. The grenade caused disorientation through sound as well as light, and they'd gotten a full dose of it. Still, disorientation didn't put them completely out of the fight.

One of the men lifted his AK-47, and Pike and Bekah both opened fire, knocking him back. Blood covered the wall behind him. Another man got off a short burst that chopped through the wall next to Pike. Holding his ground, Pike fired, and the terrorist jerked back and slumped to the ground.

The third man threw down his weapon and held his hands up, speaking rapidly in broken English. "I surrender. Do not kill me."

Pike held his rifle centered on the man, and Bekah thought he was going to pull the trigger anyway.

"What's the matter, Muhammad? Not ready for all those rivers of wine and virgins?"

"Do not kill me. I beg of you." The al-Shabaab terrorist placed his forehead on the ground.

Pike fished a zip tie from his kit and moved forward. "Cover me."

Bekah did, but she also opened her team channel on the MBITR. "Trudy."

"Yes."

"You guys okay down there?"

"Yes. You and Pike?"

"We're fine."

Pike finished binding the terrorist's hands behind his back and stood with his rifle.

"That truck's coming back."

Bekah moved to the window, mirrored by Pike, and they both looked out to see the pickup truck with the machine gunner mounted in the rear deck racing back through the alley below. The machine gunner blazed away at the buildings.

Bekah watched helplessly as the pickup driver suddenly braked and shouted, throwing his arm out the window in the direction of the wall. From the way he'd come, the Marines hiding behind the wall were visible. "Indigo Eight, move. They've seen you."

The three Marines got to their feet and retreated as the al-Shabaab vehicle opened fire.

Bekah shoved her weapon through the open window and squeezed the trigger, managing to take out the machine gunner before the other gunmen drove her back. She hated feeling helpless, knowing that her team was about to get cut to ribbons.

The pickup swerved into position below the window but remained where it could cover the Marines on the ground as well. Another al-Shabaab man had already taken over the machine gun and had opened fire, driving the three stranded Marines to cover.

Bekah knew she had to get down there and turned to get Pike, surprised that he wasn't at the window with her.

Pike picked up one of the dead men from the ground and easily carried the body over to the window. Shots thudded into the dead terrorist, but Pike ignored them while he reached for an oil lantern that sat on the floor. He opened the lantern, emptied the contents over the dead man, then tucked a spherical antipersonnel grenade into the corpse's pocket. Taking a flare from his kit, he set the corpse ablaze, pulled the grenade pin, and heaved the dead man through the window.

The gunfire from below intensified for a moment.

Horrified by what she'd just witnessed, certain that Pike was the most callous man she'd ever met, Bekah watched the dead man plummet toward the bed of the pickup truck. His arms and legs flailed, and for an instant he looked like he was still alive.

Then the corpse landed amid the al-Shabaab gunmen, and the burning oil spread among them. Someone grabbed the dead man's foot in an effort to yank the body clear of the pickup. Then the grenade went off. Shrapnel blew through the surrounding gunmen, killing or wounding everyone in the back of the pickup.

By then Pike had heaved himself over the window as well and hung by his fingers to stretch out to his full height, then let go. The drop to the ground was about fifteen feet. He landed on his feet and went down into a three-point crouch before lifting his rifle to the ready.

Although she didn't like the risk of turning an ankle, Bekah liked the idea of leaving Pike on his own even less. She threw a leg over the window ledge and followed suit, hanging by her fingers, then releasing. She didn't try to land standing up. She tucked and rolled, dissipating the force of the landing, and came up with her rifle in her hands.

Pike was already in motion, running toward the driver's side of the pickup.

One of the men who had been blown free of the pickup by the grenade lay on the ground nearby and tried to point his pistol at Pike. Bekah raised her weapon and fired from ten feet away, killing the man at once.

At the driver's window, Pike slapped aside the rifle muzzle that someone tried to thrust into his face. He shoved his own weapon into the pickup cab, ducked, and emptied the clip. He slid away as the vehicle jerked into sluggish motion, shoving another magazine into his weapon automatically.

The pickup rolled to a stop a few feet away. Pike went forward, yanked the door open, and stepped back from the driver's body as it spilled out. Bekah flanked him, peered over his shoulder at the dead men inside.

"We're clear here." Pike scanned the nearby rooftops.

Bekah did the same, thinking that surely some of the al-Shabaab were still present, still wanting to close the jaws of their trap. But no one was there.

23

"**YOUR DEATH** does not have to be a painful thing, old man. It can be a simple passing from this place to the next." Korfa Haroun gazed at the bound man lying at his feet.

The man was a withered bag of bones. His days of strength were years behind him. He lay naked and ashamed on the hot ground. Dark bruises already blossomed on his face, chest, arms, and legs. One thing was certain: the old man could take a beating.

That wasn't courage, though. That was pride and stubbornness. The old man knew he was going to die and was determined to be as troublesome as he could be.

Remaining in a squatting position beside the old man, Haroun gazed up at the small collection of families that lived southwest of Mogadishu. Less than a hundred people camped near one of the small, seasonal tributaries that trickled into the Shebelle River. The tributary was nearly a memory now and scarcely flowed from a light rain that had occurred days ago.

Soon the stream would turn poisonous due to stagnation. Then the old man and his people would have had to move on. Of course, now they wouldn't be going anywhere.

Those people stood under a nearby copse of junipers, watching the events unfold. There was no fight left in them. The men had their heads bowed in shame because there was nothing they could do to prevent the death of their elder— or their own deaths, for that matter. The women huddled behind the men, holding their crying children to their breasts and trying to soothe them. They had been without water to drink all morning. Haroun had seen to that. He knew the cries of the children ate at the minds of the adults.

Haroun had children of his own, and he knew how much parents could love them and want to protect them. He loved his own children. But things had to be kept in perspective. In this instance, children were a means to an end.

The children of such people as these, people who were unable to care for themselves and refused to align themselves with him and with the true path of Islam, were lice upon the earth. All they existed to do was take up precious resources and get in the way. They would grow up and be as demanding as their parents—and as helpless to care for themselves.

Haroun was surprised that the man he pursued didn't see these people that way as well. Or perhaps he did and used them as surely as Haroun now did, but for his own ends. Haroun intended to ask that man those questions if he got the opportunity when he caught up to him. And he would catch up to the man.

"Are you still listening, old man?" Haroun stood and kicked his captive in the side when the man did not respond.

The old man bleated in pain and struggled to roll away from his tormentor, but that was not permitted. Haroun stepped on the old man's shoulder and pinned him to the ground. The old man squinted up against the blinding glare of the sun beating down on all of them.

Haroun kept his face uncovered and let the man see him. "Defy me, and I will kill one of the children and drown you in his blood."

"I hear you."

"Good. I tire of your pathetic resistance."

"Why do you do this to us, Haroun? We have done nothing to you."

Haroun smiled. "How is it you know my name, old man?"

"I lived in the city. Before this. I lived there and I knew who you were."

"Good. Then you know what I am capable of."

The old man closed his eyes for a moment and shuddered. "I do know."

Haroun reached down and picked up the rope that was tied to the old man's feet. The other end of the rope was secured to the rear bumper of a pickup only a short distance away. "Your death can be very hard."

"You intend to kill me no matter what I do."

Haroun nodded. "I do. Your death will be a much louder message to the man I seek. And to those who would take the meager gifts he leaves. I will find him, and I will kill him for the trouble he has caused me."

The old man's face constricted like a wrinkled fist, and he closed his eyes tightly. Tears trickled from under his lids, and Haroun knew the old man would regret those.

That weakness did not touch Haroun. He had seen men break before. He had broken many of them. It was not a hard thing to do with the proper leverage.

"Kill me if you must." The old man spoke hoarsely.

"I must."

"But spare the others."

Haroun paused as if he were giving the matter serious contemplation. Then he shook his head. "No. The only option you have is for a swift, painless death or a slow one filled with agony. The future of those people was written when they took that man's goods."

The man swallowed, and calmness descended over him. In that moment, Haroun knew the old man had accepted his death and the deaths of all the people who looked to him for direction. "Ask me what you will."

"What is the name of the man who brought you the medicines and other supplies?"

"He did not give a name. I did not ask."

"Why?"

"Because one does not question God's generosity."

The answer displeased Haroun, and he slapped the old man's face. "You do not get God's generosity from someone such as that man, you old fool. For generosity you must ask me."

"You were not here to ask."

Haroun smiled. "Did anyone else call this man by name?"

"No."

"Did you hear any other names?"

The old man thought for a long moment as blood trickled over his lips from the injury caused by the slap. "There was a man. His companion. A tall, powerful man. He called this man Afrah."

"Afrah." Haroun had heard the name mentioned in other places. He still did not know who this Afrah was any more than he knew the man Rageh Daud. Still, the answer was enough to let him know he was on the proper path.

"Yes."

"Was the leader called Daud?"

"I never heard that name."

Haroun touched his fingers to the right side of his own face. "Was he burned here?"

"He was. And on his neck and arms. The burns looked recent."

That was another detail that remained consistent with the stories that Haroun heard. With those burn scars, the man could have been a soldier, but he was not American nor with the United Nations. Daud had killed UN soldiers and taken an American physician from the Doctors Without Borders program only days ago.

"Do you know that the supplies this man Daud brought to you once belonged to me?"

"No. If I did, we would not have accepted them."

"But you did, and in doing that you have doomed yourselves."

"Not if you believe in God's justice."

"God blesses only those he favors." He smiled. "I punish his enemies, the American Satans and those who would side with them. God favors me and will give me riches beyond belief when my time here is done."

The old man faced him then and swallowed. "You are a vain, despicable creature, Korfa Haroun. One day you will know this, and you will tremble at the emptiness of your soul."

Angry, Haroun stepped back and waved curtly. In response, the pickup truck started and rolled forward, gathering speed. The old man's calm demeanor shattered in that moment, and he cried out fearfully. Haroun gazed down at his captive. "Die, old man. Die in agony."

The rope slack played out and the old man jerked forward, skipping across the rocky terrain and raising small puffs of dust. His pain-filled yells and screams lost strength quickly. The pickup driver steered through the wide shallows of the tributary.

The displaced people watched in horror. Haroun saw the fear on their faces, and he liked the look of it. They did not understand that to live well in this land a man had to be hard and fierce. Now they would never have the chance to learn such things.

The pickup drove in a wide circle around the copse of trees. The old man fell silent, and his body bounced and careened over the ground. After a few minutes, Haroun waved the driver back. When the vehicle arrived, it deposited the torn and broken meat that had once been the old man in front of the people.

They cried and called on God. They asked for mercy and begged for forgiveness.

Haroun walked to them and inspected them. He saw the hope in their eyes then, and he loved the power he had over them. They were nothing, lice to be crushed underfoot, only a heartbeat removed from carrion.

A tall boy, perhaps ten years old, peered fearfully at Haroun from under his mother's protective embrace. Haroun approached the mother and child.

The mother looked up at Haroun and held her son more tightly. Silver tears cascaded down her cheeks. "Please. Do not hurt my son."

Haroun shook his head. "I will not hurt your son."

"Thank you." But even after he'd told her that, the mother didn't relax. She didn't trust him.

Haroun studied the boy, noticing how thin he was. But there was something different about him too. He did not completely look away when Haroun fixed his eyes on him. "What is your name, boy?"

The mother tried to answer for him. "His name is—"

Haroun interrupted her. "I asked the boy. Know your place, woman, or I will have the tongue from your head."

Frightened, the mother looked at the ground.

The boy met Haroun's stare. "I am called Kufow."

"It is a good name."

"I was named for my father."

The pride in the boy's tone amused Haroun. "Where is your father?"

"He died in the city."

"How?"

"Fighting the al-Shabaab devils. He was a soldier. A very brave soldier."

The mother reached for her child and tried to cover his mouth with a hand. She shushed him.

Haroun laughed and took the boy's shoulder. "I like you, boy. I am going to let you live to carry my message to this man Daud who lives with his death wish."

The boy fought and tried to escape Haroun's grip. Failing that, Kufow grabbed Haroun's hand and bit him. Cursing, Haroun punched the boy in the face hard enough to daze him. His knees turned to rubber and he almost fell. Haroun grabbed him again, this time by the back of the neck like he would a young pup.

"Bite me or strike me again, Kufow, and I will snap your neck." Haroun squeezed hard enough to make the boy yelp. "I can always choose another."

"Then choose another."

The boy's defiance intrigued Haroun. "No. You are the one I want. You will not be broken so easily." He dragged Kufow several feet away and turned back to face the people. "Take a look at your mother there, Kufow. Look at all of those people." He knelt beside the boy. "I know you think you hate me, but your heart is capable of more hate. Much more. This is my gift to you. You shall grow up and learn to hate the American Satans and the Westerners because they have caused what is about to happen here this day. And you will also hate the man who led me to you. This man Rageh Daud."

Kufow said nothing.

Across from them, the people shifted nervously, alert now to the fact that they were not through with their suffering.

Haroun whispered into Kufow's ear, but he kept his grip locked on the boy's neck. "Do you believe me?"

"It is you I will hate."

Haroun laughed. "Yes, but you will hate us all." Lifting his voice, he addressed his men. "Kill them."

"No!" Kufow struggled to get away, to get back to his mother. There was no time.

Machine gunners in the backs of the trucks parked near the captives opened fire immediately. The heavy machine gun rounds chopped into the people and dropped their corpses where they stood. The parched earth quickly soaked up their blood.

After a moment, the men stopped firing and the staccato roar of the machine guns faded away.

Kufow stood silent and shaking. Tears ran down his thin face.

"Now, Kufow." Haroun stood and looked into the boy's face. "Tell me who you hate."

24

BEKAH SAT ON A hard wooden bench outside the room that had been turned into a temporary morgue for the Marines who had fallen earlier that day. She felt empty and exhausted. She still wore her bloodstained fatigues.

The images wouldn't leave her mind. The memories of Ralph Caxton at the auto parts store and at the airport warred with the ones of him dying as she held his hand.

Although it had been less than two weeks since she'd last seen Travis and her granny, it already felt like so long ago. The perception of that time difference made her feel even more distant from her family. There was no transition going from back home to the middle of a war zone. It felt like she had just appeared here.

Or worse, that one of the two lives she led was just a figment of her imagination. Putting those two halves together was hard, especially when there were so many emotions attached to each of them.

She supposed it was because Ralph Caxton was the first Marine she'd known back in the real world and then seen die on the battlefield. All of the others she'd first met back in training or on a tour of duty. They had been Marines when she'd met them. Not the young guy who had sold her a carburetor. Not someone behind that safety net back in Oklahoma.

Bekah sipped a breath and tried to focus on the voices down the hall. It sounded like there were three or four people, but she couldn't tell what they were talking about because they spoke in low voices.

Footsteps approached, and Bekah leaned her head down on her raised knee, like she was catching a few winks and not going through . . . whatever it was she was going through. There was a lot of talk about military personnel coming back with post-traumatic stress disorder. If that happened to her, if she ended up with PTSD, would child welfare take Travis away from her? Could she be a fit mother? Would she continue to be someone Travis felt safe with?

Her son knew she was a Marine. He knew she carried a gun. When he got older and realized what that job really meant and where his mother had served, how would he feel about what she had done? Bekah didn't know. She wrapped her arms tightly around her leg and kept her eyes closed. She didn't want to be around anyone. That was why she avoided the barracks and the mess. She just wanted to get her head clear and find a way to sleep, but she knew she couldn't. She was too wound up.

The footsteps passed her, then stopped. A gentle voice spoke softly. "Hey, Marine. Are you okay?"

Bekah looked up because she was afraid it might be an

officer. Lieutenant Bridger had been through the area earlier gathering dog tags and information on the dead Marines. She still owed him an after-action report that she was working on in the small notepad she carried in her uniform. Lieutenant Bridger had been typing his on his iPad, inputting information like some kind of machine.

She'd resented him for the cool reserve he showed.

The man who stopped in the hallway was maybe ten years older than her, in his midthirties, and wore green scrubs. He was lean and looked fit, had a nice tan, but his brown hair was scruffy and he had three or four days of beard growth.

"Yes. I'm fine. Thank you." Bekah wanted him to keep moving, to leave her alone till she got her head straightened out.

Instead, he looked around, then back at her. "Are you here with anyone?"

"No."

His eyes drifted over her BDUs and took in the bloodstains. "Are you one of the Marines who got caught in that ambush earlier today?"

"Yes." *Go. Away.*

"Should you be alone right now?"

"I'm fine. Thank you for your concern."

He hesitated and ran a hand across the back of his neck. He glanced at the room across the hall, and it must have clicked that this was the place being used as the temporary morgue till the bodies could be transferred to the ships waiting out in the harbor. From there they'd be returned home.

Private Ralph Caxton was going back home only days after receiving his orders.

The man stuck his hand out. "Sorry. I should have introduced myself. I'm Matthew Cline. One of the doctors who helped . . . who helped today when this happened."

Bekah stood and took the man's hand. His grip was firm, confident. "Lance Corporal Bekah Shaw, Charlie Company, Marine Corps."

"Pleasure to meet you, Lance Corporal Shaw. Wish it could have been under different circumstances." Matthew took back his hand. "You lost somebody today?"

The bluntness of the question surprised Bekah. Back home, from someone she'd known for a long time, she could have expected something like that. But not from a stranger. And especially not under the present circumstances.

"Six Marines died today, Dr. Cline. We *all* lost somebody." Bekah regretted the edge in her voice, but she couldn't hold it in check.

"I know. I was attending when I lost one of them on the table, but I helped work on three other Marines who are going to be fine."

The casualties in the Indigo Rifle Platoon weren't limited to the dead. Several Marines had been wounded. New Marines were going to have to be pulled in.

For the first time Bekah realized that Matthew Cline didn't look like the other military doctors she was familiar with. "You don't look Marine-issue."

"Easy explanation for that. I'm not." Matthew smiled. "I'm with a contingent of Doctors Without Borders brought in to help work with the IDPs."

In Somalia, there were numerous camps of internally

displaced people fleeing the violence between the TFG and the Islamic extremist groups. And several surrounding countries were undergoing similar upheavals.

"I was here, getting a shipment ready to go out in the next few days, and heard about the ambush. Thought maybe I could lend a hand. Before I came to Somalia, I worked ER in Boston." Matthew shrugged. "Some people insist that's a war zone too." He smiled to let her know he was joking.

"That was awfully kind of you."

Matthew shook his head. "Saving people. That's kind of why I'm here."

"Yeah, I guess you are."

Matthew made a show of looking up and down the hall. "Uh, I don't really know anyone here, and I'm kind of wound up from pulling long hours in surgery. Maybe you want to be alone right now, but I'd like a little company. I mean, if that's okay."

It wasn't, but Bekah didn't have the heart to tell him that. Her granny had raised her to be hospitable. "Sure. This bench gets hard after a while." She returned to her seat.

Matthew sat and folded his arms over his chest. He was silent for a few minutes, obviously uncomfortable. Bekah wasn't going to save him from that. He'd chosen his row, now he had to hoe it.

"This is my first time in Mogadishu. How about you?"

"Yeah."

"Been anywhere else? Overseas, I mean."

"Iraq and Afghanistan."

Matthew nodded. "I've seen the news. Those spots were pretty rough too."

"Yeah, they were."

A brief silence stretched between them before Matthew continued speaking. "You from Texas?"

"Oklahoma."

"Sounds a lot like Texas."

"Maybe to an untrained ear."

Matthew smiled. "I guess so. A lot of people think everybody in Massachusetts sounds a lot like everybody in Boston."

Bekah leaned back against the wall and closed her eyes. But she knew her granny wouldn't be happy with her for ignoring the man after he'd gone out of his way to check on her. "So why come here?"

"Mogadishu?"

"Yes."

"I didn't choose to come to Mogadishu. Not really. I wanted to do a stint with Doctors Without Borders. Kind of clear my head."

Bekah looked at him then. "You came to a war zone to clear your head?"

Matthew grinned, tried to suppress it, then chuckled with good-natured humor. "I suppose that sounds a little crazy, huh?"

"A little."

He sighed and leaned his head back against the wall. "You ever think you had your whole life lined out, Lance Corporal Shaw?"

"Just call me Bekah."

"All right. But the question stands."

After a moment, Bekah nodded. It felt good talking to Matthew. Even though it was just inane, getting-to-know-you stuff, it was familiar and distracting from thoughts of Private Ralph Caxton lying cold in the next room. Bekah had always marveled at how some people could deal with death. Her granny often told her that folks didn't really have a choice about dealing with death. It was as common and mysterious as birth. A person had to accept death and keep moving because it was bound to come.

"I've thought I had my life planned out a couple times."

"Being a Marine was part of it?"

Bekah smiled. "No. Definitely not. I planned to get married, have children, and make a home for my husband and kids. I enlisted in the Marine Reserve after the divorce as a means of taking care of my son. I never planned on serving overseas in war zones either."

"You have a son?"

"I do. Travis."

"How old?"

"He's six."

"You don't look old enough to have a six-year-old."

"I had him when I was nineteen. Married right out of high school. My granny said I was too young to marry." Bekah stopped herself. "No, Granny never said that. She said that my ex-husband was too young to marry. She was right. My granny is right about a lot of things." She looked at him. "Do you have kids?"

"Me?" Matthew shook his head. "No. I'm not against the

idea. It just hasn't happened yet. First there needs to be a Mrs. Matthew Cline." He looked wistful. "There almost was."

"What happened?"

"Two years ago, I met a woman I thought was perfect for me. We dated. We got engaged. We planned the wedding. A week before we were supposed to get married, she called it off."

"Why?"

Matthew hesitated, then gave a sad smile. "I had a chance to quit working at the hospital and join a group of doctors that specialized in cosmetic surgery." He held out his hands. "You may not know this, but I've been told these are the hands of an artist. You put a scalpel in my hand, I can do amazing things." He grinned. "It's kind of hard to say that and sound modest."

Bekah smiled at him.

"I gave the idea of changing jobs some thought. I could be a good plastic surgeon. I did some pretty amazing stuff in the ER."

"Modestly, of course."

"Of course. But amazing procedures nonetheless. My fiancée gave the idea some thought too. She really liked the change because it would mean seeing more of me. Better hours. Long vacations. Bigger paychecks. A nice deal all the way around, to her mind."

"Sounds like everything was working. So what went wrong?"

"Me. I went wrong. My fiancée told me that, and she told all of her friends that. The more I thought about the new job, the more I realized I'd miss my old job. In the ER, I help people who really need it at the time they need it. I save lives. To me, that's a lot better than giving someone a new nose or a tummy tuck or liposuction. I help people hang on to the most precious thing they could lose."

"I think that's commendable."

"Me too." Matthew smiled. "I could respect a guy like me. I look in the mirror, I'm proud of who I turned out to be. But my fiancée took my decision to stay with the hospital as a personal insult. She wanted the bigger checks, the long vacations, and the prestige of being a plastic surgeon's wife. She stopped the wedding and broke off the engagement."

"I'm sorry."

"Me too. I really loved her. I guess I still do." Matthew looked at Bekah. "How long have you been divorced?"

"Six years. He left right before our son was born."

"I'm sorry."

Bekah shook her head. "No. Billy Roy was a lousy husband. He would have been an even worse dad. I'm glad my boy doesn't have anything to do with him. It's better this way."

Matthew nodded. "Can I ask you a personal question?"

"Have you asked one that wasn't?" Bekah was surprised at the way her mood had changed while talking.

He grinned. "I suppose not. Do those feelings you had for someone you loved ever go away?"

Bekah looked at him and saw the pain in his blue eyes. "Yes. It takes a long time, but eventually they do." Her granny had told her that, but she knew in her heart that it hadn't quite happened with Billy Roy. Maybe she didn't love him anymore, didn't daydream about what it was like being with him, but he could still hurt her.

"Good to know, because trying to deal with all of this has been hard."

"That's why you joined Doctors Without Borders?"

"No. I wanted to do that before, but my fiancée wouldn't hear of it. When one of my buddies found out I was single again, he told me there was a position opening, and I took it." Matthew smiled. "I loved medical school. It was fascinating learning all the details of anatomy, physiology. But you know what I learned in the ER?"

Bekah shook her head, not knowing where he was going.

"That it mattered." Matthew spoke softly. "That it *really* mattered. I don't know where you are when it comes to faith. For me, I kept remembering how Jesus didn't just talk at people; he saw them in desperate need, and he reached out and did something about it. Maybe I can't save the whole world, but in the ER, I've been able to straighten out lives that come in wrecked. I've been able to save lives that would otherwise be lost. That's a huge responsibility, really humbling."

"Not all doctors feel that way. Some of them feel pretty godlike themselves."

Matthew laughed. "I suppose they do. But that's not me. I just appreciate this chance to serve. Maybe I have to sacrifice some creature comforts, some time, but I make a difference." He paused and shook his head. "I'm probably preaching to the choir here, though. I bet you feel the same way about being in the Corps."

His words touched Bekah's heart and made her feel a little lighter. "Sometimes. Sometimes I do. When I don't get lost in missing my son."

"If we weren't sacrificing something, what we give wouldn't be the same."

For a quiet moment, Bekah thought about that. She knew her granny would agree immediately. Her granny was giving up a lot by helping her and Travis. And Bekah knew at times she felt the same way herself.

Matthew sat up. "You know what this bench really needs? Coffee, and I mean something other than the weak stuff they're serving in the nurses' station. Do you know where we can get some?"

"They have some in the cantina." Bekah got up, slid the strap of her rifle over her shoulder, and picked up her helmet. She led the way out of the building and tried not to feel guilty leaving Ralph Caxton behind.

25

THE BOY WAITS THERE *with the dead.*

The thought pummeled the inside of Daud's skull. He had first heard about the massacre two hours ago when he and his men had visited with another group of displaced people. He had given away more of the cargo he'd taken from the UN convoy. In return, he had added six more young men to his band.

He had also gotten the attention of Korfa Haroun.

"You realize this may be a trap, Rageh." Afrah sat behind the steering wheel of the truck he drove. The headlight beams cut holes in the dark night ahead of them as they followed the narrow, winding trail.

"Of course I do. If it is a trap, we will come back."

"It might be too late."

"It will not be too late." Daud looked into the darkness that shrouded the landscape. He tried to remember this group of displaced people, how many children they had among them. He couldn't recall coming this way. There had been too many trips through the countryside, too many people who desperately needed help they weren't getting.

"This is just one boy." Afrah shrugged. "He is probably already dead."

"But he may not be."

"And if he is?" Afrah looked at him.

"Then it is God's will." Daud knew Afrah held Islam at arm's length. Why had he said such a thing when he wasn't sure he believed it himself? But the image of that boy sitting there in the midst of those corpses was powerful and unsettling. He'd reached instinctively for his faith.

Afrah put his attention back on the road. "What if he is not dead?"

Truthfully, Daud had not let himself think that far. Thinking like that would mean giving in to hope, and he did not wish to get his hopes up. It was maddening to think of a child sitting out there in the night surrounded by the bodies of his family and friends.

Daud tightened his grip on his AK-47, then forced himself to relax. If the boy still lived, then Daud would take him away from there. What he would do with him after that, Daud was not certain.

He could not help thinking of Ibrahim and how he had laid his son's fragile body into the unwelcoming earth. Daud took a breath and promised himself that if the boy was dead, he would bury him. Then he would hunt Haroun all the harder.

★　★　★

They left the trucks a couple miles from where the group of displaced people had set up their little village. Daud walked into the darkness with ten men, including Afrah, and left the others with the trucks and jeeps in case they needed reinforcements or an escape. They had radios now for communication, though they used them sparingly because the Westerners and the al-Shabaab monitored the radio waves.

Afrah walked silently beside Daud. The man carried an AK-47 that looked like a child's toy in his big arms. He wore an RPG-7 strapped over his shoulder and a pouch of warheads at his side. Since Daud had made his decision to go into the night, Afrah had said nothing further.

The moon sat deep in the night sky, pale and wan, barely illuminating the terrain around them. As they neared the streambed that ran by the area where the people had established their village, Daud heard frogs croaking and the slow trickle of water wending through the stream to his right.

He walked near the water, down in the shallow ditch the stream had carved from the earth over generations. As he made his way, he kept thinking of Ibrahim, remembering how he had taught his son to walk, to throw a ball, to fish off the pier down at the harbor. There were so many things he had done with his boy that his own father had not done with him.

Ibrahim's laughter and innocence were the things Daud most missed about his son. Ibrahim had been much happier and more open to things in life than Daud had ever been.

Sometimes seeing those things in his son had worried Daud, making him realize how vulnerable Ibrahim was.

His wife had seen him fret over such things, but she hadn't known the reason for his anxiety. She worried about Ibrahim, too, but she never concerned herself with whether Daud could protect her. She had died, and he had not been there.

A short distance farther, Daud came to a halt and took out his binoculars as he stood in the shadow of a boswellia tree. The ragged bark pressed against his right cheek, but he couldn't feel it where the nerves had burned in his face. He scanned the area ahead and spotted the boy sitting under a towering juniper tree. The people had built *aqals* under and around the junipers, using the natural brush line to disguise the structures.

These people hadn't been easy to find. Without the map that Daud had taken from the UN driver, he wouldn't have found them at all.

"There is no one about." Daud lowered his binoculars. "Only the boy."

"There is something in the tree." Afrah stood only a few feet away.

"What is it?"

"I don't know." Afrah remained still and trained his binoculars on the tree. "Looks like giant bats."

Daud looked again, and this time he studied the tree. Strange shapes did hang from it, but he couldn't make them out. Silently, he put the binoculars away, then resumed his walk. There was no way he could leave the boy there alone.

★　★　★

As he approached the boy, Daud thought he might be asleep. And then he thought the boy might be dead. The man who had brought the message to Daud had reported that the boy was alive when he'd left him but that the boy refused to accompany him.

The boy waits there with the dead.

Thirty feet from the tree, Daud identified what hung from the branches. Haroun had hung the bodies of at least twenty men, women, and children upside down by their ankles. The eyes of the dead were open and gleamed in the weak moonlight as they stared around.

The boy's chin was on his chest, but his shoulders rose and fell with his breath. He was alive. For the first time since he'd buried his son, Daud felt a little hope come alive within him. He didn't know whether to hang onto it or crush it before it could grow. There was only so much pain he could endure.

"Boy." He spoke softly and let the wind carry his voice to the boy.

The boy looked in Daud's direction. His eyes were as dead as those of the corpses that hung above him.

"Do you know me?" Daud took another few steps forward, alert to every nuance of the land around him. He knew Haroun could have left a team of snipers. Or maybe he had mined the area. He might even have wired the boy with an explosive. There were so many things the al-Shabaab leader might have done.

"I know you." The boy's words were listless and dry, and Daud could tell that he'd had nothing to drink for a very long time. "You are Daud."

"I am Daud."

"Korfa Haroun wants you to know that he will kill you one day soon."

Daud took another few steps. "That remains to be seen. I intend to kill him."

The boy watched him carefully. "Haroun commands many warriors."

"I learned a long time ago, when I was your age, that it only takes one dedicated individual and one bullet to kill a man. Haroun is not invincible."

"He is a killer."

"I know. You were offered a chance to leave by a fellow tribesman after Haroun left. Why did you not go?"

"Where is there to go?"

"You cannot stay here."

The boy looked at Daud with his dead eyes. "My father died fighting the al-Shabaab in the name of the Transitional Federal Government that swore to take care of us. My mother said we could not stay in our home. So we left. When we stopped here and made our village, there was nowhere else for us." He paused. "I have nowhere to go."

"Then what will you do?"

"Stay here."

"You will die."

"It is better to die. Then I will not miss my father and I will not miss my mother."

Lowering his rifle, Daud strode to the boy's side. "A boy so young should not think so much of death."

The boy looked up at the tree. "It is all around us. How can I not think of it?" He pointed at the body of a woman. "That is my mother."

Daud looked at the woman. "Do you wish to bury her?"

A tear trickled from the boy's eye, but his face remained resolute. "Yes, but I cannot. I want to climb the tree, but I am afraid."

"Fear is something you should put behind you now. The men that did this took everything from you that caused you to be fearful. Live unafraid now. Live to kill your enemies. It is all they have left to you." Daud held out his hand. "I will help you bury your mother."

★　　★　　★

Digging the grave took an hour. Daud labored with quiet intensity, not speaking because the boy did not speak. Somehow their combined silence gave them strength. They used shovels from one of the trucks that had now set up a perimeter around the area. The sharp edges of the shovels sliced into the ground, and the going was easier than Daud dared hope since the stream was so close and the earth was not baked rock-hard.

Afrah stood guard, also without speaking, but the big man's hard face spoke volumes to someone who knew him. Their time there displeased Afrah, and Daud could not blame his friend for that.

Still, he knew he would not be able to get the boy to go with him until they had buried the mother.

Near the end of the grave digging, the boy got sick and threw up. For a moment Daud believed he had gone as far as he could, but the boy wiped his mouth with a trembling hand and took a fresh hold on his shovel.

They continued working till it was done. Then Daud ordered that a canvas tarp be brought from one of the trucks. Together, he and the boy placed the dead woman on the tarp, though Daud had to do most of the lifting. When they were finished, they wrapped the woman in the canvas, cinched it with rope, and dragged it toward the open grave.

Because he did not want to simply drop the body into the hole in front of the boy, Daud climbed into the grave and took hold of the corpse. The raw, moist stink of the earth around him reminded him of burying Ibrahim with his mother. The emotions that Daud had worked so hard to suppress almost broke free. He pulled the dead woman into the grave with him, then climbed back out.

Together, he and the boy filled the grave. When they had finished, the boy stared at the mound of fresh-turned earth.

"Do you wish to say something?" Daud stood at the boy's side.

The boy was quiet for a time. "What should I say?"

"Good-bye. That you loved her. And that you wish her a safe journey."

"Where is she going?"

"I don't know."

"My mother talked of heaven."

"Then perhaps that is where she has gone."

The boy looked at him. "Do you not believe in heaven?"

Daud answered him honestly. "There is not much I believe in these days."

Quietly, the boy lowered his head, bade his mother good-bye and safe journey, and said that he loved her. Then he looked at Daud again. "Haroun said I should hate you."

"Why?"

"Because you helped cause my mother's death."

"I was not here."

"Haroun said he killed my mother—killed all of them—so you would get the message he wanted me to give. He said if you had not done what you have been doing, he would not have come looking for you."

"Perhaps this is true."

"Then I should hate you."

"If you wish, you may."

The boy was quiet again.

"Haroun does not remember me." Daud spoke softly. "But not many months ago I was living in the city with my wife and child. We bothered no one. My son Ibrahim was about your age. I loved him very much, and I loved his mother as well."

"Were you a soldier?"

Daud shook his head. "I was just a husband. A father. Haroun had no cause to know me. But Haroun and his warriors killed my family. After I buried them, I swore that I would fight the al-Shabaab until there were no more of them or until they killed me. This is what I do."

"You are going to fight Haroun?"

Daud looked at the boy. "I am going to kill Haroun."

"Then I will go with you, and I will kill Haroun as well."

"This isn't work for a child."

"A child does not bury his mother. I am a man now. Give me a gun. Teach me how to use it. I will kill Haroun with you."

Daud dropped to one knee and looked at the boy. "Do you have nowhere else to go? No other relatives?"

The boy shook his head. "I can stay here and die, or I can go with you."

"If those are your only options, you may accompany me."

The boy reached out a hand and touched the dead parts of Daud's face. "I am Kufow."

Daud stood and took the boy by the hand, leading him to one of the jeeps. A few minutes later, they were once more traveling through the night. Only a short time after that, the boy fell asleep in the seat between Daud and Afrah. Twisting slightly, Daud made the boy more comfortable and just listened to the soft sigh of his breathing. He ran his hand over the boy's head and thought that it was time to find out more about Haroun and where the man was.

26

THE NEXT TWO WEEKS passed in a blur for Bekah. From sunup to sundown, she was on patrol through the streets of Mogadishu. She even managed a few short hops outside the city on mercy missions to take food and medicines to internally displaced people living outside the metropolitan area. The Indigo Rifle Platoon was rebuilt, bringing in other Marines. When they weren't on patrol, they were training, getting to know each other, learning that they could trust each other.

The patrols turned bloody on three different occasions as the al-Shabaab continued sniping attacks and suicide bombings. Marines—and civilians for that matter—remained spread out as they traveled through the city streets. No one wanted to be part of a group that was large enough to attract enemy attention. The snipers were the worst, able to drop four or five people before Marines, UN peacekeeping forces, or the Somali military could take them down.

More and more soldiers from different countries hit the ground in Mogadishu to provide aid and supplies. AMISOM, the regional peacekeeping mission led by the African Union under the auspices of the United Nations, had trouble keeping up with all the comings and goings. Managing the men and materials proved almost impossible, and it left holes in their security.

With all the influx of goods, the military had to tighten security as well. Even then, shipments and cargo went missing, later turning up on the black market.

In the evenings she met up with Matthew Cline for dinner or coffee, depending on how their schedules matched. He was kept busy caring for patients in the city and preparing treks outside the metro area that would provide care for displaced people afraid to enter Mogadishu again.

On Thursday of the third week, their paths crossed during the day when she and her team were assigned to guard Matthew's clinic in the city's interior. The clinic was housed in a bombed-out building that had been cleared but not restored. Plywood covered the windows, and even that had to be guarded because people would steal it to make personal shelters. Bits of cracked plaster stubbornly clung to the brick walls pocked with bullet scars.

After the ambush she'd been through, Bekah maintained a stark vigilance as she manned the post inside the clinic. She stood to one side clad in full battle gear, her rifle across her chest in ready position. Sick children and sick and anxious parents kept watch over her the whole time she was there. After hours of standing guard duty, she was beginning to think she was more of a negative influence than a positive one. But someone had to protect the people.

Matthew worked with an interpreter as he checked over the children who were brought to him. Only a few had any appreciable English, and hardly any Americans were proficient in the local languages. Matthew's command of the Somali language had grown admirably in the past three weeks, but he still didn't want to talk to parents without the interpreter.

He worked hard, and Bekah respected that. He arrived at the clinic at daybreak and didn't leave until the sun was setting. Travel after dark was limited, and most people wanted to return to wherever they were living within the city by then. A large number of the people were homeless, either because their residences had been destroyed or because they'd come in from villages outside Mogadishu.

They lived in tent cities in alleys, courtyards, and wrecked buildings. Bekah had been through some of the areas and felt bad for the people, but they were living. That was what people learned to do when they had nothing. Bekah had seen that in Callum's Creek.

★   ★   ★

"The kids like you." Bekah walked beside Matthew as she escorted him to the break area. He didn't take breaks often, usually only long enough to grab a sandwich and a bottle of water and go to the bathroom. He was gone on break usually ten minutes tops, then he was back in that receiving room facing a long line of ailing children. She didn't know how he did it.

Matthew smiled, and some of the fatigue etched into his face briefly lifted. "I like the kids. It's a simple relationship. They're sick or hurt, and I fix them. And I thank God I've got the medicine and the staff to get that accomplished."

"I've seen some of the other medical people working with them. Those kids don't like everyone."

The break area was a small room with a few groceries kept in ice chests. Two small, round tables in the center of the room were flanked by mismatched chairs. Another rectangular table occupied a spot against the wall. The ice chests containing the food sat atop it.

Matthew opened one of the chests and glanced at Bekah. "Sandwich?"

"I can make my own."

"I'm sure you can, but I'm willing to do it for you."

"Thank you." Bekah kept the sandwich simple, ham and cheese and vegetables with mustard.

Matthew fixed both sandwiches, wrapped them in paper towels from a nearby roll, took two more towels to use as napkins, and grabbed two diet soft drinks. He turned toward the tables and smiled. "Looks like we have our choice of seating."

Bekah went to the nearest table, put her rifle on the floor, and placed her helmet in the chair next to her. She accepted the sandwich when Matthew offered it, then waited for him to settle in.

Cries of sick and wounded children carried into the break area. It was a constant undercurrent of noise. Bekah was certain it would join the other nightmares she already suffered every night.

Matthew gazed at her. "How are you doing?"

Bekah picked at her sandwich. "I'm okay."

"You look tired."

"Long days will do that to you." She gave him a slight grin. "Having people shoot at you kind of adds to the stress level."

Matthew laughed, but she knew he only did that out of reflex. There was nothing amusing about the situation they were in.

He sipped his drink. "Are you sleeping all right?"

"I am."

"Because you don't look like you're getting enough sleep."

"Have you seen a mirror lately?"

Matthew grinned, and she liked the easy way that expression appeared on his face. "Okay, I'll back off. I was just concerned about you. So far, I haven't lost a friend over here. You have."

"I'm working through it." Bekah took a bite of her sandwich. "What about you?"

"What about me?"

"Is this everything you thought it would be?"

Matthew sighed and slumped back in his chair. For a moment Bekah feared she'd gone too far.

"Sorry. I didn't mean to pry."

"Yes you did." Matthew smiled at her wearily. "I think we both meant to pry. It's what we do when we're in a situation we don't have control of and don't completely understand. We check the people around us and see how they're feeling about things. I'm sure you have someone like that at home."

Bekah thought about that for a moment. "My granny.

Every time I was going through something—when I was pregnant with Travis, when I was going through my divorce, when I was first activated to come overseas—she was the one I talked to." She smiled at the memories and was surprised at how much comfort they brought her. "We usually have our best talks when we're hanging laundry."

"You hang laundry?"

"Yep. Clothesline. Clothespins. The works. Granny likes the way everything smells when it's dried in the sun. For that matter, so do I."

"What do you do in the winter?"

"We use the dryer. Oklahoma isn't exactly the Old West. We do have modern conveniences. Like indoor plumbin' and 'lectricity."

Matthew looked chagrined. "I didn't think—" He stopped himself. "Well, yes, I guess I did think maybe it was. Not all of it, but maybe where you were from."

Bekah laughed at his discomfort, and it felt good to do so. "I've got some pictures on my camera to prove it. I'll show them to you sometime."

"I'd like that."

Bekah was surprised how comfortable she felt around Matthew, especially since they came from two very different walks of life.

"In answer to your question, being here is a lot different than I thought it would be." Matthew took a bite of his sandwich. "I just didn't realize how . . . *overpowering* helping these people would be. Especially the kids. I love working with the kids. That's the one thing I've always been certain of, the one thing I believe God gave me to do. And I believe God put me here to help."

"You could have helped kids in Boston. You didn't have to come all the way out here."

Matthew shook his head. "It wouldn't have been the same. It *wasn't* the same. This . . . this is different. I feel like I was called to this place, at this time. Haven't you ever felt like God put you somewhere?"

Bekah was quiet for a moment, then decided to be honest. "I don't think God has much of an interest in my life."

Matthew frowned. "How can you say something like that?"

"Because if there's any place I should be, it's back home with my son and my granny. Travis needs raising, and my granny needs help on that little bit of family land we've hung on to." Bekah shook her head. "And when I get back, I've got to find another steady job. I lost the last one."

"I'm sorry to hear that."

Bekah shrugged. "I can find another job."

"That wasn't what I was talking about. I was talking about the fact that you don't feel God is working in your life. That's got to be an awful lonely feeling."

"If he's been around, I haven't seen any signposts. And I don't know what he would expect me to do."

"You're raising your son and helping your grandmother."

"When I'm there." Bekah tried not to sound bitter, but she suspected she wasn't quite pulling it off.

"Keep an open mind. You might be surprised at what you see one day." Matthew nodded at the people standing in line to be examined. "These people come to me for medical aid, but I want to give them more than that. I talk to them about God as I work. A lot of these people's souls are wounded worse than their bodies."

Over the last couple days, Bekah had overheard Matthew talking about God's love and salvation, praying with patients, and encouraging them, and many times she had felt better for it.

Matthew smiled. "Some of these people are Christians already. Others just need to be shown the way. God cares about them. They need to be told that until they can see it for themselves. Everyone needs that sometimes."

Bekah nodded, but she didn't think so. She was certain that if God had any interest in her life, she'd have known it before now.

★ ★ ★

The attack on the clinic came during shift change for the Marines, and it was perfectly camouflaged.

Bekah walked out of the building feeling guilty at leaving Matthew Cline behind, but she knew her team needed the precious little rest they were getting, and they had orders to stay together. It was after eighteen hundred hours, and the line to get medical attention wrapped around the building. Parents and children sat on the ground. Mothers held blankets over small children to protect them from the heat of the sun. They swatted at flies that tried to feast on the children's open sores.

A man and a boy caught Bekah's attention, and she didn't

know what it was at first. Something just wasn't right. The fact that a mother wasn't present wasn't surprising. Many of the mothers were dead, victims of the violence and sickness that ravaged the city. Then she realized it was the way the man and boy were sitting in line together.

The man was in his early twenties, and the boy was eleven or twelve, though age was sometimes hard to determine in the young because malnutrition often kept them small. But the man had to be an older brother, perhaps an uncle.

Bekah couldn't help wondering where the parents were, or where other siblings might be. But even that could be explained—all kinds of people came to the clinic.

These two sat side by side and stared at the building across the alley, like they were looking but seeing nothing. They weren't talking. But many of the other people waiting outside weren't talking either. Several of them slept or sat listlessly while trapped in fever or pain. Some parents held animated, sometimes irritated, conversations with their children. Or the children entertained each other or themselves.

The boy beside the man sat stiff and looked scared.

The man glanced over at Bekah and wore a hard look. When his eyes met Bekah's gaze, he quickly looked away.

Warning bells went off in Bekah's head. The boy wasn't acting right either, and it wasn't sickness or pain or even worry about the doctor that had him acting so strangely.

Bekah spoke in a low voice that barely carried. "Pike."

"Yeah." Pike turned to her.

"There's a man and a boy over here at four o'clock."

"Got them." Pike's expression remained neutral.

"Something's not right."

"They look okay to me."

"Trust me. The boy's not okay." She still couldn't put into words what bothered her about the scene, but she knew the disturbance was real.

Pike nodded. "What do you want me to do?"

"Wait here with the others. Cover me."

"What are you thinking?"

"I don't know. But that kid's not acting right."

"All right."

Bekah split off from her team and headed over to the line of waiting patients. The man looked at her suspiciously, but the boy never moved. Quietly, Bekah walked along the line of people and carried her rifle at the ready. She acted like she was checking the severity of the patients' conditions, something that had gone on all day because Matthew wanted the weakest and sickest patients brought in immediately. Nurses and Marines had been making triage examinations, so her presence there wasn't out of the ordinary.

Except that she had her team waiting on her.

The man's dark gaze slid from her to the three Marines standing only a short distance away. He shifted nervously, his hands hidden inside his long coat. Bekah was eight people away when the man leaned over and spoke to the boy. The boy ignored him, continuing to stare at the blank wall across the alley. The man spoke again, more sharply this time.

Woodenly, the boy got to his feet and turned toward the clinic door. His eyes were vacant, but it wasn't from sickness. It was from fear. The look in his eyes reminded Bekah of the time Travis had discovered a rat snake in the henhouse eating chicks. Bekah had been with him, and he'd looked like he had seen a monster.

That was the way this boy looked now.

"Hey." Bekah stepped in front of the boy. "Are you all right?" She didn't know if he spoke any English.

Although the boy stopped, he didn't look up at her. He stood there like a statue.

Behind him, the man barked an order.

The boy shook for a moment, then lifted his hands and pulled the pin from a grenade he'd been hiding under his shirt.

Adrenaline hit Bekah, flooding her with that old, familiar fight-or-flight response. Somewhere in the back of her mind, she remembered that the grenade only had a three- or five-second delay before it detonated. The kill radius could be as much as fifteen yards. Several of the people waiting in line saw the grenade and went into a panic as they ran for their lives.

Knowing that she couldn't run and get away in time, Bekah grabbed for the grenade. The boy tried desperately to hang on to the explosive, but she managed to knock it from his grasp, and it bounced onto the ground and rolled toward the man who accompanied him.

Seeing the grenade, the man kicked at it but missed. He had a pistol in one hand and fired three or four shots.

Everything moved slowly for Bekah. She felt like she was mired in molasses, a fly trapped in amber, and she thought of Travis and Granny and how she'd never get to see them again.

At the same time, though, she was moving, rushing toward the man with the gun in spite of the weapon.

She knew she had to cover the grenade. The Marines had trained her for a situation just like this. It was better for one Marine to die than a half dozen, better that one Marine die instead of dozens of men, women, and children who had been seeking medical attention. And in the back of her mind, she thought of Matthew Cline's words about the meaning of sacrifice.

The man pushed himself away from the wall and at her, evidently thinking he wanted to live a little longer. His path took him into Bekah's way. Single-mindedly intent on diving to the ground, Bekah hit the man in the stomach with her shoulder. They went down in a tangle, flailing, and when they hit, Bekah was on top of him and the grenade was only inches away.

The man lay facedown, squalling in fear and struggling to get up. Acting on impulse, thinking only to cover the grenade, Bekah caught the explosive in a cupped palm and shoveled it under the terrorist. The grenade slid right under the man's midsection, and she barely had time to get her hand and arm out before it detonated.

The horrific boom deafened her immediately and white noise buzzed through her head. She felt the man's body jump beneath her and blood was suddenly everywhere, splattered across the ground and over the wall only a foot away. The air left her in a rush as the concussive force slammed into her through the terrorist's body, and she felt something strike her body armor.

After a moment, she realized she was still alive, but blood was dripping into her right eye. She tried to get up, but her arms and legs wouldn't work.

Then Pike was there, lifting her in his strong arms and holding her so he could survey her. Trudy and Tyler had set up a field-of-fire perimeter and were searching the crowd for anyone else who might have been involved with the attack.

Pike looked her in the eye. *"Are you all right?"*

Bekah couldn't hear him, but she read the big man's lips. She nodded, and her head spun.

"You're one crazy broad, do you know that?"

Bekah knew she was lucky. She'd intended on covering the grenade with her own body. She just hadn't been able to.

Using his thumb, Pike wiped blood from her eye. *"C'mon, hero. We gotta have the doc take a look at you."*

She went with him, managing to walk under her own power despite her shaking legs. The boy stood there watching her, tears tracking down his face. Tentatively, not knowing what kind of response she would get, Bekah held an arm out to the boy. He hesitated, then came to her in a rush and wrapped his arms around her, holding tight as he cried.

27

SEATED IN THE COMMAND POST and nursing a cold cup of coffee, Heath Bridger studied the court papers on Lance Corporal Bekah Shaw on his iPad. He'd already been through them a few times. He grimaced at what he was reading.

"Have you been oversampling the local cuisine again?"

Startled, Heath looked up and spotted Gunney Towers entering the room. Despite the long day, he looked immaculate and ready to go. The man was almost old enough to be Heath's father, and he seemed to have energy to burn.

"I told you that your stomach is too tender for some of those spices." Towers set a big stack of folders on Heath's desk.

"It's not the food." Heath sighed and placed the iPad on the desk.

"I've seen that look before. There's something that ain't setting right with you."

"Lance Corporal Shaw's court case."

Towers lifted a mocking eyebrow. "So, did she turn out to be some kind of felon after all?"

Heath shook his head. "From everything I'm seeing here—and I'm having to do a lot of reading between the lines to get the whole story—Bekah was trapped into a fight with a local guy."

"Bekah? Not Lance Corporal Shaw?"

Heath frowned at Towers, who held his hands up in surrender.

"I assume you're looking more favorably at . . . Bekah." Towers didn't crack a smile, but his dark eyes twinkled.

"I think I may have jumped to conclusions."

"You were tired. Jet-lagged. She talks like a hillbilly girl, and you just figured she was a troublemaker."

"Maybe." But Heath knew that wasn't all of it. Growing irritation filled him at the fact that Mark Kluger still hadn't gotten in touch with him regarding the motion to set aside Darnell Lester's death sentence. He hadn't liked leaving things unsettled. No one at his father's firm would shepherd Darnell the way Heath wanted the case handled, and he felt guilty about leaving the man.

"The girl's getting railroaded?"

"Yeah. And I don't know why. In a town that small, she should be some kind of hero."

Towers sat in a chair in front of the desk and crossed his arms. "Not trying to say that I know more than you—"

"Of course not." Heath waved a hand to get the gunney to continue.

"—but maybe when it comes to small towns, maybe I know more than you." Towers grinned. "Heroes are particular things in small towns. Most people believe in them, and they support them because generally they know them. But sometimes jealousy gets in the way."

"Jealousy?"

Towers nodded. "You take this little slip of a girl that's become a Marine. Probably not many in her hometown joined up in the military. Got too many responsibilities at home. Got a family. Got a better job than the military pays." He paused. "Or maybe none of them boys wants to run the risk of catching a bullet. A girl like Lance Corporal Bekah Shaw would stand out in a town like that."

Heath sat back and listened.

"You've experienced it yourself anytime you've been in public in your fatigues or your uniform. Sometimes people give you respect. A nod. A hello. You might be in a restaurant and somebody picks up your dinner tab. And sometimes other people fight shy of you, look anywhere but at you."

Heath knew that was true.

"I don't know what our lance corporal has got going on back home, but I'm betting that part of it is the fact that she don't quite fit in no more. She makes people uncomfortable. She's been out in the world. The *big* world. And she's seen more trouble than them people are ever gonna see. The problem is, they don't know her no more—if they ever did—and they ain't sure they want to be on her team."

"Because she's an outsider." Heath understood that. He

was an outsider in his father's world; that had been apparent since he'd become a man.

"Bingo." Towers smiled.

"Do you think that's what's going on here?"

"Me?" Towers smiled again. "Wasn't me come in here full of questions."

"You asked me first."

"Only if you had indigestion. You brought up the rest of it."

Heath grinned and leaned forward again. "I guess I did, didn't I?"

"Yep."

"At any rate, I got the paperwork filed for her." Working through military channels was easier than dealing with his father's law firm. That was one of the things Heath loved about being a Marine. "She's good to go till she gets back."

"At which time she's still facing whatever charge she left behind."

"We'll see." Heath picked up his iPad. "In the meantime, we've drawn a new assignment."

"Something more than street sweeping?"

"Yeah. Command wants Indigo to accompany a medical relief effort to the southwest. There's an IDP facility a few days out that's in desperate need of resupplying and medical personnel."

Towers thought about that for a time. "We've still got a lot of green Marines attached to this unit. That ambush set us back."

"I know. We're also supposed to do some recon while

we're in the bush." Heath pushed the iPad toward Towers to reveal the face of the man on the screen.

Towers picked up the iPad and studied the scarred face of the man revealed there. "Who's this?"

"Rageh Daud. He's running what appears to be an independent operation out in the bush."

"What kind of operation?"

"He's been taking down medical shipments. A few weeks ago Daud attacked a medical convoy, killed several military guardsmen, took all the cargo, and kidnapped a doctor." Heath motioned for Towers to scroll through the pictures he'd gotten with the file, showing the burned remains of two jeeps and corpses littering the ground.

"Man knows his business."

Heath nodded.

"What happened to the doctor?"

"Daud took him to a small village, had him treat some of the people there who needed an actual doctor, not just medicines, and later let him go outside of Mogadishu. Marines around the city found Dr. Brandon Sykes stumbling around in the wilderness and brought him back into our care."

"Was he hurt?"

Heath shook his head. "Totally freaked by everything that happened, but otherwise in good health."

"Sounds like Daud is running his own care package."

"If you don't count the people he killed to take that cargo."

"Well, that's a fly in the buttermilk."

"Command didn't quite put it that way. They want us to

find Daud. If we can, we're supposed to bring him in or put him down."

"They care which?"

"No. Interestingly enough, it appears the al-Shabaab is also hunting Daud. In particular, Haroun is tracking him. Or trying to. Evidently Daud is a ghost out there somewhere. He's got a small team, keeps it moving, and doesn't step into anything he can't handle."

"Chasing a fox."

"Haroun is, and so are we. Command is of the opinion that we might be able to find Daud and Haroun somewhere close together out there. CIA intel from assets in those areas seems to point to the same eventuality."

"I take it Command is thinking we can take out two birds with one stone?"

"They are. When we find one—or both—we're supposed to call in a drone attack and try to put them down."

Towers passed the iPad back. "Sounds easy enough, but you and I know things don't really work out that way."

The search for Haroun's underground bomb-making factory had been a grim reminder of that.

Towers leaned back in his chair with his hands in his lap. "How did we get Daud's picture?"

"One of the CIA assets had a digital camera. Dropped it in the city to his handler, and it filtered to us."

"We know anything about Daud?"

Heath frowned. "Not much. The CIA and military intelligence managed to track him back nine years, which is surprising given the state of records and bookkeeping in the area. Until a few months ago, Daud was a stand-up guy. He went to work, had a family, and kept his head down."

"What happened?"

"His family got killed in an al-Shabaab attack. Daud lost his wife and son. After that, he disappeared."

"Until he reappeared and started boosting medical cargoes."

"That's right. The CIA's asset also stated that Daud is actively recruiting from among the groups he helps."

"He's trading medicines for young men." Towers stroked his massive chin. "Be an easy thing to do. Roll into one of those groups living hand to mouth, show them how they could be living if they followed him, and he'd have a lot of young boys flocking to him. Selling the dream."

Heath nodded.

"So what's Daud's endgame? What does he want out of all this?"

"CIA thinks maybe Daud's in it for revenge."

Towers shook his head. "Then what? This guy is old enough to know that revenge isn't going to be enough."

"For the moment, that may be all he has. I think he's out of control. He's hurting, and he's going to hurt people back."

Towers's eyes narrowed. "Got some experience with this, do you?"

"Back in the real world, I've represented a lot of guys for my father's firm who were exactly like this. They live in small worlds, places only they can go to. A guy like Daud builds himself a prison of grief, and he can't get out of it by himself. He's got to let someone in."

"Surrounding himself with a bunch of greedy guns and people mad at the world isn't going to provide that person."

"No. That's why prisons don't work for the most part."

"Felons I've run across in my life don't ever change their ways. They start out a bully or addict or killer, they generally die that way. You ever seen a convict change on the inside of a penitentiary?"

Heath thought of Darnell Lester and heard the man's gentle voice inside his head. *Then I'll be askin' God to look over you too.* Heath had heard that promise again and again over the last few weeks. It wouldn't leave his mind.

"I have, Gunney. He's a good man who just got caught up in a bad situation."

"Then we're talking about different men." Towers spoke softly. "I'm talking about truly evil men. Do we have anything else on Daud?"

Heath flicked through the files on the iPad. "The CIA made a connect to another name, but there's nothing concrete that links Rageh Daud to this other guy."

"Who?"

"A man named Parvez Daud."

"No relation?"

"None that can be found, but the CIA has picked up whispers that there is a connection through a man named Afrah. Parvez Daud was an ex-Somali soldier turned bandit. He abandoned the military and began looking out for himself. Judging by the file on him, banditry suited him well." Heath paused. "Until he got himself killed ten years ago."

"About the time Rageh Daud showed up in Mogadishu."

Heath grinned. "You caught that."

"I'm smarter than I look." Towers grinned back. "So Rageh Daud walked away from his father's business, found himself a straight civilian life, lost his family, and returned to what he knew."

"That's what it looks like to me."

"What about the CIA?"

"The agent I talked to believes that Rageh Daud was working some kind of angle. They're looking into a link between Daud and Haroun to see if Daud was working with the al-Shabaab and got caught with his hand in the cookie jar and that was why his family was targeted."

"Anything to support that?"

Heath shook his head. "Nothing that I can see here."

"Then they're playing guessing games. Doesn't sound like Daud was hiding."

"He had a job and stayed with it."

"The al-Shabaab could have found him there easily enough and taken him off the board."

"I agree."

"The way this shapes up, we've got one really bad man out there and a loose cannon gunning for him."

"And Indigo Rifle Platoon is going to be in the middle of it."

Towers toasted with his coffee cup. "Good times."

"We're going to have our jobs cut out for us keeping everybody alive."

"That's why they're sending Marines."

28

TWO DAYS AFTER the attack on the clinic, Bekah sat in the passenger seat of an armored Humvee and watched the countryside while Pike drove. Trudy and Tyler were in the back, with the latter on the M60 machine gun mounted on the rear deck. The heat beat down on them, and Bekah's fatigues were damp despite the air circulating through the vehicle. The MBITRs kept up a constant chatter between the fire teams responsible for reconning the area for the medical convoy a hundred yards to the left.

Most of the platoon was on edge. Two hundred plus miles out from Mogadishu and nearer to Kenya now, they were a long way from help if something went bad.

Pike looked totally at ease, though. He sat solid and calm behind the wheel as he steered through the uneven terrain. His eyes were hidden behind his dark sunglasses, and Bekah had no idea what he was thinking. She remembered how he had run toward her when the grenade had spilled out onto the ground at the medical clinic, arriving within a heartbeat instead of running from the danger. That had impressed her.

He was a hard guy to figure and didn't talk much. But he was there when she needed him. An interesting thing she had noticed was the tattoo that coiled around his neck, barely meeting Marine standards. The Corps was the strictest military branch for tattoos. She wanted to know what the tattoo depicted, but she knew she wasn't going to ask him.

Pain pulsed on the right side of Bekah's forehead. She'd caught a piece of flying shrapnel when the grenade had gone off. Other people had been wounded as well, but no one except the terrorist had died. She didn't know what had become of the boy who had tried to take the grenade into the clinic, but she hoped he was all right. The wound from the shrapnel had taken eleven stitches to close, but Matthew had told her he'd put them in close enough that there shouldn't be much of a scar left behind.

Bekah didn't worry about the scar. She still had two eyes, and she was still alive to go home to Travis. That was all that mattered.

She opened the Velcro tab on her left sleeve pocket and looked at the man's face there. Rageh Daud looked haunted and tired in the picture, and the white, uneven burn scarring stood out proudly against his dark skin.

"I don't think you're gonna memorize that face any more than you already have." Pike glanced over at her, and his lips twitched a little in a maybe smile.

"I know. I'm just trying to figure him out."

"What do you mean?"

Bekah thought about the briefing Lieutenant Bridger had delivered the previous night, detailing the mission's objectives and parameters. "This guy was on the straight and narrow till he lost his family."

"Then he went back to his old ways. It happens to a guy who doesn't have anything else to hang on to." Pike looked back at the terrain and concentrated on his driving. "A bad guy is a bad guy, Bekah. You don't change from that."

Bekah thought about Billy Roy and silently agreed. He'd never been responsible, and he never would be.

"Just stick to the program." Pike downshifted and eased through a gully. "Don't try to overthink this. Daud is a guy we gotta put down."

That left Bekah feeling unsettled. "Do you think people are that simple, Pike? Just black or white? No gray areas?"

"Yep. I know bad guys. I've been around them all my life."

Trudy leaned forward from the back. "How is it you know so much about bad guys?"

Pike flashed her a cold smile in the rearview mirror. "Because I'm a bad guy. Don't make the mistake of thinking otherwise. You'll only get disappointed."

Trudy didn't know what to say to that and leaned back in the seat. She went back to looking out the window.

A small chill crept over Bekah because she knew Pike was speaking the truth as he saw it. She'd sensed the darkness in him, but she didn't think he was as bleak as he believed he was. She turned her attention to their surroundings as well and absently listened to the chatter over the MBITRs, responding when she needed to check in.

★　★　★

The IDP camp sat near a slow trickle of water that wound through a small valley. According to the map Bekah had, the tributary was seasonal, probably only there now because of the rains a few days ago. On both sides of the stream, dome-shaped huts stood covered in colorful blankets, cargo tarps, and scraps of cloth. They looked like misshapen mushrooms that had sprouted up in wild abandon.

As the Marine vehicles approached, the people squatting outside the huts stood uncertainly, not knowing for sure what to expect. All of them wore ragged clothing and looked emaciated. A few men came out of the huts carrying single-shot rifles and machetes. None of them looked eager to fight, but they stood ready.

"Wow." Trudy leaned between the seats and gazed through the bug- and dust-encrusted windshield. "I don't think any-one was anticipating quite so many of them."

Looking out over the huts, Bekah estimated there were between three and four hundred people settled in the area. She knew there was no way the camp could have supported so many people if they were depending on foraging for food. There wasn't enough game and no crops to speak of. If it hadn't been for the routine deliveries of supplies, they would have all died of starvation or sickness by now.

"I guess the success of the camp has brought more of them here." Tyler stood beside the machine gun. "Others must have found out these guys were on a regular delivery schedule and decided to migrate."

They found hope here, and hope is a very powerful thing. Bekah knew the truth of that, and it was one of the things that kept her going—hope that Travis would turn out happy and healthy. But hope was something that threatened these people even more than the hardships they'd faced on their own. Whatever the numbers had been before the recent migration, the present population was putting even more of a strain on the camp's resources.

Bekah got out of the Humvee with her rifle in hand and watched as the scout vehicle rolled on ahead to meet with a small group of men coming from the camp. Two Marines and a Somali interpreter got out of the vehicle and talked to the camp representatives.

After a moment, Lieutenant Bridger's calm voice came over the MBITRs. "Okay, Marines, let's move in and get squared away. These people are depending on us."

★   ★   ★

The Marines took turns standing guard and unpacking some of the supplies they'd brought. In short order, the camp women turned out, laid fires, and hung large pots to cook an evening meal. Some of the children ran around and talked to the new arrivals, chattering away like magpies. Other children lay in the shade, stricken with disease and malnutrition.

Bekah helped set up the big tent Matthew Cline was going to use for his treatment center. One of the nurses organized the distribution of the medicines and medical supplies. Matthew and the other doctor, a younger guy named Keith Reilly, walked among the sick and injured, organizing them into groups to separate the more severe cases that needed immediate attention.

Once the tent was set up, Matthew moved his efforts inside. The sound of crying children and worried mothers filled the air. Bekah had just stopped to take a drink of water when Tyler approached her with a grim look on his face.

Bekah turned to face him. "Something wrong?"

"Yeah." Tyler looked pale. "Doc asked if you could come give a hand with one of the patients."

"He's got three nurses." Bekah had been looking forward to sitting down and catching her breath. The smell of the beans and rice and stew floating up from the cook pots was enticing. She was also looking forward to rack time later that evening. She and her team were going to be standing early watch the next morning, so getting to bed early was important.

"All the nurses are busy tending patients. And this doesn't need a nurse."

Curious, Bekah walked over to the medical tent and stepped through the flap. The tent was large enough that four examination beds had been set up. All of the beds were filled. Portable containers of medicines and supplies sat around the outer edge. Electric lamps, powered by generators mounted on the trucks, lit the interior.

Across the tent, Matthew stood talking earnestly to a young woman holding a baby to her chest. The woman was shaking her head and pushing Matthew away.

Bekah crossed over to Matthew. "Tyler said you wanted me." She looked more closely at the woman and the baby.

The woman looked like she was all of sixteen or seventeen,

not much more than a girl and at least ten pounds under-weight. Tears streamed down her face as she continued to shake her head in denial. The baby was small, surely not much more than a newborn, and lay with its face against her breast.

Matthew spoke in a whisper. "I need to get her out of here."

"What's wrong?"

"I can't do anything for her."

"Yes, you can." The young woman spoke in broken English. "Make my son well."

Matthew looked at Bekah, and she saw the sadness in his eyes. "Her baby has passed. He's been gone for a couple days. The other women tried to take him away from her as well, but she won't let go."

Bekah's heart chilled, but she kept control of herself.

"I need the bed space. There are a lot of kids out there who need the help I can give." Matthew shook his head. "I don't want to sound coldhearted, God knows I don't, but there's nothing I can do for the baby."

"Yes." The woman struck Matthew with a balled-up fist. "You can make my son well." As she leaned forward again, the baby's head twisted and exposed his face. The tiny eyes were open and unseeing.

Bekah took a deep breath, but that only made things worse as the smells of alcohol, cleansers, and body odor filled her nose. She breathed more shallowly. She spoke to Matthew. "Does she not have any family here?"

Matthew shook his head. "I was told that she wandered in a few days ago. The baby had a fever. Some of the women tried to help her with the baby, but there was nothing they could do. She has no one."

Bekah faced the woman, stepping in between Matthew and her. "Do you speak much English?"

The woman calmed somewhat. She cupped the back of her baby's head and brought it back to her breast. "Yes. A little."

"My name is Bekah. What's your name?"

"Varisha."

"Varisha, I wish I could have met you under better circumstances. I truly do." Bekah thought desperately, searching for words to say, and tried to imagine what her granny would do. But she knew. Granny would tell the truth. In the end, that was all there was. Just the truth.

"Make him help."

Bekah shook her head. "He can't help."

"He can. Make him."

"Varisha, your baby is gone."

"No, this is not true. He is just sick."

Taking out her phone, Bekah brought up a picture of Travis. "I'm a momma too, Varisha. This is my boy. His name is Travis, and I love him with all my heart. I would not ever want to lose him. I can only imagine what you're going through."

"My baby is just sick. This man lies."

"No." Bekah put her phone away. "Your baby is gone, and you're gonna have to let him go. You can't hang on to him." Despite her control, tears slipped down Bekah's cheeks. She took hold of the girl's elbow and pulled gently. "Please. Come with me."

"No. I want this man to help my baby." Varisha's voice was hoarse.

"Varisha, look at me." Bekah locked eyes with the woman. "There are other babies out there that need help. The doctor can help those babies. But he can't help yours. You need to let him do what he can for those children so they don't end up like your little one."

The woman cried and shook as she held her dead child. "No. *No.*" Her words turned into a plaintive cry that tore at Bekah's heart.

"You know this is true. You know your baby is gone. You need to be strong now. Let me help. We need to find a resting place for your son." Quietly, gently, Bekah pulled the young woman and her dead child into her embrace. Reluctantly at first, the woman came to her, then finally clung to her fiercely. Slowly, Bekah led the grieving mother from the room.

★   ★   ★

On a small hillside under the moonlight, Bekah dug a tiny grave for the child while his mother sat on the ground and quietly rocked him. Bekah's muscles ached from the labor, and her heart felt broken. She didn't know how much longer she could go on, but the grave needed to be deep enough.

"Need a hand?"

Startled, Bekah brushed hair out of her face and looked up to find Heath Bridger holding a shovel.

He looked uncomfortable. "I was asking around for you when I saw you'd gone off without your team."

Bekah nodded. "It's my fault. Not theirs. I asked them

to give me some privacy. Under the circumstances, they understood."

Heath nodded. "So do I, but I also know you're tired and worn out. And all this work can't be doing that head wound any good."

The pounding in Bekah's forehead had been almost non-stop. She'd felt it with every bite the shovel took from the earth.

"If you don't mind, maybe I could help out."

Bekah looked at him gratefully. If he'd simply come along and tried to take over, she knew she would have gotten angry with him. But he had asked permission. He was her commanding officer and she'd disobeyed some of his direct orders, and he wasn't reprimanding her for that either. He was there as a man.

"Yes sir. I would appreciate it." Bekah climbed up from the grave and let him step into it.

Heath worked carefully and respectfully, taking time with the task and not just getting through it. He squared the sides of the grave better than Bekah had been doing, and he went deeper than she thought she'd have been able to manage on her own.

When he was finished, he climbed up from the grave without a word and stepped to one side. He leaned on the shovel, sweat gleaming on his face. He didn't look like a lawyer then. He didn't even truly look like a Marine. He looked like a man who was in over his head and was still trying to do the right thing. He waited silently, like he had all the time in the world when she knew he didn't.

Quietly, Bekah coaxed Varisha into surrendering her dead son. Together they bundled the tiny body in one of the new blankets from the cargo that had been brought in the trucks. On their knees, they reached a long way into the grave to lay the body on the earth.

The woman wept on her knees, wiping tears helplessly with her hands as she shook and shivered. Gently as they could, Bekah and Heath shoveled the earth in on top of the baby. When they were finished, they packed the ground down tightly.

Putting the shovel aside, Bekah joined the woman on her knees and took one of her hands. Heath hesitated for just a moment, then dropped to his knees on Varisha's other side and sat there in silence as well until Varisha began to speak.

The bereft mother prayed for a long time, and Bekah didn't know how she could do such a thing. Yet the words flowed from her.

Touched by the raw emotion, Bekah silently gave thanks that her son was healthy and safe, and she asked that she be rejoined with him soon. And it surprised her how soothing that small prayer felt.

★   ★   ★

Back at the camp, Bekah found a group of women willing to take care of the grieving mother. They welcomed Varisha with open arms, and this time she went with them. Before she left, though, she gave Bekah a hug, then tried to speak, but couldn't.

Bekah couldn't speak either. She hugged the woman back and returned to the Marine group. Heath fell into step beside her.

"That was an amazing thing you did back there." His voice was soft but sounded tired.

"Helping that woman put her baby in the ground?" Bekah knew she sounded angry, but she couldn't help herself. She *was* angry.

"Yes. The Marines don't train you for something like that."

"That's because we're supposed to be saving lives, not burying victims."

"We are saving lives." Heath took her by the elbow, stopping her in her tracks. Then he nodded out toward the camp. "Look at all those people. There are a lot of lives we're saving out there today. We don't get to save them all, Bekah. That's just not in the cards. And the ones we don't get to save? We'll grieve over them and sometimes help bury them . . . and we'll remember them. That's all we can do, and if people stop doing that, then the world will fall apart."

Bekah folded her arms over her chest. "I know." She took a shuddering breath. His words mixed with Matthew Cline's and her granny's, and she knew they were all true. It felt as though pieces of her heart were locking into place and some of her worries and doubts were fading. Everyone had the same message. So why wasn't she listening better? "I tell myself that nearly every day."

"Have you eaten?"

She shook her head.

"Me neither."

"After that, I don't have much of an appetite."

"Then eat because you need to, because you do need it. You'll feel better once you've eaten. We've got a lot to do tomorrow, and it's going to come early. Let's go find dinner."

Bekah knew that was something else her granny would have said, and it was good advice. So she nodded and trailed after Heath as he headed for one of the cook fires.

29

DAUD SAT HUNKERED at the campfire and watched the boy sleeping on a blanket on the ground beside him. Gently, Daud picked up a corner of the blanket and tossed it over the boy, covering him from the night's chill.

Over the days since he had found the boy and brought him away from the tree where his campmates had been left hanging like grisly trophies, Kufow had never left Daud's side. The boy did not speak except when spoken to, and his eyes remained haunted.

Daud thought maybe some of that trauma would one day leave the boy's mind, but there would be scars. They just wouldn't be as prominent as the burn scarring on Daud's face. In a way, though, Daud's scars were easier to carry. People saw them and recognized that something had happened and respected his desire to be left alone. The boy would not have that built-in defense and warning system.

Sometimes when Daud watched the boy, he thought of Ibrahim and felt guilty. The loss of his son pained him, and having Kufow there hurt even more. But there was a solace in having the boy with him. Caring for Kufow gave Daud something beyond plotting revenge and attacks. He had never thought he would feel anything like that again.

"How is he?" Afrah stood on the other side of the fire. The giant looked like he'd been carved from the night sky above him.

"He is sleeping." Daud got up easily and walked a short distance from the fire so their voices would not disturb Kufow's slumber. "He does not always sleep because there are too many nightmares."

Afrah walked beside Daud. Around them, men lounged at their own fires and talked. Some of them slept under the cargo trucks and pickups. Others stood guard beyond them at perimeter posts. They had been traveling hard these past few days, and they had occasionally spotted some of Haroun's out-riders. Twice they had taken down scouting patrols and killed the men, then siphoned their petrol to use in their own vehicles. The whole time, the boy had watched in stone-faced silence.

They had never spoken of the incidents, and Daud didn't know if the boy felt justified in the killings or if he was further horrified by the violence. He had no way of knowing.

"We all have our nightmares, my friend." Afrah came to a stop beside Daud. "No one is safe from them in this place."

"I know."

"Have you thought about what you are going to do with the boy?"

Daud studied Afrah's hard face and tried to figure out what was on the big man's mind. "What do you mean?"

Afrah hesitated as if choosing his words carefully. "This thing that we are doing, it is very dangerous. We are hunted men, Rageh. Haroun and the al-Shabaab search for us, and we have no allies among the TFG or the Westerners. They, too, would kill us. Or lock us up. I am concerned about the boy."

"As am I."

Slowly, Afrah nodded. "Do you think, perhaps, we endanger him by bringing him with us?"

By *we*, Daud knew Afrah meant *you*. For a moment a spark of anger sizzled within him, and he almost let his temper soar. Then he realized he did not have the heart for it. "The boy is fine. While he is with us, we can feed him and see to his needs. No one else out here can do that."

"Of course." Afrah put his large hand on Daud's shoulder. "I would only not wish to see you hurt again. We lead very dangerous lives. If we care too much, we will stumble. I prefer our way of seizing our lives from those who would take them from us or those who would put us in boxes and feed us whenever they wished. If they even continued to remember us. We have had enough of that. I prefer a full belly when I go to sleep at night."

"Then we shall keep doing what we are doing."

Afrah nodded. "I wish you good sleep. I will see you in the morning."

Daud watched Afrah walk into the darkness away from the campfire and mostly disappear. Only a shadow among shadows remained. Daud did not like being questioned about the boy because he knew no one would care for Kufow the way he did. The boy was safer now than he had been his whole life. Daud refused to believe anything else.

He gazed up at the stars for a time and crowded his anger into the recesses of his mind where it would bother him no further. Then he returned to his campfire. As he watched the boy sleep, he thought of Ibrahim, of the way he had held and cherished his son, and of the way Ibrahim had grown into a tall and straight likeness of Rageh.

Although he tried to keep it at bay, Daud thought of the hard way his son had died too, and that pain ate through him like a cancer. Gently, he pulled the blanket higher over the sleeping boy and watched him breathe until those old memories finally lay at rest again.

★   ★   ★

Daud and his band arrived at the next camp early the following morning. They hoped to replace some of the men lost in the last confrontation with Haroun's people. Every time they had stopped somewhere, they had gotten new recruits. Daud expected this stop would be no less successful. But something about the elder's response put Daud's senses on edge.

The camp elder was in his early sixties, a gnarled little man who depended on a shepherd's crook to help him walk. The man's pungent body odor was strong enough to make Daud breathe through his mouth.

Kufow stood at his customary place beside Daud and wore the bulletproof vest and helmet Daud had gotten from the UN cargo and forced the boy to wear. As usual, the boy didn't speak, only watched with cold, hard eyes as the negotiations were made.

"I have medicines and food on these trucks." Daud's pitch was always the same, simple and direct.

The elder gazed at the trucks, but his attention snapped back to Daud. He spoke quietly, gingerly, and his voice sounded strained. "I see that you do, but we are poor and have nothing to trade."

"I ask nothing in trade." That was the deal Daud always made with the camps. Then he selected young men who were willing to come with him when he left. When he met up with black market dealers in various locations, he traded the goods for petrol. So far his group had managed to meet their needs. Men could be purchased so much more cheaply than fuel.

"Then you are most welcome." The elder waved to the center of the camp. "Join us."

Something about the old man's behavior set Daud on edge. Usually the camps were not so willing to accept visits from outsiders even when they arrived in peacekeeping vehicles. Daud and his men were not Westerners and did not wear uniforms. The villagers' first impression was always the truth: that they were bandits and outcasts.

Daud looked over the village, trying to figure out what made him so ill at ease. Everything was still, and the camp dwellers stared nervously at the trucks. That wasn't anything new. Strangers were always dangerous in Somalia.

Then the boy seized Daud's hand and yanked, pointing to movement in the scraggly bushes behind one of the *aqals*.

In that brief glimpse, Daud spotted a man carrying an assault rifle. He turned to his men.

"Get back on the trucks!"

Because most of them lacked training, many of Daud's men hesitated a moment before moving. Bullets sprayed over them, taking some of them down immediately.

"Traitor!" Daud lifted his rifle and aimed at the elder.

The old man held his hands up before him. "No! Please! The al-Shabaab forced us to—"

The burst from Daud's AK-47 silenced the man and punched him backward, sprawling his body across the ground. Turning, Daud caught the boy's elbow and hurried him toward the pickup where Afrah was already sliding behind the wheel.

Just when Kufow had almost reached the pickup, he suddenly went down. Daud reached for the boy and grabbed his arm, thinking that a round had hit the Kevlar armor and knocked him down. Then he saw the bright blood streaming from the boy's right side where the body armor had ridden up high.

"No!" Daud watched in horror as Kufow tried weakly to get to his feet, clawing as though trying to swim to the pickup.

Getting control of himself, aware of the bullets punching into the pickup and tearing craters into the ground, Daud slid his rifle over his shoulder and reached down for the boy, lifting him in his arms. He placed Kufow inside the truck, on the floorboard so the body of the vehicle would better protect him. Daud closed the door and leaped into the pickup's bed.

One of his men on a machine gun poured a torrent of 7.62mm rounds over the camp. Gunmen as well as people who lived in the camp died or went down in a bloody wave.

Daud slammed the pickup cab with the flat of his hand. "Go! Go!" Then he braced himself as Afrah engaged the transmission and the rear wheels spun and grabbed traction. Daud lifted his AK-47 and added his fire to that of his men as they hosed the camp with high-velocity death.

A number of tents flew to pieces as jeeps tore through from within. Evidently the gunmen had been there long enough to hide their vehicles. The jeeps roared over the dead bodies of the camp dwellers as well as fallen comrades.

A bullet pierced the head of the man working the machine gun and emptied his skull in a rush that threw blood over Daud. The man feeding the ammunition belt to the weapon froze in alarm as the dead body sprawled across him. More bullets ripped through the pickup's rear window and shattered the glass. Afrah kept the vehicle on course, though, so Daud knew the man still lived.

Dropping his assault rifle, Daud moved across the bouncing pickup bed to the machine gun. He gripped the weapon, found the trigger, and swung the heavy barrel to cover the lead pursuing jeep. "Feed the ammunition!" He kicked out with a leg and knocked the corpse from the other man. "Feed the ammunition or I will kill you myself!"

The man worked the belts, keeping them coming quickly from the containers as Daud fired long bursts. It took him a moment to find the range, but when he did, he pelted the jeep unmercifully. The rounds cored through the radiator and chopped into the hood. Some of them skimmed across the flat surface and tore into the men inside the vehicle.

The driver's head vanished in a crimson burst, and the jeep lurched out of control and smacked into another pursuer. The two vehicles jockeyed back and forth for a moment, until the driverless jeep hit a rocky outcrop that caused it to overturn on the other vehicle. Both of them became hopelessly tangled.

Daud fired into the wrecked vehicles repeatedly, managing to stay on target despite the way the pickup beneath him jounced across the terrain. Just as Afrah swung the wheel hard to take a sudden turn back onto the trail they'd followed to the camp, the two jeeps blew up. Daud didn't know if the explosion was caused by the bullets creating sparks that ignited the fuel or if one of the men onboard had dropped a grenade. Either way, a sudden fireball enveloped both jeeps in a roil of orange flames and black smoke.

Tracking immediately, Daud lowered the gunsights over another pursuing jeep and squeezed the trigger. Brass spilled out of the machine gun in a sun-kissed torrent. A few of the superheated casings brushed his cheek but he ignored them, focusing on his enemies. He kept seeing the blood that had spilled from beneath Kufow's body armor, and he cursed himself for not making the boy stay inside the pickup. Kufow would have been safer there.

A rocket warhead landed just ahead of them, and Afrah swerved to miss the crater it left as the horrendous *boom!* echoed around them. Daud hung on to the machine gun grimly as the pickup swayed and skipped across the ground, momentarily losing traction. Then the vehicle settled down again and ran flat out.

"Rageh!" Afrah shouted through the open window and slapped his hand against the door. "Over here! On this side! Quickly!"

Daud swung the machine gun around to face the newest threat.

Another al-Shabaab jeep, this one driven by men wearing the red-and-white-checked *keffiyehs*, swooped in from the left. Just as Daud laid eyes on them, the machine gunner mounted on their rear deck opened fire. Bullets cut the air around Daud's head, skimmed over the top of the cab, and thudded into the side of the pickup bed. One of them punched through the bed and hammered into the machine gun feeder's chest, bursting it in an arterial spray.

Focused on his enemy, Daud swayed and bent his knees, locking himself in behind the machine gun. He aimed low and opened fire, slightly leading the jeep at first, then inching back. The 7.62mm rounds chopped into the jeep's front-passenger tire, then steadily climbed upward, knocking holes in the jeep's body and exploding the windshield.

The tire shredded by the machine gun bullets came apart, and the metal rim dug into the ground. When the rim caught the ground firmly enough, the jeep's momentum flipped the vehicle over, pancaking it onto the unforgiving ground. A couple men flew free, but the rest were buried beneath the wrecked vehicle that suddenly went up in flames. One of the men staggered to his feet. Daud took aim and fired through the remainder of the ammunition belt loaded into the weapon. The rounds struck the al-Shabaab man and knocked him backward.

Dropping to the pickup bed, Daud shoved the dead man aside and opened another ammunition box. He hauled out the heavy belt and loaded it into the machine gun, slamming down the receiver and working the first round into position.

Breathing rapidly, Daud glanced at the boy through the shattered back window and saw that Kufow remained curled up on the floorboard. Blood covered the boy's side and pooled on the dirty floor. Daud cursed, then turned his attention to the countryside.

A thick cloud of dust hung behind them, and the whining roar of the pickup engine filled his ears. Through the dust, he barely made out the other trucks racing after them. He almost pulled the trigger to fire on them before he realized they were part of his group.

One other al-Shabaab vehicle trailed them, but it quickly gave up the chase when bullets caromed off its front end. A moment later, one of Daud's men—probably one of his father's old crew—got off a shot with an RPG-7, and the rocket turned the pursuing pickup into a bonfire that rolled listlessly across the ground.

Satisfied they were no longer in immediate danger, Daud threw a leg over the side of the pickup bed and stepped down onto the running board. He swung the door open just enough to crawl inside. Daud unbuckled the body armor from the boy's thin body, then cut off the boy's shirt with a knife. Gently, he picked up the boy and held him, pressing his hands against the boy's wounds.

There was one in front and one in back, proof that the round had gone through. Thankfully the bullet had been a small round, a 5.56mm instead of the larger 7.62mm. The exit was much larger than the entry.

Kufow breathed raggedly and was barely conscious, a result of shock.

Afrah looked at Daud. "How is the boy?"

"Alive. As soon as we can, we need to stop so I can tend to his wounds."

Afrah nodded.

Daud held the boy and whispered over and over into his ear. "Stay with me. You will be all right. Just stay with me."

But he knew not to put any faith in such words. He had told Ibrahim the same thing up until the moment his son had died.

★　★　★

An hour later, they pulled off the trail and followed a creek bed that had gone dry months ago. The earth was baked hard and withstood even the heavy weight of the larger cargo trucks.

Carrying the boy in his arms, Daud found shade under a small copse of trees, then had Afrah add to it by draping a cargo tarp over the trees to extend and complete the shade.

"Get some antiseptic from the trucks, Afrah."

Kufow looked at Daud, and fear shined sharply in the boy's dark eyes. He panted like a dog in the heat. "Am I going to die?"

Daud shook his head even though he didn't know the answer to that. "No. I will not let you die." *Not again.*

"May I have some water?"

"Not yet." Daud couldn't let the boy have water until he knew the extent of the injuries, and there was no way he would know how badly Kufow had been torn up internally.

"I am so thirsty."

"I know. Be strong."

When Afrah brought the antiseptic back, along with a painkiller and a bundle of sterile wipes, Daud injected the boy, waited till the anesthetic took hold, then tenderly cleaned both wounds. By the time he'd finished, the boy was asleep. That worried him because Ibrahim had slipped away in his sleep—gone between breaths. But the boy's breath and heartbeat remained strong enough.

Drenched in sweat, almost numb from the emotions swirling around inside him, Daud sat back. "I will need a needle and surgical thread."

Afrah went to get those things and returned.

When Daud had been a boy, his father had taught him how to sew up wounds and bandage men. On four different occasions, Daud had sewn up his father, and there had been dozens of other instances with the men. Afrah had worn stitches Daud had put in at least three times. Once, Daud had sewn up his own leg to prove to his father that he was a man. He was nine, and the wound had come from the knife of a man who had tried to kill him. His father had killed the man.

Slowly, Daud inserted the needle and pulled it through the flesh. He cut the string, then pulled the flesh together and tied off the stitch. Over and over he did this, putting six in the boy's back and thirty-two in his stomach just over his hip bone to stop the bleeding. When he finished, there was only a little blood.

"Did the bullet miss his organs?" Afrah had watched the whole process in silence.

"I do not know." Daud put the needle away, and only then did his hands begin to shake.

"Then the boy's fate is in the hands of God."

"No." Daud shook his head. "His fate is in my hands. I do not trust God. God has not cared about me. He has not cared about this boy. I am all that he has."

"Then what are you going to do? There could be something badly wrong with him, and you would not know until he was dead. In this heat, under these conditions, infection can easily set in."

Daud knew that. If all the boy's organs were in good shape, the risk of infection was the next greatest threat.

"We need to take him to a doctor." Daud took the map from his pocket. "There is an IDP camp on this route that is supposed to have medical personnel. We will go there."

Afrah was quiet for a moment. "If we go there, Rageh, we run the risk of being recognized."

"Among the crowds of sick and wounded people, we will not be noticed." Daud put the map away. "We will succeed at this, Afrah. I will not allow anything less."

30

KORFA HAROUN STOOD atop the old stone fort that an archaeologist had told him dated back to the sixteenth century. The archaeologist, an Englishman who traded in illegally obtained antiquities, had been excited when Haroun had invited him and his crew out to the place.

According to the Englishman, the fort had probably been built by Muslim warriors during the wars with the Abyssinian Christians from what was now known as Ethiopia. The fort had been picked over in the intervening centuries, and no treasure remained.

But that wasn't what Haroun had told the man. The Englishman had been convinced that Haroun wanted to divest himself of some rare antiquities. Haroun had salted the man's interest by purchasing other antiquities and passing them off as items he had discovered himself. The man had been greedy enough to immediately believe the story.

All Haroun had wanted was the Englishman's client list. The bodies of the Englishman and his retinue had been left out in the parched land, and jackals had feasted on them.

Since that time, Haroun had used the fort as a retreat when things became too dangerous in Mogadishu, as they had been since the al-Shabaab had withdrawn from the city. From that place of protection, he and his men could strike as they wished.

The structure sat on a low hill that provided a 360-degree view of the surrounding land. No one could approach them without being seen, and the wall around the fort—over twelve feet tall and three feet thick—was largely intact. Only a few breaches existed, and those he had ordered packed with rubble to forestall attempts by nomads or anyone else to gain entry.

A covered tunnel ran from the outer wall to an inner wall, providing access to a courtyard only through two points of entry. This inner courtyard held a large main building and two smaller ones. Haroun and his men slept in the three-story main building and used the smaller ones as a storehouse and as a confinement area for the prisoners and women they sometimes took.

Water was not a problem at the fort due to the artesian well that had never gone dry despite the worst summers Haroun had seen. The old engineers had found good water, and their construction had been magnificent.

Eleven years ago, when Haroun found the fort, a group of nomads had laid claim to the place. Their bodies had been the first Haroun had ordered dumped out onto the land. Since that time, and even since the time of the English archaeologist, several bodies had been added to that number.

He knelt on his prayer rug and asked for continued success against the nonbelievers and his enemies. Islam demanded obedience, and he would not be remiss by breaking those tenets in front of his men. When he was finished, he pulled the rug over his shoulder and walked through the courtyard. New "temporary" brides awaited him inside, and he had an appetite for them.

He would have gone to the women had he not been troubled. Of late, food and other materials had become an issue. The constant raiding by the scar-faced man plagued him. Haroun didn't know the man's reason for doing what he did, and he didn't care to know it. He only wanted to know the date of the man's death—the sooner the better.

As he crossed the courtyard, Haroun heard the sound of engines and paused where he was to look at the east gate in the inner wall. The huge wooden gates swung open as the guards pulled them back.

Haroun knew that whoever approached did so because they were allowed. But his hand snaked under his *jellabiya* to close around the butt of the American Colt 45 revolver he'd taken from another unfortunate business partner who had considered himself a cowboy. His bones, too, bleached in the sun not far away.

Three jeeps sped into the courtyard and came to a stop in a cloud of dust. The men got out, many of them wearing bloodstained clothing, but there were far fewer of them than there should have been, and five of the jeeps were missing.

Qaim, the fierce man with the hawk nose who had been head of Haroun's warriors for the last eight years, approached. The blood on his clothing didn't appear to be his own because he walked easily over to join Haroun.

"Things did not go as we had wished." Sand and dust threaded through his beard and mustache and made him look older than he was. His lean face and high cheekbones made his appearance stark.

"What happened?"

"The burn-faced man escaped us."

Anger flared through Haroun. He was tired of this man and his games. No one should have been able to take so much, dare so often, and yet live so long. "How did such a thing occur?"

"The boy with him spotted one of my men before we sprung the trap. The burn-faced man and his compatriots did not enter the camp as we had hoped."

"You pursued?"

"We did, and we lost several vehicles in doing so."

Haroun turned to walk away because he did not want to lose self-control in front of his men or demean Qaim in any way. The man was too valuable to him, too savvy in combat, and too willing to kill. The burn-faced man had gotten away. The man had luck on his side. But only for the moment. Haroun knew that he served the will of God, and that would triumph in the end.

"There is something else that might aid us in seeking this burn-faced man."

Haroun paused. "What?"

"I recognized the boy who was with this man."

"Who was he?"

"Do you remember the camp where we killed all the people who lived there and left the boy beneath their bodies hanging in the trees?"

Haroun did remember. That had been the first time he had been so inspired to strike fear into the heart of an enemy. Unfortunately, this was the first time he'd had an enemy so tenacious as this man Daud.

"I remember the boy."

"The burn-faced man had the boy with him. He knows we are hunting him."

"I intended that he know it." Haroun understood that fear could also make the man more wary. "What good does it do to know the boy was there?"

"The boy was badly wounded. I saw him go down, and I saw the blood cover him. During that battle, with his life in the balance, the burn-faced man picked up the boy from the ground and placed him within the vehicle they escaped in."

"The boy was not dead?"

"He was not then. But his wound was bad. He may have died shortly thereafter." Qaim licked his chapped lips. "I was thinking, however, that if the boy still lives, the burn-faced man might seek out medical attention for him. There are not many places nearby where he can hope to find help for a bullet wound."

Haroun knew what Qaim referred to then. "The camp where the Marines have brought in fresh supplies and medical staff." That place waited like a fat prize. He had lusted after it as well, wishing not only to steal everything of value, but also to crush the foothold the Westerners had made in helping the displaced people there.

Too many of those people were nomads and might discover Haroun's operation and where the fort was. And the camp was growing, its threat increasing.

"This man might take the boy there." Haroun pulled at his beard.

"So I was thinking."

"Alert our people there. Let them know to watch for this boy and that burn-faced man."

Qaim bowed his head and hurried away.

Haroun continued his walk toward the main building, and his appetite for his new brides increased as he considered his coming success.

31

BEKAH SAT IN THE DARKNESS away from the campfire with a blanket wrapped around her shoulders. She had divided her day between patrol and helping out in the medical ward. Although she hadn't wanted it to, her attention kept drifting to that grave on the low hill not so distant from the camp. She couldn't help thinking of the small body lying within the earth.

She wanted to be home. She wanted to be in Granny's kitchen and listening to Travis ask her question after question. In all her life, she'd never known anyone who could ask as many questions as her boy. She didn't think she'd ever been so curious at his age. Granny always insisted she'd been a handful, though.

She spooned up more rice and beans and thought about how much better Granny's tasted than what she was eating now. The conversation had always been better back home too, and there had been the special nights she and Granny had watched *The Amazing Race* or old *Perry Mason* reruns. Bekah missed those moments terribly as she thought about that little grave.

The loss of that child stung horribly. Earlier in the day, she'd gone to check on Varisha. The young girl had acted dazed and disconsolate, but the other women were able to take care of her now, making sure she was eating and resting. Something like this would take time. Bekah knew that was what Granny would say, and she'd go on to tell her that nothing could substitute for that time. Varisha and her son took up so much of Bekah's attention that even when she tried to keep her mind on the good she was doing at the camp, her thoughts veered back to the suffering mother.

We are God's handiwork, created in Christ Jesus to do good works, which God prepared in advance for us to do.

Bekah wasn't sure how that old memory cropped up. It was one of Granny's favorite verses from the Bible—Ephesians 2:10. She'd made Bekah memorize it when she was a small girl and felt frustrated by life. That was just something to say, though. Bekah had never felt anything really happen when she'd said it. Now, though, as she reflected on all she'd been through since arriving in Somalia, she felt closer to that truth.

She finished the bowl of rice and beans, set it aside, and looked over her team. Tyler and Pike were passed out on the ground, and Trudy wrote in the journal she'd been keeping. She also wrote letters to her class, to let them know she was all right and thinking of them.

Bekah felt guilty watching her because she hadn't written Travis or Granny in days. She owed them a letter. As she reached to retrieve her pack, she saw Heath walking her direction. She started to get to her feet.

"At ease, Marine."

"Thank you, sir."

Heath had his iPad in hand. He pointed at a place on the ground beside Bekah. "May I sit?"

"Of course."

Heath folded himself and sat easily. "I've been studying the satellite maps of the area and found something interesting." He tapped the iPad and brought up a map. "There's a structure, looks like an ancient fortification, about twenty, twenty-five klicks south-southwest of our present position."

Bekah studied the glowing monitor. The fortification, if that was what it was, didn't look clear on the map. "Are you sure that's a fort?"

Heath shook his head. "Nope. But I keep thinking about Haroun and Daud. Those guys must each have someplace they're disappearing to in this area. I thought maybe you and Indigo Seven could take a quick run up that way in the morning and do a brief recon. Two teams, in and out."

"Sure."

"It should be pretty safe there and back. We don't have reports of any hostile activity in this immediate area. You guys should be able to make it round-trip within a few hours. And you can maintain radio contact."

"Yes sir. When do you want us to leave?"

"A half hour before dawn. That should put you at your

objective just about first light." Heath tapped the iPad. "Time it right, you can set up somewhere to the east of the site. That will put the sun in the eyes of anyone out there. If there is anyone. Then you can report back."

"Yes sir."

"I've pulled your people out of rotation for tonight. Get a good night's sleep and start early."

"Yes sir."

Heath stood. "This should give you a chance to get some distance from what happened last night, Bekah."

Bekah smiled at him, knowing he'd noticed her watching the grave site. She felt awkward and insecure about it, but she also felt relieved that she was going to get a chance to be away from the sick children and all the suffering going on at the camp.

"Thank you, sir."

"Just be careful. Don't take any chances, and get back home."

"Yes sir." Bekah watched him walk away and couldn't help noticing how broad his shoulders were and how self-confident he seemed. Lieutenant Heath Bridger was shaping up a lot differently than she'd expected.

★   ★   ★

The next morning, Bekah woke twelve minutes before she'd scheduled one of the night guards to wake her. She lay there for a few moments, enjoying the warmth of her sleeping bag just a little longer, and waved the Marine off before he reached her.

Then she went to wake the rest of her team. Pike was already awake and dressed, a cup of steaming coffee in his hand. He nodded at her and reached to shake Tyler's shoulder. The other man woke readily enough, but he wasn't happy about it.

Trudy woke as well and took a deep sniff of her uniform blouse. "I can't wait to get back to base. This is too long without a shower, people. Pretty soon I won't need an M4 to defend myself."

Bekah grinned at that but refrained from saying anything. She didn't care for the grungy state she was in either, but it couldn't be helped. This far out, there was precious little water to spare. The best they could manage was cleaning themselves with baby wipes, and even that was an extravagance.

Within a few minutes, they'd grabbed breakfast MREs and climbed into the Humvee. Indigo Seven was right on their heels.

Bekah took her place in the passenger seat while Pike slid behind the steering wheel. He turned over the engine and it caught on the first try. Then they were headed out of the camp. Bekah locked her assault rifle beside Pike's as they bounced over the terrain. The vehicle's lights cut through the darkness, but the eastern sky was already starting to lighten.

★   ★   ★

By the time full morning hit, the two Humvees were in place east of the fortification. The heat of the day was already starting to bear down on them.

"Looks like the lieutenant was right about the fort." Pike

lay on the ground beside Bekah and held a pair of binoculars to his face.

"Yeah." Bekah studied the structure and was amazed at how it looked up on the hill. If she'd stayed in Oklahoma, if her marriage with Billy Roy had worked out, she'd never have seen anything like this. The most she would have hoped for were occasional trips to Dallas, maybe a vacation or two to Branson, Missouri.

When she'd been in high school, she'd enjoyed the history classes all right. Stories about people living in different parts of the world were fascinating, but that sense of timelessness had never truly touched her. Oklahoma had only been a state a little over a hundred years. That building on the hilltop was—according to the intel Heath had sent—nearly five times that.

The al-Shabaab troops standing guard on the fort were new.

Bekah took a Marine-issue high-speed digital camera from her kit and snapped pictures of the fort and the men. She wished they could get a look inside the fort to see the extent of the manpower. Judging from the number of vehicles they watched arriving and leaving, there were a lot of people.

After a few more pictures, she put the camera back in her pack. "We need to get going. We've probably pressed our luck long enough out here. We hang around too long, we're gonna get seen."

Pike nodded, but the thought of getting seen didn't seem to bother him too much. "A place like that? It's gonna be hard to bring down."

"That's why we're gonna wait for backup. Our first objective is to keep that camp safe." Bekah withdrew slowly till they were on the other side of the small hill they'd used for cover. She got to her feet and headed back to the two waiting Humvees.

As she reached the vehicle, her MBITR flared to life. "Indigo Eight, do you read?"

Recognizing Heath's voice, Bekah keyed the transmit button immediately. "Affirmative, Indigo Leader. I read you five by five."

Over the connection, shots sounded plainly amid screams of frightened people.

"The camp's under attack. We need you back here ASAP, but you're going to have to be careful. They're all around us."

Bekah pulled herself into the seat and reached for the safety harness just as Pike pressed the ignition button and got the Humvee into gear. "On our way."

32

DURING THE NIGHT, the boy got worse. Daud watched over him the whole time and was happy to see that the wounds had stopped seeping blood. However, a fever had set in, plaguing the boy with sweats and then chills, with precious little rest in between.

By morning, Daud felt he had little time to act if he was to save the boy's life. He called Afrah to him.

"I am going to take him in."

Afrah looked at Daud for a moment. "Into the medical camp?"

"Yes. There is no choice. His fever climbs steadily. If I don't do something for him, he will die."

"You do not know that."

Calmly, Daud pulled back the bandage from the wound on the boy's stomach. The flesh was dark and angry with infection, and the swelling strained at the wound enough that he feared it might burst open.

Afrah sighed. "If you go into the medical camp, they will recognize you." He touched his own face.

Daud shook his head. "I can disguise my face with bandages enough to keep them from recognizing me. With so many people scarred by the struggles that sweep this land, do you truly think I will stick out any more than another man with burns? Especially in a medical facility? No. They will only think that I am another of our country's walking wounded." He looked at the boy. "But he needs medical attention, Afrah. He needs more than I can give him."

"We could all go."

"No. Only the wounded shall accompany me. That way there will be less attention paid to us." There were two other men who needed medical attention. One of them had a bullet in his shoulder that Daud hadn't been able to get to, and the other had a broken thigh that needed a proper setting if he was going to keep the use of the limb. "The boy and our men need help."

"I know, but I fear for you." Afrah dropped a heavy hand on Daud's shoulder. "Should these Americans realize you were the one who killed the UN soldiers, it would go very badly for you."

Daud looked at the boy. "If this boy dies while he is in my care, things will go even worse. I cannot bear to watch this happen again."

"I understand. The rest of us, Rageh, will be here should you need us."

"Thank you." Without thinking about what he was doing, Daud wrapped his arms around Afrah. For a moment the big man held him, and it was almost like his father was there again. Then he broke the embrace, turned to the boy, and picked him up. "Help the others get to one of the pickups."

★   ★   ★

As he approached the camp along the weather-beaten road that led to the collection of military vehicles and *aqals*, Daud's stomach threatened sickness. He wanted to run, to turn around and go back as quickly as he could. The boy lay beside him in the seat, and he was attuned to the boy's rapid panting and plaintive groans as he lay trapped in a feverish delirium.

A pair of Marines waved him to a stop between two Humvees.

Heart beating rapidly, Daud glanced in the rearview mirror to make certain the bandaging on the scarred side of his face was in proper position. Satisfied, he applied his foot to the brake and slowed the pickup. He didn't carry a weapon. Neither did the two men in the back of the vehicle.

A young Marine stepped to the door with one hand on his pistol. Another Marine stood behind his partner with an assault rifle in both hands.

"May I help you, sir?"

Daud pointed to the boy and to the two men in the back of the pickup. "I have wounded. We were attacked by al-Shabaab at a nearby camp."

The Marine looked at the boy. "What's wrong with him?"

Daud lifted the bandage from the boy's side to reveal the ugly wound, knowing that the Marine's attention would be focused on that. "He was shot and now is fevered."

The Marine cursed and shook his head. "He's young."

"Yes."

"Give me a sec." The Marine stepped back and talked quickly on the radio. Then he pointed to a Humvee that pulled up in front of the pickup. "Follow that Marine. He'll take you to the doc."

Daud nodded. "Thank you."

"Good luck with everything. The doc's good. He'll get him fixed up." The Marine waved them forward, and Daud lifted his foot from the brake and applied it to the accelerator. He rolled into the camp without any problems.

Daud followed the Humvee and pulled over when it stopped at the center of the camp. The driver pointed to the large tent nearby. Daud nodded and waved, then switched off the engine and gathered the boy into his arms.

Nurses spotted Daud carrying the boy and came over to him with concerned expressions. One of them reached for the boy. "Let me help you."

Daud held the boy more tightly to his chest. "I have him. One of the men in the pickup has a broken leg. He will need your help more than I do. Thank you for your offer."

The nurses went away, one of them to the pickup and the other to get a litter and two men to help her with the wounded man.

Daud strode into the tent and looked around. "I need a doctor. Quickly. This boy has been shot."

One of the men in scrubs came over and lifted the bandage that covered the boy's wound. "I'm Dr. Cline. Is this your son?"

Daud answered without hesitation. "Yes."

"When was he shot?" Gently, the doctor took the boy from Daud's arms.

Daud felt empty and more frantic as he followed the doctor to a nearby operating table. "Yesterday."

"Who stitched the wounds?"

"I did. To stop the bleeding."

"You did a good job, but I'm going to have to open him up and clean those wounds out. I'll also need to take a look around and make sure everything's intact."

"Of course." Daud stood by helplessly as the doctor placed the boy on the table.

Working quickly, talking to two nurses who came over to assist him, the doctor cut the boy's shirt from his body, then removed the bandages, applied yellow-orange-tinted antibacterial, and used a scalpel to cut the stitches. Freed of the stitches, the wound opened on its own and wept infection.

"Will he be all right?" Daud kept remembering how he'd been forced to put Ibrahim in the grave with his mother. He could hear the whistle of the night air as he'd accomplished that, and he could taste the salt of his tears on his tongue.

"We're going to do our best, and our best is very good." The doctor smiled at Daud and kept working, calling out instructions, which the nurses carried out professionally and with speed.

Daud began to feel a little better.

"How badly are you injured?"

The doctor's question caught Daud off guard, but then

he realized the man was referring to the bandages he wore. "I am fine. Please attend to the boy."

"If you're in pain—"

"Please, this is nothing. The bandages are there to keep the flies from the wound. Take care of the boy. I will be fine."

The doctor nodded and continued working. Within minutes he had cleaned out the boy's wounds, inspected the damage, and pronounced the boy to be luckily free of life-threatening or debilitating damage.

Some of the tension that had filled Daud vanished in that moment, and he took his first relaxed breath. His next feat was to get back out of the camp without alerting suspicion.

Then a nearby explosion blew out the side of the tent and killed a nurse and the man Daud had brought in with the broken leg. The concussive wave blew people and supplies in all directions.

Daud threw himself across the boy in an effort to protect him, but when the second and third explosions arrived, he didn't think any of them had long to live.

33

"INDIGO LEADER!"

"INDIGO LEADER!"

Hearing the note of panic in the Marine's voice, Heath answered immediately. "This is Leader." He halted near the center of camp and looked around, not seeing anything that would warrant the tone.

"This is Indigo Two! Bogeys are coming in from the north! They're rolling fast!"

"Affirmative, Two." Indigo Two was one of the scout teams presently watching the camp's security perimeter.

Heath looked to the north and thought he detected a smudge of dust against the early-morning sky. Before he could be sure, however, mortar explosions went off inside the camp and he knew their security had already been compromised. The ground quivered under his feet.

Two of the *aqals* took direct hits and went up in gouts of flame. Bodies hit the ground several yards from the impact area.

Heath lifted a woman to her feet, picked up the small child beside her, and hustled both of them toward one of the cargo trucks. There wasn't going to be enough time to evacuate the camp in the trucks, but Heath was hoping that whoever was attacking them was after the cargo and wouldn't want to risk damaging it.

Many of the people were already heading out of the camp. They knew from a long association with violence that staying in one spot didn't bode well in an attack.

More mortars fell into the camp, bringing mass destruction all around. Heath worked as swiftly as he was able, grabbing more people who were nearby and directing them to the truck. Then, realizing that there were too many, and that he was having to fight against those fleeing, he headed for a Humvee and spotted Gunney Towers legging it in that direction as well.

They reached the vehicle at the same time. Towers clambered into the rear deck and manned the .50-caliber machine gun. Heath slid behind the steering wheel and pressed the starter button. The engine blasted to vibrant life, and he released the clutch as he floored the accelerator.

"Two, do you have eyes on the mortar teams?" Heath headed north, toward the incoming vehicles. If he'd set up a vehicle attack on the camp, he would have set up a defensive line the vehicles could fall back to. Gunney Towers seemed to be willing to go along for the ride.

"Affirmative, Leader. North. Same as the bogeys."

Glancing over his shoulder, Heath saw that three other Humvees were now in pursuit. "What kind of vehicles are the bogeys?"

"Pickups and light jeeps. Armed with machine guns and shooters."

The dust cloud to the north was definite now, a solid line that revealed the vehicles racing toward the camp.

"How many bogeys?"

"Six. No . . . eight. I see *eight*."

Heath steered straight at the enemy vehicles. The Humvees were more heavily armored, practically tanks compared to the al-Shabaab's civilian vehicles, which had few upgrades beyond the machine guns. The Humvees had reinforced bumpers capable of dealing damage in a collision.

A moment later, Heath spotted the first of the vehicles. Gunney Towers did too, and the big fifty-cal spoke in a voice of thunder. Rounds chewed up the ground in front of the approaching pickup, then smashed through the radiator and the engine. Flames burst out from under the hood.

Out of control, the stricken vehicle veered to the side and slowed down, becoming a roadblock for the jeep behind it. Gunney Towers tracked to the new target and lit it up as well. The driver must have tried to take evasive action, but the effort ended in disaster when the jeep turned turtle on the rough ground and ended up rolling over and over while slinging passengers from it like rag dolls.

Looking back at the camp, Heath watched as a new salvo of mortars slammed into the tents.

Gunney Towers reached down and slapped Heath on the helmet. "Nine o'clock. Now."

Responding immediately, Heath pulled on the steering wheel and felt the vehicle buck and rear as the tires fought the uneven terrain. It looked like they'd caught a massive dust cloud and were dragging it after them.

"Mortar team."

Heath spotted them then. A three-man team hunkered down under a low ridge that hid them from the camp. He steered for them as Gunney Towers opened up with the machine gun. Fifty-cal bullets tore one man to pieces and took the legs out from under another. The third escaped, but only because Heath bore down on him so quickly that he was out of range of the machine gun's field of fire. Heath adjusted the steering wheel and chased the man down, thinking of the women and children he'd seen lying dead on the ground. There was no mercy in his heart, only the desire to subdue the enemy.

The al-Shabaab man was there one instant, then he was under the wheels. As Heath made another tight turn, he looked back the way he'd come and saw the corpse the Humvee had left behind. Then he was looking for new targets, knowing they could save lives if they acted quickly enough.

★　★　★

Dazed, Daud peered up from where he lay on his back on the ground. His first thought was of the boy, and he couldn't remember how they had gotten separated. He believed one of the last explosions must have knocked him away.

Frantic about the boy's safety, Daud forced himself to stand and peered at the operating table where the boy had lain. He breathed a sigh of relief to see the boy still there.

Several dead men and women lay in the tent. Both of the

men he had brought there were now corpses that joined some of the medical staff and other patients.

Before Daud could cross to the boy, four men dressed in tattered clothing entered the tent through the large hole in the back. They carried machine pistols that they brought out of their loose clothing. One of them was a hawk-faced man with a fierce beard whom Daud immediately recognized as Qaim, one of Haroun's lieutenants.

Reluctantly, wishing he had a weapon, Daud gave ground before the men.

"You are certain you saw him come in here?" Qaim gazed around the wreckage belligerently.

"I am certain." The speaker suddenly pointed at Daud. "There. With his head bandaged."

Qaim lifted his machine pistol.

Hurling himself forward, Daud dodged through the front entrance of the tent as bullets ripped through the air where he'd been. He immediately went low once outside the tent, scrabbling at the earth with his hands like an animal.

A Marine wheeled and looked back at him, pulling his weapon to his shoulder. Daud didn't know if the man would have shot him or not, because in the next instant bullets from inside the tent struck the American in the face.

Even as the corpse fell, Daud reached out for the fallen Marine's rifle and pulled it to him. Still bent low, Daud ran and dove behind the pickup he had driven into the camp. On the other side of the vehicle, breathing raggedly, he yanked the captured weapon to his shoulder and peered at the tent.

One of the al-Shabaab men appeared in the tent's

doorway. Daud centered the rifle's sights over the man's chest and opened fire, squeezing off two three-round bursts that drove the corpse back into the tent. Then he waited, hoping another man got brave enough to do the same thing.

Only no one did.

Gathering himself, getting a bad feeling about the lack of response from the al-Shabaab men, Daud slid away from the pickup and returned to the tent. Instead of going through the entrance, he made his way around to the section blown out at the side. He remained low and duck-walked into the tent.

One of the al-Shabaab men remained inside. The man watched the tent's front entrance nervously, but he split his attention between the other open sections of the tent as well. He noticed Daud coming through the opening too late, but he tried to bring his weapon up anyway.

Wanting to take the man alive, Daud shot him in the right elbow as he turned. The bullet's impact knocked the machine pistol from the man's grip. He screamed in pain and stared in shock at the crimson threading down his numb arm.

Approaching him, Daud covered the room. The other two men had gone.

The boy was gone as well, as was the doctor who had been attending him.

Turning, the wounded al-Shabaab man tried to escape, but he was in shock and not moving very well. Daud grabbed the man by his shirt collar and bent him backward over the nearest operating table with the heated rifle muzzle under the man's chin.

"Where is the boy?"

The man didn't speak.

"Talk." Daud's tone was cold and dispassionate. "If you do not, I will kill you right here."

"They took him. They took the boy."

"Why?"

"Qaim knew they could not stay here. When they saw the boy, Qaim said that since we had not killed you, Haroun would be happy with the boy as a compromise. They left to take the boy and the two doctors to Haroun."

"Why would they do this?"

"As hostages. To keep the Americans at bay, and to draw you to Haroun." The man grimaced in pain. "Haroun has promised to kill you."

Daud thought only of the boy and how yanking Kufow around as Qaim and his compatriot were doing couldn't be good for his injuries. The boy needed medical treatment and a chance to rest.

"Where did they go?"

The man nodded toward the back of the tent. "There. They went that way."

Yanking the man forward, Daud hauled him from the table. "If you make one wrong move, it will be your last."

Holding his injured arm, the man stumbled forward. Daud followed him to the hole in the rear of the tent and stepped out into the open. He gazed in all directions, but all he saw was madness, people fleeing, a mixture of vehicles among them. There was no sign of the boy.

"Lower the weapon." The voice sounded behind Daud

and held grim intensity and lethal conviction. "I'm not going to tell you again."

Recognizing the accent as American, Daud gingerly placed the M4A1 on the ground and held up his hands. "This man is one of those who attacked this place. He is al-Shabaab."

"We'll get all that figured out soon enough. You just take three steps away from that weapon and drop to your knees. Do it now."

Angry and frustrated that he had lost the boy, Daud complied with the order, then locked his hands behind his head as he was also told to do. He stared at the crowd of people running from the camp and tried not to feel helpless. Afrah was still out there. Something could yet be done.

"I want to speak to your commanding officer."

The Marine stepped forward and grabbed Daud's left wrist. "We'll have to see about that."

Moving quickly, knowing that if he wasn't in a position to force a negotiation, he would have nothing, Daud captured the Marine's wrist and jerked him forward, headbutting the man in the face. Spinning on the ground, he swept the Marine's feet from beneath him as the assault rifle cracked rounds into the ground. He grabbed the Marine's MARPAT uniform and pulled him forward again, keeping him off balance, then slammed his head into the man's face again. Cartilage snapped and blood spurted from the Marine's broken nose. His legs went boneless and he dropped.

Daud captured the falling rifle and pointed it at the al-Shabaab man as the terrorist tried to get to his feet. "No."

The man froze.

"Sit."

Reluctantly, the man did as he was told. "I am bleeding. I need medical attention."

"You should have thought of that before you blew up the medical facilities. Be thankful you yet live." Daud remained seated and waited, raking the bandages from his head. If the Marines knew of him, now it was time for them to know he was here. He knew he did not have enough people to attempt to rescue the boy. He did not even know where Haroun was.

But he felt certain the Marines would know more. He would get their information, and then he would decide what to do.

★　★　★

The attackers turned tail without warning.

Heath almost pursued, buzzing with adrenaline, but he knew that would be a mistake. They could be leading him and his team into a second ambush.

"Hold your positions, Indigo. Let's get a new perimeter established and see if we can take care of our people." Heath turned the Humvee around and headed back to the camp. Smoke crawled into the sky from the burning *aqals*.

"Indigo Leader, this is Indigo Three."

Three had been left behind at the camp. "Go, Three."

"We have a situation here. Are you coming back?"

"On my way now." Heath put his foot a little harder on the accelerator, wondering what had happened now, doubting that things could get any worse than they already were.

★   ★   ★

When he saw Rageh Daud holding a rifle to Private Thomas Ruiz's head just outside the medical tent while a dozen other Marines held weapons on him, Heath thought maybe he should reevaluate his earlier assessment.

"Are you the commanding officer?" Daud spoke calmly, and Heath figured that was a good sign.

"I am. Lieutenant Heath Bridger." Heath let his rifle hang at his side, not bothering to point the weapon at the man. If Daud shot Ruiz or moved his rifle in anyone else's direction, he was a dead man.

"I have a proposition for you."

"I'm listening."

"We have a common foe, Lieutenant Bridger. Korfa Haroun. I trust that you know this name."

"I do."

"A man acting on Haroun's behalf has taken a boy I brought here, a boy I do not wish to see come to any harm."

Heath didn't say anything.

"This man, Qaim, also took two of your medical personnel as hostages."

"How do you know this?"

Daud pointed to the wounded man sitting close by. "Because this man is al-Shabaab. He was with the team that came to assassinate me. He told me. And nurses inside the medical facility will confirm that."

Heath pointed at the destruction that had been done to the camp. "You think all of this was because of you?"

"No. I think Haroun wanted to strike at you as well. Perhaps to get the cargo you brought." Daud shrugged. "However you choose to look at it, we have both lost something to Haroun. He has more men than you do. He has more men than I do. But together, with the information the man can give us—" he nodded toward the wounded man— "I think perhaps we might have a chance of getting those people back."

Heath paused for a moment. "I can call for help."

"Do that and Haroun will be gone before anyone can get here. You are days away from Mogadishu, and even the planes you use will be hours away, if they can muster a rescue effort so quickly." Daud glanced at the sun. "It is eleven o'clock now."

Taking a glance at his watch, Heath discovered Daud was only eight minutes off. Impressive.

"Your military command will take time to form a strategy and follow through on an operation to rescue those doctors. And before they do that, they will want someone to investigate Haroun's hiding place."

Heath nodded.

"You see how this agreement benefits both of us."

"Yeah. The problem is, how do I know I can trust you?"

"The same way I know I can trust you. Because in this instance, we must trust each other."

Before Heath could say anything, Daud removed the rifle from Thomas Ruiz's head and tossed it away. Immediately two Marines rushed in to take him into custody.

"Stand down, Marines." Heath surprised himself at how quickly he'd made up his mind about the situation.

But everything Daud had said, including the need to recon Haroun's fortress, was true. "How many men do you have?"

"Twenty-six."

Heath estimated he had perhaps that many Marines who could take the field. "How many men does Haroun have?"

"According to this man—" Daud nodded toward the wounded al-Shabaab terrorist—"Haroun had a hundred and twenty."

Heath smiled grimly, thinking of the carnage he and Gunney Towers had left scattered all over the outskirts of the camp. "Well, it's safe to say that Haroun doesn't have that many anymore." He took a breath. "Call your men in. Let's see what we can put together."

Daud nodded and looked around, then back at Heath. "Perhaps I could borrow a vehicle."

34

FOR THE FIRST FEW HOURS back at the camp, Bekah rotated in and out of patrol. The sight of the destruction in the camp took her breath away. Even though she'd been somewhat prepared by her radio conversations with fellow Marines, she hadn't realized the actual impact. When she wasn't patrolling, she split her time between helping out with the wounded and grave duty. There was no time to bury anyone. That would have to be attended to later, but it was important to know where the bodies were and who had died.

Gathering the Marine dog tags of the six dead was the hardest. She couldn't help feeling that Charlie Company's Indigo Platoon had to have some of the hardest luck in the Corps.

She also hoped that Matthew Cline was still alive.

While she, along with most of Indigo, stayed occupied, Heath and Gunney Towers remained locked up with Rageh

Daud and the al-Shabaab terrorist Daud had captured during the attack.

Then, finally, Heath called them in to the briefing.

★　★　★

Seated in the briefing room, which was one of the surviving tents, Bekah studied the handmade map on the board as Heath covered the fortification where Haroun had holed up.

"From the intel we've gathered, Haroun has between a hundred and a hundred twenty armed men inside the fort." Heath stood in front of the mixed group of Marines and Rageh Daud's bandits.

The tension in the room was so thick it could have been cut with a knife. Everyone—Marine and bandit—kept their hands close to their weapons, and Bekah couldn't believe Heath had kept bloodshed from breaking out already.

The bandits had lost friends and loved ones to the al-Shabaab, though. Some of them had lost entire families. So their focus on Haroun as the larger enemy was easy to see. The Marines were bound by a desire to strike back for lost comrades and to carry out their mission to eliminate the al-Shabaab from Somalia.

"There's no getting around the fact that you're going to be outnumbered two to one once we're inside that fort." Heath didn't hold anything back, and Bekah believed all the listeners respected him for that. "But that's where training and desire will make a difference."

Several of the bandits who knew English translated Heath's words for their cohorts.

"Our main objective is to get a good assessment of the fortification. If we can't get our people out, then we're going to be able to hand solid intel over to the Marines arriving in the morning. Whatever we don't finish tonight when we attack *will* be finished in the morning."

One of Daud's men, a giant with savage scars, grinned coldly. "Perhaps they will only be here in the morning to applaud our success."

Heath grinned back at the man. "If we manage to pull that off, then we'll deserve the applause."

Looking at the bandits, Bekah couldn't help thinking about the innocent UN and Somali soldiers the men had killed while stealing medicines and cargo from convoys, trying to help the displaced people. In some respects, they weren't much different from the al-Shabaab.

However, she forced herself to remember that the bandits were displaced as well. In fact, all of the warriors gathered in this room were displaced—the Marines had been called from their homes and thrown into a foreign battlefield to protect the innocent and the weak. Bekah had never really thought about things in that light before. It was a revelation of sorts.

"We're going in at dark." Heath spoke flatly, with a calm orator's voice, and it required hardly any effort for Bekah to imagine him up in front of a jury in a courtroom. "We only get one shot at this, and here is how we're going to do it." He turned back to the map. "A skeleton group of Daud's men under the guidance of one of my corporals will pull the Humvees up to the front of the fort as night falls. They will stay out of mortar range and put on a show of attacking the fort. While the al-Shabaab are engaged on the front, the rest of us will attempt to breach the rear of the structure. With luck, we should be able to get inside before we're discovered. Once we're there, we put down every al-Shabaab man we find while we search for the prisoners."

Bekah swallowed and her ears popped.

Heath faced his troops. "Are there any questions?"

There were none.

"Then let's move out."

★   ★   ★

Two hours later, Bekah lay along a ridgeline on the east side of the fort. As she gazed through the darkness on the other side of the structure, she saw the Humvees arrive. The vehicles' lights glowed brightly in the black night.

Lights inside the fort immediately shifted as guards raced toward the front of the structure.

"Well, those Humvees have got their attention. Definitely not in stealth mode." Pike lay to Bekah's right. His face, like hers, was striped in cosmetic black to reduce the glare and make them part of the shadows. They wore MARPAT digital camouflage, which rendered them harder to see.

Almost immediately, the al-Shabaab launched an attack, and the Humvees returned fire. Most of the mortars and rockets landed well short of either side, but the machine guns definitely had the range.

"All right." Heath's voice was calm over the MBITR. "That's not going to hold their attention forever, and if Haroun decides to send out a tactical team to recon those vehicles, they're going to discover this is a feint. Let's move in."

Bekah rose to her feet and went forward, trotting to keep pace with the wave of Marines she was assigned to. She thought about Travis and Matthew Cline, torn between staying safe for one and rescuing the other. She focused on the job at hand. That was what she'd sworn to do the day she took the oath.

Marine first.

At the wall, still undiscovered, Bekah shook out one of the padded grappling hooks they'd set up for the assault. The first teams whirled their hooks overhead and let fly. The hooks sailed easily over the wall, and Bekah pulled the slack out of her line.

The crack and bang of the al-Shabaab weapons rolled through the hillside around them.

Bracing her boots against the wall, Bekah swarmed up the line while the next Marine behind her grabbed the rope and steadied it. She halted at the top and slid her rifle into her arms while she hung there. After making certain no one was in the passageway between the inner and outer walls, she threw a leg over the wall and dropped to the hard ground between the ramparts. She had the rifle up at once and held her position while her team and the other teams did the same.

When the second wave of Marines clambered over and dropped, Bekah led her group toward the east gate. She flipped down her night-vision goggles and peered into the courtyard.

Several al-Shabaab were in evidence in the open area, but

most of them were heading toward the west wall where the action was. Beside her, Pike was calmly chewing gum and even looked like he was bored. "Shooting gallery. Should be fun."

"Make sure you keep it tight." Bekah threw a glance at Tyler and Trudy as well.

All of them nodded.

Heath came up between them. "All right. We're all here. Let's roll." He led the way, with Gunney Towers at his heels.

Bekah followed after Heath with her team dogging her. They didn't know what the two outbuildings were for. Several jeeps and pickups were parked in the courtyard. Two of the fire teams, backed by some of Daud's bandits, were assigned to investigate those buildings. Everyone else concentrated on the main building.

Guards along the front of the building had maintained their posts. Heath crept up alongside the building and slipped the knife from his combat harness while sliding his rifle over one shoulder. Bekah turned off the horror screaming inside her mind as she saw Heath move silently forward behind one of the guards.

She had been trained in hand-to-hand combat, had been taught to kill an opponent with a knife, but she'd never done it. The idea appalled her because it seemed so much more personal than shooting someone. The thought was idiocy, of course. Dead was dead, but she hoped she never had to do something like that.

Heath was on the terrorist before he knew it. Placing the knife at his throat, Heath bent the man's head forward.

In the movies, the hero always yanked an opponent's head backward to expose the throat, but that only flexed the neck muscles and made the cut harder to perform. Pushing the head forward relaxed those muscles. Heath drew the knife across in one smooth motion.

The man grabbed for his throat and dropped the AK-47 that he'd been holding. The noise alerted the al-Shabaab terrorist standing only a few feet away, in spite of the noise along the west wall. Startled, the terrorist turned and brought his rifle up.

Gunney Towers shot the man in the face twice, and the body dropped to the stones.

The half-dozen guards standing in front of the building's entrance spun quickly and began firing. Heath waved the Marines back behind the corner, held on to the dead man, and withdrew a grenade. He flipped the explosive into the center of the group, swung back around the corner himself, and pushed the dead man from him. He had his rifle in his hands before the grenade went off.

Partially deafened from the close-proximity blast, Bekah surged forward after Heath and Gunney Towers. The two men advanced at a deliberate pace, rifles held to shoulders and knees bent to make them smaller targets. Bekah flanked Heath on the left, and Pike flanked Gunney Towers on the right.

Most of the al-Shabaab terrorists had been killed by the shrapnel from the grenade, but a couple lived and opened fire. Others came from the courtyard, drawn by the explosion.

Bekah found targets in all directions and fired in rapid three-round bursts. Men went down and she stepped in their blood, feeling it slick beneath her boots. A few rounds thudded into her body armor and another round ricocheted from the top of her helmet or caught her NVGs—she wasn't sure.

The Marines stayed in a group and ducked in through the entrance.

The interior of the fort hadn't been improved much in the last five hundred years. Evidently when whatever occupying force had left, no one had taken much interest in the place. The big room was lit by large electric lights powered by generators somewhere on the premises.

More al-Shabaab stood guard within, scattered around the room along the second floor. The first floor had no windows, making it easier to defend in case invaders breached the outer walls. But the battle to take the second floor would be hard. The second floor had a lot of vantage points that allowed for snipers. Back in the sixteenth century, those snipers had probably been archers, but the sniper posts were a lot more dangerous with men armed with rifles.

Bullets cracked against the stone walls and the paved floor. Beside Bekah, Trudy went down. Bekah spun at once to check her teammate and saw that she'd been hit in the calf. Bekah glanced up at Tyler. "Get her out of here. Stop the bleeding."

Tyler nodded and shouldered his weapon. He grabbed Trudy under the arms and dragged her out of the building as bullets cracked the stone around them.

Pike pulled a grenade from his combat harness and yanked the pin. "Fire in the hole!" He threw the grenade onto the stairway landing, where a group of al-Shabaab had collected.

Ducking her head, Bekah ran along the wall, following Heath to the bottom of the stairs and hunkering down. The grenade went off, and bodies slid down the stairs. By that time, Heath was already in motion, sprinting over the fallen bodies and spraying bullets into those men who had survived the initial blast.

"Bekah, take your group and track the generators. Find them and take them out."

Bekah knew that Heath must not have seen Trudy go down, or that she had assigned Tyler to drag her to safety. Pike instantly joined her, his dark gaze following the electrical lines tacked to the walls. All of the wiring led to a doorway under the curved stairwell.

"On it." Bekah turned and made for the door.

Heath was at the top of the stairs, firing again and again while Gunney Towers guarded his back. "Indigo Four, you're with Eight."

"On it." The three surviving members of Fire Team Indigo Four peeled off from the group and sprinted after Bekah and Pike.

"We've got company." Pike's growl barely reached Bekah's ears, but she caught his nod toward Daud and a group of his men, including the big man, who were accompanying them.

Daud acknowledged Bekah with a nod. "Rats always

leave a route they can use for escape. I do not think Haroun will have left himself nowhere to run."

Bekah silently agreed and continued to follow the thick, snakelike cables bundled into a cluster. She passed through the door to another hallway that had not been lighted and spotted a group of al-Shabaab lying in wait in the darkness.

35

BEKAH BARELY HAD TIME to throw an arm in front of Pike and get herself back to the safety of the doorway before bullets raked the walls and ricocheted down the hallway. Pike scrambled back as well, cursing the whole time.

Shouldering her rifle for the moment, Bekah plucked two grenades from her combat harness. She pulled the pins from the explosives, counted off a second, then heaved them into the hallway. Pike shadowed her toss with his own grenades a split second later.

Bekah covered her ears and waited. The explosives ripped through the hallway, magnified inside the constrained space. And a cloud of dust and stone fragments vomited out of the doorway in a rush.

The lights in the main room went out, and Bekah realized the explosions must have taken out the electrical cables in the hallway. But lights in the building's upper stories remained, so she guessed that other wiring paths still existed. She hoped all of the generators were kept in the same area.

She flipped down her NVGs and found them still operable. Then she led the way into the hallway with Pike on her right.

Several of the al-Shabaab waiting to ambush them were dead or heavily wounded. Only a few remained alive and willing to fight. She spotted them in the green imagery afforded by the NVGs and opened fire as Pike did the same. They left dead men in the hallway as they kept advancing at a rapid pace.

Daud was behind her, breathing heavily. He kept his fingers resting lightly on her shoulder, and she knew it was because he couldn't see in the darkness. The thought of him being there unnerved her, but she concentrated on the job Heath had assigned her to do.

The hallway ran straight another fifty yards, then turned sharply to the right and began a steep descent. There was only enough room for three people to walk side by side. Another group of al-Shabaab waited in the darkness at the bottom, but they couldn't see the Marines advancing until she and Pike had opened fire and left them sprawled across the floor.

They kept moving forward. Daud stumbled momentarily over one of the dead men, but he maintained contact. Bekah couldn't help wondering what drove the man so fiercely. Heath had mentioned that Daud had brought in a boy to be treated at the medical facility, but she knew from the intel briefing on Daud that the man's son had been killed in an attack engineered by Haroun and the al-Shabaab. Vengeance might have brought Daud along, but Bekah couldn't stop thinking about the boy, and her thoughts kept connecting him with the baby she'd buried and with Travis.

She knew how she'd feel if anything happened to Travis and if she knew who was responsible, but it was more than that. When the boy had tried to smuggle the grenade into the medical clinic in Mogadishu, Bekah had tried to protect him as well. In her eyes, he'd been an innocent, just a tool the al-Shabaab had constructed to carry out their war.

Daud's hand left Bekah's shoulder as the glow of electric lights dawned in the tunnel ahead. Before she knew it, Daud ran past her. She tried to call him back, but he wasn't listening, and the big man and the other bandits ran at their leader's heels.

Then Bekah heard the generators ahead of them. More than that, the rumble of truck engines punctuated the growl of the generators. Realizing there were vehicles up ahead, Bekah picked up her own pace.

Heath's voice came over the comm and the connection sounded scratchy, no doubt strained by the stone separating them. "Bekah, we've just discovered the building's been mined. We've found two emplacements so far, both of them attached to structural supports. This place has been rigged to bring it down. Do you copy?"

"Copy, Leader. We're in a tunnel beneath the fort. We've found the generators, and there are vehicles up ahead as well."

"Understood, but you need to clear the building. Haroun has this place wired to implode. We're pulling out now."

"Affirmative, but we're out of the blast zone, I think. Going back would take too long."

Heath paused just a second. "Good luck then. I'll see you on the other side." Then he was gone.

Ahead, the tunnel widened into a cave that held a dozen generators and four jeeps. The noise was intense, and the men waiting in the jeeps didn't notice the Marines and Daud's people converging on them from out of the darkness.

Beyond the jeeps, a large tunnel continued, swallowed in darkness beyond where the jeep headlights could penetrate. Daud had been correct. The original builders had designed an escape strategy in the event they were overrun. It was a tactical necessity for any fort that stood out in the wilderness not far from enemy territory.

Bekah lifted her NVGs and followed Daud into the cave. Movement on the right side of the cave drew her attention, and she spotted Haroun emerging from a tunnel there. A dozen men guarded him, and two of them pushed Matthew Cline and one of the other doctors ahead of them. Another man carried a young boy, and Bekah realized that it must be the boy Daud had brought to the camp.

Haroun wasted no time heading toward the waiting jeeps.

Daud took cover behind one of the throbbing generators and raised his AK-47. He fired without warning and Bekah was certain his target was Haroun, but one of the al-Shabaab stepped forward at that moment and the bullet caught that man instead. The harsh *crack!* of the rifle ignited a powder keg of action as the al-Shabaab suddenly reacted like an irritated wasp's nest.

"Shoot the drivers!" Bekah took cover behind one of the generators as well, then aimed for the lead jeep driver on the left, hoping to create more confusion. She sighted on the man's head and squeezed the trigger. Her first shot missed because the man jerked his head around to look over his shoulder, but her second round cored into his cheek and killed him instantly.

When the dead driver's foot slipped off the clutch, the jeep jerked forward and the engine stalled, causing just enough movement to roll into the jeep beside it and form a logjam.

Pike took out two of the other drivers in quick snap shots. Those vehicles also sputtered and died, ramming into each other.

Rolling around the generator's side, Bekah went forward, intent on the al-Shabaab guards holding Matthew and the other man prisoner. Pike followed on her heels as they stayed low behind the generators. Bekah spoke over the comm, knowing her fellow Marines—including Pike—would hear her. "I've got the man on the left."

"Cool. Whenever you're ready."

"Let's get as close as we can. We'll need to get the hostages out of the way."

The two guards never knew Bekah and Pike were on them till the last second. They reacted instantly then, trying to sweep their weapons up and around.

"Now." Bekah bracketed the man's chest and squeezed off a three-round burst. Pike fired a heartbeat behind her.

Bekah's bullets drove the al-Shabaab man back and down, and he was gone before he hit the floor. The other terrorist went down as well, his face now a gory mask.

Bekah raced forward and threw an arm out to catch

Matthew, who stood stunned in the middle of everything with fresh blood staining his scrubs. Her arm went around his waist and knocked him backward into relative safety behind one of the jeeps. Bekah forced him flat on the ground and yelled into his ear. "Stay!"

Matthew nodded and lay fearfully as Pike planted the other doctor next to him. Then the two Marines returned to a standing crouch at the jeep's back bumper. Bekah pulled her rifle to her shoulder and loaded a fresh magazine into the weapon since she knew she only had a few rounds left.

The assault had set off a miniature gun battle that left more al-Shabaab strewn on the ground. Some of Daud's men and one of the Marines were down as well.

Bekah estimated that out of the twenty-three al-Shabaab terrorists she had counted in the cave, nine remained. She and Pike and Daud and his lieutenant were still standing, along with two other Marines and two more of Daud's men.

They were almost evenly matched, all of them taking cover where they could. Bekah breathed frantically, tasting the oily smoke from the generators and feeling it burn into her throat and sinuses. The rasp of her breathing sounded loud in her ears even with the generators banging away.

"Take out the generators." Bekah lifted her rifle and fired at the generators. Pike and the other Marines opened fire as well. Sparks and flames flew, and the lights in the cave went out.

The al-Shabaab and the bandits panicked, and muzzle flashes tore holes in the darkness. Then Haroun's voice rose above all the clamor and confusion.

"Stop! Stop shooting! Listen to me!"

Bekah flipped down her NVGs and powered them on. The green imagery chased away the darkness, and she focused on Haroun's position. The al-Shabaab leader remained hidden behind the jeep where he'd taken cover.

"Haroun." Daud's voice was a harsh bark. "You will not leave this place alive."

Bekah crept toward the front of the jeep she sheltered behind, closing on Haroun's position. The crepe soles of her boots made no noise.

"I will, Rageh Daud, or I will kill the boy."

For the first time, Bekah realized she'd lost track of the boy in all the confusion.

"Do you hear me, Rageh Daud? I will put a bullet in his head, and you will be helpless to do anything."

"The Marines care nothing for that boy." Anguish made Daud's voice rough.

"Are you listening, Americans?"

Bekah glanced at Pike and nodded. The Muslim leader wouldn't like dealing with a woman, and Bekah didn't want to give away her position.

"We're listening."

"I have the building above mined with explosives. If you do not allow me to leave this place, I will detonate those explosives and bring this fort down on top of your comrades."

"There's nothing to stop you from doing that once you leave this cave." Pike sounded cold and hard, like a man who didn't care about anything. "Me, I'd rather bury you down here than take a chance on trusting you."

Bekah didn't know if the Marines on the upper floors had all gotten clear of the building. She knew they wouldn't just leave her and the others here, and she didn't know how big the danger zone was. She took another step forward in the darkness, trusting that Haroun and his people were blind as she left the safety of the jeep to get a better angle on Haroun.

"You are a fool, American. I am giving you a chance to save your comrades."

"I don't believe you."

Moving in a crouch, sliding her feet from side to side so she didn't cross over and trip herself, Bekah took four more steps to the side and brought Haroun into view. He was crouched behind the jeep. The boy lay on the ground, held in place by one of the al-Shabaab. Haroun held a remote control device in his right hand.

"Then you are a greater fool. This is the only chance you will have."

"Surrender. That's the only chance *you* have."

Another shadow crept in from the right. Bekah recognized Daud crawling forward on his belly and knew the man was moving blindly, making his way by feel, closing in on the sound of Haroun's voice.

A surge of fear filled Bekah. She stared at Haroun, and her thoughts were of the boy. If she did not have the position, if she did not have this shot, she thought the boy might die. The Marines above and the Marines below in this tunnel might die. The chance to eliminate Haroun and further destroy the grip the al-Shabaab had on Mogadishu might not exist.

For an instant, the fear held her. Then she remembered

the verse her granny had taught her so long ago. *We are God's handiwork, created in Christ Jesus to do good works, which God prepared in advance for us to do.*

Had God brought her here, to this moment, to this job, halfway around the world? Was this part of the work God had planned for her? Could eliminating a man—even an evil man—be considered a good work?

Those conversations with Matthew Cline, with Heath Bridger, and with her granny came tumbling back through her head. Anyone else could have been here. Anyone else could have made the shot she knew she needed to make.

But she was the one who was here, and she knew she could do the job before her. It was what she had trained to do.

In this moment, she had more clarity about her place in life than she'd ever known. She'd been torn between family and duty, called to serve her country, but this calling was higher than that. She remembered that small prayer she'd allowed herself when she'd helped Varisha bury her son, and she thought about how Matthew Cline believed so strongly that God had a plan for everyone who wished to make a difference in this world.

That plan—that moment—now stretched before her, and she knew it. *God, if this is what you have in mind for me today, let it be done. In Jesus' name, please let me shoot straight.*

She centered her aim at Haroun's right shoulder. In training, she'd been told about the brachial nerve, which controlled the arm. Hostage rescuers were trained to make that shot, and if it was successful, the wound would cause the arm to go dead.

God, please, if this is part of the plan you have for me, then be with me now. Bekah felt the warmth and confidence surround her, banishing her fear and uplifting her courage. Her finger slid over the trigger and she squeezed.

The rifle banged against Bekah's shoulder, and she lost sight of Haroun in the sudden onslaught of light from the muzzle flash. Then, when her vision cleared and she caught sight of the Muslim leader again, she saw that he had fallen back with a look of surprise.

The detonator lay on the ground near the boy.

Desperate, Haroun tried to reach for the detonator with his other hand. Bekah shot him in the face twice, and his body flopped back. Tracking on, she shifted her aim to the man holding the boy to the ground and put a three-round burst into the man's chest.

By that time, the Marines were up and taking advantage of the darkness and the NVGs. Two more al-Shabaab went down before the rest threw away their rifles, lay flat on the ground, and begged for their lives.

"Kufow!" Daud sounded fearful.

"I am here."

"Thank God." Daud pushed himself to his feet and fumbled through the darkness to the boy's side.

Bekah reached the boy first and reached out for the detonator. She took it apart quickly and removed the battery. By then, Daud had the boy in his arms and was weeping.

"Bekah?" The comm connection to Heath sounded clearer and stronger.

"We're here." Bekah took a ragged breath. "Haroun is

down. I've secured the remote detonator." Standing on shaky legs, she looked over the battlefield and gave silent thanks, not just for their survival, but for the peace she felt.

★   ★   ★

Matthew Cline and the other doctor worked on the wounded Marines and the injuries Daud's bandits had sustained, but they also checked the boy, Kufow. Bekah stood nearby watching. Although the uneasy truce had been negotiated between Heath and Daud, the tension between the Marines and Daud's men still continued—no one relaxed. They were all displaced, all in enemy territory. If the two sides hadn't been so evenly matched, so cut off from support, if they hadn't just walked away from one battle and weren't now mourning their dead from that confrontation, Bekah suspected neither Heath nor Daud would have agreed to the cease-fire.

But continuing that fight would have left so many more people dead. No one could afford any more losses. And as Heath pointed out, Haroun had been a much bigger fish than Daud was. HQ would be happy with what they'd gotten. Daud would be a battle to fight another day.

Daud stayed with the boy, never leaving his side, just as the big man who accompanied the bandit leader never left him.

Driven by her own maternal feelings, Bekah approached Daud. "What are you going to do with him?"

Daud looked at her in surprise. "I am going to protect him and care for him. I did not come all this way just to leave him to the vagaries of fate. This place is too hostile for that."

Bekah hesitated for a moment, then thought of what her granny would say and spoke softly, with compassion. "No."

"No?" Daud's eyes tightened in anger, and the giant at his side stepped forward.

Pike stepped forward too, though Bekah hadn't until that moment realized the Marine was there.

Daud waved the big man down, eliciting a curse.

Bekah spoke tersely and with unflinching resolve. "You are a fugitive, Daud. Once we're gone from this place, once this is over, you're going to be hunted. I know Lieutenant Bridger has given you a pass on getting out of here, but come tomorrow morning he's going to be hunting you again. The Marine Corps will be hunting you again. *I* will be hunting you again. And the al-Shabaab will kill you on sight."

"I have lived a long time under such threats."

Bekah nodded. "You have. You're obviously good at what you do. You're a bad man in my book, but you've also got a love for this boy. You need to look at that and think about the life you're going to drag him into. He's already nearly been killed twice in as many days. He's just a boy. How long do you think he can survive under circumstances like that?"

Daud had no answer.

"I know you lost your son. I can only guess what that feels like. But I've got a son too, and I know I would not expose him to the kind of danger you're going to be facing. Someday, somewhere, someone is going to catch up with you. And when they do, you're going to die. Do you want this boy to die with you? Do you want him to see you die?"

For a moment Daud stood there gazing at Kufow, who watched him quietly. Then, without a word, he walked over and kissed the child on the forehead. The boy reached for him and held him tightly, crying plaintively as he lay on a makeshift bed in the back of a Humvee.

"No." The boy spoke in a ragged whisper. "Do not go. Please."

Daud pulled away, kissed the boy on the forehead one more time, and looked at him with tears in his eyes. "I must. You need a life, Kufow. I trust this woman. What she says is the truth. I have no home, no life to give you except hardship and death. Know that I love you. Grow up straight and tall."

Kufow cried helplessly and wrapped his arms around himself. "Please."

Daud forced himself to turn away from the boy. "Promise me that you will see to his welfare."

Bekah nodded and extended her hand. "I give you my word."

Daud took her hand, shook it briefly, then turned and walked away. The big man and the rest of the bandits silently followed him to the collection of pickups and jeeps. They took the vehicles and drove away, disappearing through the gate.

Pike stepped up beside Bekah as the child wept. Tears ran down Bekah's cheeks as well. "I know that wasn't easy, and I know it hurt, but what you did, Bekah, that was stand-up."

Bekah nodded and went to Kufow so he wouldn't be alone. He wouldn't look at her, but she hoped that one day he might understand.

★   ★   ★

Pike stood beside Heath and watched Daud and his men pull out of the area.

One of the medics, a young Marine from Iowa, approached the lieutenant. "Do you really think letting Daud go is the best decision, Lieutenant Bridger?" the medic blurted out.

Heath glanced at the man. "After everything we've been through, do you really think getting into another firefight is something we should do?"

The man paused for a moment, then shook his head and walked away.

Standing nearby, Pike took a deep breath. Before he knew it, he was speaking. "Sir, it's the right thing to do. Avoiding a firefight isn't the only reason, though."

"What's another?"

Staring at the disappearing figure, Pike Morgan knew what was really going on with Daud. "That man's had his world rocked. He's lost his family." He thought of Petey in that moment, and he knew some of the loss that Daud was going through. "He's a bad man, but he's not evil. There's a difference."

"Daud killed civilians and medical people."

"Yeah. He did what he thought he had to do to survive. Given the right time and circumstances, Lieutenant, you might be surprised at how much you'd have in common with a man like that."

Heath stared at Pike for a moment, then let whatever question he had in mind go unasked.

Pike figured it was probably better for both of them that way.

★   ★   ★

"Coffee, Marine?"

Hearing the familiar voice, Bekah turned and found Matthew Cline standing behind her. He looked worn and weary, dirt smudging his face, but she knew she didn't look any better.

"Sure." She accepted the cup of coffee he offered and took a sip.

"I want to look at the wound on your head. Make sure the stitches are intact."

"I'm standing perimeter guard."

Matthew smiled at her. "I know. I had to ask where you were. I can look at your wound while you stand guard."

"All right." Bekah stood still while he checked the wound.

"I'll want to dress that again later. When you have the chance."

"I'll make sure to stop off when I can."

"Do that." Matthew regarded her with those startling blue eyes. Then his smile got even bigger. "Don't get me wrong, we all look like a mess, but you look more at peace than I've ever seen you."

Smiling even though she tried to keep a straight face, Bekah nodded. "I feel pretty good." She took in a deep breath and let it out. "I found something out there that I wasn't expecting."

Matthew nodded. "That's the way it usually works."

EPILOGUE

"MS. SHAW, are you certain your attorney knows the court date is today?"

Seated at the defendant's table, Bekah was filled with nervous anxiety. It was early December, and she'd gotten back from Mogadishu only six days ago. She was fervently hoping she wasn't going to be in jail for the holidays. She wanted to spend Christmas with Travis and her granny.

They sat in the courtroom and watched her, smiling when she looked in their direction.

Judge Warren Harrelson sat quietly at the bench, awaiting an answer.

Bekah glanced at her watch. Her attorney was already ten minutes late. She didn't know what would happen to her if the attorney didn't show up. She supposed it was possible she'd be remanded to the jail, and she didn't want to be separated from Travis.

"Your Honor, I talked with him a couple days ago. He assured me he would be here."

The prosecuting attorney, an officious little man who had a reputation for going for the throat when he had a case that appeared to be a slam dunk, stood and sighed theatrically. "Your Honor, if it please the court, we've already granted a considerable extension to the defendant in this matter. The county would like to see justice done sometime in the near future. If Ms. Shaw's attorney—"

"Not *Ms.* Shaw." A familiar voice rang out strongly over the courtroom. "She is Corporal Shaw of the United States Marine Corps. I'd appreciate it, Your Honor, if the prosecuting attorney referred to my client correctly if he's going to speak of her."

Bekah turned around and saw Heath striding toward the front of the court. He looked immaculate in his Marine dress uniform, complete with white gloves and his cover tucked neatly under his arm.

The judge lifted an amused eyebrow. "And who might you be?"

"Lieutenant Heath Bridger of the United States Marine Corps. I'll be representing Corporal Shaw in this matter. I apologize for my lateness, but I've never been here before and the GPS isn't quite accurate."

"That's the way it is in some of these small towns." Judge Harrelson waved Heath forward. "Welcome, Lieutenant. Have a seat."

Heath placed his briefcase on top of the table where Bekah sat and shot her a wink. "Thank you, Judge."

"Bridger, you say?"

"Yes, Your Honor." Heath stood at parade rest.

"I know an attorney named Lionel Bridger."

"My father, Your Honor."

Bekah didn't know anything about Lionel Bridger, but the prosecuting attorney suddenly looked like he'd swallowed a toad.

"I see." The judge leaned back in his seat and steepled his hands together in front of him. "Well then, this should be interesting."

Heath smiled confidently. "To the best of my ability, Your Honor." He sat and looked at Bekah. "Relax, Corporal. You're in good hands."

Bekah smiled helplessly. "Thank you."

"My pleasure."

★   ★   ★

Afterward, Bekah wasn't sure exactly what had taken place, but the trial was over a lot more quickly than she'd expected. Heath had somehow harassed the prosecuting attorney at every turn, challenged facts and witness testimony, and torn Deputy Trimble to pieces on the stand.

When everything was said and done, she was free and a warrant had been issued for Buck Miller's arrest.

Granny invited Heath back to the farm for a late lunch. Bekah wasn't pleased with the idea of Heath coming to their home when he was so obviously accustomed to wealth, but she didn't want to just watch him leave as quickly as he'd come.

She'd gotten to know him, and herself, in Mogadishu,

and she'd hated parting ways only a tad bit less than she had looked forward to seeing Travis.

Heath received a phone call and momentarily excused himself. As Bekah set the table, she tried not to overhear his conversation, but she picked up on the fact that Heath wasn't happy. He returned to the table a few minutes later.

Bekah looked at him, noticing the glow of the earlier win was missing. "Bad news?"

"Another case isn't going exactly the way I'd hoped, but the jury's not out, so to speak. I'll make it happen." Heath sipped his tea and lunch was served.

"Do you know how to throw a football?" Travis looked at Heath while holding a spoonful of macaroni and cheese.

"As a matter of fact, I do." Heath smiled, and some of the bleakness brought by the phone call lifted from him.

"He does." Granny nodded. "Lieutenant Bridger was one of the best quarterbacks Oklahoma State University ever turned out."

Heath grinned self-consciously. "Do you follow college ball?"

Granny nodded as she cut another slice of cherry pie and put it on Heath's plate. "Bekah never got interested in watching football. Not much of a sports fan at all, but she'd watch a little baseball with her granddaddy now and again."

Bekah felt embarrassed.

"Momma can't throw a football." Travis ate his spoonful of macaroni and cheese. "Can you show me how?"

"Sure."

"Now? Or do you have to keep your clothes clean?"

"Actually, I think I can keep my clothes clean and teach you to throw a football."

Afterward, Bekah stood at the large window and stared out into the yard as Heath taught her son the basics of holding the football. Travis's puppy chased around them, barking and whining.

Granny stood beside Bekah and watched. "He's a good teacher. Gentle and patient."

"Yeah."

Granny looked at her and smiled. "Quite an interesting man, this lieutenant of yours."

Embarrassment singed Bekah's cheeks. "He's not my lieutenant. The next time I get deployed, I'll probably be assigned to someone else."

"We'll see. You know, he must think highly of you to have come all this way to represent you in that case this morning."

Bekah shrugged. "That's just how the Marines are."

"Maybe, but you never know what God has planned."

For the first time in her life, Bekah totally believed that.

ABOUT THE AUTHOR

MEL ODOM is the author of the Alex Award–winning novel *The Rover* and the Christy Award runner-up *Apocalypse Dawn*. Odom has been inducted into the Oklahoma Professional Writers Hall of Fame (at the age of 37—otherwise mentioning such an award makes him sound very old and retired). He lives in Moore, Oklahoma, where he coached Little League for years, and teaches professional writing classes at the University of Oklahoma. Since first being published in 1988, Mel has written more than 160 books in various fields, which he blames on his ADHD, desperation (five children), and opportunity.

GO MILITARY.

Best-selling author **MEL ODOM** explores the Tribulation through the lives of the men and women serving in the U.S. military.

APOCALYPSE DAWN

The end of the world is at hand.

APOCALYPSE CRUCIBLE

The Tribulation has begun, but the darkest days may lie ahead.

APOCALYPSE BURNING

With lives—souls—on the line, the fires of the apocalypse burn ever higher.

APOCALYPSE UNLEASHED

In the earth's last days, the battle rages on.

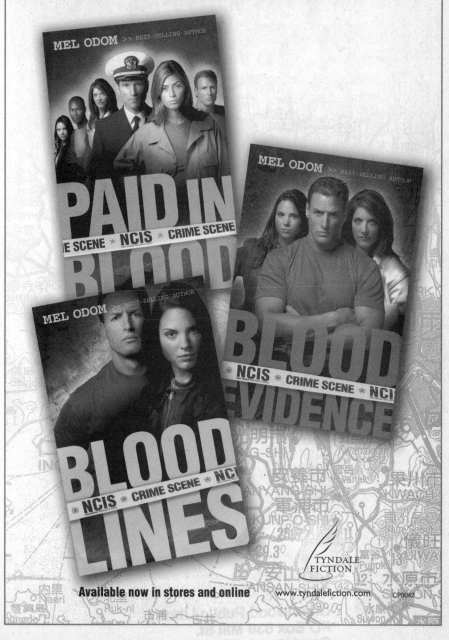

Have you visited
TYNDALE FICTION.COM

lately?

Greenwood Public Library
PO Box 839 Mill St.
Greenwood, DE 19950